This Book Belongs To

THE
BRIDE
FROM
DAIRAPASKA

THE BRIDE

FROM
DAIRAPASKA

ODESSA MOON

PESCHEL PRESS ~ HERSHEY, PA.

www.odessamoon.com

Cover design by Jake Caleb / jcalebdesign.com

ISBN-13: 978-1724456052

ISBN-10: 1724456059

Library of Congress Control Number: 2018953237

First printing: August 2018, version 1.0

For Bill,
I love you now and forever

And for
Fido, Muffy, Mariah, and Maxie,
You are all brave, loyal, good and true.

Table of Contents

Cast of Characters

Debbie Miller: She did the best she could under the circumstances.

Ghita Acconcio: The oldest daughter. Loved despite her unfortunate gender.

Aldo Acconcio: An unpleasant man, assigned but not chosen.

Carina Acconcio: The middle daughter. It was even more unfortunate that she was a girl.

Mrs. Acconcio: Not the mother-in-law you hope for.

Mr. Acconcio: He didn't rule his own roost.

An unnamed baby: A girl, and so of no value to anyone.

Spotty: Brave, loyal, good, and true. He was smarter than he looked.

The old daimyo of Dairapaska: He didn't believe in asking sheep what they wanted.

The old daimyo of Shelleen: Also of the firm opinion that serfs didn't have any more rights than sheep.

The new daimyo of Shelleen: The new boss. He had reasons he did not disclose for why he sent peasants out to almost certain death.

The daimyo's overseer: He did the best he could with a difficult job, although the peasants did not agree.

The village headman: He had a thankless and impossible job.

A woman on the road: She didn't take her own good advice.

The way-station attendant: He helped more than he knew.

Yannick: A Hand of Kenyatta and a man with a troublesome past.

Harley: A boy with a future.

Tyr: Another boy with a future.

Two wolf-dogs: Four times Spotty's size, and they made sure he knew it.

Otis: Another Hand of Kenyatta who knows Yannick's past

very, very well.

Gray Gal: A very patient mare saddled with an unhappy rider.

Chika: She knew a witchy woman when she saw one.

Kerill: A boy with a troublesome past and hopes of a better future.

Niall: Another boy with an unhappy past but a better future ahead.

Leon: He hoped his children would listen to him and sometimes, they did.

Remus Kenyatta: He came to understand why the new daimyo of Shelleen did what he did and he admitted he would have done the same.

Moswen: A wise woman, she collected names for future people and remembered those who had passed on.

Anchali: Moswen's grandfather, currently residing in an oak tree.

Alison: She believed in facing facts, no matter how unpleasant they were.

Barb: A gossip who wanted things to be the way she thought they should be.

Preston Kenyatta: Remus' second and someone Debbie got to know rather better than she would have liked.

Avalon Kenyatta: A lady of the Four Hundred, yet she nursed her baby like any peasant woman.

Hiroshi Kenyatta: He was the first to realize why the new daimyo of Shelleen did what he did.

Azi: Another boy with a future.

The Post-Mistress of Kenyatta: She knew what was the right thing to do.

The Post-Master of Dairapaska: He ignored his sworn duty.

The Post-Master of Shelleen: He did what was easy and not what was right.

Debbie's mother: She missed her daughter more than words would ever say.

Alice: The luckiest of the 24 Brides from Dairapaska.

Lupita: She won and she lost in the bride trade.

Pia: One of the 24 Brides from Shelleen.

Blanca: Another of the 24 Brides from Shelleen.

Fulvia: She couldn't accept was done to her family so she took out her anger on people who didn't deserve it.

Lysander: Yannick's brother who wonders a great deal about Debbie.

Erissa: Lysander's wife, who goes to the trouble to find out who that stranger is.

Mandy: Otis' wife, who also goes to the trouble to find out who that stranger is.

Maureen: Someone who Yannick knows very, very well. She burns everyone she touches.

Andrew: A bodyguard from Purnell. His opinion of Maureen never wavers.

Dave: A bodyguard from Purnell. His opinion of Maureen matches Andrew's.

Sal: She wanted to get paid and hard coin was better than barter any day, even if it did mean putting up with someone she despised.

Maureen's most recent lover: Entitled, wealthy, and vindictive.

Their newborn son: Unwanted by Maureen and unknown to his abusive father and she needed to keep it that way.

The new daimyo of Dairapaska: He had to clean up what his predecessor did without losing face.

Howard Shelleen: He selfishly made things far worse for the peasants than they needed to be.

The Kennel-Master of Kenyatta: He didn't get the results he planned

Trapped In Misery

EBBIE STARED AT THE BRUISES on Ghita's arms as her oldest daughter whimpered softly, the tears running down her face. The dull purple splotches blooming against her olive-green skin could not be denied. Aldo had slapped Ghita.

She had to do something, besides uselessly share tears with Ghita. Debbie thought of what her grandmother would say, so far away and so long ago in Dairapaska, and shoved the memories away. She could no longer pretend to make the best of it. The undeniable evidence was in front of her, pushing her to do something other than to endure. There was no question in her mind on that subject, not anymore. The new question was: What was she going to do about it?

Debbie looked at the dirt walls hemming them in and blocking the light and air and avoided her daughter's red eyes. She hated living in Shelleen, she always had, and trying to manage in the new village trapped in the middle of nowhere was even worse. Not that she had had any choice in one single damn thing that had happened to her since she was sixteen. Her choice had always been limited to how she chose to cope with what was done to her. Now she had to cope with what was being done to her daughters.

Her thoughts refused to stay still and focused, a skill that normally allowed her to plod forward, putting one foot in front of the other, over and over until the day was done and she could escape into her dreams. The past reared up with all its ugly, painful memories, forcing her to see it again.

She remembered being shipped off to Shelleen with as much input into the decision as a sheep would get. Every day since her arrival, she had tried so hard, never complaining, never arguing, working as hard as she could and trying to be grateful for the good things and small mercies that came her way; but Aldo striking their daughter was unacceptable. She could no longer keep her head down and just endure. Debbie blinked and tried to pay attention to her daughter, huddled up against her and shaking.

"Ghita, angel, let me put some cold water on those bruises," she said softly.

"Yes, mommy," Ghita whispered.

Debbie was grateful that she had stopped crying. Aldo hated it when the kids cried, and it would be just like him to walk in from the stony fields with Ghita still in tears, no matter how quietly she wept. She wiped her own escaped tear away with a corner of her apron, knowing how the sight of it would infuriate her husband and upset her daughter still further.

"I want you to stay away from your father. Can you do that?"

"Yes, mommy."

"And I want you to find your sister Carina and tell her to stay away from your father. You two be quiet little mice and go weed the vegetable patch. Remember to push the terraformers back into the dirt. Maybe it will help. And keep Spotty away from him. Can you do that?"

"Yes, mommy."

Ghita looked so sad, her eyes downcast and her mouth trembling. Aldo hadn't been any prize but he had never hurt one of the kids before they left for the new village. He was, Debbie supposed, an adequate husband. He didn't drink that much, he worked most of the time, and when he came to her at night, he got it over with quickly so she could fall back into an exhausted sleep.

Debbie watched Ghita leave the gloomy soddy and when the door closed — blocking the sunshine and leaving her inside its dank embrace — she slumped down onto the splintery bench, ignoring the endless work waiting for her.

She remembered the tears at leaving Dairapaska, hers and all the other girls and all their families, now so far away. The train ride across what felt like half of Mars had been endless. The only relief had been to stare out the windows at the steppes in the government corridor and the road alongside the train. The road had had people of all sorts walking along it, people choosing where they wanted to go. Debbie had watched them through red-rimmed eyes and wished desperately that she could have joined them.

The grass of the steppes had blown and waved under the wind, filling the world to the horizon, free and spreading forever. The government corridors were not farmed like Dairapaska was or Shelleen, she supposed. There was no wheat, no barley, no oats, no maize, no peas and beans, just grasses of every shade of green filling the world and growing as they pleased. No man told them what to do.

She and the other twenty-three brides had known so little about what waited for them in Shelleen. It was Northern Agricultural Tier, like Dairapaska, and they were needed there. They would be married into the families of Shelleen, bringing much-needed new blood unrelated to anyone in the quadrant. The daimyos had been heartily pleased with their deal, improving the fertility of the peasants of both demesnes with a single, bold action. The peasant families involved, she reflected sourly, had felt differently.

That was all that they had been told. The brides speculated endlessly, chewing over what little they did know until the words were empty of meaning, leaving only loss behind.

A noise outside startled her, yanking Debbie back from the past to her surroundings. She tensed and leaped to her feet, praying that it was not Aldo. She had learned long ago to never be caught sitting and doing nothing. It was not Aldo and Debbie was grateful for that tiny mercy. The nameless baby woke up, demanding her attention. Debbie picked up the baby and stared at her sweet face in the dim light. She was only six months old, but it seemed so much longer.

Aldo hated the new baby. He had refused to name her or carve her a kuksa as was customary, and he had resented every moment of Debbie's time that she took. The baby had been colicky and that had enraged him still further. It would have been so different if this baby had been the desperately needed son.

Debbie slumped back on the stool and let the nameless baby latch on, hungry again. Aldo had been so happy when she had caught this baby. It had quickened early on during the endless trek away from the old village, grown slowly as they had struggled to build a new village out on the steppes.

"A son," he had said over and over. "A son at last." He had been kinder. Letters from his family had been sweeter in tone when they had mentioned her. His mother, Mrs. Acconcio, had even been gracious enough to acknowledge her existence without adding a complaint about her daughter-in-law's many faults.

And then the baby had been born in its own time in the grim soddy in the hateful, desolate village and it had been a girl. Aldo had screamed at her in his fury, cursed the midwife, and thrown the bloody afterbirth at her. The midwife had left as soon as she decently could and when the door was closed, Aldo struck Debbie but not for the first time.

She had to do something. She could not stay here anymore with her children. But what could she do? She was trapped, hundreds of klicks from nowhere and even further away from the family she still missed every day.

It would have been so much better for all of them if they had not been chosen to settle the new village out on the steppes. His family would not have been happy with another girl but a grandchild was a grandchild and they desperately wanted more. But Aldo had been chosen, the last man to be selected as a pioneer, and so Debbie and their daughters had to leave their home, too.

The noise started up again and got louder, becoming a clatter of wagons, neighing horses, and coarse shouts from outriders to get out of the way. Yapping dogs added to the clamor, alerting anyone who didn't already know that something had happened. Debbie jumped up again, startling the baby into a howl. She knew the sound of wagons, but this rumble and grumble went on and on as wagons rattled and bumped down the corduroy road that wound by the cluster of soddys. A wagon meant the daimyo's overseer had returned with letters from relatives left behind, news of the villages, a few desperately needed supplies, and instructions from the daimyo. But the overseer had never before arrived with this much noise. He rarely traveled with more than his crew, a single wagon, and a string of packhorses.

Word would spread quickly and Aldo would return early from the fields with the other men. Debbie soothed the baby hastily while looking around the soddy to see if she had missed any of the day's chores. There was nothing amiss that would upset Aldo, so she walked outside into the sunshine, blinking at the brightness after the dim soddy.

A visit from the overseer was important. He would expect every peasant in the village, young and old, to gather quickly and listen to him pass along the daimyo's requirements.

Debbie clustered with the other silent, anxious women near the village hall and stared, her hand to her mouth, as the overseer's crew unloaded crates of mil-rats from the many wagons into the hall. They were famine food. It was true the fields were yielding poorly. Every plant the farmers tried struggled to grow. Nothing thrived and everyone went around with a growling belly as they tried to make the supplies they brought with them last. But to see *this*, crate after crate of mil-rats being unpacked, was a frightening omen. She forced herself to be still, commanded her heart to stop racing. Rumors would spread quickly enough, racing up and down the dirt lanes between the soddys, growing far better than the barley or cabbages did, but those rumors would not be true. Nothing official, nothing accurate would be said until the overseer was ready. She would have to wait for his words.

Debbie refused to speculate with the other women of the village. "There's no use borrowing trouble," was all she was willing to say when she was asked.

As the wagons were unloaded, the word spread to the

peasants to assemble two hours before sunset in the village square, a grand name for an empty rectangle of beaten down, dusty, orange-tinged soil. Everyone had to be there, from the oldest to the youngest, and no exception was given for illness or infirmity or work that had to be done. So Debbie attended, carrying the new baby, and with Ghita and Carina clinging to her skirts. She was grateful that the new baby wasn't crying, unlike some of the other babies and toddlers. The colic seemed to have finally run its course.

Aldo chose not to stand with his wife and daughters, causing sidelong glances and disapproving murmurs that he chose to ignore. The midwife's husband in particular was, Debbie noticed, contemptuous of Aldo's decision. She chose to be quietly grateful for his absence as she waited patiently for the overseer to speak.

The overseer stood on a wooden platform in the center of the village square, and he spoke loudly and clear, so his voice could be heard over the unhappy babies. He told the silent, resentful adults and their silent, sullen children and whimpering babies what the daimyo expected from them and how disappointed he was in their performance. Things weren't moving quickly enough. Not enough sod had been broken for the new barley fields. Not enough stone had been moved.

He told the peasants that the new daimyo was generous and understood their plight. To that end, he had delivered the wagonloads of mil-rats. It would feed the peasants and their children over the winter as they continued to break the sod, move more stone, and build new, better houses to shelter in.

This brought murmurs of rage and fear from the huddled serfs, which the overseer ignored. They had been told when they first set out that when winter came, they would be allowed to retreat back to the old villages for the worst of the season, rather than freeze on the steppes. It was something that everyone looked forward to. They would see their much-missed families and have a break from the endless, thankless work trapped in the middle of nowhere.

The overseer finished with a grand flourish, telling all the peasants how lucky they were to have such a kind and caring daimyo and how fortunate they were to be the first people in the new village. They and their children would have status for generations to come. Their names would be listed forever in the cadastre, showing exactly which family held the rights to every piece of land surrounding the new village. They were the ancestors of the greatness to come. Their labors were building a golden future for Shelleen.

He did not circulate among the crowd of peasants afterwards to receive their effusive thanks, but instead retreated to the luxury of his guarded tent with its thick, warm carpets, lanterns, and soft bed on the hill overlooking the village of dank soddys.

Debbie silently took her children back to their dark, grim soddy and got back to work preparing supper of boiled grain and a few herbs. Everyone else went back to their assigned tasks, in the village or out in the fields. Before he trudged back to his own barren field, Aldo hit her again and then, right in front of her, slapped Ghita for being disrespectful.

Shortly after dawn, word spread again, carried from soddy to soddy by anxious children tasked with the job. Another assembly had been called. Everyone in the village trooped wearily to the village square to hear what new blessing they were to be granted.

The village headman stood on the wooden platform this time. He told everyone that most of the men in the village would be going out to a further set of fields and would spend the next three days there, breaking sod. They would stay overnight, so as to get more work done. If they camped where they labored, they could start work earlier and stay later as they would not have to waste precious time walking back and forth.

He did not look happy about his announcement, his eyes darting back and forth resentfully towards the stone-faced overseer watching him closely, his arms crossed. No one else was happy either, but they did not dare say anything with the overseer's guards watching and ready for signs of trouble.

The headman then named every man he expected to see at dawn the next day; every man who would have the privilege of breaking new sod for the benefit of Shelleen. The first name he called was Aldo's.

That evening, Debbie made every effort to keep her daughters meek, obedient, and quiet, and she did the same herself. She busied herself making sure that Aldo would have everything he needed for the next three days out on the steppes. It worked well enough as he did not berate his older daughters and he ignored, as always, the new baby. He did not ignore Debbie and found fault with everything she did.

That night, Debbie found solace and freedom in her dreams as she always did and, in the morning, she knew what she could do. She saw Aldo off as always, and as soon as the chosen men left for the far off new fields, she took Ghita and Carina aside and spoke to them.

"Girls, I want you to trust me. We're leaving the new village. Ghita, I want you to find, rinse, and fill every waterskin we have. Carina, I want you to watch the baby and try and neaten up the soddy. I will be back as soon as I can. Do not speak to anybody, and do not leave the soddy."

Debbie slipped quietly through the lane winding among the soddys to the village center. It was deserted as everyone, from the tots to the oldest, was working in the desolate fields, hoeing the struggling vegetable plots, searching for eggs from half-molted chickens, milking scrawny goats, or slaving in their hovels. The usual workload was heavy enough, but with most of the men gone, the same amount of work still remained to be done, now parceled out among the remaining villagers.

Inside the hall, she quietly took as many mil-rats as she could carry in her pack, taking the time to fit them in tightly. She filled the pockets of her kirtle and apron as well. She took care to rearrange the heaps that remained, so that what she took did not show.

She had eaten them before; everyone had. The brick-like bars were starvation food when there was nothing else available. The lords of a demesne only supplied them when famine threatened. It was thought that having them widely available to the peasants encouraged sloth and idleness. Why they thought this was strange, as nobody would normally eat mil-rats if anything better was available. They were a chewing exercise that filled the belly and nothing more.

Today, Debbie looked on them as a gift, a gift that would allow her to escape.

2

Escape Into the Steppes

ER HEAD DOWN, DEBBIE WALKED quietly and quickly back to her soddy, following the dusty path winding between the other soddys. She was grateful that no one paid attention to her, but not surprised. With most of the men gone, the few remaining were overwhelmed with the workload. The women whose husbands had left had their chores heaped on their plate as well as their own. At the soddy, she was relieved to see that Ghita had completed the morning chores, with Carina helping. They had found all the waterskins and filled them. She was grateful again at what good girls they were.

She checked carefully so there would be nothing left behind to show what she was planning to do. Anyone who stopped by would assume she was busy elsewhere.

Debbie found a sack for each girl and looked around the soddy. She could not take anything with her that would tell people that she had run away with her daughters. She had to have the waterskins but that couldn't be helped. She had to pray that their disappearance would go unnoticed. She finally settled on changes of clothing for the baby and her little knife.

She studied the sacks again. Did she really need both of them? She held them up to the morning sunlight spilling in through the doorway, its rays not reaching into the far, gloomy corners. They were coarsely woven, ragged with wear, and not something anyone would steal. They could use them as blankets at night and if they found something to eat along the way, the girls would be able to carry it in the sacks, as they could carry the extra mil-rats loaded in her pockets.

In the end, she took both sacks as a sign of hope. They had water to drink and mil-rats to eat, the clothes on their backs, and that would just have to do. Debbie took a moment to be grateful that it was late summer. It was starting to get cool at night, but not cold. The weather had been dry, and she hoped it would stay that way.

She led her daughters out of the soddy, carrying the still-unnamed baby in a sling, along with the pack on her back. She would lead them north, across the steppes, to the border of Shelleen and to the road in the government corridor that ran alongside the railroad. This was the road she had seen so long ago from the train window, a road that went someplace else, a road traveled by people who had made the decision to go to a place of their own choosing.

As they slipped out of the confines of the village, unnoticed by anyone, the first problem presented itself. They owned, like almost everyone, a small spotted terrier, mostly dirty white with plenty of splotches in shades of muddy brown. Spotty, like all the other village terriers, earned his keep by keeping down rodents and other vermin that threatened the grain stores. He fed himself that way as there was never any food in the new village to spare for a dog.

Debbie sometimes wondered if he would let her have a rat he had caught to make a broth but he never would. He was hungry and, it was his food. As far as Debbie was concerned, even if it was a rat, it was still meat and it had been a very long time since she and the girls had had anything other than the few off-tasting eggs from the scrawny chickens. In the old village, Aldo had insisted on eating most of what little meat they had and here there was less.

Spotty barked if strangers came around, but all the terriers did that. They also barked when strangers didn't come around so Debbie often wondered why they bothered barking at all. The dogs of Dairapaska had been better trained. In her spare moments, she had taught Spotty to come when called and to sit. He was a smart dog, and she was trying to get him to understand when to bark and when not to.

Ghita and Carina adored Spotty and when they had free time they played with him along with all the other village children and their barking terriers. He had been a gift from their grandfather in the old village. Spotty was their almost constant companion and slept with them every night.

"Mommy," Carina whined, "we can't leave Spotty. He would be sad."

"Mommy," Ghita said more soberly, "father might hurt Spotty if we don't take him with us."

Debbie felt even more tired, but Ghita was right. Aldo would take out his anger on the dog. Spotty was tolerable to Aldo only because of his vermin-hunting. Her husband disliked cats and so they had never had one. It was just as well as any cats out here in the steppes would have been eaten by hawks. The terriers were too big for a hawk to carry off although they would snatch puppies when given the chance.

"All right. He can come with us," Debbie replied. She was rewarded with her daughters' smiles, something they rarely showed in the new village. And it was possible, she thought, that Spotty might be useful on their journey through the steppes. He was accustomed to finding his own food, and he would bark at anything that came near them.

They walked and walked, Debbie carrying the heavy pack, the baby, and the waterskins. The girls carried their sacks, with a few mil-rats to make them feel useful, and another waterskin apiece. They did not complain, just walked silently, and followed their mother into the endless sea of ankle-high, lank and weedy grasses.

Debbie fretted over the weight of what they were carrying. The pack was so heavy, but it would get lighter fast as they ate the mil-rats. The waterskins were so heavy, but as they drank the water, they would empty out. She feared that later on they would miss the weight of food and water and wish they had more.

She had to trust that they had enough to make it to the road, sixty, maybe even seventy klicks ahead of them. She was unsure of the precise distance as no one had ever told the peasants where the new village was exactly located. The daimyo's overseer said they did not need to know. He had even refused to tell the village headman.

At the road in the government corridor, there were waystations every so often and every one of them was stocked with mil-rats and water. You had to ask, but you would be given what you needed. That's what she had been told on the train ride so many years ago, when she had watched all those people walking along, going to someplace of their own choosing. She hoped it was still true.

Debbie wanted to make it to the road and then she would decide what to do next. It would take them many days to walk to the road, but she hoped no more than five if all went well. They would sleep along the way, in a nest of grass. That's what she told her daughters.

Ghita and Carina both liked the idea of a nest of grass and they became more cheerful as they plodded along in the sunshine. Spotty turned out to be useful as he kept the girls entertained with his antics. They slowly walked north until sunset, always keeping at right angles to the sun. Debbie was deeply grateful that it was warm and dry and the weather looked like it would stay pleasant.

As they plodded along, Debbie would check behind her to see if anyone had noticed them escaping, but no one did. The land rose and fell in gentle, low hills and they quickly concealed the village of brown and green soddys. By late afternoon, the grasses on the steppes were growing almost calf-high, and not quite as sparse and lank. Debbie would look back and see the path they had made, knocking down the different grasses, and she fretted over leaving such a clear trail. But it was windy and it looked like the grasses recovered and stood up again, concealing their passage through them. Each rise they crested added another notch to the distance between them and the new village. Each rise they crested opened up another sea of grass, flowing almost unchanging to the horizon in a carpet of green and brown.

She contented herself with thinking of the daylong head-start they had, perhaps more. Who would come looking for her and Ghita and Carina and the nameless baby? No one in the village was her friend and so no one cared very much. They were all too busy anyway, struggling under their own burdens. It might take until Aldo came back with the rest of the men, three days from now, for anyone to notice their absence. Three days was a long time, long enough to be lost to Shelleen forever.

When the sun began to set, they made the promised nest in

the grass, trampling a small circle and cutting extra grass with the little knife that Debbie brought to lay on, and settled in. As the night deepened, the stars came out; filling the velvety black sky with sparkles and glimmers. The Milky Way formed a river of light that split the sky in two, crammed with too many stars to count. The constellations showed her that she was keeping a fairly good path to the north.

There was no one to hear so Debbie sang to her daughters, a rare treat for all of them.

Spotty turned out again to be useful as he cuddled up with them, helping them to stay warm under the coarse sacks and on top of the cut grass. He never once barked that night, and Debbie assumed that it was because there was nothing to bark at.

It took them five more days to reach the road.

During the journey, Spotty stayed with them, trotting alongside when he didn't dart off to snatch a field mouse to swallow whole. Debbie had expected him to run off and get lost, but he never did. He would sometimes run ahead and proved himself one day when he barked like a mad thing at something hidden in the grass.

Debbie had the girls stay back and when she checked what Spotty was barking at, she saw a snake, very long and as thick around as her wrist. Its scales gleamed red in the sunlight. It lifted its head to watch them, the eyes a flat black divided by a line of gold. The snake's tongue flickered in and out, testing the air for their scent. They carefully detoured around it.

Debbie was grateful to see the road at last and more grateful that they had not run out of food before they reached it. She had been very careful with the water, letting each girl have enough and no more, and they still had a few swallows left. Each day as they walked, she fretted over how long it was taking, but she could not walk faster than Carina.

At the road, she had all three girls sit well away from it, behind a low rise so they would not be seen. Spotty stayed with them, keeping them company and guarding them.

Debbie took the empty pack and all the waterskins and cautiously made her way to the road. There were people walking in both directions, just as she had remembered. Some were in small groups and some were in large, but nobody seemed to be alone as she was. Debbie waited patiently, crouched behind a taller clump of grasses, until she saw someone she thought might speak to her. The friendly-looking woman was lagging behind a larger group and she waved at Debbie when she spotted her. Debbie rose and went over to her and when she asked, the woman told her where the way-station was. Debbie was grateful again to hear that it was only a klick away to the west.

The woman claimed to be part of a family, walking along to the east towards Purnell. She was chatty and helpful and told Debbie what to watch out for, particularly about staying well away from men, whether in groups or alone.

"It's not safe," the woman told her. "Attach yourself to a family group or some women alone. Don't go anywhere by yourself."

"Thank you," said Debbie. "I'm alone with my daughters. I was thinking we could go to Purnell."

The woman smiled, a smile of commiseration and shared fatigue. "You're running away from some bastard man, I would guess. That must be why you're alone on the road."

"No, that's not it," Debbie lied. She thought it would be better to not reveal any information about her situation, even to a stranger like this woman.

"On the road a woman alone is assumed to be a prostitute or a target," the woman replied, her voice suddenly flat and dead and her smile gone.

Debbie wanted to cry. "I have little daughters. Doesn't that mean anything to anybody?"

The woman inclined her head up towards the north. "I've heard that north, where the horsemen live, they take in any woman. They're not fussy. They're savages though. They spend their whole lives on a horse, eating and sleeping and chasing after wild animals. They live in tents, even in the winter." She shuddered theatrically.

"Really?" Debbie asked, her eyes going very wide. Shelleen was at the northern edge of the Northern Agricultural Zone and it suffered from brutal winters, far worse than Dairapaska had endured. Debbie had never quite got used to them, despite her years of practice.

A rough-looking, ragged man looked back, and called harshly to them. "Quit flapping your jaws and get over here! We need to get a move on."

The woman looked around, biting her lip, her expression suddenly tight and frightened. "Don't come with us. Go north. You'll be safer there," she whispered and scuttled away, towards the man frowning at her and the small group he was with.

"Thank you," Debbie said and she backed away quickly, towards the steppes and away from the road and the hostile stares of the woman's companions. To her intense relief, none of them followed her into the steppes. Nonetheless, Debbie did not take a direct path through the grass, straight back to her daughters. She took her time, weaving through the grass and trying to keep her head low so she would not be seen.

When she returned, Debbie was deeply grateful that all three girls had stayed quietly where she had left them and not wandered off. Ghita and Carina had made chains of flowers to wear and entertained the baby by waving grass plumes for her to snatch at. They had not been seen or bothered.

Ghita said, "Spotty didn't bark once, mommy."

"But he sat up when you came back," added Carina. "I'm so glad you let us keep him."

"I'm glad Spotty listened for me," Debbie replied. "We're going to walk near the road to the west to the way-station. We'll get food there and water."

"We can't walk on the road, mommy?" asked Ghita. "The road would be easier than the grass." The grass was now almost knee-high and thicker and wading through it had been slow going. It tired both girls, even with Debbie breaking a path for them.

"I know, angel, but it would be more dangerous."

Debbie sat down in the grass and nursed the unnamed baby, hungry again, and thought about what she would say at the way-station. When the baby was finished, she wearily got back to her feet, tucked the baby in her sling, picked up the pack and the waterskins, and she and her daughters plodded to the west, Spotty trotting alongside them. Debbie noticed that Spotty always wanted to stay to her right, between her daughters and the road. Previously he had not cared which side he trotted on. She wondered if he could hear or smell something that she could not.

At the way-station, a sturdy, low building built of red sandstone, Debbie had the girls hide with Spotty while she cautiously approached it, waiting until the road was empty to get closer. She peered around the corner of the building and saw a bored attendant and a few people getting a ration and some water. She backed away and waited off the road, crouched in the grass, until everyone had left and she could see no one approaching in either direction when she dared to peek around the building's sides. She swallowed and straightened herself up and walked over to him.

"Excuse me sir," asked Debbie, carefully keeping her eyes on the ground, "I would like some rations and to fill my waterskins."

"Sure, lady, take what you need."

"Thank you."

She went back and got the girls and Spotty and they drank their fill, rinsed and filled their waterskins, and took as many of the mil-rats as the attendant would allow.

"There's more along the way, you know. You don't have to carry a lot," he said.

Debbie was unsure if the attendant was concerned or if he had to ration what he gave out. She had to say something he could accept.

"Yes, sir, but I was warned to be careful, and I don't want to have any trouble," Debbie answered as respectfully as she could. She tried very hard to not let her fear show in her voice.

The attendant eyed her and her daughters and the small spotted dog. They were ragged, dirty, barefoot, and unaccompanied by any sort of protection that he could see. Only the dog made eye contact, glaring back at him. His decision made, the attendant said, "Take as much as you need, lady."

"Thank you." Debbie filled her pack and stuffed a few extra mil-rats into Ghita's sack and a few more into Carina's. Afterwards, they walked across the road, trying hard to not be noticed, or scurry like frightened rabbits. There weren't very many people here, only the few who had come along while Debbie had filled her pack and the waterskins and she was grateful for that. A few stared at them, but nobody said anything. She chose to take that as a good sign.

They reached the train tracks, five of them lined up and stretching east and west to the horizon. Debbie had the girls look carefully in both directions as trains moved very fast compared to people and they walked across the sets of tracks and away from the road and into the unknown north.

The attendant watched them go, then walked over to the bulletin board, inside the building near the dormitories. He looked over all the notices, piled one on top of the other, but did not see anything related to a runaway woman and her children so he put it out of his mind.

Debbie continued trudging northward, patiently enduring the never-ending grass. Ghita and Carina would get tired so they kept having to stop to rest and the journey was taking her longer than she thought it would. The woman she spoke to when she first got to the road had frightened her, as had the looks she and the girls had received from some of the other sparse foot traffic. The north sounded better than the road, and they could live in a tent. It couldn't be worse than a soddy, always damp and musty and dark.

She knew she was taking a tremendous risk going into another demesne. There was always the chance that she would be sent back to Shelleen. On the other hand, maybe she would be returned to Dairapaska. She wondered if anyone there still remembered her with ten years of distance between them.

The daimyo of Shelleen refused to allow any of the twenty-four girls to write home to their families, and Aldo and his family had agreed with that ruling and often said so. "Your place is here in Shelleen now" her mother-in-law had said. "You don't need those Dairapaska serfs anymore."

Debbie refused to think of the alternative fates that could await in the northern demesne. She wished she had asked the attendant what its name was. He would have known. She and the girls could eventually walk to Purnell, but what would await her and them there? She had no money. She could not keep her daughters safe, and she did not want them to end up as whores, begging in the street. She thought of the little knife she had brought along. It wasn't much protection, but if she had to, she could make sure that her daughters could never be hurt again.

She had thought of walking back to the west and Dairapaska, but that was so far away. Winter would have come and gone by the time she and her daughters got anywhere near to it, and then there were always the dangers of the road. The north seemed safer. No one at Shelleen would think that she ran away there. They rarely spoke of the North, and when they did, they cursed and spat and swore about the winter winds that came howling down from there, winds that tore flesh from bone and chilled you to your very soul.

The little group plodded along, and the grasses on the steppes got taller, bushier, and more varied than the grasses of Shelleen. It became harder to forge a path through them, and much slower. Every night, Debbie checked the stars and every day she readjusted her route, always keeping the morning sun at right angles to her and the girls.

It wasn't unpleasant. The sun shone almost every day. It was warm and the air was filled with birdsong. The bugs didn't bother them as much as she had feared. Sometimes it would rain, but never for very long. They would plod along in the rain, slowing down, and wait for it to end and for the sun to return and dry them out. Best of all, Ghita and Carina stopped looking and acting as much like timid mice. They were relaxing and starting to laugh and run. It had been a long time since Debbie had seen them happy and unworried. She had her own worries, but even so, she could feel her soul ease with each step further away from Aldo, his family, and Shelleen.

She sang to them as they trudged forward, teaching Ghita and Carina the songs she had learned so long ago in Dairapaska. There were songs for bringing in the wheat, songs to praise the rain, the return of summer, the rising sun, songs of thanksgiving and gratitude. Shelleen had songs of its own, and she sang them too, her daughters able to sing along with her. Sometimes it seemed like the birds would join them like a chorus.

They tried to count the birds, seeing how many different kinds there were and there were many; far more than there had been in the new village. Ghita picked flowers when they rested and made chains of them to wear as they walked. Carina picked the grass stems with the fluffiest tops to wave at the baby and make her burble. Spotty pranced alongside them, darting off into the grass and coming back with a satisfied look. He did that more often than he had before and Debbie wondered if there were more little rodents for him to eat than on the other side of the road in the government corridor. His fur was getting sleeker, his ribs not so prominent. At night, they would watch the stars come out and Debbie would tell the girls stories about the constellations and how they were leading them to the north.

The night sky was beautiful, brilliant with glittering stars strewn across the Milky Way. The night stars over Dairapaska had been arranged a little differently, but not too different from what she had learned to recognize at Shelleen. The moons would race across the sky, just as they had in Dairapaska. The stars and the moons shown down uncaring and cold but they meant no more harm than the clouds and the grass and the wind. They were indifferent to Debbie and Ghita and Carina and the unnamed baby and their fates. Nonetheless, they gave their beauty willingly, indifferently, unconcerned with anyone's opinion of them, and only for the sheer joy of being beautiful whether anyone cared to see them or not.

The baby turned out to be easier than Debbie expected her to be. She was willing to nurse in the sling that Debbie had rigged up so they could keep walking. Debbie kept the baby's bottom as clean as she could, wiping her off, and keeping the diaper she wore lined with the softest leaves and moss. Ghita and Carina helped her find the best mosses every time they had to stop.

The baby was the happiest of them all. She was getting constant attention from Debbie and her sisters rather than being ignored in a cradle while Debbie worked, her little feet weren't sore from walking, she wasn't hungry, and no one was angry with her for existing.

Debbie worried that Ghita and Carina would ask about their father, but they never did. They did not seem to miss him at all. When they had left the old village, they had cried over leaving their grandmother and grandfather and the aunties and uncles. Aldo had been short with them and angry about their grief. The girls had quickly learned not to cry in front of him over their hurt and loss. They had not cried once during the long trek north and Debbie was grateful for that mercy.

Days passed and Debbie was beginning to wonder how she would know when she reached the northern demesne. Demesnes were huge and some were mostly empty of people. That was true of Dairapaska as well as Shelleen. It had been a big event when the population of the old villages had grown enough to allow the founding of a new village.

Debbie did wonder about that. She hadn't thought any of the old villages were large enough to spare people to found a new village. If anything, the old villages of Shelleen weren't even quite as large as what she remembered of Dairapaska. But the daimyo of Shelleen had said the population was large enough to settle a new place, so maybe it was true. She stewed over that thought as it did not seem true to her.

She kept thinking about that as they plodded north, wading patiently through the seas of fluttering grass that carpeted each hill and vale. Maybe he had another reason for putting a village there. It wouldn't be something that she would ever know; it might not even be something that the village headman would ever be told. But the daimyo wanted a village out in the middle of nowhere badly enough to force the peasants to winter over even though they were woefully unprepared. It was likely that even with the mil-rats, many of the serfs and their children would die from cold and hunger.

Debbie smiled at the dragonflies dancing over the endless ocean of grass. If she was at all lucky, she would never find out why the new daimyo of Shelleen had done what he had done to the peasants in the old villages. He had torn apart families for his own reasons, just as the old daimyo of Shelleen and the daimyo of Dairapaska had torn apart families for their own purposes. She would keep plodding forward to a different future, one that she was choosing, and she would never go back to Shelleen, the new village or the old ones, and to Aldo and his family.

Even if she and her daughters were lost in the endless steppes and died, it would be better and less painful than going back to Shelleen.

Several more days passed as the little group doggedly trudged through the ocean of rolling grass. With each klick northward, the grass was imperceptibly higher and more varied, yet at the end of the day, Debbie could see the difference. It kept getting harder to break a path through the dense plants for her daughters. The mil-rats were running low, and there was very little water left.

Debbie saw it first when she wearily crested another ridge. A flash caught her eye and there it was, over to her right and ahead. A tower of glinting gray stones stacked neatly one on top of another broke the horizon. It was not natural; rearing out of the grass like a fir tree made of rock. The top stone caught the sunlight and flashed again. Perhaps it was the boundary to the demesne and perhaps some of the wild riders would be there and they would have food and water. She did not allow herself think of what they would expect in payment.

She said to her daughters, "Look! A tower of stones. We'll go there and rest."

Ghita looked up trustingly. "Will we get water there, mommy?"

"I hope so."

The land was deceptive as always, and it took hours more to walk to the tower of stones. As they grew closer, they saw it was built on a low rise of earth, making it even taller. The stones were piled in a great pyramidal mass, much taller than the tallest man and as broad across at the base as a man lying down.

Long ago, a small troupe of entertainers had come through Dairapaska and Debbie vividly remembered the men in brightly colored, striped clothes tossing each other through the air. Acrobatics, they had called it. The daimyo of Dairapaska had let everyone take the day off to watch and had even provided a feast. She had never seen anything like it beforehand, and she had never seen anything like it since.

This tower of stones stood as high as when one acrobat stood on another man's shoulders. She wondered if someone had done something like that to construct this great pile of stones. She wondered more about the men who had done the backbreaking work of hauling stone to this hill through the endless seas of grass. The stones had been carefully selected for size and color, larger darker stones on the bottom and towards the top the stones got progressively lighter. Only the palest gray stones with flecks of mica to sparkle and flash had been chosen to make the top of the pile. The tower was crowned with a fist-sized lump of white quartz, gleaming brightly in the sun like a chunk of ice on fire.

Ghita and Carina were astonished and stared, open-mouthed. They had never seen a tower so high since they had left the old village. There was nothing like it in the new village, just the soddys and the village hall, also built of sod. They approached cautiously but there was no one around, no sound other than the hum of insects, cries of birds, and the whisper of the wind tousling the grass. Spotty scampered up the hill and ran around and around the base of the tower, sniffing and exploring. He yipped with excitement but he didn't bark his "strangers here" yelps.

Debbie walked cautiously around the hill supporting the tower and on the north side of the hill, hidden from view, discovered a soddy sunk into the ground. The tightly fitted bamboo door had no lock so she opened it slowly. She peered in to see a room lined with shelves, cunningly roofed over, floored, and backed with bamboo to keep the small space dry. There were mil-rats on the shelves and objects that Debbie did not recognize. As she and the girls marveled over their good fortune, Spotty began yipping louder and more franticly.

She went back outside, followed the yips, and discovered a pump that stood over a red sandstone trough, big enough for a man to lie in. A few pulls on the pump and she got water; fresh, clean, clear, and ice-cold. She knew that meant a well or a cistern.

Debbie was overwhelmed with her good fortune. She and her daughters would not starve, nor would they die of thirst. She would no longer have to ration what they had left. It was a treat to finish off the last of the mil-rats they had carried from the way-station, even giving some to Spotty who ate them eagerly.

They washed off at the pump, rinsed and filled all the waterskins, and saw that the sun was getting low.

"Mommy," said Ghita, all smiles, "can we stay here forever?"

Debbie smiled fondly at her daughter. "No, angel, only

overnight. We'll make a grass nest and bring it into the soddy and we'll eat our fill and, in the morning, we'll keep walking north."

It was a great pleasure to sit on the side of the tower's hill, backs against the warm stones, and watch the sun sink slowly into the west, painting the sky with reds and oranges. They weren't hungry, had plenty of water, and the chance of a good night's sleep; snug, dry, safe, and warm. The nights had been slowly getting colder as they plodded north, a harbinger of the coming fall. During each night huddled together in the grass nest, Debbie had to push away worries about what to do as the season marched forward on its never-ending wheel. On this blessed night, she had no such concerns and could relax.

As she watched the sunset, Debbie took the time to make dolls for each of the girls out of grass. They were simple dolls but Ghita and Carina were delighted. She had had to leave their two rag dolls back in the new village since if she had taken them, it might have been noticed.

Debbie was very grateful that they had found the soddy at the base of the tower as that night a storm moved through. It rained on and off during the night, waking her, but she, her daughters, and Spotty stayed snug and dry.

This soddy, unlike the ones that the villagers had built, had a ceiling and walls that kept the insides dry. Debbie wondered how the builders had done it. Even the floor stayed dry. But it made sense that the unknown builders would do this because if they had not, the mil-rats and the other things would have been ruined by dampness.

She was impressed and grateful for their thoughtfulness and planning.

In the morning, she and the girls, even the baby, washed off with the cold water in the pump, drank their fill, and ate as much as they wanted. There was no one to say no and Debbie decided to take advantage of it. She didn't know if they would find another tower with a storeroom of treasure like this one.

She borrowed a comb she found on a shelf and took the time to thoroughly comb out and rebraid everyone's hair. Their own carved horn comb had been left behind in the soddy, making this one a small gift. She wore her own hair in one long brown plait down her back. Ghita's and Carina's hair was arranged in one braid to each side as was customary with girls of their age. The unnamed baby's hair was still very short and fluffy, barely concealing her scalp. It would be a long time before she had enough hair to braid. Regretfully, Debbie returned the comb to where she found it; she could live without it, and the mil-rats were more important.

She and the girls cleaned up as best they could, hauling out the grass nest and scattering it about as they had done every night before. They tried making everything look neat, but as with all the other grass nests, anyone could see that someone had been there.

Moreover, Ghita and Carina had pressed their muddy handprints on the bamboo walls by the door, and Debbie could not bring herself to wash them off. It showed that they had been there; her happy living daughters and that they mattered. She decided right then to add the baby's tiny handprints too, getting her little hands muddy and pressing first one and then the other to the wall to show that she had been there too. Ghita and Carina giggled at the sight and added more muddy handprints to make a design around the baby's tiny ones.

Debbie chose not to add her own, enjoying the novel sensation of saying "no, I won't."

The ground was soft from the rain and as they walked around, they left some footprints in the bare, wet soil near the red sandstone trough. Debbie thought about how it showed that they had been there enough to leave another mark. There was nothing she could do about it so she chose to ignore it and as they walked the soil dried enough that they didn't leave obvious footprints any more.

The sun shone as they headed north, trudging along what seemed to be a road. At any rate, the grass wasn't as high and dense as it was off to the sides and that made the walking easier. There had been a similar road running east to west in front of the tower, but it did not go north so she ignored it. Debbie wondered how the mysterious tower builders maintained a grass road, but she was grateful to not have to wade through the suddenly waist-high grass, breaking a trail for her daughters.

They had full bellies and full packs and full waterskins. Debbie and her daughters were feeling happier and more hopeful than they had for many, many months.

They walked another full day and as the sun began setting, Debbie and the girls settled in for the night in another grass nest. Ghita and Carina played with their grass dolls, and the baby played with the fluffy grass tops Debbie waved for her, and Spotty sniffed about, snatching something small and squeaky that he eagerly swallowed. It did not rain that night and Debbie was grateful again. She wondered how long she would be lucky like that. There was nothing she could do about it but endure so she finally chose to push those worries away.

3

Discovered

N THE MORNING, THEY CONTINUED plodding to the north. The overnight rain from the day before had brought some coolness with it, making for a chillier night, and so the morning sun was even more welcome and warming. They had walked for some time, slowly warming up, when Spotty trotting alongside them suddenly stopped. He pricked his ears, his head was up and alert, his eyes searching, and he sniffed the air vigorously.

At first Debbie thought it was another snake but he spun around and began barking fiercely back towards the way they had come, back towards the tower of stones, south, and Shelleen now so far away. Spotty flung himself up into the air with the force of his barking; he was leaping and jumping in a noisy frenzy and she knew at once that this would be a problem much bigger than a snake.

"Girls, we have to hide. Something is coming."

She was trying to get her frightened daughters to move quickly, looking for a place to hide in the waist-high grass, when she heard much bigger dogs barking. She led them over the hill and then they were surrounded by large, fierce dogs circling her and her daughters and barking loud, deep, hunting barks. She fell to her knees, then down on the ground, trying to shield her daughters with her body.

Spotty was as hysterical as she had ever seen him, barking and lunging at the much bigger dogs who snapped at him with gleaming fangs.

Debbie screamed at the dogs to go away, and Ghita and Ca-

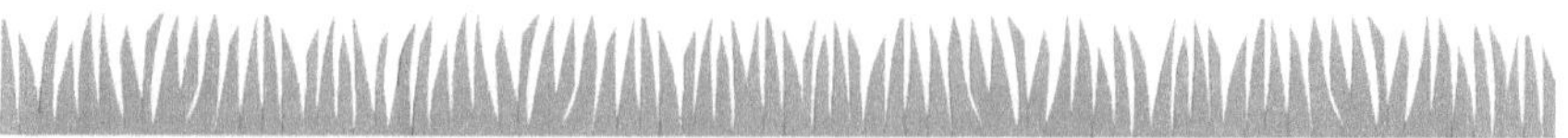

rina and the nameless baby wailed in terror. The dogs were as big as the wolves that she and everyone else in the new village had been endlessly warned about so long ago, back in the old village when they had been chosen to be pioneers.

Debbie had not worried about wolves when she began the trek north, having decided that it was a story to keep the serfs terrified and in their place. Nevertheless, these dogs *were* wolves, with rough heavy fur, fierce eyes and slavering jaws lined with bright fangs as long as her little fingers.

But the wolves didn't leap on them and tear them apart as wolves should have done. They circled, close enough to touch if Debbie would have dared. They kept snapping at Spotty but didn't rip him apart even though he tried hard to bite them. These wolves were as big to Spotty as he was to the rats and mice he caught and ate, but he didn't care. He fiercely defended Debbie and Ghita and Carina and the unnamed baby and through her terror, she spared a moment's gratitude for bringing him with them.

She forced her head up to look down the path, beyond a circling, snarling wolf-dog, and felt her heart stutter and want to stop. Some men, shaggier than she had ever seen before, riding shaggy horses were bearing down on them. These must be the northern savages the woman at the road had mentioned. They were more frightening than their wolf-dogs and Debbie could only pray that they would stop after raping and murdering her and leave her daughters alive.

The men did not speak as they rode up and they wheeled their horses to a stop. They were a mix of men and teenage boys riding, all with long braided hair pulled back, the two men with thick, heavy beards and mustaches and the boys with just a straggle, and all were dressed in dull wools. The leader whistled to the wolf-dogs who at once settled down, alert but no longer barking and circling them.

Spotty recognized this new, more dangerous threat and charged the horses, barking fiercely and getting kicked at for his pains. The leader yelled something to one of the boys who pulled out some ropes and stones tied together that he spun at high speed around his head and threw it at Spotty as he leapt into the air, trying hard to bite the riders.

Debbie was horrified to see Spotty crash to the ground, his

legs tightly bound by the cords. Spotty kept barking hysterically, wiggling on the ground and fighting his bonds, as the boy leapt off his horse, ran over to Spotty and muzzled him with a piece of rope, silencing him.

Ghita and Carina were so frightened that they had stopped screaming, unable to do anything except huddle on the ground, clutching at her and sobbing. The baby more than made up for them, crying as loudly as Debbie had ever heard her, and she pulled the baby to her chest in the sling, hoping to sooth her. She struggled to her knees, trying to keep her daughters behind her, her mind frozen and empty.

The leader swung down from his horse and walked over to her and stopped a few paces away, pausing to study her, her daughters, and Spotty. As near as she could tell behind the beard and mustache, he was openly puzzled, his head cocked to one side.

He turned to the other man and the boys and his hands flew into a series of gestures. The second man and one of the boys began riding very slowly, followed by two of the wolf-dogs, circling around Debbie and her daughters huddled on the ground, making wider and wider circles into the waist-high grass, moving gradually away from them. They studied the ground and the low hills as they went, alert and watching for something she could not see.

The leader of the riders had a loose braid of hair as long as hers hanging down his back, almost as black as his piercing eyes. There were some bits of color in it, shining against his dark hair. His ears were pierced and he wore an orange feather in each one, the same color as the setting sun.

As he stared at Debbie, she found her voice and cried out over her screaming baby, "Please, don't hurt my daughters! I'll do anything, don't hurt my daughters, please, I beg you."

"Not gonna hurt you or your daughters, doll." His voice was deep and gravelly, his accent strange. "Are you alone?"

"My daughters, please don't hurt them!"

"Tell me who you are. Are you alone? Besides your guard dog, I mean?"

Debbie made herself nod, then tried to speak without screaming or crying. "Yes, we're alone."

"No one forced you here? Kidnapped you?"

She shook her head more forcefully and struggled to her feet. Ghita and Carina clung, shuddering, to her skirts, hiding their faces in the patched cloth as though if they could not see, they could not be seen. She could feel them shaking as they clutched her legs and hear their spasmodic breaths as they gasped for air. The baby had stopped crying and was whimpering, a gasping, hopeless, sobbing sound that tore at her.

"No, we're alone." Debbie made herself stop and breathe and meet his eyes, something that she had learned long ago not to ever do to a man. "I'm Debbie. I'm from Shelleen, and I'm not going back there, not me and not my daughters."

The leader studied her, his head cocked to one side, and said disbelievingly, "You walked here from Shelleen? You and these little girls and your guard dog alone?"

Debbie nodded vigorously, not trusting herself to speak.

"That was you at the cairn then, yeah?"

"I don't know what you mean," she answered dully.

"The stone tower atop the soddy. Hand prints all over the walls."

"Yes, that was us." She closed her eyes in despair. It had seemed so harmless, so joyful at the time.

He walked slowly towards her, while the wolf-dogs and the two boys watched quietly, alert for any movement from her. Spotty began shaking harder, trying desperately to bark and tear free from his bonds. The leader quirked a smile at him and Spotty did his best to growl back despite the muzzle.

"Big dog in a little dog's body. So why'd you run away from Shelleen? Where's your man?"

"Don't send me back to him! Please, I'll do anything to keep my daughters safe. Don't send us back, please."

The man scowled at her, suddenly angry in a way he had not been before. "You ran away from your husband. You stole his kids."

Debbie was more afraid than ever. All men were alike. None of them cared what they did to women. They used them as they saw fit.

She made herself speak, forcing down her terror of him and every other man who did as he pleased when he bore none of the cost.

"I won't go back and be beaten by him anymore." Debbie

struggled with the words, saying out loud what she had never spoken of. "I won't let him hit my daughters anymore. I would rather die out here on the steppes and be free of him than go back. He'll kill me and then he'll murder them, starting with the baby."

The man stopped scowling at Debbie, but he did not look happy.

"We'll sort this out with Kenyatta."

"I don't know what that means."

He smiled without any humor. "Kenyatta is where you are. You're gonna get to meet the daimyo, also Kenyatta. That's how we do it up here." He scowled at her, angry again. "Let him deal with you."

The man and older boy who had ridden off returned and their hands flew. The leader turned back to Debbie, saying, "Well, that part of your story seems to be true. You're alone."

"It's all true." Debbie held her chin high and met his dark, hostile eyes. There was no point in keeping anything back. She chose to speak the truth and reveal herself to him as she had never spoken to anyone before, not since the bride trade so many years ago. There was nothing left to lose.

"The daimyo of Shelleen made us set up a new village months ago and things weren't going well and most of the men had to go out to break new fields for three days, and I took my chance and ran away with my daughters. No one there wants me. I'm not from Shelleen and I'm not one of them and I never will be. I'm from Dairapaska and I was made to go to Shelleen and forced to marry Aldo. He hits me, and after the new baby was born, he started hitting my daughters and he told me that he wished the new baby would die so I could catch a new baby sooner."

"No man would do that," the leader said. The riders, one and all, looked angry and shocked.

"Yes, they would," she replied in a flat, dead voice. "The new baby is a girl and Aldo wanted a boy. He wouldn't name her. He wouldn't let me nurse her when he was around. He wanted her to die. I won't go back."

The leader sighed deeply, his face a complex mix of emotions. He clenched his fists, making Debbie cringe and look away. "I'm Yannick. Ever ridden a horse before? You and your girls?"

Debbie shook her head, staring into the trampled grass. "Didn't think so."

He turned to the other man and the boys and his hands flew. This time, they answered back, their hands flying. Debbie watched them and wondered if they were arguing. It looked from the men's faces that they were.

Ghita and Carina had stopped whimpering into her skirts although they still shuddered violently. She knew they had been listening. The baby still sobbed and she took the chance to try and sooth her.

Yannick. What a strange name, Debbie thought, cuddling the nameless baby to her breast. He and the other man looked so strange and shaggy. The male serfs of Shelleen and Dairapaska before that had close-cropped hair and kept their beards trimmed short. She had never seen men with feathers dangling from their ears, like a woman would wear.

Debbie marveled at what she had done. She had never said out loud to anyone what Aldo had been doing to her or how he wanted the new baby to die. Aldo had usually been careful to hit her when the girls weren't around. She was not sure how much Ghita and Carina knew but now, there were very few secrets left.

The argument seemed to be over, the young rider who had captured Spotty mounted his horse and rode off, and Yannick turned back to Debbie.

"This is what we're gonna do. You and your little girls and your dog are going with me, Harley, and Tyr. We're gonna ride to the manor house and the village as soon as Harley gets back with a horse for you and some extra gear."

He paused; studying the group huddled before him. "I got something for your girls."

He pulled out of his shirt two of the grass dolls she had made for Ghita and Carina when they had spent the night in the soddy. She thought she had found them all, but these two had been left behind. "Found these dolls in the soddy, tucked up on the shelf."

He knelt down within arm's reach of her and held out the two dolls, now dry and brown, one in each hand. "Thought you might like them back."

There was a long silence and then Ghita reached out a shaking hand and snatched the doll and pressed herself back into Debbie's skirts, hiding her face. Another long silence and then Carina did the same.

"Thank you," said Debbie. "We forgot them."

"That was worrying. Finding dolls and little hand prints out here at the border. We get bandits come through sometimes, with women and kids they've stolen."

"We aren't stolen. And we won't go back to Shelleen." Debbie wondered if she could reach her little knife and wondered more if she could do anything with it before this man stopped her.

Yannick crouched down to look at Spotty who rewarded him with renewed growling and struggling. "And what am I gonna do with you?"

Ghita spoke for the first time, her voice shrill. "Don't hurt my doggie! Please don't hurt Spotty."

Carina started to cry again, joined by Ghita and the nameless baby. Debbie sank back to the ground and pulled her daughters into her lap and they huddled together, the four of them.

Debbie alone was silent. She was distraught and overwhelmed by despair. She had tried so hard to keep them all safe and she had succeeded too. There was nothing to say that she had not already said to Yannick.

"The dog will come with us. If you can't control him, he'll have to go hogtied and muzzled."

Debbie thought about this as her daughters' sobs slowed down to hiccups and gasps. "I don't know," she said finally. "Spotty is a smart dog but I don't know if I can get him to understand. He followed us when we left the village and he's been with us ever since."

"He's doing his job."

"Yes, I suppose he is." Debbie was lost, answering mechanically. She had no idea what to do anymore.

"You been eating anything but mil-rats?"

"No, not since we left the village." Some defiance crept into her voice. "I took them so my daughters wouldn't starve when we ran away."

Yannick looked puzzled again. "I thought them dirt lords didn't let their serfs have mil-rats. You have to feed yourselves or starve."

Debbie forced herself to meet his dark eyes again. "The

daimyo of Shelleen told us when we were forced to make the new village that we could go back to the old villages for the deep winter and the thin time. Then he changed his mind and told us we had to winter over. He sent wagonloads of mil-rats so not so many of us would starve over the winter. Then the men had to go break new fields, far away, camping out on the steppes. I stole the mil-rats so we could run away and never come back." She let her bitterness show, something she had learned long ago not to do. It didn't matter anymore.

He curled his lip with distaste, but at what, Debbie wasn't sure. "You could have chosen the road," Yannick said flatly.

Debbie swallowed, her mouth dry as the dust she was crouched in. "It didn't seem safe. We were alone, and I have no money. A woman I met said to go north. She said it would be safer and so I did."

"You'll be safe. You have my word on it, Yannick of Kenyatta."

He stood up and stretched. He called to the silent, intently listening riders behind him, "Tyr! Make a fire. We need some tea."

Tyr turned out to be the youngest of the boys, not much more than fifteen, Debbie thought. He dismounted his horse and, in a few minutes, had a tiny fire going, a small tinker's kettle of water over it that he produced from one of his saddlebags. He poured dried leaves from a small drawstring bag into the water and Debbie could smell their clean mintyness cutting through the air, welcoming and comforting.

Ghita and Carina watched Tyr silently, peeking around her skirts, and then stared, entranced, into the dancing flames. Debbie had never made a fire on their trek north as she wanted to leave fewer traces of their journey. Besides, it would have meant taking the precious tinder and flint from the soddy and that would have been noticed right away. She shifted the whimpering baby around so she, too, could see the flames.

"We're gonna have our tea," Yannick said. "Harley should be back soon, and then we'll get you and your daughters moving to meet Kenyatta."

Debbie wondered how they were going to drink their tea in the middle of nowhere and watched as every one of the riders produced a kuksa from somewhere.

She had left their wooden cups behind as she knew it would be noticed if they were missing. There were four in their soddy, one for each of them; but not one for her nameless daughter. It was traditional for a new baby to have a kuksa carved within the first week of life so the baby could play with the cup and then learn to drink from it.

When Aldo realized that the new baby was a girl, he had refused to carve her a cup. Everyone in the village knew what he had meant by that. He didn't care what they thought and not one other man in the new village had stepped in to carve the new baby a cup. Debbie knew that the other peasants disapproved of Aldo's behavior, but not enough to risk his fury.

The kuksas of the riders were stained black from long usage. She wondered if they had the same custom of carving a wooden cup for each new baby, a cup that would be used for your entire life and then buried with you.

Yannick asked, "You need cups?"

Debbie nodded, afraid to say anything.

"Cups got left behind? Even the baby's?"

To Debbie's surprise, Ghita spoke up. "Father wouldn't carve one for the baby. He said she didn't deserve one."

Debbie was more surprised at the raw bitterness in Ghita's voice. She had not thought that Ghita understood what Aldo's actions had meant.

"Everyone in the village knew that father didn't want the new baby. They said it meant the baby should die because she wasn't a boy."

Debbie did not know what to say, other than to pull Ghita closer to her and Carina and the nameless baby.

Yannick and the other man and the boys looked appalled. He turned back to the riders and their hands flew.

Tyr poured the tea, sharp and clean with mint, into every rider's kuksa. Yannick walked over to Debbie and without a word, handed her his cup, Tyr did the same with his to Ghita, and the other man gave his cup to Carina.

Debbie was overwhelmed. No one in the village, old or new, liked sharing their cups within the family, much less with a stranger. She vividly remembered having her hand slapped away by her mother-in-law when she had absentmindedly picked up the wrong cup. Aldo had resented taking the time to carve a cup for her and she had had to use a gourd cup while she waited for a kuksa of her own.

None of the girls from Dairapaska had been allowed to bring their cups to Shelleen. They'd been told that they needed to break clean with the past, as they would never return to their homes and families. The new families in Shelleen would be their future and new kuksas would cement that bond.

She drank the tea slowly, trying to get her thoughts in order. It was hot and good and crisp, and the heat worked its way into her stomach, warming her again. Ghita and Carina blew on theirs to cool it and sipped it greedily. Mint tea didn't often come their way in the new village and they usually had to be content with water or whey or sometimes milk if there was some left over from making cheese.

When she had finished the tea, Debbie handed the kuksa back to Yannick. Tyr had already made more tea so he and Yannick and the second man could have their tea.

Debbie was astonished all over again. In both villages, old and new, the women always drank after the men had been served. It had been true in Dairapaska as well.

"Get you some cups as soon as we can. What's your girls' names?"

"Ghita is my older daughter. Carina is my younger girl." Debbie held them tightly to her and the baby.

"And the baby?"

"She doesn't have a name. Aldo wouldn't let me name her."

Yannick scowled at her. "He ain't here. Baby needs a name. She'll be part of Kenyatta now. Whatever name you chose is fine as long as it's not being used by someone else."

Debbie stared up at him. Did this mean *she* could choose a name she wanted for her baby? But not a name that someone else was using. What did he mean by that?

"I don't understand. Two people can have the same name."

"No, they can't. Not in the North. We never share names cause a name belongs to one person and one person only. Everyone is unique and so their name has to be too."

Debbie was surprised again. Aldo and his family had told her that the first boy she bore would be named after his grandfather, the second would be named after his father, and the third would be named after Aldo. She would have no choice in the matter. Ghita and Carina had both been named after relatives of her in-laws, with no input from Debbie other than saying how pretty those names were.

"We don't reuse names either," Yannick went on. "A name belongs to the person it's given to and no other, not till that person's done with that name, however long it takes."

Again, Debbie didn't know what to say, so she said nothing, just stared at him.

"But what about our names?" she asked after thinking it over. "What if someone else has our names?"

"I don't believe anyone in Kenyatta has those names right now so no worries, yeah?"

"I'll think on it."

The baby began to fuss again, a different fussing, one that said she was hungry and hoping that Debbie would be able to nurse her. The days and days of walking had allowed Debbie to nurse the baby whenever the baby wanted to and she had gotten used to this attention and she liked it.

Back in the new village, Debbie had often had to make the baby wait, something neither of them had liked. But could Debbie allow her to nurse while these strangers waited on her?

The baby began wailing louder and Ghita said, very softly, "Mommy, baby's hungry."

Ghita had quickly learned to take the baby when she fussed if Aldo was around and he wanted Debbie's attention and he always did, rather than share her with the unwanted baby. Ghita pulled at the sling trying to take the baby.

"Baby need you? We have to wait on Harley anyway."

Debbie turned, and walked a few paces away, hunched over. She looked like a scared rabbit but she could not help herself. It felt so vulnerable to expose herself and the baby to these strangers. She sat down on the edge of the grass road, where the taller grass grew so thick and let the baby latch on. The grasses gave her the illusion of a shield. Ghita and Carina followed her closely and they huddled up against her, peeking sometimes over their shoulders to see what the riders were doing.

In a way, Debbie was grateful that the baby wanted to eat as it gave her time to think. She was alive, her daughters were alive, Spotty was alive, and it didn't look like the riders or their dogs would harm them. At least not yet. And they had been far kinder to her than Aldo would have been.

She would choose to go north with them to Kenyatta. She knew that she didn't really have a choice, but she could pretend that she did, making what was happening easier to swallow. What a strange name Kenyatta was. She had never known the name of the demesne to the north, and she had not cared either. For the first time since leaving Dairapaska, Debbie began to wonder what else she did not know about what was outside of Shelleen.

She could hear the men and the boys talking in low tones behind her, low enough that she couldn't make out the words. Debbie looked down at the new baby, who was very happy suckling away. Such a little thing she was, with her wisps of brown hair and brown eyes set in her olive-green face. She looked like Ghita and Carina did as babies.

As she sat and thought, hugging the baby tight against her, Yannick came up and laid down Spotty next to her and Ghita and Carina, then walked away. Spotty was still tied and muzzled and he struggled mightily to snarl and bite Yannick but was unsuccessful. As soon as Yannick laid him on the ground, Spotty settled down, with Ghita and Carina petting him, and telling him what a good doggie he was. He wagged his tail for them, thumping it on the ground.

Behind her the dogs barked sharply, startling her, and making Ghita and Carina flinch and whimper and Spotty struggle against his bonds. The baby jerked away and began to wail again. Debbie picked herself up and turned around, the sobbing baby tucked back into her sling and Ghita and Carina clinging again to her skirts.

The boy Yannick had called Harley had come back, leading a horse laden with baggage and another rider accompanying him, a new rider. This one was a little older than the boys but not yet a man. Like the others, he had bright bits of color in his hair, more than the other boys, but not as many as the two men.

"Harley! You made good time, lad." Yannick uncoiled himself from the ground where he had been sitting. "Debbie, this is what we're gonna do. You and the baby will ride the new horse, Harley will take Ghita and Tyr will take Carina. Harley! Tyr! You both got little sisters and I expect you to take care of these little ones as if they were your own sisters. We'll ride out to Kenyatta and the daimyo can decide what to do next."

Debbie stared at the horse in horror. It was enormous and shaggy, gray with a black mane and tail, and gray stockings. "I've never been on a horse. Ever. I don't know what to do. None of us do."

He quirked a tiny smile at her. "Didn't think so. You'll learn quick and we'll take it slow. We got over 150 klicks to get to the village and even as slow as we're gonna go, it'll be quicker than walking."

"The baby. My daughters. We can walk, we're used to it."

"We ain't got the time to fool around. Baby will go with you in the sling. All our women do that and it works just fine."

As Yannick spoke, Harley and Tyr had been moving things around from the extra horse to their own mounts.

Yannick said to the second man and the other boys, "Otis, I want you and the lads to trace Debbie's trail back to the road, make sure no one's coming after her and mess it up so none of those dirt-eaters can follow her into our territory. I'll be back at the cairn with Harley and Tyr in nine days, less if I can."

He turned back to Debbie. "You're next. Give the baby to Ghita to hold."

Debbie obediently handed over the nameless baby to Ghita and gave her the sling. She didn't know what else to do. This was as bad as being back in the village. But they hadn't hurt her and it didn't look as if they were going to. That was something to be grateful for, although it was a struggle.

The gray dappled horse looked enormous, looming over her. There was a sort of blanket cinched over its back made of heavy dun wool. Its back was as almost as tall as her shoulders and she had no idea how she was supposed to jump up on top of it and then control the animal once she was up there.

She realized that Yannick was speaking to her. "I'm gonna lift you up. Hold onto the reins loosely and put your feet in the stirrups." As he spoke, he held up first one thing and then the other and Debbie realized those were the names of the things he was talking about.

He put his hands around her waist and effortlessly lifted her up and she tried clumsily to put her legs around the horse, her skirts hiking up and showing her bare legs up to her thighs. It was humiliating and she could do nothing about it. She sat, trembling, on the horse, trying desperately to hold on to the blanket.

Yannick sighed. "Hold onto Gray Gal's mane and stick your feet into the stirrups. I'll take the reins and lead you around."

And he did, walking the horse around slowly while Debbie clung to its back, her fingers holding tightly to the horse's black mane. The horse did not seem to mind how tightly she gripped the hair and it didn't try to turn and bite her. Debbie was deeply relieved.

They spent the next hour or so with Yannick helping Debbie up and down off Gray Gal and leading the horse around in a circle while she held on for dear life. Ghita and Carina and the baby watched in open-mouthed awe, staying well away. Spotty looked on disapprovingly from within his muzzle and bonds but he could not do anything about her situation, any more than she could.

It was exhausting and Debbie, as she clung to Gray Gal's mane, wondered how well she could walk afterwards. She had always believed that it would be easier to ride an animal than it was to walk but now, feeling the strain in her legs, she had her doubts. Yannick kept telling her how to sit and hold on and at first she had no idea what he meant. Gradually as the afternoon wore on, she began to relax.

At that point, he said, "great! We're ready to go."

Debbie looked down at him in horror and for the first time since leaving Dairapaska all those years ago, she directly contradicted what was told to her when she answered, "You are crazy and I won't do it."

He grinned up at her, the first time he had smiled at her since he had called off the wolf-dogs. "Yes, you will, doll. You'll be fine."

While he had been walking her around on Gray Gal, the gear had been distributed among the other horses, all except one blanket rolled up on the ground. Yannick lifted her down from the gray mare and as soon as her feet touched the ground, she sat down, trembling and shaking. Ghita and Carina came scuttling up and they watched him tie up the last rolled blanket on Gray Gal's back.

Harley mounted his horse and Yannick picked up Ghita and carried her over to him and set her in front of Harley on the horse. She didn't fight him but her terror showed in her face.

Harley put an arm around her, holding her tightly and whispered something to her and began letting the horse amble in a circle. Carina was next, in front of Tyr on the brown horse and she was just as frightened, trying to squeeze back her tears and failing.

Then it was Spotty's turn. He was tied across the front of the blanket on Yannick's horse, in the same spot as Ghita and Carina were sitting. He tried hard to bite Yannick through his muzzle and failed again.

Yannick lifted Debbie back up onto Gray Gal, then gave her the sling to arrange across her body. The baby was next, handed up by Otis, and Debbie tucked her in tightly, tying the sling so she could not fall.

Yannick mounted his horse last, ignoring Spotty as though he wasn't there, and they set off to the east at a slow pace, accompanied by two of the wolf-dogs.

Debbie was petrified that she would drop the baby and petrified that she would fall off so she kept one hand clutched on the baby in her sling and the other tight in Gray Gal's mane. Yannick had the reins to her horse in one hand, his own horse's in the other, and she was amazed at how he could control both huge animals so easily.

Ghita and Carina sat stiffly as they ambled along, hanging on desperately despite being held by Harley and Tyr. Spotty gave up struggling and hung limply. Only the baby enjoyed the ride, staring at the world wide-eyed at her new vantage point.

4

Riding to Kenyatta

THEY TRAVELED THIS WAY FOR what seemed like hours until Yannick called a halt. He swung down from his horse easily, got Debbie and the baby down off Gray Gal and as soon as he let go, she promptly collapsed onto the ground, the thick grass cushioning her as she sprawled, legs aching. Ghita and Carina joined her moments later and then Spotty, still tied and muzzled, was unceremoniously dumped next to them.

They huddled together, sore and stiff, and watched unspeaking as Yannick and Harley and Tyr set up camp, start a fire, and then Harley and Tyr both remounted their horses and set off into the grasslands with one of the wolf-dogs as though they hadn't already been riding for hours.

"Where's Harley going?" Ghita asked shrilly, breaking the quiet. "Is he leaving us here?"

"Him and Tyr are gonna hunt some game for supper. Hares or prairie chickens most likely," answered Yannick.

Debbie looked around for the first time and saw how far off they were from right angles with the late afternoon sun. This was not the way she had been traveling.

"Why are we going east? I thought we had to go north?"

Yannick looked over at her, puzzled again. "Nothing north but steppes and critters till you reach the government corridor, some 300 klicks of tall grass and rolling hills in all. The manor house, the villages are all in the southeast corner of Kenyatta, the corner closest to Purnell. I know Shelleen does it this way. Everybody does."

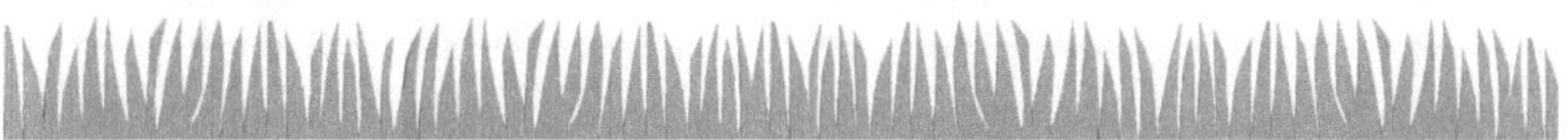

Debbie sat back, silent again and horrified. Never once during the slow trek north had she thought about how demesnes were arranged. The ruling family's manor house and the main villages were always in the corner of the demesne closest to the quad's free-city. Farther away from the populated areas, many demesnes were a wilderness of grasslands and wild animals. Not many demesnes had large enough populations to fill all the available land with villages and farms. Shelleen certainly didn't and neither did Dairapaska. She had known that. How could she have thought that the cold wastelands of the north would be different?

"You didn't think about that, did you?"

She shook her head vigorously, pulling the baby closer to her and edging closer to Ghita and Carina.

He huffed, "Good thing we found you. We got a main path running south to north, with way-stations too. But they're all set up for riders and the path is empty most of the time. You and your little ones woulda got lost and died out in the grass."

Debbie shut her eyes tight with despair. She had been so stupid. She could feel the tears leak out and that made her more miserable. She had spent so many years never showing any face to the world other than one of patient, pleasant endurance. Concealing what she felt and thought had become second nature and it had allowed her, for so many years, to keep her innermost self free from the strictures of Aldo, his family, and Shelleen. Even Ghita and Carina had never known how unhappy she was as she had been even more careful to not burden them.

The baby began to fuss again and Debbie wrenched herself away from her thoughts to care for her. Ghita and Carina huddled next to her, whispering to each other, and clutching their grass dolls. The dolls had turned brown and were becoming brittle at the edges. She would have to make some more.

Thinking about making more dolls allowed Debbie to think about something else other than dying on the steppes. The terror she had felt when the wolf-dogs had surrounded her and her daughters and the relief afterwards when they had not been ripped into bloody bits and devoured had made her rethink her position on dying in the grass. Whatever was going to happen to them in Kenyatta was preferable to dying. They had some value or Yannick would not have been so careful of them. The steppes were still better than going back to Shelleen and Aldo.

She tried to count the days since they had left the new village. It had been several weeks, perhaps almost a month. Each day had blended into the next, calm, empty, and quiet, as Debbie and her daughters had plodded north. Only the road in the corridor, then finding the cairn, and finally being found by Yannick and his crew, had broken the serenity.

If Aldo were to find her now, Debbie was sure of it, as sure as she was sure of breathing, he would beat her to death for her disloyalty and for taking Ghita and Carina away from him. He would most likely murder the unwanted and nameless baby too, leaving both of their bodies on the steppes for beasts to devour. She wondered if he would allow Ghita and Carina to live. Aldo would be angry enough that in his rage he might not care what his family back in the old village would say.

She would not go back and she would not let her daughters go back. It would not matter what the daimyo of Kenyatta had to say to her.

Harley and Tyr came riding back in triumph making the wolf-dog who had stayed at the camp sit up and bark vigorously. The wolf-dog with Harley and Tyr answered with more barking. Spotty growled through his muzzle and flopped around against his bonds. The wolf-dogs' barking frightened Ghita and Carina and the baby. They cringed back against her, the girls whimpering and the baby crying again. Debbie thought of how Aldo would have reacted to their tears and fears and was grateful again that she had seized the chance that fate had given her and run away from him forever.

She did not notice Yannick quietly observing them.

Ghita and Carina settled down quickly when they realized why the wolf-dogs had barked, but the baby took longer to sooth. By the time Debbie had gotten her calm again, the hares the boys had caught had been skinned and spitted and were roasting over a fire. The smell of cooking meat tore at her stomach. It had been a very, very long time since she had eaten rabbit. Weeks of mil-rats satisfied hunger but they weren't the same as real food, like the grains and beans she and her daughters were accustomed to. The roasting hares were considerably bigger than the rabbits she was familiar with, but they looked much the same, with their long ears, dappled tan bodies, and much longer legs.

Yannick strode up to her and nudged Spotty with the toe of his boot. Spotty tried to snarl but he was worn out, thirsty, and hungry. She petted him, telling him what a good dog he was as did Ghita and Carina.

"I got to untie him so he can eat. Tyr! Bring over some of those guts," Yannick said.

Tyr came over holding the skin of one of the hares like a bag. He spilled the steaming entrails onto the ground by Spotty who stared at them longingly and sniffed the air with enthusiasm. He whapped his tail on the ground to show his approval at this feast laying before him. The rest of the entrails had been devoured by the two wolf-dogs. They stared at what was being given to Spotty with envious eyes. He saw this and tried to growl at them through his muzzle, making them growl back. Yannick undid Spotty's legs and then his muzzle. Spotty lunged for the banquet and snapped it up, every messy, bloody scrap.

When he was finished, he snarled at the two big dogs who pointedly ignored him, then at Yannick and Harley and Tyr who all laughed while their hands flew.

Before he could be hogtied again, Ghita roused herself and grabbed Spotty and sat down, clutching him to her thin body. Carina joined her and the two girls petted him, telling him again and again what a good doggie he was. He let them do it, whining, shuddering, and wagging his tail, and did not snarl any more. Debbie wondered if Spotty had had his fill and if he would tolerate these strangers around his people.

"He'll have to be muzzled if he bites," said Yannick, anticipating her thoughts. "I shouldn't have to tie him again. You think he can keep up with the horses, running alongside?"

Debbie looked over up at Yannick, then at Spotty having his tummy rubbed by her daughters while the wolf-dogs lying nearby pretended not to notice the attention being lavished on him.

"I don't know," she answered slowly. "When we left the old

village, we all walked and the dogs walked with us. They were always able to keep up."

"We won't be riding too fast at first, so we'll see how it goes." Yannick tore a back leg off of one of the roasted hares and sprinkled it with a bit of salt from a tiny pouch he then tucked back into a pocket.

"Hare? Better'n mil-rats."

Spotty looked up eagerly as Debbie took the hare leg. It was so good, hot and rich, and the taste flooded her mouth and warmed her down to her stomach but she did not offer him a tidbit. She tore the meat off, ravenous, and broke the bone to suck out the creamy marrow, disappointing Spotty again. Ghita and Carina had their own hot pieces of hare and were enjoying every messy bite, blowing on their burning fingers and licking off the grease. It tasted as good as any rabbit Debbie had ever eaten.

All of the hares were quickly eaten and washed down with water as the last rays of the setting sun played over them. The bones and remaining scraps were tossed to the wolf-dogs who snapped them up, leaving Spotty disappointed once more.

In the fading light, Yannick and the boys unrolled the blankets by the fire, one for Debbie to share with her girls, and one for each of them.

Harley unrolled his bedroll and fussed with it, laying it out to his liking, clearing away any little stones from underneath. Spotty had been watching him intently. When Harley stepped away to finish cleaning up the campsite, Spotty wiggled free from Ghita's lap and scampered over to the bedroll. He looked around to see who was watching and then deliberately lifted his leg and peed on Harley's blanket.

Harley saw him from across the campsite.

"I'm gonna kill that fucking mutt!" he screamed.

He lunged after Spotty who bounded nimbly out of his way, barking joyously and springing into the air. He deftly evaded Harley, always bouncing a little out of reach and yapping derisively, enraging Harley still further as he struggled to catch Spotty and failed repeatedly.

Debbie and Carina sat horrified while Yannick and Tyr laughed themselves silly.

"Smart dog!" Yannick was finally able to say. "Remembers who muzzled and hogtied him."

The wolf-dogs looked on with open amusement from where they lay watching the show, as did the horses.

Ghita also chased after Spotty, all the while screaming at Harley to stop, and Spotty finally let her snatch him up after Harley grabbed him by the tail, forcing him to sacrifice a big tuft of his fur to escape.

"Leave my doggie alone!" she screamed up at Harley, clutching Spotty to her chest. Harley looked fit to burst, spluttering and glaring at Ghita who glared back up at him, while Spotty smirked at him from the safety of her arms. Finally, he stormed off into the darkness, swearing terribly.

"Is Harley going to hurt my Spotty? I won't let him," cried Ghita.

"He'll get over it," answered Yannick, still snickering. "Should have been watching for it, though. Dogs remember what people do to them. Harley won't forget that now."

They settled themselves in for the night; Debbie and the baby and Ghita and Carina and Spotty snuggled up together. Yannick lay down alongside her and Tyr arranged himself alongside Ghita. The wolf-dogs lay close by with the horses hobbled within easy reach. Harley finally came stomping out of the darkness and rolled himself up as far away from Spotty as he could, doing his best to avoid the rank, wet stain.

Spotty yawned hugely, his fangs flashing in the firelight. He felt vindicated after his capture and humiliation. He had vanquished Harley and gotten away with it, he had a tummy full of hare guts, and he had successfully defended his family. They were alive, safe, fed, and all because of him. He settled in contentedly at Ghita's side, feeling very pleased with himself.

Debbie lay in the darkness, the baby snug by her side, and felt deeply grateful. She and her daughters and her dog were warm, well fed, safe in the center of the group and, for right now, that was enough. She did not sing to her daughters, and they did not ask; they knew she never sang in front of others. As she drifted off into exhausted sleep, she wondered what name she would choose for the new baby. How wonderful that thought was. She could name her daughter as she saw fit.

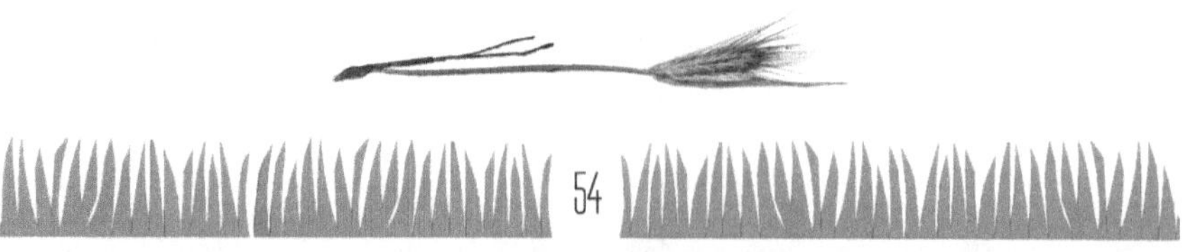

The dawn woke everyone. The fire had gone out so Tyr set to work, bringing it back to life and setting up for a breakfast of grains boiled in water, with shreds of dried meat thrown in. Yannick saw to the horses and dogs as Harley stomped around tearing down the campsite, erasing every trace that they had been there. Every time he passed Spotty, he snarled wordlessly at him. Spotty returned the favor but he made sure to stay out of Harley's way and close to Ghita.

Debbie was stiff and sore and she was not looking forward to spending an entire day learning how to ride a horse whether she liked it or not. She did not see the romance in it at all, compared to the ease and practicality of walking. Ghita and Carina were quickly developing a more positive viewpoint towards riding versus walking. Trudging through tall, dense, scratchy grass for weeks had been hard for them. On horseback, the horse did the work and they could see much farther. The baby was unconcerned as she rode in someone's arms all the time anyway.

They were finally on their way. Spotty was behaving himself and so did not get muzzled. He trotted alongside Debbie, perched frighteningly high on Gray Gal, and since the pace was slow, he kept up easily. He kept well away from Ghita as she was again riding pillion with Harley.

As they rode east into the rising sun, Debbie thought about what awaited her and her daughters in Kenyatta. Should she dare ask questions? She would not get answers if she didn't. Being high up on the horse was still terrifying and she was desperately afraid she would fall off, or worse, drop the baby. She spared a moment to be grateful that Ghita and Carina seemed to be safe with Harley and Tyr. Even better, Harley did not seem angry with Ghita over how Spotty had behaved towards him.

Yannick rode alongside her, effortlessly controlling his own horse as well as hers. She thought about him and his reactions. He wasn't happy with her for running away from her husband and stealing his children, that was clear enough. She didn't think that any man would ever approve, no matter how awful the husband. Debbie reflected bitterly that wives could and did get beaten and few men other than a father or brother could be counted on to step in. It had been true in Dairapaska as well as Shelleen.

Aldo hitting his daughters; that was different. He would have been ostracized if anyone had known about it. No one cared what he did to Debbie. She was just a wife with no family around to care and wives could be replaced. Ghita and Carina, despite being girls, were the only grandchildren in his family. His relatives one and all, if they knew, would have been furious with him. Aldo had often been unhappy with Debbie, for what she never knew, but he had never struck her until the forced march from the old village. He had never been especially interested in his daughters but he had also never been routinely angry with them as he was now.

Debbie knew that Aldo could control himself. He did all the time since he only struck her when no one could see. He had been even more careful with Ghita and Carina. He only showed his rage publicly with the new baby, refusing to carve her a kuksa and grumbling continuously and openly about her sex.

Despite the new baby being a girl, Debbie understood that if they had not been forced to set up the new village so far away, Aldo would have eventually gotten over it. His family would have said exactly what the peasants of the new village said to him. "Debbie is young and healthy and fertile. She has the chance of many more babies ahead of her." The difference was that he would have listened to his family. His family would have had plenty to say to *her* about delivering a girl instead of a boy, but a grandchild was a grandchild, and they desperately wanted more.

If the daimyo of Shelleen had not wanted the new village plopped down in the middle of nowhere, she would still be living with Aldo and she would have never, no matter how secretly unhappy she was, run away as she had.

How strange that another action over which she had no control whatsoever should have resulted in her life changing so very much again. She would have lived out her life and gone to her grave in the old village in Shelleen, and everyone would have said, "Patient Debbie. Pleasant Debbie. Dull Debbie. Debbie the ox. Nothing ever bothered her."

But that was only true on the outside. On the inside, it bothered her very much, but since she took care that no one ever knew, it came to much the same thing. And then she ran away, taking her daughters with her. What would the peasants left behind in the new village make of it? They would speculate forever and by now, depending on the overseer's schedule, word might have already reached the old village, Aldo's family, and the rest of Shelleen.

But no one would ever know exactly what she did or why or even where she went. Nobody would say "Debbie the ox" ever again even as they chewed over the story endlessly for decades to come. It was a comforting thought, making her smile.

How different would her situation be in Kenyatta? Would it be better? Would she have much say in how her life ran, more than she had in Shelleen? It was impossible to say. Debbie thought about that and decided that it was possible to say. Yannick, the other rider, and the boys valued her enough to keep her safe and cared for, along with her daughters. Even Spotty, trotting alongside her, had been kept safe and fed.

They had not liked it at all, what Aldo had done to the nameless baby by refusing her.

Perhaps she would have a little say in her own life. She would get to choose the baby's name.

And there was something else she could ask about, while they were riding through the endless seas of grass into the east. She could wait until they made camp, but if she asked while they were riding, it would be harder for Yannick to hit her if it turned out to be a bad question. She fretted over the thought of waiting. Better to do it now, she finally decided, and hope he got over being angry by the time they made camp.

It would mean turning to look at him. Debbie tightened her grip on the baby with one hand and Gray Gal's mane with the other and cautiously turned her head towards him. She didn't fall off the horse right away, nor did the baby fall, for both of which she was deeply grateful. Gray Gal did not appear to even notice Debbie cautiously shifting her weight.

"Yannick? May I ask some questions?"

He looked over at her, surprised. "Sure, doll. What do you wanta know?"

She took a deep breath, gathering her strength. "Will Kenyatta keep me, rather than sending me back to Shelleen to Aldo? And keep my daughters?"

He looked angry for a moment, but she wasn't sure at what.

Not at her, she hoped.

"Yeah, he'll keep you here at Kenyatta. Ghita's been talking to Harley. He told me this morning she said as how her dad hit her. Seems that part of your story's true. Carina won't talk to Tyr. She just looks scared and shuts up when he asks her to tell him about you and her dad, but she'll talk plenty about the village. Not a good sign. You won't be sent back and neither will your girls."

Debbie was deeply relieved, feeling a worry slide away. "Thank you. It means everything to me, keeping them safe. We can live in tents forever if it means not going back."

He looked offended. "We don't live in tents. I mean we do, depends on what we're doing, but we got houses."

Debbie risked another look at him, taking her eyes off Gray Gal's ears. The baby chose that moment to wiggle around in the sling and she gasped and clutched harder at both the baby in the sling and Gray Gal's mane. She turned her eyes resolutely forward and they rode in silence for a few moments.

When it didn't seem like anything would happen with the baby sliding to her death, Debbie tried again. "I have something else," she began hesitantly.

"Yeah?"

"You know I'm from Dairapaska. I can't go back because it would cause problems with them and Shelleen. Would it be okay if I wrote to my family there? None of the girls from Dairapaska were ever allowed to write home. Everyone there must think we're dead."

This earned her a long stare from Yannick. "You weren't allowed to write letters?"

"Never. And I do know how to read and write. We all could. But we were told, all of us, that Shelleen was our home now and we couldn't ever write back to let our families know what happened to us."

"Did they want you to be unhappy?"

Debbie thought about this carefully before answering him, wanting to be sure she explained properly to this hawk-eyed man. "I don't think that anybody cared what we thought or wanted. And I think it was the same with the Shelleen girls. I never heard of any of them writing back to Shelleen from Dairapaska. That couldn't have been hidden. So we never heard back about our families that way either.”

“You can write as much as you want.” Yannick paused, thinking about it, and added, “You should probably tell your family right off that you’re not at Shelleen anymore and they shouldn’t say anything to anybody about how you ran off. Save Kenyatta some trouble, yeah?”

Debbie puzzled over this, then realized, “Oh! You mean that they’ll know I’m writing from Kenyatta and how did I get there? They’ll want to know everything that happened and all the other families will want to know what happened to their sisters and daughters.” She stopped and thought some more.

“But I don’t see what it would matter to the lords, even in Kenyatta. Nobody would ever talk to them, ever. We’re serfs. Lords don’t talk to us. They don’t much care what we do as long as we work and don’t cause trouble.”

Yannick laughed sourly. “Word gets around and pretty soon every last person in Dairapaska, from low to high, will know that you ran away from your husband and stole his kids away from him.”

Debbie looked down at the nameless baby. The baby was watching everything around her with wide eyes and sucking on her thumb. Her other little hand clutched the sling.

“I had to,” she finally mumbled.

“I know that,” Yannick said patiently. “What I’m saying is that a story like this gets told and retold and eventually the daimyo of Dairapaska will hear it. Maybe he’ll say something to Shelleen and maybe he won’t. Maybe he’ll say something to Kenyatta and maybe he won’t. Dairapaska’s a dirt demesne a long ways away on the western half and we got nothing to do with them. But this is a good story. Eventually Shelleen may hear something and he *could* make trouble for Kenyatta. Shelleen’s part of the quad and we got to work with those dirt-eaters even if we don’t like them.”

She watched Gray Gal’s ears twitching at the occasional fly as they ambled along.

“Maybe I shouldn’t. It’s been many years and who would care anymore?” The thought was heartbreaking, that people she missed desperately might no longer care about her or her fate.

“You still care and so will they. Nobody forgets losing the

people they love, ever. Write to them. Bring them joy."

The baby chose that moment to wail. Debbie looked down fondly at her little face. "We'll have to stop for a while. She's hungry."

Yannick sighed. "I don't suppose you can nurse her while we keep moving?"

Debbie stared openmouthed at Gray Gal's ears as she thought about all the things that could go wrong, culminating with the baby falling and being trampled into bloody paste under the horse's unconcerned hooves. "Um, no, I don't think I can."

Yannick sighed again. "This is gonna take even longer than I thought. Harley! Tyr! Baby needs her mamma so we're gonna make camp. I'll need some tea."

"I'm sorry."

Yannick twisted in his saddle to meet her eyes. "It can't be helped. She needs you. Try and come up with a name. We can't keep calling her 'baby'."

They stopped, made camp, and Debbie settled in with the nameless baby. Ghita and Carina were happy to stop as well and they collected grass plumes to wave at the baby, distracting her from her business until Debbie sharply told them to let her nurse in peace. After that, they waved the grass plumes to make Spotty leap and yap, annoying everyone.

Yannick, Harley, and the wolf-dogs swiftly disappeared into the steppes once Spotty started barking at the grass plumes. Tyr got to stay with them, build a fire, and make the tea. When the other two didn't come back right away, Tyr explained that they would take this chance to hunt something for dinner.

The thought of eating made her stomach growl and the girls both looked up.

"Mommy, I'm hungry," said Ghita.

"Me too, mommy," added Carina.

Debbie thought regretfully about the pack full of mil-rats. Yannick had insisted that they be returned to the cairn she had taken them from. If she had that pack, she would have had enough to share but would they have lasted until they reached Kenyatta? One hundred and fifty klicks were a long way, even on horses to make the trip faster.

Her pack, filled to the brim, had lasted to the road for just her and the girls, and then another pack, the one from the way-station, had lasted until the cairn. Both trips had only been about 50 or 60 klicks, although she was not sure. One hundred and fifty klicks were three times longer than what a pack of mil-rats for the three of them would last.

She watched Tyr, walking slowly around the camp and watching the steppes around them. He would crouch down sometimes and look at a plant and write something in a little notebook. She did not know what he was doing, but she did know one thing. Boys ate a lot. A boy like him could eat as much as her, Ghita, and Carina combined. Her pack would have been emptied out even faster than before.

Debbie had to trust that Yannick knew what he was doing. He hadn't seemed worried about getting enough to eat, for him and the boys or for her and her daughters.

The baby finished up, burped hugely, and was ready to play with grass plumes. Debbie took her opportunity to make more grass dolls for Ghita and Carina, while at the same time trying to keep the baby from eating the grass she was waving about. She had finished the second doll when Yannick and Harley returned.

They were both grinning, Harley especially so. He had a long-legged animal slung over his shoulders, a type she had never seen before.

"Harley brought down a gazelle," said Yannick proudly. "Dogs already ate when we field-dressed it."

Both wolf-dogs looked happy, their long tongues searching for the last bits of blood on their muzzles. Spotty sidled up to them, sniffing with interest and got snapped at for his pains. He retreated back to Ghita and the grass plumes.

The gazelle was butchered more cleanly, the scraps going to all three dogs, and after spit-cooking, everyone got to eat their fill, including a slice of the roasted liver. Debbie enjoyed every morsel, as did her daughters.

Afterwards, Yannick said, "weather's gonna turn on us and it'll be raining by twilight. If we push faster, we can make the shelter." He studied Debbie, his expression noncommittal. "Otherwise, we'll camp in the rain."

Debbie cringed. She was already riding at a terrifying speed but she really did not want to stay outside overnight in the rain.

When the serfs had walked from the old village to the site

of the new one, they had encountered rainstorms many times. Those days had been a misery, whether walking along in the driving rain during the day or huddled together under sodden blankets, trying to sleep so as to be ready for the next day's trek through the mud. The chill of the rain had soaked their clothes down into their bones, taking days of dry weather to slowly drain the wetness away, letting dryness and warmth seep back in. The heavy wool kept them from freezing, but there was nothing pleasant about enduring its thick, smelly, sodden weight.

One of the babies on the trip had died from the cold, soaking rain but the daimyo's armed men had insisted that they continue on to the site of the new village rather than take time to grieve. It had made the serfs even more resentful.

Debbie looked down at her nameless, laughing baby, clutching a grass plume in her fat little fist and waving it around in delighted awe, and stared up at Yannick, her eyes huge and filled with fear. "I'll try. I have to have the baby snug and tight so she doesn't fall."

"I won't let that happen. Harley! Tyr! Break camp now cause we're gonna ride for the shelter."

It seemed only moments later that Debbie was back on top of Gray Gal, with the baby more tightly secured, the camp broken down, and everyone else on their horses. Yannick set the pace, at first as slowly as they had ridden before and Debbie felt herself relax. Then he spurred his horse to a slow trot and Gray Gal kept right up.

Debbie clung tightly to Gray Gal's mane, trying to stay upright and hold onto the baby. This was terrifyingly fast and she felt dangerously unmoored, trying to hold onto Gray Gal with her legs. She didn't dare look around her to see if Ghita and Carina were all right. She had to assume that Harley and Tyr were keeping them safe. She hoped that Spotty was keeping up but she was even more afraid of looking down at the ground racing past underfoot than looking around.

They were riding much faster than before and she wondered how fast they would have to go to find the shelter before the rain came. The sun gradually lowered itself in the sky and the clouds began to shift and build, making the light dim down faster.

Debbie had hoped that Yannick had lied about a storm coming to force the group to move faster, but it seemed that a storm really was coming. She could hear, far off in the distance, a rumble of thunder, and her heart sank. Walking in a thunderstorm was bad enough but riding a horse in one would be a true misery. She and her girls would freeze in their thin, patched kirtles and aprons.

Yannick increased their speed again, and they went faster still. Debbie focused on holding on to Gray Gal and the baby and not thinking about anything else.

The storm grew closer, the thunder louder, the sky darkened further and the wind picked up. Yannick called to Harley and Tyr something she didn't understand, and they bolted past her, moving far swifter than they had been riding before. That was when Debbie realized how fast a horse could run.

She did not dare turn to Yannick to ask why Harley and Tyr had ridden ahead with her daughters. She did not even dare try to think about his reasons. All her effort was focused on hanging on, clutching the baby, and ignoring how much her arms and legs, back and rear end were hurting.

They kept trotting, and Yannick increased the pace again, but they never moved as fast as Harley and Tyr had. They had long since disappeared down the trail with her daughters. The wolf-dogs didn't seem to have followed them so Debbie assumed they were still following Yannick. She hoped that Spotty was too but she didn't dare turn to look.

They rode into a mist of rain, cold and damp, and then the first fat raindrops began falling. It was gentle at first, and then they began hitting Debbie with greater force. She didn't know if the rain hit harder because it was a fierce storm on its way or because she was riding fast in it.

The sun had disappeared behind clouds and the horizon, light was failing and twilight was coming on when she saw a glint of a fire far off in the distance. She prayed that it was the shelter and to her infinite relief, it was.

The shelter wasn't much. It was a small, three-sided building with a low, sloped roof that was open to the south, away from the direction of the storm. But it had a roof and walls to keep out the worst of the wind and rain and that was far more than the serfs had had on the endless forced march to the new village. Debbie was truly grateful to see it, with her daughters, Harley and Tyr, their horses, and the welcoming warm fire crowded inside of it.

She didn't object when Yannick urged Gray Gal still faster and then they were inside, under the roof, and out of the rain and wind. Harley was already helping her down from Gray Girl, even before she could catch her breath.

Debbie staggered to the fire on burning legs and collapsed in front of it. The warmth of a fire had never felt so good. Ghita and Carina were already there and they made room for her. She was very content to sit, one daughter on each side and her baby in her lap, out of the wind and the rain.

"Mommy, we went so fast!" Ghita said. Her eyes were sparkling. "It was the most fun ever."

Carina was nodding her head in agreement, her eyes bright, too. They were both wrapped up in striped wool blankets. The stripes were shades of tan and cream, and Debbie recognized it as being undyed wool. Yet someone had still cared enough to alternate the shades of undyed wool, varying the stripes from top to bottom to make a pattern. She wondered who that someone was, who made a shelter blanket a little more beautiful.

"We beat the rain and Harley and Tyr got the fire going and the horses settled and look! The floor stays dry. It's not raining inside like the soddy did," Ghita marveled.

It was true. They were dry. The soddy had been miserable after a rain. It took a long time for the cold wetness to seep and drip away after a storm. That's what came of building a house from bricks made of sod. When it finally dried out, the next storm came and soaked it again.

Debbie shivered in front of the fire, both from the cold and from the frightening ride in. How much faster had Ghita and Carina been riding that they had beaten the rain and had time to get the horses into the shelter and the fire started? She hoped that her girls had had the sense to stay out of the way while Harley and Tyr worked.

Someone — she looked up and saw that it was Yannick — draped a wool blanket over her shoulders, and she gratefully wrapped herself and the baby in it.

As she settled in, she noticed that the shelter had a floor of bamboo, sloped towards the open side. If any rain came in, it would drain back outside. There were shelves and hooks lining the back wall, along with some closed cabinets. She had thought the horses were inside the shelter and they were, but there was a low wall dividing the space in two. The horses were on their own side, where they could watch the doings on the people side.

The fire pit made of stone sat in the center of the people side of the shelter, with low walls to keep the fire away from the bamboo floor and more stone edging around it for sparks. Someone, Tyr probably, had already set two pots hanging over it, one of mint tea and another of stewed grains with the shredded, dried meat.

It was a good design. The pit was large enough to cook over and to sit around for warmth. The fire would not be a danger and the stones would get hot and radiate heat all night. Even though there wasn't a chimney that she could see, the smoke left the shelter. Through the open front, she supposed. Well, it was a shelter and not a house.

"Mommy? Where's Spotty?" asked Ghita.

"Uh, following us?" she answered, at a complete loss. Debbie didn't want to even think of him being lost in the storm, not after he had been such a good dog on the trek north.

And then the wolf-dogs came barreling into the shelter, followed a few minutes later by Spotty, running after them hard. Yannick was on his feet at once, shoving the dogs to the front and side and when they started to shake off, Debbie knew why.

Spotty shaking didn't make that much of a mess, but the wolf-dogs shed so much rain it was like being back outside. When they were finished, the dogs tried to wedge themselves as close to the fire as they could without actually touching the hot stone edging. Spotty flopped himself between Debbie and Ghita, panting, and when a wolf-dog came up alongside Carina to lie down, he only snarled a tiny bit and received only a small growl in return.

"Debbie."

She looked up to see Yannick holding out a kuksa full of steaming hot tea. She took it gratefully, and sipped it slowly, enjoying the sensation of heat curling through her body. Ghita and Carina had cups of tea as well; soon everyone did but the dogs and they sat around the fire in companionable silence, drinking the hot tea and watching the rain.

It was a great pleasure to observe the rain from a safe, dry, warm vantage point. Debbie, Ghita, and Carina had not watched rain while being able to stay dry since they had left the old village all those months ago.

5

Debbie Begins to Reveal Her Past

THE STEW TYR MADE WAS HOT and filling and hunger made it taste better than it actually was. When it was all eaten, they settled in for the night. Debbie kept Ghita and Carina and the baby tucked close. As tired and worn out as she was — and she hurt all over from desperately hanging onto Gray Gal during that dreadful ride — she did not find sleep easy.

She lay quietly by the fire amusing the baby, and idly listened to Yannick quizzing the boys on the plants and animals they had seen during the day, things that she knew very little about. She wondered how they recognized what they saw while riding so fast. He spent time discussing what he saw in the sky as well; how the clouds had come boiling up from the north filling the sky and what that meant when combined with the direction and speed of the wind and the dampness he felt in the air.

Ghita and Carina listened very quietly, sometimes timidly asking a question about a bird or a bug and it was always answered, and in some detail. Yannick seemed to know something about everything they saw on the steppes.

Debbie did not ask questions.

It bothered her very much why these strangers were being so kind to them. She could not understand it. She was a penniless serf, a runaway, and from far, far away with no family connections to speak of. She had no value other than the work she could do. Or what a woman could always offer but they didn't seem to want her that way either, for which she was intensely grateful.

She lay in the fire-lit shelter, listening to the rain beating on the ground and the night sounds of the horses and dogs and Yannick and the boys and her daughters. Yannick had not been happy, at all, about her leaving Aldo and taking his children, even if he was starting to accept why she did it. Yet here he was, hauling her and her daughters off to Kenyatta and interrupting whatever he had been doing out on the steppes. He seemed very sure that they would take her in.

She wanted to ask why. Should she?

Debbie had heard all the lurid stories about slavers stealing people for the equator plantations. Everyone in Dairapaska knew them and so did everyone in Shelleen, telling and retelling similar tales of agony, fear, and woe. If she and her daughters were to be sold to the equator plantations, then why were they being so careful of her and the baby's needs? Slavers did not behave decently with their captives. All the stories agreed on that point.

Or perhaps the stories about the equator slave trade were just that: stories to keep the serfs afraid and obedient and not striking out on their own for the government corridors and the free-cities. Everybody knew that city air was free air, just like everybody knew that within a demesne, the law was whatever the daimyo said it was.

The stories she had been told about wolf packs had turned out not to be true. The northern dogs looked like wolves with their huge shaggy, toothy fierceness but they were dogs. Debbie did not know much about wolves but she was pretty sure that no wolf would ever wag its tail or obey a human master like these beasts did. That made them dogs. Nobody would dare tousle the ears of a wolf, like Yannick did with these dogs, nor would a wolf beg for more petting.

Other stories said you couldn't successfully escape. That wasn't true either. Debbie had proved that a woman with small children could walk from a village to the border to the road and all on her own. Maybe you couldn't walk the hundreds of klicks from a village deep inside a demesne all the way to the government corridor without being found out but a border village? It wasn't possible. It was doable. She had done it and on the spur of the moment without any planning at all.

Debbie knew she had been lucky. The mil-rats had been

available, it had been late summer, the men had been off in the fields for several days, and the guards had gone with them. But she had still been able to slip away. This meant other people could do it too. Families with their kids could quietly walk off and disappear. No one ever did but maybe it was because they didn't think they could and the dreadful stories that were told had reinforced that belief.

What would happen when she wrote to her family in Dairapaska and word got around? Yannick was right on that point. Word would get around and fast, like dry tinder catching a flame.

She remembered how in Dairapaska stories were told and retold about what everyone did, even out in the far villages. Anything that was even the slightest bit out of the ordinary was chewed over endlessly. She knew stories about distant relatives who had been dead for a generation and the amazing thing that they had said or done. She even knew stories about distant relatives who lived in the other demesnes in the Dairapaska quad; people whose immediate relatives had passed into memory but who nonetheless still wrote long, detailed letters about every aspect of their lives, letters that were passed around endlessly so everyone could memorize them.

The same had been true of the villages in Shelleen. Everybody in Shelleen would be talking about her and her escape for generations to come, and they would do the same in Dairapaska within minutes of her first letter's arrival.

But Yannick did not seem to be concerned. She wondered if he had considered what a taste of freedom might mean for the serfs of Dairapaska and Shelleen.

The more she thought about it, the less difference Debbie saw between her situation and that of the slaves she had learned about in the village school all those years ago. She hadn't had any choice about where she lived. She belonged to someone not of her choosing. She had little say about anything she did. She never saw any reward for the work she did, other than to have to do it all over again the next day, never getting ahead, never accumulating wealth and security for her family. Didn't that make her a slave? And then she had run away, something a slave would do.

Why didn't Yannick and Harley and Tyr run away? They

had horses and gear. They knew how to camp and hunt game and probably find water too. There had been village hunters in Dairapaska and a few in Shelleen, but most of the peasants did not go out onto the steppes to hunt at all. They did not know how to catch anything bigger than a rabbit and they spent most of every day in the fields, weather permitting. At the close of day, they huddled with their families in their cottages in exhausted slumber and waited for the night to pass. Rarely did people go outside to watch the stars and tell stories and when they did, they never left the familiar confines of the village for the inky black steppes beyond. Certainly, no one ever willingly *slept* out of doors overnight, even within the village borders. It just wasn't done.

Nevertheless, Yannick and the boys must have slept outdoors all the time and the terrors of the black night did not bother them one bit. Debbie had been afraid of sleeping outside but nothing had happened to her and her girls in their grass nests. She *had* been lucky that it hadn't rained at night and that the night temperatures were still mild. Cold rain would have been a misery. But nothing had bothered them. Maybe because Spotty was with them? But he was a little dog, not a huge wolf-dog like the two monsters snoring away at her feet. Maybe the terrors of the dark night were another lie, like the slave plantation stories, that the lords told the serfs to keep them in line.

Moreover, there was no daimyo's man supervising Yannick and Harley and Tyr or the other man, Otis, and the boys who had been left behind back at the stone tower. This fact was astonishing all by itself.

When the new village had been set up, the daimyo of Shelleen had sent an overseer along with armed guards to escort the peasants on the long march and then they stayed to see that everyone got settled in and got to work. The overseer regularly visited after that, always with armed guards to ensure that nobody did other than what they were supposed to do.

The village headman always did his best to negotiate for his village, but in the end, it was what the overseer for the daimyo wanted that mattered, not what was good for the serfs. That was unusual too. The peasants did the day-to-day labor on the land and they knew what they were doing. The daimyo knew that too, since in the old villages the peasants toiled without close supervision. Yet, in the new village, he did not seem to care that the strange things *he* wanted were not what the peasants needed to do. Why didn't he care?

Yannick and Harley and Tyr could have gone wherever they chose, but they still chose to stay in Kenyatta. Perhaps it was a good place. They must have families that they did not want to leave behind. But they were all capable enough that she was sure that they could take their families with them, if they wanted to escape to a free-city for a better life.

But they didn't. So, Kenyatta must be a decent place to live for the peasants.

Debbie smiled into the darkness. Maybe it would be a decent place for her and her daughters, too. She would ask Yannick in the morning why he was so sure that Kenyatta would accept her. She would be careful and wait until they were riding, like she had asked about writing letters today. If she made him angry with her questions, he wouldn't hit her while she was on Gray Gal and risk her dropping the baby and by the time they stopped, he might be over it. Maybe he wouldn't even get angry with her. He hadn't yet.

Debbie lay quietly, Yannick rolled up in his blanket asleep. His long, lean body was warm next to her and with her daughters snuggled up on her other side, she was the coziest she had been in a very long time.

She rolled it over and over in her mind. It was such a pleasant thought. She could ask Yannick a question and he would not get angry with her and he would even answer it as he had patiently answered her daughter's questions about the birds they had seen. She would do it. Debbie could feel another knot in her soul loosen, knowing that he would most likely not harm her, and then she was able to sleep.

When dawn came, the rain had slowed to a thin mist but it had not vanished with the night. Debbie woke to the smell of mint tea and the sight of Yannick silhouetted in front of the cloud-obscured, rising sun. He stood studying the leaden sky and drumming his fingers on the side of the shelter.

The baby woke up and decided she was hungry and that took her attention for a while. It was a pleasure to be able to take care of her baby without worrying about what Aldo would say or do. Debbie was grateful again that she had taken her opportunity to run away. Even if things did not turn out well, she had had these beautiful, golden days with her littlest daughter, days she would have never had back in the new village.

Yannick walked over to her, a set look on his face. He crouched down next to her.

"Debbie, the weather's not gonna get much better, not for hours. I wanta push on, to the next shelter. That'll mean a long, wet day but we'll sleep dry and under cover instead of out in the open. I know you're sore. Can you do it?"

Debbie stared up at him and then down at the fire, her mind empty of everything except the shock that someone had asked her opinion about something important. She could choose.

"Debbie, you listening to me?"

She turned her face back up towards his own intent gaze. "Yes. I'll try." The baby gurgled and tried to grab at the flames and she at once scooted them further away. "Is there a way for the baby to stay dry?"

"We got ponchos. They shed the rain pretty well." He smiled at the baby who smiled back, and then made a grab for his beard, and succeeded to her gurgling delight.

Debbie was horrified, but Yannick only laughed. "Hah! Have to be more careful." He very gently uncurled her tiny fingers from his beard and stood up, smiling at some memory. "They grow up fast."

"Harley! Tyr!" he called out. "We're gonna ride out, not wait for the weather to clear."

Debbie soon found herself back on Gray Gal, with the baby back in her sling, but this time covered with a hooded poncho that enveloped them both. She fretted as she tried to keep hold of Gray Gal, the baby in her sling and the poncho, debating if she had made a good choice. She was grateful that she had time to get used to wearing it in the shelter before riding out into the thin rain.

Ghita and Carina were tucked up inside Harley and Tyr's ponchos, only their faces peeking out. Both boys also wore big, wide-brimmed leather hats that she had not seen before. More things that they carried in their bulging saddlebags, she supposed. Or maybe they came out of the shelter cupboards.

Yannick was dressed similarly, a heavy wool poncho over his clothes and another wide-brimmed, dark brown leather hat to shed the rain.

The wolf-dogs did not have ponchos or rain-shedding hats and they did not look eager to run into the cool, gray drizzle any more than the horses did.

Yannick led the way out into the rain, and whistled for the wolf-dogs, with Harley and Tyr following behind. Debbie did not dare look back to see if Spotty was following.

As they trotted along, Spotty came racing alongside Gray Gal, yapping up at her. He was not happy about being out in the rain and he barked and snarled to tell her so until one of the wolf-dogs ran alongside and growled at him. After that, he settled down.

As they settled in, Yannick set a faster pace and they maintained it for hours. The baby slept in her sling, snug and cozy and rocking against Debbie's body. She was undecided if she should be grateful or not. It was easier to ride when the baby slept, but that might mean she would be up all night and that wouldn't be pleasant for anyone.

The rain gradually thinned to a fine mist and then the mist burned off before the face of the noonday sun. Yannick asked, "You need to stop, Debbie?"

She risked a look away from Gray Gal's ears and said no and they continued riding into the east. Sometime later on, the baby finally woke and cried and then it was time for a break.

The ground wasn't too muddy, there were almost dry, stony outcroppings to sit on, and it was very pleasant to get out of the wet wool ponchos, now spread out on the grass to dry in the thin sunshine. Wool didn't become killing cold no matter how wet it got, but wet wool made you forcibly remember the sheep it came from.

The baby was nursing vigorously, Tyr had made tea for everyone, and everyone had a cup. There had been some spares in the shelter and Harley had packed them for the journey.

Ghita held up her kuksa, marveling at how clean the wood was. It did not look like it had ever been used. "Doesn't this belong to someone?" she asked curiously, turning the cup over and over as she admired it.

"Nah," Harley answered, "these are practice cups. It'd be a waste to not use them so everybody's practice cups, the ones that don't get burned, go into shelters. In case somebody loses one on the steppes, yeah?"

Carina held up her cup into the watery sun, running her fingers over the pale, smooth wood. "Can we keep these?"

Tyr chuckled. "Sure, for now. Someone'll carve you a nicer one when you're in Kenyatta. It'll have your name, some flowers and everything. Make it pretty, yeah?"

Debbie thought about that. Tyr seemed very sure of his answer. Why would someone do that? It took some time to choose the wood and carve a nice kuksa and there was always something more important to do than carve extra ones for guests who did not bring their own. That's what gourds or sections of bamboo were for. If you were rich you owned china mugs, but those were precious and jealously guarded so they didn't get broken.

The baby stopped nursing and burped tremendously, making everyone laugh. She laughed too, a joyous burble that thrilled Debbie. The baby had babbled and smiled more and more since they had begun the long trek north. She was happy, and it showed.

Yannick was pacing, studying the gathering clouds that filled the view to the north with fluffy, gray-tinged pink mounds. He did not look happy. He came back to the group around the campfire and said, "This is one of them storms. It'll come in bands, never too bad, but it won't stop either. If we want to make the shelter and sleep dry, we have to get moving."

Harley and Tyr were on their feet at once, breaking the camp down and repacking the horses. Debbie was happy to see that Ghita and Carina stayed out of their way, helping when they could do so.

"Debbie," Yannick said as he crouched down next to her. "We got to move faster to beat the weather, and we'll be riding in the rain anyway for the last part of it. Can you do this?"

The baby wiggled in her lap trying to grab at a plume of grass and she thought of the terror of riding so fast the night before and the worse terror of the baby getting sick from the cold rain, like had happened to that other baby during the endless walk to the new village. She could not let that happen.

"Yes, do what you have to," Debbie replied, looking up at Yannick's face. It was becoming easier to meet his dark, intent eyes. "A baby died when we marched from the old village to the new because of the rain. We weren't allowed to stop."

Yannick looked away, appalled, and swore softly. "When we hit the shelter tonight, I need to know what happened on that march the dirt daimyo made you do. And how you got from Dairapaska to Shelleen. I can see I got a lot of stuff to tell Kenyatta when we get home."

He lifted her back onto Gray Gal and they were off, riding faster than before. Debbie was feeling mildly more comfortable on top of the horse than she had been, but she did not think she would ever get to like it.

"Debbie!" She risked turning her head to hear Yannick better. "I don't want to stop again, if you can help it. When we get closer, I'll send Harley and Tyr ahead with the girls. Ready to go faster?"

She swallowed and said, "Yes, I'm ready."

He spurred his horse and they moved faster still. Debbie focused on holding on and trying to find a way to stay more comfortable and in tune with Gray Gal's movements. Yannick and the boys must have been riding since childhood to be so effortless at it. Maybe Ghita and Carina would become equally effortless at riding. Did they even let girls ride the way boys did? Kirtles did not work well for riding, not like pants. She would find out when they reached Kenyatta, and she contented herself with that.

The sun slowly moved overhead on its journey to the west and as it did so, the clouds darkened, thickened, and the wind picked up. The air began to fill with mist and then the mist changed back into a light drizzle.

The poncho helped keep the worst of it off, and Debbie was grateful for the unknown maker who had woven it so tightly, allowing it to shed most of the water, keep her and the baby warm, and block the questing fingers of the winds.

The afternoon passed endlessly and the baby, to Debbie's infinite gratitude, chose to nap rather than fuss. The rain passed in stages overhead, never quite turning into a downpour and never really stopping either. It was a cold, wet, bleak, interminable day, and the sun never came out.

Debbie thought of how awful the day would have been without the ponchos and how much ponchos would have meant during the long march from the old village to the new. It had been miserable when it rained, day or night.

The poncho she was wearing would not have been hard to make. It was just a square with a rectangle sewed on for a hood at the neck opening and a drawstring to pull it snug. It was plain, undyed wool, but very tightly woven and felted. Shelleen had sheep and wool and weavers. They could have brought ponchos for the long march. It would have made the trip so much easier, and the ponchos would have been usable as blankets at night and for long afterwards.

Why hadn't the daimyo of Shelleen supplied them better for the long journey? Whenever it rained, many of the peasants had coughed afterwards for days. And that baby had died. It was surprising that no one else had died. If the daimyo wanted the new village so badly, then why did he take so little care of the peasants who had to settle it? The more she thought about it, the less sense it made to her.

Shelleen did not have people to spare. It was the reason behind Debbie and the other girls from Dairapaska being traded with the girls from Shelleen in the first place. Fertile, unrelated brides made for more people. So why did the daimyo not care that the peasants had to get to the new village so quickly that a baby died and that the peasants got sick? They had had so few supplies, no ponchos, only a few goats and chickens, nothing to help the peasants set up the new village out on the steppes far from anywhere. As time went on, sometimes more supplies arrived in wagons with the overseer, but there was never enough to meet more than the barest needs.

Debbie remembered quite well the stories told at Dairapaska about setting up a new village. They were never much more than a full day's walk away from an existing village, a road would be built between the two to make travel between them easier, and the peasants who volunteered to go would have better status in the new village than in the old. They would have first pick of the virgin land and their descendants would have more respect as being the children of the first settlers. Their family names would be listed first in the cadastre, never to be removed, even if that line died out generations later. There were always volunteers; that was what she had been told. Their descendants were proud of their pioneering ancestors and always made sure to mention their great-grandparents' courage and fortitude.

Moreover, you had to have plenty of extra people to settle a new village as those people would not be coming back to the old ones. It was never haphazard or rushed; building, settling and supplying a new village took time, planning and effort. Just building the new road took weeks of backbreaking work and that was for the distance of a day's journey. A new village had to succeed, grow and thrive, and eventually add to the wealth of the daimyo of Dairapaska or the resources poured into it were lost.

The daimyo of Shelleen did not seem to know or care anything about those procedures and that was very, very strange. Debbie recalled all the stories she had been told at Shelleen about splitting off new villages and realized that the Shelleen peasants knew exactly how strange it was. In her misery and shock at her and Aldo being selected, she had not paid much attention to the talk raging around her about how strange it all was. So why had the new daimyo done it?

As she pondered on this, Yannick urged Gray Gal to a faster trot. Debbie decided that she would wait until the shelter to ask Yannick why he was so sure about her and her daughters being accepted by Kenyatta. They were moving too fast to risk a conversation and she would have to yell to be heard over the wind and the rain. Better and safer to wait.

Yes, definitely, better to wait and ask Yannick after she told him all about the long march. The more he heard about Shelleen, the less he liked it. He was much less likely to be angry at her questions if he was already angry about what had been done to her and the rest of the serfs.

That was strange too. Kenyatta must treat its peasants very differently for them to care how other serfs were treated, especially strangers. Relatives, no matter how far away in consanguinity, would be different.

It got darker and the rain got heavier, and Debbie wondered how long it was until sunset. She did not like the idea of riding in the dark wet night; that was even scarier than riding in the day, no matter how dim the sun was. Did horses see in the dark? What if Gray Gal tripped and fell, dumping her and the baby onto the ground and crushed them? This was a truly terrifying thought and Debbie tried to force it from her mind. She had to trust that Yannick knew what he was doing.

He whistled sharply, breaking into her thoughts and she was grateful for that distraction. Harley and Tyr spurred their horses and they again, as they had the previous day, raced past her and into the darkness, carrying Ghita and Carina with them. They could not be terribly far from the shelter.

The baby chose that moment to start wriggling and fussing. Yannick slowed the horses down and asked "do you have to stop?"

Debbie was in a quandary. Should she stop in the growing twilight and the steady rain or wait out the baby's tears? She could, she knew, ignore the baby for hours. She had been forced to when Aldo was around and both she and the baby had survived. But they had both hated it. And every minute they spent on the trail in the rain was going to be cold and wet and make the journey to the shelter take even longer.

She risked turning her head to him, enveloped in the poncho, while keeping the fussing baby from falling. "Yes, just for a minute to get her calmer and more secure. She can wait, we both can, if we have to."

He reined in his horse and Gray Gal, and Debbie rearranged the baby under the poncho while he held the horses steady and rock solid. The baby did not like it one bit and said so, loudly. Debbie resigned herself to listening to her baby wail, something she had hoped she would not have to do again with Aldo gone from their lives. She could only make sure that the baby had her thumb handy.

They were on their way again, the baby loudly unhappy while Debbie gritted her teeth and did her best to ignore her aching body, her swollen breasts, and her sobbing, squirming baby. It took a long time to reach the shelter and she was grateful when the baby finally accepted her thumb as a poor substitute for Debbie. The baby wasn't happy at all and she regularly took her thumb out of her mouth to scream out her hurt and hunger and frustration.

Yannick didn't say one word to Debbie about the baby's screams during the dreadful ride and she was grateful that he didn't. Aldo had always had something unkind to say when the baby cried. Yannick picked up the pace every time the baby's wails slowed down, trying to get them to the shelter faster.

At last they saw the firelight glimmering in the rainy darkness and as before, Yannick rode his horse and led hers into the shelter and Harley was waiting to help her off as soon as they were inside.

Debbie collapsed next to the fire, her body aching all over, and got the baby out of the sling and latched onto her breast and got the blessed silence that she sought at last. The baby was happy too; she was finally getting to eat and have attention paid to her. She had gotten used to having her needs met quickly on the long plod north and she did not like going back to the way things had been done before.

Ghita was waiting with a kuksa of mint tea and a wool blanket, and Debbie sipped the hot liquid gratefully and pulled the blanket over herself and the baby. Dinner of a grain and meat stew followed and then the dogs showed up, eager to get out of the rain and hopeful for something to eat. Tyr was ready with strips of something dried and they snapped them up, all three of them, with a minimum of growling at each other.

"Harley told me the big dogs follow the trail the horses leave and they know the way. They're very smart dogs! And Spotty follows them, that's why he's not getting lost, even in the rain." Ghita was very proud of herself for knowing something her mother did not.

"Tyr said there's shelters all around the border of Kenyatta. We have two more to go before we get to the village and the manor house," said Carina, also pleased at being able to tell her mother something she didn't know.

"Two more. My goodness," Debbie said. She turned to Yannick who was stretched on his back on the floor besides her, his head pillowed on his bedroll and a wolf-dog pressed up next to him, sharing their warmth. "Are they as far apart as these two have been?"

He smiled a little. "If you're asking if the ride between them is as long, yeah, it is. The shelters are set up for riders with dogs. Without dogs, we can ride from the manor house to the cairn where we found you in two days. Long days, but we can do it, yeah?"

Debbie thought about this. Yannick and the boys seemed so self-sufficient and resourceful. "Why do you need dogs?"

"Wolves, big cats, other critters. Dogs watch out for all kinds of varmints, including two-legged ones like bandits. They can feed themselves if they have to and make it possible for us to sleep at night without having to set a watch." He sat up enough to ruffle the ears of the wolf-dog wedged up against him. The dog whapped his tail in appreciation on the bamboo floor.

Debbie sat back with her mouth open, closed it, then squeaked, "There are wolves? Really?"

"Sure are. The packs are at the northern end of Kenyatta now, following the wild herds, but there's always the chance of them coming south early. Didn't you know that?"

"I, uh, thought it was just a story the lords tell the serfs to keep us from trying to escape."

He sat up to better see her face in the dim, fire-lit space. "You're lucky, you know that? We don't have many wolf packs in the north but we do have some. You have to have the big predators to eat the grazers and keep them bunched up and moving. I don't care for them myself, but the ecologists at the manor insist that we have to have them."

"Predators."

"All kinds, wolves and coyotes and foxes and jackals, and the cats, big cougars, cheetahs, bobcats, and the little ones that look like barn cats only they're not. Having Spotty along helped you a lot."

Debbie did not know what to say.

Ghita said, her eyes very wide, "we never saw anything like that."

"You wouldn't. The littler ones won't bother you. They're shy and you're too big to eat. The big ones, well, you don't usually see them until it's too late. But you were also coming up from Shelleen and across the corridor. The dirt demesnes don't have the range of critters that we do and the corridors with roads in them aren't much better, at least not on the dirt side. Dirt daimyos don't know how to manage their land to make the soil better. Better soil means better vegetation and more of it and that means more critters of every kind."

Debbie wanted to faint. "There really are wolves?" She was repeating herself, but she could not help it.

"There really are. Tyr! Get Debbie some more tea. She needs it bad."

Debbie held out her cup and Tyr poured her another helping of mint tea and she drank it automatically, letting its warmth wrap around her.

"Would you have run away from your husband if you'd known?" Yannick asked carefully.

Debbie stared into the fire while she thought over his question. "Yes," she finally said. "I would have. I couldn't let him hurt my daughters any more, especially the baby. The wolves would have been a huge risk but maybe they wouldn't have found us. Aldo was getting worse, the longer we were in the new village. He hated it there, and he took it out on us."

"Why'd you choose him anyway? You weren't real clear about your situation."

"I didn't have any choice," she answered, her voice dull. She cuddled the nameless baby closer, petting her wisps of hair.

"Tell me. Start at the beginning. Kenyatta will need to know."

So she did, starting with her selection along with the other Dairapaska girls, back when she was sixteen, and how her family could not pay the bribe to keep her home. As she spoke, slowly, of every painful event, leading up to being assigned to Aldo, the shelter grew quieter.

"When I was sixteen, the daimyo of Dairapaska made a deal with the daimyo of Shelleen. Nobody had ever heard of Shelleen before, but after that, everyone did. He had his overseer choose twenty-four girls and we were to be traded with twenty-four girls from Shelleen, sent halfway across Mars.

"I suppose it made sense. There were no ties between anyone in Dairapaska or Shelleen, even counting out to twelve degrees of consanguinity. Every match was almost guaranteed to be fertile. You know how important that is."

Debbie looked over at Yannick and he nodded his head.

"Family lines would continue, and the children would be fully fertile and so would the grandchildren. We were told the daimyos were very happy with the deal. They wanted more people for the health of the demesne and this was sure-fire.

"The daimyos were happy but nobody else was. Yes, it meant new blood for the good of the demesne, but at the cost of losing forever daughters, sisters, nieces and the children they might have borne. It was shoved down our throats. I suppose they could have asked for volunteers, but they didn't."

Yannick spat into the fire, making it snap and crackle.

Debbie sipped more tea, trying to wet her throat, and thought of the differences between slaves and peasants.

"The daimyo's overseer had all the unmarried girls age sixteen and older in each of the villages line up and he looked us all over, choosing who he wanted to ship off to Shelleen. We were told that he was choosing girls from more inbred lines; girls whose families were showing signs of not being fertile within the demesne.

"That's what he said. Everyone I knew thought that maybe he did choose some girls like that, but what it looked like was that if your family could pay him a bribe to let you stay, well, you got to stay. My family didn't have enough money. We never had any money to spare, we never seemed to get ahead even though we worked hard. It had never mattered before because we did all right."

She stopped for a long moment, fighting back tears.

"Now it mattered. My family didn't have anything to offer in exchange. So I got picked. I remember the tears at leaving Dairapaska, mine and all the other girls and all of their families. I remember the train ride across Mars. I had never, ever been on a train before, I had never even seen one. It was long and dull with nothing to do but watch the grasslands roll by and cry with the other girls.

"We sat together, all of us, and there were chaperones from the demesne to watch us all the time so we couldn't escape even if we wanted to. The train stopped at every station and we were never allowed off. We were told that if we tried to run off, we'd be recaptured right away, our families back home would be punished. And if we did escape, we'd end up whores starving in the gutters."

Debbie stopped again and sipped more tea, thinking about that ride so long ago. Yannick did not press her, waiting quietly in the flickering fire-cast light besides her.

"It was hard to sleep on the train, but we were fed, we were warm and dry, and we didn't have to work in the fields so I suppose that was something. All us girls talked endlessly about the same thing. 'How different would Shelleen be from Dairapaska?' Every demesne is different from every other, even when they're in the same zone. We knew that Shelleen was Northern Agricultural so they would farm like we did. That's all we knew. Nobody official would say anything else. Maybe they didn't know. Sometimes a guard would say something. That's how we learned that Shelleen was so much further north than Dairapaska. That meant it would be colder in the winter.

"We talked all the time, when we weren't crying. Everybody hoped that we would be allowed some time in the Shelleen villages to get to know the people there. They couldn't have been any happier than we were. How would they treat us? They lost daughters, sisters, nieces too. It didn't sound like the Shelleen girls got any more choice than we did. When we didn't talk, I would stare out the window at the road in the government corridor. I would watch those people walking along, all of them going someplace else. They looked poor but they all had a choice and we had none.

"I missed my family so much. My older sister was pregnant and I would never see that baby. My parents, my grandmother. My aunties and uncles. I would never see Dairapaska again. There was a boy I was friendly with. He would marry someone else and not me. Everything was gone.

"Finally, we got to Purnell. We didn't see anything of the town, we hardly saw the train station. There were wagons waiting and we were hustled into them. The guards never left us alone even for a minute. I suppose it was to make sure none of us had a chance to run off.

"But where would we have gone? None of us had any money. We didn't know how to live in a free-city. How would you find work? I mean, besides, well ..." Her voice trailed off.

"Nobody wanted to do that. We all heard the stories of what happens to girls alone in a city. You end up a whore dying in some back alley. You don't get to go home."

Debbie chose not to add, with Ghita and Carina cuddled up against her and listening intently, that there had been times since when she had wondered if that was so terrible a choice. As a whore, she'd have to service endless men as opposed to one husband but her money would be her own. And she wouldn't have to take care of them, like a husband. Those men would leave when they were done.

"We didn't know what was waiting. And we would have no one to help us. I could always ask my mother, my grandmother, my aunties if I had a question. Who would help me in Shelleen? The wagon ride was awful. It took days, bumping over that road and I kept reminding myself that it wouldn't be any better for the girls from Shelleen, but that didn't help.

"I tried hard to think about the future. Maybe we would be given time to meet people in Shelleen. To find a place for ourselves. Maybe I would meet someone kind. I know people in arranged marriages and it can work out very well, if both people set their minds to it. I knew what my grandmother would say. She'd say 'make the best of it, Debbie. That's all you can do.'

"It was late afternoon when we arrived at the gates to Shelleen and then what I found out later was the main village. We were herded into the village hall. We got food and water and we were allowed to wash up and then they locked us in for the night. I was so tired that I slept. I had terrible dreams.

"When morning came, we were given barley porridge and water, we were allowed to wash again and then they..." She stopped again.

Debbie looked over at Yannick. His face was stony and his eyes unreadable. "That's past, Debbie. Those people can't hurt you anymore. You will *never* go back to Shelleen. I swear it."

"It was like a slave auction," Debbie said slowly. "I saw pictures in the village school once in Dairapaska. The school master would talk about how much better Mars and Dairapaska was than Olde Earthe. We were so lucky to be on Mars where there were no slaves, except at the equator plantations, I mean."

She drew in a long, shuddering breath.

"They lined us up. None of us said anything and I remember

staring at the cobblestones. Some man, I never saw him again, said fine words about how we would be a blessing to Shelleen. We would bear many children for the families of Shelleen. He was somebody important, I guess. He wore the fanciest clothes, with lace whiter than snow and gold buttons. They glittered in the sun.

"While he talked, I paid some attention to the Shelleen peasants so I didn't have to listen to his blather. None of this hurt *him* or *his* family. He didn't have to care like the Shelleen peasants. They didn't sound happy or convinced. They looked as angry as our families back home in Dairapaska. They lost their girls too. I remember worrying that they would take their hurt and anger out on us.

She stopped again and swallowed more mint tea, trying to sooth her dry throat and roiling stomach.

"Then he shut up his speech. Waiting for applause I suppose but no one clapped. So he called each girl from Dairapaska by name and assigned us to strangers right then and there. They, well they weren't what I expected. All these men, they were older, in their thirties or even older. They all should have been married long since.

She breathed in slowly before continuing. "We found out later on that none of these men had fathered children. Their families had no grandchildren. Their lines would end. That's why we were there. That's how I was given to Aldo.

Debbie looked over at her silent, wide-eyed daughters, thinking hard of what to say next about their father. "Aldo was, well, not any different from the other men. He was a farmer like them. There wasn't any choice and so I took his hand like I was supposed to and I went with him to his cottage and his family. I remember trying to block out all those strangers hating me for being there when their own daughters were lost to them. I thought about my granny and what she would say. She'd say 'make the best of it, Debs. You can't always choose what happens but you can choose how you feel about it and you can choose how you cope. Try to find something to be grateful for.' So that's what I did.

"I made the best of it. And I have Ghita and Carina and my baby. I managed. The other girls from Dairapaska managed. Some better than others. Some worse. I worked hard at getting along with my mother-in-law, Mrs. Acconcio." She looked away out into the darkness, trying to keep from frowning, knowing how much her daughters had loved their grandmother. "I made the best of it."

She sighed deeply. "It worked out, I suppose. For a long time. I had my girls and I kept my thoughts and dreams to myself. My granny was right. It made things a little easier. I didn't cause trouble. I remember how happy everyone was when I became pregnant and how much happier everyone was when I was finally able to hold onto the baby, not losing it. The first grandchild for the Acconcio family. That was you, my Ghita."

Ghita's eyes were wide and bright with unshed tears, catching the light from the fire.

"Then, finally, came you, my Carina. Everyone was so happy."

Debbie chose to keep back what her mother-in-law told her when Carina was born. 'You should have had a son,' Mrs. Acconcio had snarled. 'You must have a boy to carry on the family line.' But Mrs. Acconcio, despite what she had to say to Debbie and she had plenty to say on the subject, never said anything cruel to Carina about her not being a boy. Debbie was always grateful for that tiny bit of kindness.

"That's what happened. That's how I ended up in Shelleen and married to Aldo."

Debbie knew that Ghita and Carina had very little idea of her past. It was never, ever talked about in front of them and they were so little anyway. They'd asked their grandmother back in the old village once why they only had one set of grandparents, unlike so many of the other children and they'd been told that they had all they needed. Her mother-in-law had told Debbie afterwards, very sharply, that she needed to work harder to keep her daughters happy and uncomplaining.

Ghita broke the shadow-filled silence. "Nonna said we didn't have anybody else anywhere. Do we have a nonna and a nonno in Dairapaska?"

Debbie closed her eyes in grief, thinking of her mother and father. Time had not dulled the pain of being wrenched from them. It was as raw as ever, tearing at her heart with its talons. "Yes, if they're still alive. A nonna and a nonno and uncles and aunties and cousins. They would love you just as much as nonna and nonno do, if they knew you were alive."

"But they don't know, do they mommy?"

"No, I was never allowed to write them. None of the girls from Dairapaska were and we weren't allowed to get any letters. Just like the girls from Shelleen weren't allowed either. No one was allowed to write to them."

"Like Auntie Fulvia's little sister, Blanca," Ghita said slowly. "The one who was sent away."

"Yes, like Auntie Fulvia's little sister. I know that Auntie Fulvia misses her terribly, but I didn't know she talked about her to you."

Ghita moodily picked at her wool blanket rather than meeting her mother's tear-bright eyes. "She would complain to Uncle Enzo about you. That you were trying to take her place and you couldn't."

Carina was hugging Spotty very tightly, burying her face in his tear-stained fur and sniffling. She didn't say anything.

Debbie sighed again and tried to select her words carefully. "It hurt Auntie Fulvia very much when her little sister got chosen, just like it hurt everyone in Shelleen who lost a daughter or a sister. I know the same was true in Dairapaska. I'm sure Auntie Fulvia never meant to be unkind. It was hard and cruel to everyone."

"I can't believe those dirt daimyos did that to you, just can't believe it," said Yannick. He shifted closer to her, a warm presence just far enough away so their bodies did not touch but close enough so she could hear him breath. It was oddly comforting.

Debbie looked down into the fire, trying to see a happier future in the heart of the flames. "It's true."

"I know that," he answered patiently. "It's hard for me to accept they could do that to their people. We'd never do that in the North. Never. Which leads me to the next thing I do *not* understand. Why'd that dirt daimyo send you and the rest of the serfs to set up a village in the middle of nowhere? This does not make any sense."

"It didn't make any sense to anybody," Debbie answered, grateful to be off the topic of her being torn away from everyone she had ever loved.

"No one could understand it," she continued. "They've settled new villages in Shelleen before and they did it just like Dairapaska from the stories I was told; a day's walk away when there were too many people in the old villages for the land to support.

"But not this time. The daimyo of Shelleen decided that this was the perfect spot but he didn't build a road beforehand. He claimed his surveyors said the soil was wonderful and there was plenty of water. When we got there, the soil was poor and the water was scanty. He didn't send many supplies, like house-building materials. We didn't have very many animals, chickens, dogs, or goats. Nobody got to volunteer, like you usually do when you set up a new village. One day we were told to go, all five villages had people chosen whether they wanted to or not and the villages weren't overcrowded at all, and the next day, they marched us from the old villages, over 150 klicks across the steppes. It was all so *hurried*.

"We left in early, early spring, much too soon. There was a rough trail so someone had been there before. It was dreadful. We weren't allowed to stop, no matter what the weather, and it took weeks to walk. They were in such a *rush*. Water was always a problem. People got sick. That baby got really sick and died and we couldn't wait even an hour to mourn. His mother had to carry his body the rest of the way to the new village and he was the first person buried there."

Yannick stood abruptly and began pacing. "That does not make sense. I think what Dairapaska and Shelleen did to you girls and your families was sick and mean, but it makes sense. New genes mean more fertility. But this! It's like he wanted you to die out on the steppes. Did he choose any special kind of peasants for this?"

Debbie shrugged. "Farmers and their wives and their kids. The midwife and her husband, he's a carpenter. No hunters, no potters, no shoemakers, no weavers, no thatchers, just farmers to get crops in the ground right away. No one could understand it at all. At least they let us write letters back to the old villages. The daimyo sends his overseer back and forth regularly and he carries mail so we get news sometimes. He's always bring packhorses with supplies, and a wagonload once in awhile. Nobody knows anything but everybody guesses endlessly."

"So you got people from all the villages in Shelleen?"

"All five of them." Debbie stopped and thought. "Aldo was very angry that we were sent. I was the only girl from Dairapaska to go and our names were called last. No man who was married to someone from Dairapaska was chosen until Aldo's name was called. He carried on and raged but the overseer told him to shut up and be proud he was chosen to settle the new village out on the steppes."

She huddled up against herself, holding the baby tighter, and Ghita and Carina snuggled closer. "Aldo was harder to live with after that."

"I want you to think on this, Debbie," Yannick said. "You've lived on two demesnes now, plus what you saw on the train ride between them. You were in that new village for months. Did you ever see or hear any reason why Shelleen picked this particular place?"

"I have no idea," she replied softly. "I've thought about it, everybody did, and I've thought more since running away. There was no reason. My mother-in-law had plenty to say about wasting resources out in the middle of nowhere and that's what the daimyo did. We were just hanging on, staying alive, and then the daimyo decided we had to overwinter rather than come back to the old village."

She looked up to Yannick, looming over her in the dim light. "Even with the mil-rats the daimyo sent, most of the serfs will starve. The fields weren't yielding well at all; the soil was rocky and poor. He would have to send many more wagons full of mil-rats to keep the peasants alive. Everybody knew it, but the daimyo's man wouldn't say if they were sending more. He wouldn't say anything, not even to the headman. He wouldn't even say if they were building a road."

Yannick was frowning terribly, and Debbie hoped it wasn't at her or what she had said.

"There's something else happening," he said finally, easing her tension. "There must be. No sane daimyo throws people away like rubbish. I want you to think about it, anything that's even the slightest bit strange about the soil, the steppes, the rocks, the sky, the critters you saw, the plants. Shelleen had a reason for this, he had to have, and I want to be able to tell Kenyatta as much as I can."

Ghita and Carina both yawned then, distracting him. "We'll settle in for the night and get out fast in the morning. Thank you, Debbie, for telling me this. I know it was painful. I'll have some more questions in the morning, after I think on this."

Harley banked the fire for the night, and they rolled themselves up in their wool blankets, Debbie and her daughters again in the center of the group. She thought about that again. Yannick always arranged it so she was surrounded by him, Harley and Tyr, and the wolf-dogs. Was it to make it harder for her to try and run away as she would have to climb over him and the boys, waking them? Or was it to make it harder for something else to get at her and her daughters like a wolf or a cougar?

When the serfs had walked from the old village to the new one, each night the women and kids had always slept in the center of the group, while the men and older boys arranged themselves near their families on the outer edges. Perhaps Yannick was doing the same. She did not think an equator slaver would do that. Perhaps the men of the village had had a reason as well. They knew that there were night dangers, and it wasn't just a story to keep the kids quiet.

The night stayed rainy and cooler and the baby was fussy all night long. She was fully rested from her long nap while riding and eager to play. Debbie slept fitfully and when she was awake, trying to keep the baby soothed and quiet so everyone else could sleep, she thought endlessly about the questions Yannick had asked about the new village.

It did not make sense at any level. So why did the daimyo of Shelleen do it?

6

Yannick Learns More

T HE NIGHT PASSED, COLDER than the ones before, and morning came. The rain had thinned to a mist but there was a distinct chill in the air, one that had not been there before. It was a warning of the winter to come.

Debbie woke slowly, wondering what was missing. She was warm, she was dry, the baby was gone. She sat bolt upright, terrified that the baby had crawled into the fire while she slept and there she was on the other side of the shelter. She was sitting with Ghita and Carina and Spotty and trying hard to pick up one of the shelter kuksas while the older girls giggled softly, then restacked the cups that she had knocked over.

"Let you sleep a bit. Got a long day ahead." Yannick held out a cup of tea for her and she took it and sipped it gratefully. Debbie thought again how kind this stranger had been to her, despite his distaste for her leaving her husband and stealing his children. She would have to ask him why. No one in Shelleen had been kind to her like this. She could not decide what it meant.

"Gonna be another wet day. Fall's coming on and the weather is turning. Soon as you and the baby eat, we leave."

Soon thereafter, she was back on Gray Gal, the baby in the sling and under a poncho to shed the rain. Debbie expected Yannick to ride out first, but he waved out Harley and Tyr and her daughters, and they cantered down the path into the rising sun.

"I didn't want to ask you this in front of your girls. Those burn scars on your legs. Your husband do that to you?"

Debbie closed her eyes tightly, despite her fear of being

high up on a horse and not seeing where she was going. It had been humiliating to have her kirtle hiked up so high when she rode Gray Gal that everyone could see her bare legs. That had been another good thing about the poncho. It covered her up. She didn't like showing anyone the ugly, puckered scars splashed across her calves and thighs.

She shook her head. "No. It was an accident. I spilled a pan of boiling water. Aldo wasn't anywhere around me."

She could not read his expression. Should she have lied and said Aldo did it to her? No, she had not lied to Yannick once and she wasn't going to start.

"My other question. If you'd stayed in the old village, not been sent to the new one, would you have run?"

Debbie stared at Gray Gal's ears for a long moment as the horse ambled along into the east and the new day.

"No," she replied. "He was tolerable. Aldo didn't get bad until we were picked to move to the new village. We'd still be there."

"What about the baby being a girl?"

She sighed gustily. "No one in his family would have been happy, but they would have gotten over it. Aldo wouldn't listen to the peasants in the new village but he would listen to his parents."

She huffed and scowled at Gray Gal's ears. "They would have told *me*, endlessly, that the next baby had to be a boy, but they wouldn't have said anything to the baby or to Ghita and Carina. She would have gotten a name and a kuksa and nonna would have made her a rag doll right away." She could not stop the bitterness from creeping into her voice and then decided she didn't care.

Why did he ask those questions? What did they matter? But he moved on to another subject and she put it out of her mind.

"Anything you can remember being different about the new village? Something that said why the daimyo was so keen on putting you and everyone else out in the middle of nowhere?"

"Nothing. The soil was poor and rocky, but no worse than anywhere else." She stopped short, remembering. "No, that's not true. When we walked, we had to stop every night to sleep. There were many places we slept where the soil was better. We knew what we were looking at, we're all farmers, and when we kept walking past good spots for farming, the men agreed that the new village would have wonderful soil, much better than what we had in the old villages."

She risked turning her head again to meet his dark, intent eyes. "When we got to the new village site, the village headman was horrified. All the men were, even the midwife's husband and he's a carpenter, not a farmer. The headman kept asking the overseer why he had bypassed much better spots, spots that would be easier to grow food on, that wouldn't need as much work, and that had better water sources nearby and were closer to the old villages. The overseer wouldn't say anything, just that this was the site the daimyo wanted for his new village. It had to be here and nowhere else."

"What did you think of the soil, based on what you know?"

"It was the poorest I have ever seen, anywhere," Debbie answered thoughtfully. "It would have to lay fallow for years to be worth anything and this had been lying fallow forever! It wouldn't get any better, not without decades of work and probably not then."

Yannick scowled at the mist. "The daimyo of Shelleen wants something there. That's clear enough. If it's not the soil, then it must be something underneath it. They send any miners with you?"

"No, not at all. Shelleen has a few, they have a small tin mine, I know that. One of the Dairapaska girls was married to a miner."

"Hmmm. I want you to think about every kind of grass and plant you saw, how thick they grew, how tall. Sometimes, plants can tell you what is in the soil, or underneath it. Any unusual rocks too."

They continued through the mist at a slow walk while Debbie thought about this. He was right. There were plants that grew thickly where water was close to the surface and nowhere else. There were grasses that grew only where the soil was lean and grasses that grew only where the soil was richer. The weeds growing in a field would tell you when it was time to let the field lay fallow.

She thought about the endless stones they had moved from the new fields to set between them as low walls, the stones they had moved to make paths and foundations. She had helped move plenty of stones, more than she had ever seen in her life, but none of them had looked any different from what she had seen before. Or did they?

Yannick spurred his horse, they moved faster, and Debbie readied herself for another endless day in the saddle. They caught up quickly with Harley and Tyr and continued riding into the east, the sun hidden behind its veil of clouds. The weather did not clear, giving them a cold drizzle broken only with patches of thick, damp mist. She was very grateful again for the warm wool poncho and whoever had woven it so tightly.

By late afternoon, the sun began peeking through the clouds and the rain began to thin.

"You're making better time, Debbie. Getting used to riding, yeah?"

Yannick's voice startled her. She had been focused on holding on, holding her wiggling baby, and thinking about the stones in Shelleen and their subtle differences between the old villages and the new one.

He whistled sharply and Harley and Tyr again galloped away from them to the unseen shelter further down the grass road.

She realized that despite her aches and pains and fears, she was getting used to riding Gray Gal and she was getting better at it. They had not left at dawn, Yannick had let her sleep a bit, and here they were at the next shelter and it wasn't full dark yet.

Now that she could see the shelter better in the last rays of the setting sun, Debbie was even more impressed with the builders. The shelter was built of whitewashed cob on a stone foundation, floored and walled inside with bamboo. It had a thick thatch roof with a huge overhang to keep the rain out on all sides. Cob made a good building material, even though it took a long time and a lot of labor to build a house. It was thick, withstood the cold, kept out the drafts, and there was always mud and straw available. However, it didn't like getting wet. Wet cob turned back into mud and straw. It always had to have whitewash on the outside, a foundation of stone to keep it well above the mud, and a tight roof to keep the walls dry. Then it could last forever.

As with the two previous shelters, the entire front was open to the south. What she had not noticed before was the dense, tall hedge growing around the shelter, separated from the building by a grassy strip about five meters wide. She had to assume the hedge made a large semicircle on all sides of the shelter that didn't face the road.

Once inside, Debbie noticed for the first time that the horse section of the shelter didn't have a bamboo floor. Their side was stone, which made sense. It would wear far longer under the horse hooves and would be easier to keep clean.

Yannick rode into the shelter, Debbie on Gray Gal alongside him and Harley helped her down. This time though, Harley took both horses and led them back out of the shelter. Harley and Tyr's horses were both missing.

Ghita saw her looking around at the empty stable area and knew again that she knew something her mother did not, filling her with joy.

"Mommy, the horses are in back of the shelter. There's a grazing area, that's what Harley said. He showed me the water trough and the pump."

"Did Harley tell you what the hedge is made of, Ghita?" asked Yannick.

"Osage Orange! And other bushes too, but I don't remember their names. Him and Tyr showed me and Carina all the different leaves and those big, funny-looking fruit. He said we shouldn't eat them cause they were for the horses."

"Good lad. They shoulda put up a fence to keep the horses in. Did they?"

Ghita nodded vigorously. "And I helped!"

"Good girl. They'll bring the horses back inside when it gets darker."

The dogs showed up, panting and looking tired from their long run. Debbie was grateful to see that Spotty was keeping up with the wolf-dogs. He was overjoyed to see her, Ghita, and Carina again and despite his daylong run, he still found the energy to bounce around the girls, yapping and springing into the air and wagging his tail madly, before flopping down panting on the floor at their feet.

Harley came back around the corner of the shelter and sneered at Spotty. Spotty returned the favor, then rolled onto his back to allow Ghita to rub his tummy. He stretched luxuriously, enjoying every minute of her devoted attention, while the wolf-dogs once again pointedly ignored his obsequious behavior. Spotty looked smugly at them and at Harley. He knew he was the favorite, and they were just jealous.

Tyr had gotten supper on again, and afterwards, Debbie decided to be brave and get it over with and ask Yannick why he was so sure that Kenyatta would take her and her daughters on.

He was laying stretched out alongside the fire at his ease, this time with his head pillowed on a wolf-dog who looked happy to be used that way. The wolf-dog opened his jaws, showing every fang, and yawned at Spotty who yawned back at him. Despite the long days, Yannick did not look one bit tired, any more so than Harley or Tyr did.

Debbie was tired and sore but, she was grateful to notice, not quite as tired as she had been. Maybe she was getting used to riding, at least a little bit. Ghita and Carina and the baby were full of energy and they got up and began investigating the shelves in the shelter in the last of the light with Spotty sniffing around as well. They found more kuksas, plain and clean, and began making towers of them for the baby to gleefully knock over.

"Yannick," Debbie said quietly. "May I ask more questions?"

Yannick rolled over enough to study her face. "Doll, you can always ask me, or anyone here questions. They not let you do that at Shelleen?"

Debbie looked away into the beautiful, unconcerned flames dancing in the fire-pit. "I had to be careful. Aldo and his family didn't like it if I wasn't properly respectful."

Yannick snorted in disdain. "Ask away."

"Why are you so sure that Kenyatta will accept me and my daughters? We ran away from Shelleen and you said yourself that Shelleen might make trouble for him."

Yannick breathed out deeply. "I don't like that you left your man and took his kids." He held up his hand to forestall her protest.

"I understand your reasons but I got my own for not liking what you did. I want that out of the way. The other thing you got to know about us here in the North is that we run to boys.

We got way more fertility problems in the North and that's one of them. We're always short on girls. Boys got to marry somebody and they can't if there aren't any girls.

"Your daughters, all three of them, aren't related to anybody here, at least twelve degrees of consanguinity or more. When your gals are old enough, they'll have their pick of husbands. They'll be courted by every likely boy in Kenyatta and probably our nine-square too if they don't like who they got to choose from here. Your girls will be fertile with everybody and they'll as likely bear daughters as they will sons. And their children will keep that fertility."

He looked over at her, trying to read her face in the flickering shadows. "That matters a lot. Even if you hadn't had the reasons you did to leave Shelleen, if you'd just run because you were *bored* with that *tiresome* husband of yours, Kenyatta would still take you and your girls on. He won't give a damn what Shelleen has to say."

"Second is you. You're still real young, and you'll have your pick of husbands too. You're not related to anyone up here and you have three daughters already. Any man in Kenyatta would be proud to have them girls as his daughters and you as his wife and the promise of more children to come."

Debbie hunched over, pulling up her legs and wrapping her arms to protect herself, and stared off into the darkness outside the shelter.

"I don't know if I can do that again," she answered in a thin, tight voice. "I let Aldo do what he did and I have my daughters but I don't know if I can live with that again."

Yannick scowled terribly, but Debbie did not see him. "It'll be your choice. No one will force you, ever. We don't do that up in the North."

"Thank you."

"Third is you."

Debbie looked over at him, startled. Hadn't he just said that?

"You're tough and you're brave and you're lucky. The North is challenging. Even people born and bred up here can have a hard time of it. But you, you lived through everything that got thrown at you, and when you had to and the chance appeared, you ran for it to save your girls. You walked over a hundred klicks across the steppes, just you and three little girls and a little dog and you made it.

"Debbie, what you did was amazing. You walked off into the unknown, no training at all, and you were *lucky*. The weather stayed dry, no critters bothered you, and you never ran out of water or mil-rats. You may have come close, but you didn't run into trouble. And then we found you, before you got too far north into Kenyatta."

Debbie smiled into the indifferent flames. "It didn't feel lucky at the time. It was terrifying."

"Plenty better than what would have happened to you and your girls on the road."

"Yes, that's true." Debbie told him about the woman on the road who had told her to go north. "I've thought about her and I think that the men she was with, well, she didn't want to be part of their group, but she didn't know what else to do."

"She could have walked north too, with mil-rats and waterskins from that way-station. But she didn't," Yannick replied with little sympathy in his voice. "You did. That matters, Debbie. You chose to make the hard, scary leap into the unknown and your girls may turn out to be just as tough and lucky as you are. That matters too."

"I haven't been lucky since I was sixteen and got picked for Shelleen."

"Sometimes strange things happen, things that don't seem lucky at the time, but then they turn out that way." He stopped suddenly, an odd look on his face.

"This will too," he said more slowly. "When we get to my village, you'll see Kenyatta, I'll get you fixed up with my folks so's you have a place to stay while you find your feet, and you can write to your family in Dairapaska."

Debbie was startled again. "Your folks?"

"They'll take you in, we got the space, your girls can play with my boys, and my mother will see to it that nobody bothers you. I can't say that about every woman in the villages. There's unmarried men who will want you, Debbie, and their sisters and mothers and aunties will push you to become part of their family. My mother will fend them off just as long as you need her to. And she'll be happy to show you how we do things up here in the North and she'll want to know how you did things in Dairapaska and Shelleen. We aren't afraid to learn from outsiders. Sometimes they got useful things and useful ways."

"That's very kind of you."

"Looking out for the future of my demesne, that's all. I'm a Hand of Kenyatta, a damn good one, and that's part of my job."

"There's something else. I don't want to make trouble for Kenyatta."

Yannick rolled his eyes. "Told you already Kenyatta will tell Shelleen to pound sand."

Debbie took a moment to puzzle that one out, then plunged in.

"That's not it." She paused to see if he objected to her disagreeing with him and when he did not, she continued. "I ran away and I took my daughters. Every single person in Shelleen will be talking about it and when I write home, everybody in Dairapaska will talk about it too. You know they will. In both places, we told stories about unusual things all the time, over and over. The peasants in both places will never stop talking about how I ran away with my girls.

"The thing is Yannick, serfs don't run away! We were told, all the time, about wolf packs and equator slavers and terrible things in the night that would eat us if we tried to run to a free-city, and I *did* it."

She studied the darkness outside again, the stars glittering in dark bands of night between the broken clouds. "If I can do it, with no planning and no man to help me, *anybody* can. Yes, I got lucky with the weather and the men being away and the mil-rats. But I didn't plan ahead, I just walked away. The serfs of Dairapaska and Shelleen will talk about this forever and some of them will run away now too. That may cause a problem for Kenyatta, when Shelleen's serfs start running away and causing him trouble. Same with Dairapaska. The daimyos, both of them, will make trouble for Kenyatta."

"I didn't think of that." He chuckled. "I'll warn Kenyatta, but I know what he'll say. It'll be good for them dirt daimyos. Remind them to take better care of their people, yeah? He'll keep you on. Tough and brave and lucky and smart."

Debbie didn't know what to say. Thank you seemed so inadequate. No one in years had ever said anything so nice to her. So she chose to say something else to this competent, considerate man stretched out next to her.

"I've been thinking about what you asked about the new village. The soil was the poorest I've ever seen and the rockiest. The plants were all poverty grasses, and there weren't very many animals or bugs. You know how usually there are worms and things in the soil? There weren't very many. Even the terraforming fungus and lichens and algae struggled. They grow when nothing else does, I guess that's true in the North?"

"It is. Go on, yeah?" He was listening intently, and Debbie noticed that so were Harley and Tyr as were Ghita and Carina. She wondered how long they had been listening to her conversation with Yannick.

The baby, uninterested in the doings of the older people, continued to chortle and knock over stacked cups and Ghita, Debbie was pleased to see, would quietly restack them to keep her occupied.

"When we walked north, the land changed very gradually and the soil got better. There were more plants and bugs and we saw birds, more and more of them. By the time we had walked two days, it was much better and it stayed that way until we reached the road. When we crossed the train tracks, the soil changed again. Everything grew much better, thicker and taller, and it was harder to wade through the grass."

"That was our doing," said Yannick proudly. "We run mixed herds of critters to within a few klicks of the tracks. Government's not using that land in the corridor so why shouldn't we? All those critters eat the plants and then they feed the soil. That's why you saw the difference between one side of the road and the other."

Debbie thought about this. "We always manure the fields, both in Shelleen and Dairapaska."

"Not enough," Yannick scoffed. "When you farm, you're always taking stuff out of the soil and you got to put it all back and then some. When you ranch, if you do it right and not everybody does, you put back more than you take out. Builds soil. We farm too, can't eat meat all the time, and we rotate our crops and alternate our fields with pasture and they still spend six years out of seven untilled."

"My goodness. I know we don't do that. Anyway, the soil was terrible, almost dead. I don't think the daimyo could have picked a worse spot for a village. Aldo and the other men would complain constantly. And it was rocky, more stones than soil it seemed and very sandy. Sandy can be alright but this sand was—," she stopped, puzzled.

"—Different somehow. Sometimes it seemed greasy. I'm not sure how to explain it. Nothing grew well, not the barley, not the mint, not the turnips and cabbages. It didn't seem to matter what we did, not in the fields and not in the kitchen gardens. The chickens were shabby and the goats were always sickly. They'll be very hungry this winter if the daimyo of Shelleen doesn't send more mil-rats. The water tasted a little off too, I had gotten used to it and the water at the way-station on the road tasted so much sweeter and fresher."

"So it's something in the ground that Shelleen wants. Has to be. Did you see anything in the rocks?"

"No, and I moved plenty of them. We all did, even Ghita and Carina and all the kids. We built walls around all the fields and built paths and laid foundations for the buildings that were to be built next year. The stones were everywhere, and they all had to be moved for the plows. Every house and barn will have a stone floor and walls, every single path in that village will be paved, and so will every road leading in and out and there will be a wall around every single garden and field, that's how many stones there were."

She stopped, thinking about the stones. "They were a little different than the stones in the old village in Shelleen, but I can't say why. But if you put them side by side, I think I could tell which one was which."

"I think they were more orangey, mommy," said Ghita. "All of them."

"Hmmm. Kenyatta will have to know." Yannick tapped his fingers rhythmically on the floor.

"He'll want samples," Harley said.

Yannick smiled approvingly. "Good thinking, lad."

"You can't go to the new village," Debbie protested. "You'd be crossing into Shelleen's demesne without permission."

He grinned widely at her, as did Harley and Tyr. "Only a problem if they catch us, Debbie. And none of those dirt-eaters will ever see us unless we want them to."

He seemed very confident and Debbie decided that maybe

he had reason to be. Certainly, she had not seen anything since meeting Yannick to doubt that he could do whatever he set his mind to.

Carina yawned hugely, followed by Ghita. Yannick was back on his feet at once. "Time to settle in for the night. Harley, you and I'll bring the horses into the shelter. Tyr, break out what we need for the night."

A short time later, Debbie was rolled up in wool blankets with the baby snuggled up close, Ghita and Carina next to her and Spotty keeping their feet warm. As before, Yannick was rolled up in a blanket right next to her. He was warm too.

She thought about what he had said to her, about her and her daughters being so valuable to Kenyatta. She could understand her daughters, even though their growing up enough to marry was many years away. They weren't related to anybody in the North and that came close to guaranteeing their fertility.

The idea that they could choose their husbands was novel after her years in Shelleen. But she would have chosen her own husband back in Dairapaska, and most of the village girls in Shelleen got to choose their husbands as well. It was only the girls selected for the bride trade who had been forced into marriages they would not have chosen. She thought of the boy she had liked back in Dairapaska. She struggled to remember his name and his face had faded into the past. If she had been able to stay in Dairapaska, she might be married to him now. But she would not have had Ghita, Carina, or her little, nameless baby.

What was more surprising was that Yannick thought she had value and more than just because she could possibly bear more children. Tough and brave and lucky and smart, he'd said. He did not approve of her leaving Aldo and taking his kids but he still said that to her. That was very nice of him.

And she could choose, if she wanted to. Did she want to marry again? She didn't think she would ever want to, after her marriage to Aldo, but maybe it would be different in Kenyatta. She might meet someone nice, someone who would value her and treat her decently. She could take her time and she could choose, but only if she wanted to. She would not *have* to.

Debbie could feel another knot in her soul loosen and she drifted off, listening to her daughters breathing and the other night sounds from Yannick and the boys and the dogs and the horses and the light rain that had started falling outside again.

Morning came again, another gray, dismal, drizzly damp day. Debbie studied the thin rain pattering down and decided that she had been very lucky indeed. The weather could have changed earlier and she and her daughters would have been soaked, night and day, as they plodded north. It would have been a misery and they would have become sick, maybe even died. It was good fortune that Yannick had found her.

If she understood correctly, there was one more shelter to go and then they would arrive in the evening of the following day in his village in Kenyatta. Her riding was improving, although she still hurt all over. It was amazing how much faster they traveled on horses, even moving at a slow trot. 150 some klicks from the stone tower to the village at Kenyatta and she would arrive in another day. She remembered all too well the endless journey to the new village, walking every step of a similar distance; agonizingly long days with no breaks to rest other than at night and stretching out over many, many weeks.

The daimyo of Shelleen had been in such a tearing *hurry* to get the new village settled. There had to be a reason.

As they rode through the drizzle, Debbie thought about what everyone had had to say about the new village. Aldo had gotten letters once in a while from his relatives in the old village and she had read them discreetly when he wasn't around. No one in his family in the old village could figure out what was going on, and when she had a chance to speak with the other women, they had said that their families did not understand it either.

No one in the old villages, any of them, was being told by the daimyo of Shelleen or his men why this settlement had to be built. So he did not want them to know, any more than he wanted the settlers in the new village to know why he insisted on this location and no other out in the middle of nowhere.

That was important, she could feel it. When she and the other girls had been traded between Dairapaska and Shelleen, the daimyos at both ends had spent plenty of time informing them and their families why this was such a wonderful idea and why they should be happy about doing their parts.

But the daimyo of Shelleen never said why the new village was such a good idea; not when the idea was announced, not when they settled it, and not afterwards to the peasants left behind. His representatives had talked endlessly about the good of Shelleen and the chance to start a new village as the pioneer families but not *why*, other than blather about how it would benefit everyone. There were no reasons, like more children, or less hunger in the deep winter.

The day passed slowly, never getting warmer or sunnier. Fall was definitely on its way. It was a relief to reach the last shelter and get out of the misty rain.

As before, Yannick had sent Harley and Tyr along early and the aroma of hot mint tea and spitted, roasting hares filled the air when she and Yannick arrived at the shelter.

Harley was looking very proud of himself. Ghita was bouncing up and down in her eagerness to tell Debbie about what he had done.

"We got here so early and Harley showed me how he caught Spotty with his bolas. That's how he caught the hares for supper. He did the same thing to them he did to Spotty!" she squealed, clapping her hands.

Yannick was very approving. "Good lad. You'll be a vaquero in no time."

The wolf-dogs and Spotty arrived about then, panting, tired, and ready to lay down by the fire and get off their paws. Spotty did not look approving when Harley held up his bolas to show them off, and he very quietly got back up and lay down behind Debbie. He did eat his share of hare guts despite his distaste for their provider.

As they settled in, Debbie told Yannick about how the daimyo of Shelleen had never told the serfs why he was setting up the new village, other than in the most vague generalities.

Yannick considered this as he tore at the hare leg he was eating. "He doesn't want anyone to know. And he was in a tearing hurry. You're right. That matters. Lords in general and daimyos in particular usually can't shut up about their terrific ideas. They want everybody to know how smart they are so's they can be admired."

Debbie smiled at the crackling fire. "Is that true of Kenyatta too?" She snapped her mouth shut, horrified at what she had said, and hoped desperately that Yannick wouldn't strike her for being disrespectful to his daimyo.

He laughed and said "'fraid so. Northern lords are better than any other kind, but they're still lords. It goes to their heads."

He stood up and stretched. "I want to leave at first light, so's we can get to the village earlier. Harley! Tyr! As soon as you're done eating, get everything set up so's we can get out in the morning in a hurry."

Harley and Tyr were on their feet soon after, and shortly after that, everyone, horses, dogs, and all, were bedded down for the night.

As they lay quietly in the darkness, waiting for sleep to come, Debbie rolled herself and the baby over to talk to Yannick. He was rolled up in his wool blanket next to her, still awake.

The baby made a grab for his beard and he let her chew on his long braid instead, tugging it away gently and then letting her have it again to play with, thrilling her and making her giggle. "Problem, Debbie?"

She bit her lip, undecided on what to say now that she had his attention. "I suppose I'm worried about meeting everybody at Kenyatta tomorrow," Debbie said at last. "The last time I met a village of strangers, well, it wasn't very pleasant."

"This won't be like that. No one will force you. Everybody will want to talk to you, no doubt about that, cause you're new and you've got quite a story to tell. Nine-day wonder, that's what you and your girls will be and you need to get your head around that. But no one will harm you or your little ones."

"I'll have to talk to Kenyatta? I've never spoken to a lord of any kind before."

"Remus Kenyatta is okay. Puts on his pants just like everybody else. And he will want you and your girls to stay, mark my words."

"Will you leave right away?"

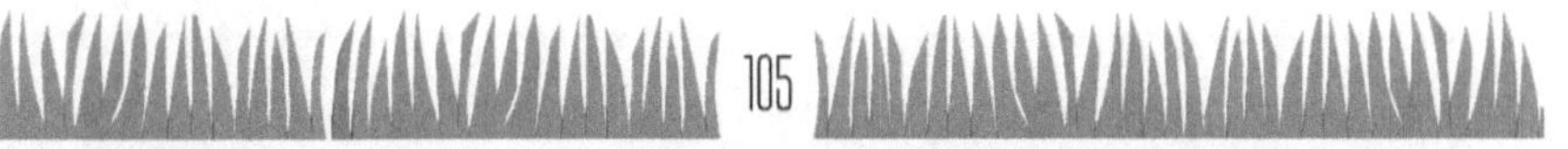

"Got to. As soon as I get you settled, Harley, Tyr, and me have to ride back to meet up with Otis and the other lads. This village of Shelleen needs looking into, and it'll be good training for the boys. Plus, we're getting set up for the fall migration. That's coming up fast."

Even in the dancing shadows cast by the fire-pit, he could see her puzzlement.

"Something we do twice a year. We move our herds, all kinds of critters mixed together, from the north down to the southern edge of the demesne almost up to the road, to make it easier for them to winter over. In the spring, they all get moved, gradually, to the northern edge, across the corridor and right up to Winzlow's borders. We don't move the natural flocks of gazelles and whatnot. They move on their own, they're not stupid and they don't like the cold either. The predators, wolves and such, follow the herds."

"Would we have run into that? If you hadn't found us?" Debbie whispered, feeling dread slip across her as she considered what might have happened to her and her daughters.

"Maybe. You had water and mil-rats and you might have made it to the next shelter on the road north before you ran out. That's if the weather hadn't got you first or one of the predators. You weren't equipped for them or bad weather, you and your girls."

"We were lucky," she said, very softly.

"Yes, you were. Luck is a strange, powerful thing." He paused, looking thoughtful and added "I think yours has been saving itself up for when you really needed it. You'll be fine in Kenyatta. You'll see. Try and sleep now, cause I want to push hard tomorrow."

He gently took his now-damp braid away from the baby and rolled over; staying close and warm. Debbie soothed the nameless baby over the loss of her new toy, tried to settle herself and eventually, sleep came to all of them.

Arrival at Yannick's Village

OVERNIGHT THE WEATHER cleared, and the early light roused her along with the sounds of movement. Harley, Tyr, and Yannick were already up and moving.

Debbie and her daughters wolfed down a hurried breakfast and were soon riding east into the rising sun and on the last leg of the journey to Kenyatta.

Ghita and Carina were excited and Debbie could hear them asking endless questions of Harley and Tyr. That alone told her that she was getting better at riding Gray Gal. She was able to pay attention to what was happening around her. Yannick noticed this and urged the horses a little faster and Debbie, to her surprised relief, noticed that she wasn't terrified.

The day passed quickly and the sun was a pleasant change from the previous wet days. It was good to be warm and dry again. At last, as the sun began wearing itself into mid-afternoon, she saw the signs of a village ahead. As in Shelleen, there were the plowed strips of land, planted in various grains and pulses and grass for hay. They were separated by strips planted with trees, with bushes underneath, and she recognized apples and hickories. There were many, many strips of pasture, thick and lush, between all the plowed fields and the orchards.

To her surprise, Yannick slowed down. "Letting the dogs catch up," he said to her.

Just like the villages of Shelleen and Dairapaska, this village in Kenyatta was a cluster of cottages, with low-walled kitchen gardens surrounding each one. Unlike them, the houses and barns and outbuildings were built of cob, whitewashed a brilliant white that reflected the sunshine. There were no wattle and daub huts here. The thick thatch roofs had patterns woven into their ridgelines, every house different. In Shelleen, only the richest peasants bothered to have patterns woven into their roofs.

The cottages were all bigger than she had expected, and every one of them had a large, stone chimney rising from the center of the roofline. Yannick rode up to a house near the center of the village, and dismounted, tying his horse to a thick bamboo bar mounted on the wall by the open door. All of the buildings she had passed had one, and she had wondered what its purpose was. Now she knew, and it made sense. You had to have a place to tie up a horse, as you could not let them run around loose in a village. It was always a bad idea to let animals run around loose, getting into the kitchen gardens or harming children, and a horse could do almost as much damage as a pig.

He helped Debbie down and she stood there in the vegetable garden feeling very awkward, clutching the nameless baby to her breasts. She could feel the eyes of other villagers on her, watching quietly to see what was going on as they went about their own tasks. In the distance, up the hill, Debbie saw the manor house overlooking the village, also keeping a weather eye on all of its doings. She had never before lived in the village closest to the manor house, where the ruling family held sway, and she didn't know what that would mean, other than closer oversight than she was used to. There were certain advantages to *not* living in the main village in a demesne. She shoved that concern away and turned back to the house standing before her, the house that Yannick called home.

This house had a brightly painted design of diamonds and triangles arranged around the front door, echoing the design painted around all of the windows, with their opened shutters. This was much fancier than the houses in Shelleen generally got. All the cottages she could see had designs, some more elaborate than others, and all of them were different. Debbie wondered if it meant something and decided it probably did.

"Ma!" Yannick called in through the open door. "Got visitors for you."

A startled older woman appeared at the door at once, rubbing her hands dry on her apron. "Yannick? What are you doing home? I thought you wouldn't be back for weeks."

"Debbie! Come here and meet my mother. Mom, this is Debbie from Shelleen and from Dairapaska before that. She's got her three little girls with her and she needs to stay with you."

Harley and Tyr had dismounted and tied up their horses and were leading Ghita and Carina forward, both looking timid and reluctant. They ran to Debbie and clutched her hands and skirt. Spotty appeared too, panting from his long run. He stayed close and wary, baring his fangs to show what a good guard dog he was. Debbie was grateful that he did not bark furiously at this stranger and she wondered if he was too tired to bark.

Debbie tried hard to paste on a smile for Yannick's mother, memories of Aldo's mother flooding over her like icy water. She held the nameless baby tightly, with Ghita and Carina trying to disappear into her skirt.

"Debbie, this is my mother, Chika. Mom?" Yannick's hands flew and his mother, after a moment, began answering back with her hands. Her expressions changed like lightning and Debbie wondered what she was being told.

Debbie waited silently, her daughters equally silent at her sides. Only the baby wiggled and cooed. When their hands stopped flying, Chika said, "you poor thing. Come inside right away, you and your girls and your dog, and have some tea. Yannick? Do you have time to say hi to your boys? I'll hunt them up."

He hugged her tightly.

"I will, when I come back with Kenyatta."

He turned to the lads, waiting patiently by their horses, the wolf-dogs flopped down panting at their feet, and called "Harley! Tyr! Go talk to the Horse-Master, get some fresh horses and fresh gear, swap out the dogs with the Kennel-Master, say hi to your mammas and sisters and tell them about Ghita and Carina, and be back here in two hours time. We'll ride out as far as we can and make a cold camp on the steppes. We got to meet Otis back at the cairn and I don't intend to keep him waiting."

He turned back to the women eying each other, Debbie cautiously and Chika with open interest. "Debbie, Chika will take care of you and your girls and I'll be back with Kenyatta as quick as I can."

The boys had mounted up, ready to go. Yannick said, "Harley, one last thing."

Harley stilled, tensed, and when he turned back, he had a wary look on his face.

"Make sure you say hi to your girl."

Harley grinned, then whistled for the wolf-dogs while Tyr rolled his eyes. Both boys set off at a trot, followed by the wolf-dogs, and disappeared between the buildings.

Yannick remounted his own horse and trotted off in a different direction, up the hill towards the manor house. It was a vast stone building with two big wings and the glitter of glass in many large windows; the better to survey its surroundings to the horizons.

Debbie found herself ushered into Chika's cottage, out of the sun, and into a chair with a cup of tea in her hands by the biggest masonry stove she had ever seen. Ghita and Carina were staring around, wide-eyed and silent. The baby was wide-eyed too and had stopped gurgling.

Spotty was undecided if he should explore this strange new space full of strange new smells or if he should stay by his people to protect them. He compromised by darting away a few steps to sniff and racing right back to Debbie's side, over and over.

There was a lot to stare at. The room was arranged differently from what she was familiar with. The masonry stove took up the center of the room, with ovens and cooking areas set into it, along with storage for wood and charcoal and cubbies for pans and an open hearth set in as well. It was so large that Debbie realized why the cottage was so large; the stove took up the extra room, leaving a cottage no bigger than what she was used to. There was a table with a lavishly embroidered tablecloth in front of the hearth in the stove and chairs with cushions embroidered to match.

The walls were whitewashed the same brilliant white as the outside walls, making the room brighter, and every window had heavy wool drapes that hung from ceiling to floor, pulled back to let the sun shine in. Debbie thought that was interesting to see all that fabric used so lavishly when the windows were smaller than those she had seen in the past in other cottages.

Shining pale bamboo cupboards lined the walls, their creamy surfaces reflecting the sunshine into corners, along with benches and stools, and there were two doors off to the side, open to reveal hallways going elsewhere. Every surface was light and bright, probably, Debbie thought, to make the endless northern winter less gloomy.

Chika beamed at the baby sitting in Debbie's lap sucking her thumb vigorously while she stared around her. "What a precious angel! You must be so proud to have three girls. A blessing from Winter to be sure. Sit and I'll have bread and butter to go with your tea in a trice."

"Mommy?" Ghita whispered to Debbie. She looked shy and worried, an expression very unlike the one she had had since they had run away. It tore at Debbie's heart. "Will we stay here?"

"For a while, I think," Debbie whispered. "Best behavior now, you and your sister."

Carina was even more subdued and was sucking her thumb, a habit that had come back when they had marched from the old village to the new and one she had stopped soon after they had left the new village to head north.

Ghita and Carina sat on their stools and sipped their tea, quiet as mice. They had gotten used to riding with Harley and Tyr all day for days on end and now, suddenly, everything had changed again. Debbie felt the same way. As soon as she got used to one thing, something else happened. Even Spotty was feeling uncomfortable and was uncharacteristically quiet.

The baby had already decided she liked the new place and this new woman smiling at her with such enthusiasm.

Chika reappeared with sliced barley bread and butter and then, to Debbie and her daughter's astonishment, proceeded to drop more butter in her tea, letting it melt into an oily slick across the top of the cup.

She laughed at their expression. "It keeps the cold out, yeah? Everyone butters their tea in the north. Don't worry. We won't make you do it."

Ghita stared at the pale-yellow film coating Chika's cup, then her own where she could see mint tea and nothing else.

She bravely said, "But Harley never did that and we drank tea at every stop. Tyr made it."

"That's because the riders don't carry butter with them out on the steppes," Chika replied. "If they could do it, they would. Eat now, you need real food after the trail and Debbie, I want you to tell me everything. Yannick told me the highlights but, well, I'm sure he missed plenty of details."

"I — you're being very kind," Debbie faltered.

"You're safe, you and your daughters. That's the important point right now and you'll stay with me and Leon as long as you need to."

"Can Spotty stay too?" Ghita ventured.

"Of course." Chika narrowed her eyes at Spotty who was carefully investigating the base of a cupboard, trying to determine what that fascinating smell was. "He'll have to mind his manners though. We have cats."

Debbie was overwhelmed. She sipped her tea and wondered what to say and then to her horror, she burst into tears.

She sobbed and sobbed, Ghita and Carina clinging to her, the baby in her lap began to wail, while Chika did her best to sooth her, coming to sit besides her and put a comforting arm over her shoulders. Debbie felt humiliated and struggled to regain her self-control, the control that had served her so well all those years in Shelleen but she could not do it.

Her sobs eventually slowed to hiccups and she opened her eyes to a refilled cup of tea being held out to her by Chika.

"Drink this and tell me everything."

So Debbie did; from being chosen for the bride trade, her life in Shelleen, the new village, and finally running away. When she was finished, Chika said, "Yannick skipped a lot and I'm sure there's still plenty more to tell." She looked significantly at Ghita and Carina who smiled bravely at her as they nibbled on their bread slices, their heads down to hide the tear tracks on their faces.

Debbie nodded. "There is." Her voice was hoarse, yet oddly, she felt better. It was like lancing a boil. You had to let the poison out for the wound to heal.

"Finish eating, while I find you and your girls some clothes and you wash up. Kenyatta will be here soon with Yannick and I'm sure you'll be more comfortable talking to the daimyo with a full tummy and a clean kirtle, clean face and hands."

While Debbie and her daughters ate, Chika bustled about, opening cupboards and pulling out clothes. "We're close enough in size that you can wear my kirtles and your daughters will get what Kerill and Niall wear until we get clothes for them. Good thing I kept that baby outfit. This little angel can wear it."

The little angel chose that moment to decide she was hungry too and that she wanted Debbie right now.

Some time later, Debbie relaxed in the chair; cleaner, fed, warm, and wearing a woven wool kirtle with a wide embroidered hem. She was taller than Chika so the kirtle fell to mid-calf on her, but it fit well enough and it had no patches on it anywhere. Ghita and Carina were wearing tunics and pants, looking like little boys except for their braids. The baby was clean again after a quick bath in a basin by the stove and ready to play.

It was, for all of them, a pleasure to wear something that had not been worn to rags. They had been able to bring very few garments with them to the new village and what they had brought, sturdy though it was, became progressively drabber, worn and ragged with time and work.

Spotty was feeling braver and was ranging further afield, sniffing in every corner but he would not pass through the open doors, either down the dim hallways or outside and risk letting his family be out of his sight. He stopped suddenly in mid-sniff at a cabinet and raced to the doorway to the outside and began barking hysterically. He was springing into the air as though he had not been running for most of the day.

Ghita and Carina cringed against Debbie and the baby began to wail again. Debbie and Chika both tried to sooth the girls as Spotty barked furiously at the entrance of Yannick and a much older, very distinguished-looking stranger.

The stranger looked over at Yannick, raised an eyebrow, and their hands flew.

Chika saw the stranger, at once walked over to him, dipped her head respectfully and said, "Welcome to our home, sir."

"Always a pleasure, Chika," he replied. "This young woman must be Debbie? And her brave little girls and her brave little dog?"

Debbie struggled to her feet to greet this new stranger. He was dressed similarly to Yannick in leather boots, wool tunic and trousers but his clothing was noticeably more finely woven, carefully dyed and lavishly embroidered, with feather trim worked in as well. Like Yannick, he had almost waist-length hair and a beard but his hair was loose, full of narrow braids and on every braid, colorful beads gleamed brilliantly against his white hair.

She tried very hard not to stare at the beads in his hair and the deep red-orange feathers at his ears as she said, "Yes, sir, I'm Debbie. I've run away from Shelleen with my daughters, Ghita, Carina, and my little one and our dog, Spotty." She wanted to keep her eyes respectfully on the floor but the beads kept distracting her. She had never before seen such a thing and certainly she would have never guessed a man would be so decked out.

Kenyatta reached out to the baby, smiling and chucking her under the chin. "This is the little one without a name, yeah? What a fool that husband of yours is. Chika will introduce you to the Names-Mistress and she'll help you find what you like that no one else has. Chika, why don't you take the girls to find Kerill and Niall, so's Yannick and I can talk with Debbie."

To Debbie's grateful amazement, the baby decided to stop wailing and smile back at the daimyo of Kenyatta, because this had to be who this man was. It was the enticing, glittery beads in his hair, she decided. She resolved to keep the baby from grabbing at them. Fortunately, Chika had found a rattle with the baby clothes and the baby accepted it now, stuffing it into her mouth.

"Of course, sir," Chika said. "Yannick, there's tea and bread and butter on the table if you or Kenyatta have a mind for them."

She took Ghita and Carina by the hands and led them, silent and apprehensive, from the room and outside. Spotty did not know what to do. Should he stay with Debbie and Yannick and this stranger or should he stay with Ghita and Carina and guard them from other strangers? He ran back and forth, between Debbie and the open door, yapping all the while, then ran after Ghita and Carina and abandoned Debbie to her fate.

The room was suddenly very quiet with Spotty gone.

Kenyatta said, "I'm Remus, daimyo of Kenyatta. Yes, you're welcome to stay with us, you and yours. Yannick told me everything that happened, but I want to hear from you about this village of Shelleen's."

Debbie took a moment to think of what to say, wondering why the new village was so important, more so than a runaway serf and stolen children. He waved her back into the chair, and she began to tell him about the new village; everything she had noticed, thought about, and what all the other Shelleen peasants thought as well.

When she was finished, Kenyatta who had been listening intently, said, "You're lucky, Debbie, make no mistake, and you'll be lucky for Kenyatta too."

To her relief, he turned his attention away from her.

"Yannick, I want you, Otis and the lads to investigate. Bring back as many samples as you can, but do not eat anything there or drink the water in the poisoned area."

"And the setup for the fall migration?" Yannick asked, looking pleased.

"I'll send Pello and his crew. This is more important than anything else."

Debbie had been listening to them talk while, at the same time, trying to keep the nameless baby distracted from Remus' shiny beads, and she caught the two vital words.

"Sir? The area is poisoned?" she blurted out in horror, not able to stop herself despite being in the presence of the daimyo of Kenyatta. He had not, after all, asked her to speak.

"From your description, yes, I think it is," he said calmly, unbothered by her interruption. "As soon as Yannick arrived, him, me, the ecologist and the geologist have been going over what you saw. It isn't natural for the terraforming lichens and fungus to struggle. There aren't many places where they can't take root and thrive. Why, we'd be knee deep in algae if everything else didn't outcompete them as soon as the soil gets better. Shelleen's up to something, putting people where the land is sick."

Debbie was distraught and frightened enough to question him further. "Will my daughters be alright? We ate what we foraged and grew and drank the water for months." She could not control the tremor in her voice or her hands.

"I think you'll be fine now that you're away from that place," answered Kenyatta. "It isn't completely poisoned or the terraformers wouldn't be growing along with the poverty grasses. Your girls saw birds and bugs not too far away and those critters won't stay." He smiled at her. "It's a good thing you got out, though."

He smiled reassuringly at her again, finished his tea and stood up. "Yannick, you and the lads are heading back out right away, yeah?"

"Yeah, I'll pick up extra pack horses from the Horse-Master. We'll need to carry samples out and I want to rotate the horses out of the poisoned area as often as I can."

"Good. Requisition anything you need. My staff will start researching the old geologic charts to see what Shelleen's got. There might be a hint."

Kenyatta paused and turned back to Debbie. "You said that it seemed like Shelleen was in the biggest hurry in the world to set up this new village?"

"Yes, sir." She kept her eyes modestly down, wincing at how bold she had been before. "It always takes several years to set up a new village and yet we were told one day that we were going, and the next day, we went."

"Something must have changed," said Kenyatta in a considering manner. "Otherwise, Shelleen would have done this years ago if he knew this was there."

"That early spring storm last year," Yannick said thoughtfully. "The huge one. Lasted for days, remember? If the winds were high enough, and they must have been, they'd have stripped off the topsoil covering whatever's there. Shelleen conducts routine border patrols, we all do. That's how they found out."

Kenyatta beamed at him. "I do believe you are correct, Yannick. Find out everything you can, do not be seen by any of Shelleen's people and come back when you're done. Good work. You brought us Debbie and her girls and discovered something that may be very important to all of us in the quad."

He fished around in a tunic pocket and tossed two bright beads to Yannick. "Good work."

Smiling broadly, Yannick easily caught them in midair and held the pair up to catch the late sun. They shone a deep orangey red, the same shade as the feathers he and Kenyatta both wore. "Thank you, sir."

Kenyatta said, "I'll leave you to it. Make sure you see your boys before you ride out. Debbie, in a few days, after you've settled a bit, Chika will bring you and your girls to the manor house. I got people who need to talk to you about what you've seen. By your leave?"

"Of course, sir," Yannick inclined his head.

Remus Kenyatta took a moment to coo at the baby who, to his amusement and Debbie's horror, dropped the rattle and tried desperately to grab at his bright beads. He then left, leaving Debbie to stare at Yannick, while holding the disappointed baby.

"Poisoned area, he said it was poisoned."

"I think he's right, Debbie. It's why nothing will grow there properly and why the water was bad." Yannick waved his long braid at the baby, changing her pout to a giggle.

"Why would Shelleen put a village where it's poisoned?"

"That we don't know, not yet. But I'm gonna make a good start on finding out." Yannick stopped and spun around slowly, looking triumphant. "You are lucky, Debbie, and you're gonna bring luck to Kenyatta. I knew I'd earn a bead, but two! And more to come, I'm sure."

"You earned a bead?" asked Debbie wonderingly. This was a lot of enthusiasm for a bead.

He laughed. "It's what we do, how we keep track. You saw all them beads in Remus's hair? I have at least as many; I just don't wear them out on the steppes. I only wear the most important ones."

He pointed to the bright bits of color in his own hair up at his temples. "They each mean something, and soon as I have the time, I'll tell you all about it."

"Dad! Dad!" A pair of whirlwinds raced into the room, followed by a yapping Spotty, Ghita, and Carina, and with Chika slowly bringing up the rear.

Yannick snatched up his sons, whirling them around the room, making them laugh and Spotty leap about and yap louder. Debbie thought of Aldo who had never once shown any enthusiasm for his daughters and was glad again she had run when she had the chance.

"I was waiting for Remus to leave, and I knew you wanted to see the boys while you could," said Chika. "Do you have any idea when you'll be back?"

"No idea, mom. This is gonna be completely different from setting up the migration or running the borders. One thing I know, the lads will benefit. Harley will be made a vaquero for sure after this."

"You have to go back out, dad?" asked the older boy.

He was a hair taller than Ghita, with Yannick's dark hair and eyes. His brother was older than Carina but not by much, with lighter hair and eyes than his brother. Like Yannick, both boys had their hair in a single, long braid heading to their waist. Their hair was as long as Ghita's and Carina's, something Debbie had never seen before on a boy. It must have never been cut.

"'fraid so, Kerill. That's what makes me a Hand. Now I want you and Niall to help Ghita and Carina settle in. Can you boys do that for me?"

Yannick spent a few more minutes with his sons, then hugged them and Chika goodbye. To Debbie and her daughters, he said, "You'll be safe and cared for. You have my word on it. I'll stop by quick when Harley, Tyr and I ride out. And I will come back."

He disappeared out the door and the room was quiet again.

Chika sighed and wiped her eyes, breaking the silence. "It's always hard when anyone leaves, isn't it? Anyway, we've got a supper to get on. Debbie, if you could help me? Boys, why don't you play with Ghita and Carina and the baby. They'll all be living with us for some time."

She stopped and gave the terrier a considering look which he returned. "Spotty too."

Chika turned out to be much easier to work with than Aldo's mother ever had been. It was very pleasant for Debbie to settle into the routine of preparing a meal in a nice cooking area with a dry floor as opposed to the dreadful soddy. As they worked, Debbie quietly told Chika more of what her life had been like in Shelleen, both before and after the move to the new village.

The last of the afternoon sun was fading when Yannick, Harley, and Tyr stopped by on their way back to the steppes, not even staying long enough to have tea. They had just enough time to say goodbye and reassure Chika and Debbie and the kids that they would return.

At supper, they were joined by Leon, Yannick's father. He admired the baby and allowed a suspicious Spotty to sniff his boots. Ghita and Carina were beginning to settle in and told Debbie all about everybody they had met in the village during her talk with Kenyatta.

After supper, Chika and Leon both insisted that Debbie write a letter to her mother in Dairapaska right away, not waiting until after the evening washing-up had been done. Debbie was surprised and grateful and filled several sheets of paper, writing quietly at the table as other people bustled around her, taking care of the after-supper work. It was an astonishing luxury. Even better was looking forward to mailing her letter in the morning.

The washing-up complete and the letter written, Chika settled into a chair with the mending, Debbie joining her, and it was so much like what she remembered about mending with her mother in Dairapaska, that she wanted to cry again. Debbie had done plenty of sewing, spinning, and knitting in Shelleen with Aldo's mother and her sister-in-laws, but they rarely wanted to hear what *she* had to say. Chika was full of questions and she listened to Debbie's answers.

Chika had more questions when she insisted on showing Debbie how to braid her hair in a style similar to her own loops and coils. "Only men in the North wear a single braid down the back. It won't do to keep your hair that way," she told Debbie. Her voice did not grate on Debbie's nerves like Aldo's mother would have, and she explained her reason, something else that Aldo's mother would never do.

All the while Debbie talked, more than she had in years. Chika was an interested, sympathetic listener, coaxing out details that Debbie had never spoken of to anyone before. There were still topics they did not cover. Both women had an unspoken agreement that there were details that did not need to be discussed in front of children.

When it was time to sleep, Debbie got another surprise. The wider hallway turned out to be lined with tiny rooms, alcoves really, each one large enough to hold a big mattress of tightly packed straw and wool, with drawers underneath, and shelves and cupboards lining the three walls. Each alcove came complete with a wide-silled, small window, heavily draped in bleached wool, and a thick, heavy cream wool curtain across the front. The ceiling was made of more bamboo, so pale it was almost white, highly polished to make the space brighter.

"For privacy," said Chika, "and to keep the heat in during the winter. Leon and I have the first cubby, Yannick is opposite us, then the boys behind us, and you'll take this bed, you and your girls, across from the boys. This will be your private space."

It was a cozy little nook, with plenty of space for Debbie and her daughters and the baby. There was even a small shelf for a rush-light if she wanted one. The deep-set window looked out onto the west and the glittering stars filling the night sky.

When everything had been done at last, and she and her girls had settled themselves inside the cubby, Spotty at their feet, Debbie lay back on the mattress, enjoying the softness and the smell of clean sheets. It was a great luxury after the shelter floors, the grass nests, and the pallet in the soddy. She had not had a mattress to sleep on since they had left the old village. It was soft and warm, feeling as if it had been made entirely of wool and not mixed with packed straw.

Ghita and Carina whispered to each other, then sank into sleep, as did the nameless baby.

Debbie did not.

She kept thinking about what Remus Kenyatta had said: "a poisoned area." What a terrible thought that was and what a terrible thing the new daimyo of Shelleen was doing to his serfs. She did not doubt for a moment that he thought it was needful and she was also sure that he did not care if the peasants died, as long as he got what he wanted.

Whatever was there was of major importance, so much so that he was willing to pay for it with the blood and lives of his serfs; serfs that his predecessor had gone to a lot of trouble over with the bride trade, trying to improve their fertility.

When she spoke to Kenyatta, she would have to be sure to tell him that. Hmmm. Then why did the new daimyo send her and Aldo? All the other Dairapaska girls and their husbands stayed behind, along with their children and their promise of fertility for the next few generations.

It was a puzzle.

The other thing that kept Debbie awake was, to her surprise, that she missed Yannick's presence next to her, along with the wolf-dogs, and Harley and Tyr. She had gotten used to them very quickly. That was strange. But then again, maybe it wasn't. They had been kind and had made sure she and her daughters were safe and cared for. And by the end of the first scary day, she had felt safer.

Debbie decided she felt safe again, as well as warm and dry, and then she was able to sleep.

The following days were a jumble of impressions. So many things in the village were like the villages of Dairapaska and Shelleen, whereas other things ranged from a little different to astonishingly strange.

The visit to the Names-Mistress the day after they arrived in the village stood out. The Names-Mistress was an old woman, still very sharp, and she wanted a written list of every single person Debbie had ever met or heard of, so she could write their names down on the rolls she kept. Her own name was Moswen.

"Yannick told you we don't reuse names, yeah?" the Names-Mistress said, her eyes twinkling.

"Yes, he did. He said I could choose my own name for my baby?"

Debbie wanted to be sure that she could and that this choice was not something that would be offered to her and then cruelly snatched away.

"Yes, you certainly can," Moswen answered, "as long as no one else is using it. A name can't be reused until the person it belonged to no longer needs it. Has Chika shown you the Sacred Grove yet?"

"No, we hadn't got that far yet," Chika replied smartly. "There's so much to do!"

Moswen tsked at her. "A baby has to have a name. That's what needed to be done. We'll walk to the Grove while I explain. Debbie, I collect names. Every Names-Mistress in the North does. Since we don't reuse names, we always need fresh ones. Your names from Dairapaska are wonderful and many of the Shelleen ones are new to Kenyatta as well. You would never know they were part of our quad, as little as they have to do with us."

Chika chuckled. "We have very little to do with them, as you know full well."

"True enough. We don't use family names in the North either, another reason why each person has to have a unique name. I'm Moswen of Kenyatta, and if I want to be formal, I say that I'm Moswen of Kenyatta, daughter of Sybil of Kenyatta. I can go back for several generations and if I need to, I can include my father and grandparents and aunts and uncles."

"That is very different," Debbie said. "Dairapaska and Shelleen both use family names for everyone who's related. Aldo's family was desperate for a baby boy. They had no male heir to carry on the family name of Acconcio and if they didn't get a boy, the land they held in trust would revert back to Shelleen. It's why he was so angry about the baby being a girl."

She kissed her baby's upturned nose and was rewarded with a burble of joy.

"Ridiculous," sniffed Moswen. "Family lineage can travel just as well through the mother's side."

Debbie stroked the baby's soft brown hair. "They don't care about that," she said softly. "The girls marry and take their husband's family name."

"That is absurd," said Chika, oozing disapproval. "That says the mother's family doesn't count!"

They crossed over the stile built into the low stone wall, Ghita and Carina following and Spotty circling them madly as he tried desperately to be in several places at once. A flowery meadow separated them from a great forest of trees, more than Debbie had ever seen. They formed a vast arc stretching across the steppes, almost as though the forest wrapped itself around the villages and the manor house of Kenyatta, shielding them from the north wind.

"This is the Sacred Grove," said Moswen, as they reached the trees. "Every demesne in the North has one."

She led Debbie through the trees to a clearing, following a path Debbie could not discern. The trees they passed were of every size from slim sapling to mighty giant. The smaller, younger trees tended to be on the outskirts of the grove, and they grew larger and taller as the group walked under them, deeper between the trees. The variety of the tree species present was enormous, far more than Debbie would have expected.

Dairapaska grew trees for timber, forage, fruit, and nuts, as did Shelleen, but this forest seemed different, less regimented and regularly spaced. The trees had been deliberately planted, giving each one space to spread, but not in any orderly fashion of this kind of tree here and that kind of tree there. The ground beneath them was thick with mosses and low, leafy plants growing in their shade. Although the weather was getting colder, none of the leaves had dropped, but they were starting to change color, with glints of red and orange, gold and brown dappled across the green canopy of leaves.

Moswen paused in front of a tall oak and laid her hand on its trunk, gazing up its trunk to the leaf-shrouded top so far above her. She turned to Debbie and said, "This is my grandfather, Anchali. Grandfather, this is Debbie and her baby and her daughters, Ghita and Carina. They are new to Kenyatta and I'm showing them our ways. Debbie has to choose a name for her baby and I hope you will guide her in her choice."

Debbie did not know what to say without sounding rude, so she said nothing, just stared at Moswen and the oak tree.

Ghita did not have any such compunctions. "Your grandfather is a tree?" She looked disbelieving, while Carina looked confused. Spotty sniffed at the roots of the oak tree.

"No, my sweet girl, his spirit is in the tree," Moswen answered serenely. "When we die in the North, our bodies are buried in the grove and as soon as we can thereafter, a tree is chosen and planted over the grave. This oak has grown strong and tall, like my grandfather. See?"

She pointed to the carving cut deep into the side of the tree. "Here is his name, Anchali. That name cannot be reused as long as his tree is alive and anyone remembers the deeds of Anchali. When both of those things become false, when he is no longer using his name, then the name of Anchali can be given to another baby boy, a boy who will grow up to be strong and brave and a leader of men, like my grandfather was.

"Every tree here contains the soul of a man or woman of Kenyatta, someone who was once alive in human form and walked among us. We come here to remember them. We celebrate our births and marriages here, and we bury our dead here. If I am very quiet, I can hear my grandfather's voice when I sit under his tree."

Chika was smiling sadly, her eyes bright with tears. "I have many family members here and I come visit them. It helps me to remember them. When I stand under my mother's tree, I know that I am still dearly loved by her. She has not forgotten me as I have not forgotten her."

"A name is very important, Debbie," Moswen said firmly. "It will live on long after the physical body no longer walks among us, as long as the spirit exists, as long as the tree lives and stories are told about that person. What name did you have in mind for your little one?"

"What if the name I want is taken? What about our names?" asked Debbie, feeling her heart constrict.

"Your names are your names," replied Moswen serenely. "They have been given to you and we will not take them away. Fortunately, no one in Kenyatta is named Debbie or Ghita or Carina, but that will not be true of other northern demesnes. I believe this is a sign that you were meant to come here."

A breeze whispered past them, rustling the oak tree's leaves, and bringing with it the rich scent of earth and moss, full of fecund life.

"Would a name used in Kenyatta be reused in one of the other Northern demesnes?" asked Debbie.

"It can be, but if that person is very famous, then most likely not. Who do you want this sweet baby to be? If you have no ideas, I have many hundreds of names on my rolls waiting for the right person to come along. Since we don't reuse names, your names from Dairapaska and Shelleen will give us even more choices."

Debbie held her nameless baby tightly. She was afraid to say her choice out loud. What if the name she wanted, had always wanted, had wanted for Ghita, had wanted for Carina, had already been given away?

"What name do you wish for your angel baby, Debbie? We will find one *you* want, one that is right for this baby."

"I want," Debbie stopped and made herself go on. "I want Espe. My grandmother said it meant hope."

Chika smiled broadly. "A beautiful name and so well suited for a baby."

Moswen leaned back against the oak tree, her eyes closed and she stayed that way for many moments while the others waited, listening to the breeze whisper among the trees. She stirred at last. "I think that no one has that name, not in Kenyatta and perhaps not in Satran either. I will have to confirm this when we go back to my house but I think, yes, Espe will be this baby's name."

She leaned over and kissed the wide-eyed baby's head. "A new baby is always hope for the future, and I believe you, Espe, are the cause of new life and new joy for your mother and sisters."

Debbie's spirits flew. She wanted to sing, to dance, to sob, but she did none of those things. Instead she sank down onto her knees, and then sat in the soft, cushiony moss in front of Anchali's oak, clutching Espe to her breasts. Her baby had a name at last, and it was one that she had chosen.

Ghita sat next to her and waved a leaf for the baby to grab. "Espe is pretty, mommy. I like it."

"So do I," said Carina. She sat on Debbie's other side and held out a finger for the baby to clutch.

Debbie felt, as she sat on the moss, the strong oak tree supporting her, that she and her daughters had found refuge at last.

When she felt able to move again, Chika and Moswen led her and her daughters around the grove, pointing out the trees of various family members, some recently dead with saplings to mark their passage into the grove and others gone for many decades; their tree grown into tall, wide, spreading adulthood.

There were many kinds of trees and Moswen explained that each person could, if they wanted, choose the tree for their grave. An oak for acorns, a pear for fruit, a hickory for nuts, a fir to provide shelter from the cold winter winds. If no choice had been given beforehand, the family would choose with the help of the Grove-Master and the Grove-Mistress, looking for a tree that would complement the others and add to the wealth and security of Kenyatta.

She stopped by a fallen giant fir tree at the center of the grove. It had lost most of its branches and the ones that remained had no needles any more. The carving of his name was obscured with heavy moss and lichens, blurring back into the bark as the tree rotted where it lay.

Moswen said, "This man, Daniel, was one of the earliest settlers of Kenyatta. He helped build the manor house and laid out the first village. He planted the first windbreak to block the north wind. Even though his tree is returning to the soil, feeding it with his life, he is still remembered. His name will not be reused in Kenyatta for many lifetimes to come."

As they slowly walked back to Moswen's house, Debbie would whisper the new baby's name to her, "Espe, Espe my little angel, you have a name at last."

When they reached her cottage, its exterior walls elaborately painted with long, sinuous lines like writing, Moswen brought out the rolls of names. They were made of long, crackling sheets of parchment, dozens of them, bound together at the top and she had many, carefully laid on shelves. She showed Debbie the newest parchment rolls where she had begun adding all the names that Debbie knew from Dairapaska and Shelleen, names that would be reused in Kenyatta but only once.

She began searching through the lists of who was alive or in the Grove as her own daughter and granddaughter prepared a lunch for Debbie and her daughters. They were both Moswen's apprentices and when Moswen passed into the grove, her daughter would be the next Names-Mistress.

When they had finished eating, a smiling Moswen reappeared. "It is as I thought. Espe has never been used in Kenyatta. This little one is Espe and she will always remain Espe. No other woman will have her name and when people speak of Espe, they will mean her and only her. She is Espe, daughter of Debbie of Dairapaska and now of Kenyatta."

Learning Village Ways

D EBBIE AND HER DAUGHTERS were gradually introduced to everyone in the village, starting with Yannick's older brother Lysander and his family and Otis's family. They were kitted out with clothes, soft wool slippers and knitted stockings, sabots for the dirty work outside, and they learned the routines of Chika's house and the village.

As they walked around, Debbie quickly noticed that, as Chika had said, only males wore their hair in a single braid down their back. That is, if they weren't wearing their hair loose, with many tiny braids covered with beads to adorn it. Any boy who had earned a bead made sure to wear it, no matter what he was doing. It was acceptable for little girls to have two braids, one on each side, but when the girls got older, they made much more elaborate constructions of plaits piled high. No woman ever wore her hair loose or down outside of her cottage or the bathhouse.

Chika had been insistent that even though she was a stranger from another demesne, Debbie keep her hair plaited and piled up despite the extra work.

"Only your lover should know how long your hair is," she had told Debbie as she combed out her hair inside the privacy of the cottage.

Debbie thought this one over and realized that no woman she had seen since her arrival ever wore her hair loose or down in a long braid. Then she blushed as she realized Yannick knew exactly how long her hair was, and indeed, had watched her unbraid it, comb it out and then rebraid in the shelter before setting out each morning. He never said anything, but she had noticed him noticing. She had thought nothing of it as she worked on her own and her daughters' hair, happy that he played with Espe while she did so. Aldo had never played with his own daughters so that had held her attention, not her taking care of their hair. Hair was cleaned by a thorough combing out, then braided to keep it neat and out of the way. Debbie had always been quietly proud of her thick, lustrous hair, but it was just hair. Now she had to wonder what Yannick's thoughts were and blushed again. Then she realized the intimacy of him lending her his comb and her cheeks burned still more.

Northern customs for hair were strange but easy to comply with so Debbie chose to follow them without comment on how silly it seemed. It saved more potential embarrassment. It also let her pretend that she had always known and had not transgressed during the journey from the cairn.

It was much harder to watch Leon teach Ghita and Carina to ride horses, something that no serf in either Dairapaska or Shelleen ever did. Debbie cringed every time she saw Leon toss Ghita or Carina up onto a horse and then lead the huge animal around, her tiny in comparison daughter clinging to its back and giggling madly. The girls thought it was great fun and did not share her fear of them falling off and being trampled. Debbie had very little interest in ever getting back on a horse. Her feet worked fine, and she did not see the need. Since no one insisted that *she* learn, she chose to avoid the subject while praying Leon knew what he was doing with her daughters.

In many other ways, daily life was like the old village in Shelleen and in Dairapaska before that. It had a similar, complex network of obligations, gifts, favors, debts, barters, trades, and relationships that would take time to learn; who owed what to whom and at what time of the day or season of the year. Family relationships, neighbors, friends, co-workers, all had to be placed into the web that bound the villages of Kenyatta together. Steppes partnerships, such as Yannick and Otis, added an additional layer of complexity as a steppes partnership could and sometimes did trump a blood relationship. In her explanation, Chika noted that Yannick was closer to Otis, his steppes partner, than he was to Lysander, his own, much older brother. Lysander, in turn, had his steppes partner to whom, depending on the circumstances, he turned to first rather than to Yannick and other blood kin. And as always, there were the obligations due to the ruling family of Kenyatta, overseen by the daimyo and enforced through custom and tradition.

The post office, however, was the same, located close to the grand manor house, overseeing the lands around it from the top of the hill. It had a cubby for every household in every village in the demesne to receive its mail from the outside world. A member of each household would pick up their mail as they saw fit or when the Post-Mistress insisted they stop in because either the cubby was stuffed full or something important had arrived from the outside world.

Chika had been dismissive of the idea of a daimyo controlling the mail that his peasants received.

"That is so wrong. What the hell does it matter who writes to you or who you write letters to? Why, I write letters to relatives all over the North and nobody ever tells *me* no."

"They usually don't," answered Debbie. "It was only with the bride trade that we had restrictions put on our mail and only between Shelleen and Dairapaska. I suppose the daimyos thought that the women would become part of their new homes quicker if they were not always remembering their old homes and families."

"And did it work?" asked Chika, looking extremely dubious.

"Well, in one or two cases maybe it sort of did," Debbie said sadly. "But for most of us from Dairapaska, not very well. It would have been hard to get mail from home, but that would have been better than being forgotten. I suppose the same must be true for the Shelleen girls. Nobody knows."

The morning after she had arrived, before they went to the Sacred Grove with Moswen, Debbie mailed her letter to her mother detailing everything that had happened; her marriage, her daughters, and her finding refuge in Kenyatta. She had made a point of asking her mother to not tell the Shelleen brides that she had run away, not wanting to cause more trouble for Dairapaska than they probably already had. It would take a week or more for her to get an answer back, if her mother was still alive to answer. Nonetheless, she and Chika stopped at the post office every day afterwards to check if an answer had arrived all the while knowing that it was too soon.

The comforting similarities of the village in Kenyatta brought into focus even more strongly how strange the new village had been. The peasants had brought almost nothing with them to build the new village out on the steppes, other than the clothes on their backs, tools for farming, food stores, things for animal husbandry yet very few animals to husband, and necessaries for running a household. Shelleen had sent so little with them, although some of that might have been due to the lack of a usable road. This was, by itself, a bizarre situation as who ever built a village without first building a proper road to make traffic back and forth possible? Debbie stored up the strangenesses to give to Kenyatta when she had her audience with him.

So far, he had yet to summon her.

She discussed it endlessly with Chika and Leon and both agreed that these little, mundane details of everyday life mattered. They all implied that Shelleen had been in a tearing hurry to get the new village set up. It was as though a deadline hovered over him, one he did not dare miss.

"It sounds, I know, that Airik Shelleen was a terrible daimyo," said Debbie as she and Chika were slicing their way through a hill of cabbages to ferment in crocks for the winter. Espe was at their feet, happily waving a rattle at a watchful tabby cat. Chika's two cats had already learned to keep their tails well away from Espe's eager reach.

"But he wasn't, not really, no more so than the daimyo of Dairapaska had been or the old daimyo of Shelleen. No one was unhappy, there were no riots or revolts, and everybody usually had enough to eat. We were normally left in peace as long as we upheld our obligations to the daimyo and everyone did."

Debbie frowned and whacked another cabbage in half with more force than necessary. "The bride trade made many people angry, very angry, but there were enough people who benefited that there were no open protests. Everyone understood the need for new genes and new blood. It was how the daimyos did it that made the families so angry."

"I think that was dreadful," said Chika, pursing her lips in disapproval. "We move girls around from demesne to demesne but only the girls who want to leave because they think the local boys are boring and the local villages are dull. And they all write back to their families and sometimes even visit! We count our relatives out to six degrees of consanguinity and I write to my own relatives across the north, many of them people I have never met in person."

She chuckled and held up the wedge of red cabbage. "Why I got the seeds for this cabbage from a distant relative in VanDenRooz! She swore they were cold hardy and they are, better than any other kind I've grown. The color keeps too, another big plus. Lovely to see it in the winter, it is."

"It's how things had been done in Dairapaska in years past," said Debbie, remembering. "I have distant relatives in the other demesnes in our quad, and we wrote letters back and forth even though nobody got to visit. I think the daimyos were afraid that if you visited, you would get off the train in the free-city and never get back on again. If you wanted to go live with distant relatives in another demesne in the quad with your family, you could petition the daimyo. If the other demesne agreed, and they nearly always did, the family would leave with an escort from the daimyo's men."

"So the family didn't disappear from the train station?"

"Yes, exactly." Debbie slashed another defenseless cabbage in half and began swiftly cutting it into narrow strips. "But we were having more and more fertility problems in Dairapaska and in the neighboring demesnes as well. That's why Dairapaska and Shelleen did the trade and with so many women. They wanted a lot of fresh genes, not just a few, and they wanted them to be as different as they could manage."

"We have our own problems with fertility," Chika said, "but there are other ways around it than just trading young women." She gave the cabbage in her hands a veiled smile. "Yannick told you that your daughters will be in demand when they grow up, yeah?"

"Yes, he did."

"I've already had several women in the villages ask me about considering their sons for them in the future."

"Ghita is seven!" Debbie sputtered.

"She won't be seven forever. That's what's being pointed out to me." Chika carefully kept her eyes on the cabbage she was packing into the stoneware crock with plenty of salt, sliced onions, juniper berries and sage leaves. "I'm being asked about you, too."

Debbie set down her knife and held onto the counter to steady herself. She could not bring herself to meet Chika's understanding face. "I don't think I can do that."

"I'm not surprised, considering what your experience with marriage has been. I'm fending them off, don't worry. You'll never be forced to marry, our winters are hard enough as it is and if you're with someone you don't like, well," — Chika began tamping the cabbage down — "there are dreadful stories about what gets found in the spring. We like to avoid that in the North.

"But you may want to consider this."

Chika looked around, checking that the older children were outside, rather than hovering underfoot with big ears. Espe did not count, as she would not be able to understand what she heard or ask unfortunately timed and embarrassing questions later on.

"Northern men make outstanding lovers. We have long winter nights and that gives plenty of time for practice." She had a complacent, satisfied smile on her face.

Debbie stopped slicing onions and stared at her. "I — I'll think about that."

"I'd bet cash money that your husband didn't have any idea of what he was doing in a bed, yeah?"

"Aldo did," answered Debbie, mystified. "I have three children."

Chika laughed, a low throaty sound, one that Debbie had not heard before from her. "If he had any notion of how to please a woman, you wouldn't be so skittish about the thought of laying with a man. So he didn't."

The sound of running footsteps made a welcome distraction for Debbie.

"Mommy! Mommy! Gramma! Gramma! Come quick!" Four whirlwinds came charging into the cottage, shouting and jumping. Unusually, they were not accompanied by a barking Spotty.

"Slow down, Kerill, what is it?"

"Ghita, where is Spotty?"

"He treed the neighbor's cat and boy is she mad!" Kerill

yelled over the noise of the other kids.

Spotty was slowly reaching an accommodation with the two tabby cats in Chika's household. He was learning to respect their claws and in exchange for not being chased, they agreed to not sleep with Debbie and her daughters, leaving that bed to Spotty, and Spotty alone. The rest of the cottage was still under furious negotiation. This state of armed détente did not exist with any of the other cats in the village.

"Oh, dear," Chika said. "Please tell me it wasn't Alison's cat?"

"It sure is, gramma. She is just spitting, says she's gonna catch Spotty and skin him for a winter muff," said Kerill with ghoulish enthusiasm.

Ghita was jumping up and down in her agitation. "You can't let her, mommy!" she shrilled. "Spotty kept us safe out on the steppes!"

"Don't worry, Ghita, sweetie. Your mom and I will take of this."

They walked outside, following an excited Kerill and Ghita, Niall and Carina down the lane winding between the cottages to an apple tree in the walled garden plot of Alison's cottage. Spotty was barking exuberantly and flinging himself into the air trying to reach his prey, while Alison swore at him and her cat hissed from the branches above.

Debbie remembered the day she met Yannick as she watched Spotty deftly evade Alison, while yapping scornfully at her pitiful efforts to catch him. "A pity that Harley isn't here with his bolas."

Chika snickered. "An outstanding idea. Kerill, you take Niall and the girls and go find your grandfather and have him bring his bolas." To Debbie, she said, "Leon is still pretty good and Spotty's gonna make it easy for him, the way he's jumping so high."

Leon soon arrived and in due course, Spotty was unceremoniously captured and carried back to the cottage yapping in indignation, Kerill climbed the tree to rescue the cat and got scratched for his trouble, Alison — who had a ten-year-old nephew's future to consider — managed to be civil to Debbie despite how her cat felt about the subject, and the amused witnesses all had a story to tell at supper that evening to the rest of the villagers. From past experience with similar situations,

Debbie knew the tale would be all over Kenyatta in the next few days.

That night, as Debbie waited for sleep, she thought about what Chika had said about Northern men making outstanding lovers. They had not been able to return to that conversation as there were too many small people running around underfoot after Spotty's capture.

She thought back to Dairapaska and the boy she had hoped to marry so long ago, the one whose name she no longer quite remembered, whose face she could no longer recall. She had enjoyed kissing him, and she had been eager for more. Would she feel differently about a man if she had had someone who had pleased her? That was something to think about, a thought she had never considered before.

At breakfast the next morning, Chika asked Leon to keep the kids out from underfoot. The plan was for her and Debbie to pickle beets and radishes for the winter, a hot smelly process involving large quantities of boiling vinegar.

Debbie agreed wholeheartedly. When she had dropped the pan of boiling water that had left her with ugly scars, she had always been grateful that Ghita had been on the other side of the cottage with her nonna rather than underfoot.

As they settled in for the long day ahead of scrubbing, chopping and slicing, Chika said, "I had another reason for getting the kids out. Someone will approach you soon enough and I'd rather it was me."

"About my marrying again?" Debbie asked. She still wasn't sure if she fancied the idea even if she did get to choose. Once was enough.

"Yannick's marriage," Chika said.

Debbie startled and looked away, not sure of where this conversation was going to go. "Oh. I did wonder what happened to his wife. He wasn't happy with me when I told him that I'd run away with my daughters."

"He wouldn't be," answered Chika. "Not at all. Yannick isn't widowed. Maureen, that was his wife, walked out on him."

Debbie stared at her — although her hands never stopped

scrubbing beets — thinking of Aldo and all the reasons he had given her to leave and yet she never had.

"But why? He's so capable and he, even when he didn't have to be, he didn't want to be! he was still kind to me and my girls. Even as scary as it was, having to ride Gray Gal, he made sure I was safe, and he told me why we had to do it. To save the time of walking."

Chika slammed her knife through a large, thick radish, slicing it cleanly so the inner rings of red glowed against the white flesh. "Yannick has his faults but he is one of the most decent men you will ever meet. I could not say any of this with Kerill and Niall around because that miserable, worthless bitch is still their mother."

"Oh." Debbie thought wearily of her mother-in-law. Mrs. Acconcio had not always held her tongue when Ghita or Carina were around to overhear what she had to say about their mother.

"Don't think I ever said anything to Maureen, because I didn't. I wasn't going to be one of *those* mother-in-laws, causing trouble with my son's wife. I'm sure she still knew how I felt, but she didn't care what anyone thought and she didn't ever hear it coming from me.

"Maureen, I don't even know where to start with her." Chika slashed apart more beets, cutting them forcefully, her face angry. "She was not from Kenyatta. She was from Lynch, one of the farther north demesnes and she'd been to three other Northern demesnes before she landed here in Kenyatta. That should have been a sign, yeah?"

"That she traveled a lot?" Debbie ventured.

"That she couldn't be happy. That she could never be satisfied. Maureen was beautiful, the most beautiful woman I'd ever seen by a wide margin. You know how every young woman is pretty?"

"Well, most of us are." Debbie made a face at the pile of beets.

"Maureen was stunning. A flame in the shape of a woman, she was so alive and vibrant and you couldn't tear your eyes away from her. And like a flame, she burned everyone she touched."

Debbie had been pretty enough but no one had ever described her as anything more than pleasant, hard-working and sturdy.

"She came here, Kerill is seven now, about nine years ago. Yannick was settled on a girl, Tamar was her name, and they were getting serious enough to want to marry. When Maureen showed up, he noticed her. All the young men did and plenty of the men old enough to know better did too. And he said that she was trouble."

Chika began chopping beets vigorously, making them smaller and smaller, into beet puree rather than beet chunks.

"Maureen took that as a challenge and she went after him like a cat on a mouse. And he ended up falling for her, desperately, totally, as though she was the only woman in the world. Poor Tamar was humiliated. Yannick broke off their betrothal and married Maureen. And Maureen was happy, for a while. But she was made to be unhappy. No matter what she wanted, once she had it, she didn't want it anymore. She could never be satisfied. It was like she had a hole inside and it could never be filled.

"She caught Kerill and for a while, she was happy again. Yannick was over the moons with joy, both for her and for the baby. Then she was unhappy again, and it didn't matter what Yannick did, he couldn't please her. Then she became pregnant with Niall and things got better, for a while. But Niall turned out to be a boy and she wanted a girl. After that, it didn't matter what Yannick did. He did everything for her, and it was never enough.

"Then, when Niall was about a year old, Yannick had come back in from a circuit on the steppes. He danced for Maureen, just like he always did, and she eventually, just like always, accepted his dance."

Chika slammed the knife through another beet, then began vigorously hacking it apart, staining the cutting board with more fresh red juice.

"Sometimes she, well, there would be doubt. The bitch. Anyway, the next morning she announced to him and to us and to everyone else in the village that she was tired of Yannick, he was dull and boring and stupid and didn't know how to please a woman. She took the boys and left for Satran, that's the demesne across the corridor. She moved in with one of their vaqueros the day she arrived, humiliating Yannick across the nine-square, not just in Kenyatta."

Debbie was horrified. She thought of all she had put up with from Aldo and his family with never so much as a cross look on her part and was horrified and unbelieving again. She put a hand on Chika's shoulder to get her to stop pulverizing the beets. The stains would never come out of her apron, the way she was battering them into submission, spraying their juices everywhere in a red haze.

"I was always afraid Yannick would hit me while we were riding from the stone tower to the village and he never did," Debbie said. "He answered my questions and showed me how to ride and never once said anything to me about Espe crying. I can't understand why Maureen would leave him. Was she crazy?"

Chika laughed sourly. "Crazy? Quite possibly. Like I said, there was something missing inside her. She stayed with that vaquero in Satran for a few months and in the end, she very publicly decided he wasn't good enough either. Maureen came riding back here with my grandsons and said to Yannick, 'I'm sick of the kids, they get in my way. Take them or I'm dumping them off in Purnell.'"

"She walked out on her kids?" Debbie couldn't believe it. She had never heard of a woman abandoning her children, other than by dying.

"She did and she never came back. Yannick took them in at once, moved back in with us and out of the bunkhouse where he'd been staying, and he spends every minute he's home with his sons. You can imagine the gossip, yeah?"

Debbie could indeed imagine the gossip; fascinated, juicy and cruel. This must have been what Yannick meant when he said that a good story would be spread everywhere and lightning fast. He had had the personal experience of being a nine-day wonder. This was a story people would talk about and embroider for generations.

"Even today," Chika went on, "years later, there's a few who will tell you that it must have been something Yannick did, despite Maureen walking out on her sons, her escapades throughout the North and how she uses and burns everybody she meets."

"Do you know where she is now?" Debbie asked.

Chika began ripping apart another pile of beets.

"I know where she's been. One thing I will say for Maureen, she cares about her mother. She writes to India regularly. I've never met India of Lynch but she writes to *me* about what Maureen is up to, so I get the true story or at least Maureen's version. She always apologizes for Maureen being the way she is, as if India could have stopped her! If it's something I can tell the boys about their mother, I do."

Chika glared at the sink and the mound of radish and beet parts, the wet, bloody chunks oozing red juice in trails across the counter and dripping onto the floor. "Usually I can't. It breaks India's heart that her daughter did this to her grandsons; she writes to them too. That bitch never does. And all the while, Maureen's been making sure that she can't ever go back anywhere. She burns her bridges but good."

"That's awful, just awful. Poor Yannick and those poor boys."

"It hurts them terribly and they never talk about their mother. They know what people say. The only one who wasn't torn to bits was Tamar. She fled to Aguillero to stay with distant relatives and met one of their vaqueros. She has children with him now. Her mother tells me she's very happy."

"My goodness. That's something, I suppose."

"Yes, it is. And it's something that Maureen brought our grandsons back to us. She could have dumped them anywhere and we likely would have never known, never found them," Chika said harshly, slashing more beets into puree.

Debbie felt deeply guilty, shutting her eyes tightly to keep back tears. "I did that to nonna and nonno. They must miss Ghita and Carina terribly."

Chika finally put down the knife and hugged Debbie to her. "Debbie, you would have never left, if it hadn't become dangerous for your daughters. Little Espe might have died, and Aldo hit your older ones. Remember that and don't feel that you did something wrong. You did what you had to do to keep your daughters and yourself safe. You are nothing like Maureen."

She began scooping up the oozy chunks into a crock along with handfuls of herbs. "Yannick will not talk about Maureen, ever. He only says two things. That she is his sons' mother and that she'll come home to them."

Debbie watched the pan of vinegar simmering over the fire.

It was about to boil, and she would pour it over the beets and radishes as soon as Chika was ready for her. This was the dangerous part, lifting the heavy, scalding-hot pan and trying to pour it cleanly, without shaking or spilling. "Does he really believe that?"

"I don't know," Chika answered. "He has never looked at another woman since then and he could have. She tore his heart out, made a fool of him across the North, stole his children and then threw them away. She'll never come back, Maureen doesn't believe in returning to the scenes of her crimes, and she still has the rest of Mars to devastate. I pray every night that she doesn't."

They carefully poured the scalding vinegar over the crocks full of beets and radishes, then topped them with salt and a clean, heavy stone for each crock to press down the contents. The crocks would sit quietly for months in the cold room, next to the crocks full of cabbage in brine, waiting for the deep winter and the thin time. They would be welcomed, adding flavor and color to meals when everything green was asleep under the snow.

That night, as Debbie waited for sleep, she thought about Maureen. How could she have done that to Yannick? There were far worse men walking around than he was. Debbie had heard plenty of stories and knew some of the participants, both in Dairapaska and in Shelleen. Although Aldo was no prize, he had been far from the most unpleasant man she had heard of.

But this explained why Yannick had been so upset at hearing her story. Chika had said how fundamentally decent he was, and it was true. He had still treated her fairly, and he had thought of the good of Kenyatta rather than wallowing in his own raw pain.

How he must have loved her. He probably still loved Maureen, to not take another wife. Debbie had already figured out that, despite the shortages of potential wives in Kenyatta, a hard-working, capable man did not have much trouble finding a woman. It was the lesser men, the ones like Aldo, who remained unmarried and alone. And that was very much like Shelleen and Dairapaska.

She fell asleep missing his long, lean warmth rolled up against her.

Finally, some days later, word came from the manor house that Debbie and her daughters needed to meet with Kenyatta and his staff in the afternoon.

Debbie had spent days thinking over the strangeness of the new village and she was feeling ready to face Remus and a roomful of aristocratic strangers. Chika insisted that they all spend the morning in the bathhouse to clean up better from the days of chopping cabbages and roots for the winter. There were still mountains of vegetables to go, as well as many other things to prepare for eating in the winter. Meeting Remus would be a nice break from that unending work.

The bathhouse was very similar to Shelleen's, with its large tubs of hot water for soaking in and women washing themselves and their daughters and babies, gossiping during the process. In Shelleen, it had always been a pleasure to settle into a tub and sometimes join the conversation.

Unfortunately, since everyone was becoming more comfortable around Debbie, the other women were now making a point of telling her about the virtues of their sons, nephews and grandsons. The more thoughtful ones asked Debbie if Ghita and Carina had been over to play with their boys so as to get to know them better.

So, when Debbie sank into the tub, she was expecting that conversation. Chika had gone off to take care of Espe, allowing Debbie some time to bathe, but also allowing another woman to come up and say, in a low significant voice, "Did anyone tell you about Yannick yet? You should know how he can be."

Debbie smiled up at her. Chika had said it would not take long for a gossip to approach her and it hadn't. From her arch look, Debbie judged that this woman had been a friend of Maureen's.

"Yes, thank you. Chika told me all about it," Debbie answered pleasantly. All the practice she'd had in Shelleen in not showing her feelings came in handy again and Debbie found herself grateful for the skill.

"Oh, well, Chika wouldn't say anything against her son," was the answer.

Behind them Debbie heard, "carrying tales again, Barb? Yannick did everything he could for that Maureen and you know it."

It was Alison's sharp voice, which surprised Debbie. She had not thought that Alison and Chika, though they were neighbors, were friends.

Then Chika appeared with the baby, scrubbed clean with a bow tied around her head to rein in her wispy hair and Barb swiftly stalked away, her back stiff with anger.

Chika sighed. "Barb again? Thank you, Alison."

"Not a problem. So you're taking Debbie and her girls to the manor house, yeah?"

"Yeah, Kenyatta wants his staff to talk to her about the new village that Shelleen built out in the middle of nowhere."

"Strange, very strange, that a daimyo would do that," Alison said. "Debbie, keep that worthless mutt of yours away from my cats and Chika, tell Kerill that I don't appreciate his spooking my chickens when he gallops past. Next time he does that, he gets to catch them and bring them back."

Chika did her best to not roll her eyes. "Of course, Alison. Anytime your chickens get out, I'll have Kerill retrieve them."

"See that you do," and Alison went back to her business.

"Well," Chika said. "Barb didn't take long, no surprise there."

"She was one of Maureen's friends?" asked Debbie as she dried herself off and combed out her hair, thinking about how she would arrange the braids. She had yet to settle on a style that was quick and easy, while still being publicly acceptable. She wondered what she would say to Ghita and Carina, who had been listening avidly. They would be sure to ask questions later. The surprise was that Ghita had not said something right then and there, and Debbie chose to be grateful for that small mercy.

"Oh, yeah. Thick as thieves, those two, and Barb thought Maureen could do no wrong. Yet she's never heard one word from Maureen since she walked out. I suppose Barb can't admit to herself what Maureen was."

"It was nice of Alison to say something."

"Alison can be hard to get along with, but she despised Maureen. She also believes that people should face facts, whether they want to or not. That doesn't make her popular with people like Barb."

"No, I would think not."

Chika had been vigorously toweling off Ghita and Carina while the two women spoke. "You girls behaved very nicely," she said, "not being rude to Barb. You're a credit to your mother, yeah?"

"That Barb was wrong about Yannick," Ghita replied loyally. "He helped us and he didn't have to. And he helped Spotty even though Spotty tried to bite him."

"And Spotty peed on Harley's blanket and Yannick wouldn't let Harley hurt Spotty," added Carina.

Chika looked amused. "Somehow Yannick failed to tell me about that, not enough time, yeah? You girls tell me about what Spotty did on the walk back to our cottage."

By the time they got back, Chika was laughing at Ghita's description of Harley chasing in vain after Spotty.

"It really was very funny," added Debbie, "even though it wasn't funny at the time."

"Not funny for Harley, I'm sure. Ghita, you've met his little sister, yeah?"

"Yes, gramma Chika, Reay's really nice. She likes Spotty."

"Make sure you tell her and her mother this story as soon as you see them. They will laugh."

All cleaned up, with freshly braided hair and new ribbons to match the baby's bow, Debbie and her daughters dressed in the finest of their fine, new-to-them clothes, and they followed Chika down the path out of the village and up the hill to the manor house that watched over the lands below.

Kerill and Niall had been told to keep Spotty busy and well away from the manor house, which they were accomplishing by having Spotty chase rodents (and cats and chickens) in one of the large, shared barns. Chika and Leon would hear about this later on, in detail, and not just from Kerill and Niall.

The manor house was a huge pile of reddish stone on the hill, with many large windows to catch every bit of the sun. It had been built with two large wings framing a south-facing stone courtyard, the wings also lined with windows and balconies on the upper floors. The central door was large enough for several men to walk abreast when both sides were open.

Debbie had seen the manor houses of Shelleen and

Dairapaska, and this one was similar, but with more elaborate carvings across the top of each big window and door. People in Kenyatta liked to decorate their houses far more than they had in Shelleen and she supposed the manor house would be no exception. She had, of course, never set foot in one. This would be a new experience.

Ghita and Carina had been carefully instructed on their behavior and Debbie had hopes that they would listen. They were generally obedient little girls so there was a good chance it would happen. As they settled into the village here in Kenyatta, they were turning back into the cheerful, active children they had been in the old village, before the long march and Aldo's unhappiness in the dreadful new village had scarred them.

They were ushered through the front door by a maidservant, one of the village girls Chika later told Debbie, and led down softly carpeted hallways with fancy pictures on the walls, up a grand staircase, down another long hallway with more pictures, and at last into a large room with a big table in the middle.

The room had large windows, with the heavy wool drapes in Kenyatta's colors of deep blue and red-orange pulled back to allow every bit of the early afternoon sun in, and many lamps as well, for when the sun went down. It was lined with shelves full of an impressively large number of books. There were cabinets as well, all made of bamboo and wood, carved and decorated. Some of them had glass fronts and were full of odd curiosities.

Remus Kenyatta was leaning over the table next to a thin, graying man. Several other people were gathered around, looking on. They were studying a large chart laid out on the table.

He turned at their entrance and said, "Ah Debbie! Just who we need. This is my second, Preston, my geologist, Hiroshi, and my ecologist, Avalon."

Debbie very respectfully dipped her head to hide her surprise that the ecologist was a woman. She hadn't thought that a woman would hold an important position in a demesne, but why not? Women had brains and demesnes were, at heart, businesses and they employed the daimyo and his family. Daimyos did not like wasting talent anymore than they liked wasting money.

They all took a moment to coo at Espe and to greet Ghita and Carina.

Like Remus, Preston and Hiroshi had long hair with beads woven in, and the heavy beards she was realizing were the hallmarks of Northern men unlike the cropped and trimmed men of Shelleen and Dairapaska.

She joined them around the table and the questions began, starting with figuring out the exact location of the new village. The charts that Remus had produced were old, some of them dating back a century or more and they were marked with the corridor, the government way-stations, the villages and the cairn.

Debbie carefully retraced her footsteps from the cairn to the way-station and backwards across the corridor.

She remembered how many days that had taken, and about how many days it had taken to walk from the old villages to the new location and the landmarks along the way. It did not take long to pinpoint, within a few klicks, where she thought the new village was located.

The next step was to lay out the village, all the building foundations and paths, the low walls, and the soddys. Ghita was helpful in remembering exactly who lived where; all the names of all the families.

At that point, Remus asked, sounding very puzzled, "So the soddys were *outside* the village foundations?"

"Yes," Debbie answered. "We were told exactly where to build by the overseer. The village headman had a lot to say to him about that, but he wouldn't listen. The soddys weren't too bad, we weren't as far from the water, but the village center was a longer walk from the well. The overseer wasn't real clear as to whether or not a new well would be dug for the village center. He insisted that we clear certain fields of stones and would ignore other fields even though the soil was a little better."

The geologist, Hiroshi, had been studying the charts and checking old books dating back to the early days of terraforming. He frowned in thought, his eyes concerned. "These stones, tell me about them."

Debbie went into great detail, everything she could remember, about moving the stones, what they looked like and their subtle differences between what had been in Shelleen, with Ghita reminding her of what she had missed. Hiroshi was particularly interested in the greasy quality of the sand, the orangey color and the wet sheen of the stones even when they were dry, and he made careful notes as they spoke.

Carina had lost interest and was examining the contents of a glass fronted cabinet with Chika and Espe when she turned and said, "Mommy, do you remember? There was that mint, it grew in a sandy spot and Speranza's mom made tea from it and everybody in her family got sick tummies."

The ecologist, Avalon, now suddenly alert, asked "what kind of mint?"

"It was a wild mint that grew there," said Debbie. "Not one of the ones we brought with us. It was definitely mint but I didn't use it for us. Aldo didn't like the smell. He said it wasn't the kind of mint he liked and he wouldn't have it in the soddy. After Speranza and her family got sick, no one used that mint."

That led to a lengthy discussion of the plants already growing on the site, how healthy they looked, and trying to identify them. The plants and seeds brought by the serfs didn't grow well: if anything, Debbie thought they grew worse than what was already in place.

"Did you notice any sicknesses in the new village? Things you hadn't seen before?" asked Avalon.

"A lot of colds and coughing, skin rashes, upset stomachs, definitely more than what we had in the old village. That was another reason why everyone wanted to go back to the old villages for the deep winter. The new village was unhealthy. The chickens and rabbits didn't seem healthy either. We had a few goats and the milk always tasted off. The eggs were wrong too."

Remus said "We have got to have those samples. It'll take Yannick some time to gather what he can and bring it back here."

Preston had been listening quietly, not speaking, but now he did. "I've met Airik Shelleen a few times and he is whip-smart. He would never do this if he didn't have a compelling reason. He doesn't like wasting resources, either money or people. The only surprises about him being made the daimyo were his age and his specialty. I'd have thought the family would want another ten winters of seasoning on him. And he's not an ag man, which is really strange for Shelleen."

"Refresh my memory. He became the daimyo soon after the great spring storm, yeah?" asked Remus.

"Yeah. Very strange, that was."

"I'm sure I know what happened," Remus said. "The storm uncovered something and the family must have decided he was the best person to deal with it. It was something major, something that needed finesse, knowledge, and ruthlessness, something that stretched outside the boundaries of Shelleen. This village has the feel of a fraud, something to show to outsiders who won't know how it should have been done."

"Strange that they would even bother," said Preston thoughtfully. "We're all pretty independent cusses and none of us give a rat's ass what the other lords think. Our land is our land and we can do as we please with it. Can't believe Shelleen would be any different."

Hiroshi gasped, went pale, sat down hard in a chair and put his head in his hands.

"Hiroshi? You know something, yeah?" asked Remus.

"It's not common knowledge," Hiroshi answered slowly. He looked up at Remus, his face pale.

"I learned this in school, when I was trained as a geologist. Hidden in a sub-clause in the charter is an option for the Martian government to take control of a demesne or a portion of one if it's deemed necessary for the terraforming."

Remus sat down hard in his own chair, also much paler. "That has to be it. Shelleen has to show they're making a good-faith effort to do something — what we don't know — so they don't lose control of their land, any part of it. He would sacrifice peasants for that. We all would."

Debbie asked wonderingly, "but why would they want poisoned soil for terraforming? Terraforming makes healthy soil and the algae and fungus grow as soon as you leave a bit of bare soil for them. That soil was awful."

"Terraforming works on many levels, Debbie," answered Remus. "There are huge industrial complexes that do many things, in addition to the lichens that grow on their own. The nuclear reactors, the Nitrogen Factories, the Icicle Works, the Magnetrons, the Heat Traps, they all need special equipment and special raw materials to operate them. You know of the Dirac mines?"

Debbie did. Everybody did. They were notorious as a place where men toiled, wrenching ore from the deep bowels of

Mars, some of them well-paid free men and many more who were unwilling prison labor. Everyone had a distant relative, sometimes not so distant, who got shipped off to the Dirac mines, usually never to return.

"There are other ores, other mines, not as well known or as common as the Dirac mines. Shelleen may have discovered one of those lodes."

"We have to have those samples," Hiroshi said firmly. "I have some ideas, I don't want to say them yet, but I'll get my testing equipment ready. That orangey, greasy sand and the stones that look wet when they aren't. I'll hit the books, see what I can find."

Avalon added, "I'll check my literature and see if the poverty grasses you described indicate any specific mineral."

"Debbie," Remus said, catching and pinning her with his eyes. "You are lucky and you are lucky for Kenyatta. You got out and you came to us, giving us a chance to know what Shelleen is up to. Shelleen's part of our quad, even if they are dirt-eaters, and if the Martin government is going to try to control their land, we need to know, we need to help Shelleen, and we need the entire quad to present a united front to those officious, grabbing bastards."

Afterwards, Debbie, Chika, and the girls walked back to Chika's house. "This is much bigger than you, Debbie," said Chika. "Let's stop at the post office. Your mother may have written back, and with luck, there will be a letter waiting for you."

There wasn't, but the next day, there was.

The First Letters

EBBIE STARED AT THE FAT letter the Post-Mistress had given her. Her mother had written back. The letter had arrived so quickly that she must have written her reply the same day Debbie's own letter arrived and mailed it the next. Now that she had the letter in her hand, recognizing her mother's handwriting despite years of not seeing it, she did not know if she wanted to read it or not.

What had happened to her family in Dairapaska? Her mother was still alive. Did she want to know what had happened to everyone else? Sometimes not knowing was easier because then you could pretend that nothing bad had happened.

Debbie stood rooted to the floor in the post office, pale and shaking, clutching the letter to her heart and struggling to hold back tears. Chika noticed her distress and took charge, taking Espe from her mother's trembling arms and gathering Ghita and Carina to her.

"We need to get back to the cottage. Girls, while your mother reads her letter, you are going to help me get supper on. Grampie Leon and Kerill and Niall will be hungry."

Back at the cottage, Debbie took Espe and went off silently to her sleeping alcove, climbed in, pulling the wool curtain closed behind her and stared out the window, west towards Dairapaska, so far away in years and distance. Finally, she used her little knife to slit the envelope open and began to read. Espe sat in her lap shaking her rattle and uninterested in the contents of a letter, other than to grab at the pages and chew on them.

Her mother was well. Her grandmother had died. Debbie stopped reading as her heart clenched and tears filled her eyes.

Her grandmother would never know that she had lived, that she had born three children, that she had escaped. Her grandmother had gone to her grave not knowing that her wise counsel had enabled Debbie to survive. She thought of the walnut tree in the Sacred Grove that held the soul of Chika's mother and wished she had a tree for her grandmother, a tree to sit under and remember and grieve, but there was not and there never would be. She breathed slowly, deeply, let her tears flow, and then Debbie was able to begin to read again, afraid of what else was waiting in her mother's words but needing to know more than ever.

Her father had been ill but looked like he would be doing better soon, especially as they now knew that Debbie was still alive and healthy. They were overjoyed to receive her letter. The entire family, every single relative spread across the village, had had her letter read aloud to them, and then again, and then a third time. Everyone in the family was overjoyed. She had daughters of her own. Her mother was jubilant and dearly wished she could meet her granddaughters. Could Debbie receive packages? If so, her mother and her grandmother and her aunties and sister and cousins were ready to send whatever she wanted.

Debbie's mother went on to describe everything important that had happened in Dairapaska in the many years she had been gone. There had been unrest and widespread unhappiness. The work still got done and the obligations to the daimyo were being met, but it was an uneasy and resentful peace. The Shelleen brides had more or less fit in but they desperately missed their homes and families.

Debbie put the letter down again to breathe slowly and wipe away more tears. That sounded so much like the experiences of the Dairapaska brides. So those girls had suffered the same, just as she had thought all those years ago.

Debbie's mother went on to beg Debbie to write back as soon as she could. Word of her letter was spreading like wildfire through the villages. The other families in Dairapaska who had lost a daughter to Shelleen were desperate to know what had happened to their own girls. Did Debbie know? Where they alive? Did they have children? Were their marriages better than the one she had been forced into with Aldo? Could

Debbie please tell them? Any news at all was welcome.

Her mother finished with another entreaty to write back, please, and to say again how much she and the family missed her, loved her, had prayed for her every day and now they had three granddaughters to miss, to love, and to pray for.

Debbie sat for a long time, holding Espe close to her, as she stared out the window to the west, towards her lost family so far away. The sun slowly shifted down to late afternoon, the same sun that was shining over Dairapaska's morning. At last, Espe began to fuss so she nursed her baby and as she did so, Debbie composed in her mind her letter back to her mother. When Espe was finished, Debbie climbed out of the alcove and found Chika working over supper with Ghita helping a lot and Carina not so much.

Leon had returned while Debbie was reading her mother's letter and soon after followed Kerill and Niall with Spotty, yet she had never heard any of them come in. Debbie asked Leon to watch Espe and she returned to the alcove with fresh paper.

Debbie began writing the second letter to Dairapaska.

She started with herself, detailing the family she had married into, all their names and who was related to whom. Then she listed the first of the remaining twenty-three brides of Dairapaska, and every detail she could remember as to who Alice was married to, how it had gone, and the children she had borne.

Debbie was careful to write only what she was sure of; what she had seen with her own eyes, heard with her own ears from one of the brides, and not any of the speculation and rumors about the other brides, their husbands and in-laws, and how they were treated by those families.

She carefully drew family trees so the families in Dairapaska could see the interlocking relationships in Shelleen. The families of Dairapaska did much the same thing because it was always important to know who was related to whom and how, so Debbie knew they would want every detail she could provide.

As she did so, Debbie realized that many of the Dairapaska brides came from families that were unrelated and did not have much to do with each other. But now, these families had something very important in common. They had lost daughters to Shelleen and maybe, perhaps, like the families in

Shelleen, they had had a stranger given to them.

But not always and sometimes, it was indirect. Her own sister-in-law, Fulvia, had lost her little sister to the bride trade and had gained a Dairapaska sister-in-law. Some families got even less. Many of the Shelleen families had lost a daughter, a sister, and no woman from Dairapaska had been given to them in exchange. This had to be true in Dairapaska as well. Did that matter?

Debbie thought about this. Would it make a family angrier to receive an unhappy stranger in the place of a loved daughter? Or would it make them more accepting of that stranger, understanding a little bit of how that stranger felt, alone and bereft, lost in a strange land. Fulvia had never gotten over resenting her even though she, Debbie, had had no more choice in the matter than Fulvia's little sister Blanca had.

And the families who lost a daughter but gained no one? Would their anger and hurt and resentment be deeper still? They had even fewer grandchildren as a result of the trade as those children who were born were on the other side of Mars. They did not benefit at all.

The families who gained a Shelleen daughter-in-law, but who were fortunate enough to keep their own daughters, were they really fortunate? Or would the losing twenty-four families envy them and cause them trouble? They had gained a daughter-in-law, with fresh genes and many grandchildren, and had lost nothing. Could they accept the precious gift they had been given? Could the losing families of Dairapaska accept that they had suffered while others did not?

As she wrote, Debbie wondered what the result of her letter would be. Would she be lancing a boil, old and festering, but now able to heal with her words of what had happened to daughters and sisters? Or would she reopen terrible old wounds and pour salt onto them, making them hurt even more? Possibly it would be both.

She stopped writing to stare out the window, watching the sky fade into orange and red and purple bruises as the sun sank into the arms of the west. Should she send this letter and cause more pain to people who had already endured so much?

Debbie studied the words she had written, the ink so black against the dull white paper. Like the stars beginning to appear high in the darkening sky, they were indifferent to the feelings of the people who would read them, just as they were indifferent to her own emotions as she wrote them. They were what they were, unconcerned and uncaring, yet like the stars overhead they offered what you needed, if you wanted to take it; leaving them as they were before, forever untouched and unchanged.

The stars overhead offered beauty to anyone who cared to look. These words of hers offered information, true information. It would be painful to some, perhaps to many, but it would fill the dreadful void of not knowing, of always wondering what had happened.

If her mother's letter was any indication, the other families of the brides from Dairapaska missed their daughters more than words could ever say. She knew it was true of the families of the Shelleen brides so why would it not be true of Dairapaska?

Debbie had speculated endlessly with the other brides from Dairapaska if her family remembered her and missed her. Her mother's letter confirmed that they grieved deeply. She wished desperately she could write to them in Shelleen and let the other young women know that they were missed and loved and mourned. They had not been forgotten.

But she couldn't do that, daren't do that or she would cause trouble for Kenyatta. So, Debbie wrote everything she knew to be true for the families of Dairapaska. She could not do anything for the other twenty-three young women still trapped in Shelleen, but she could offer knowledge to their families left behind, so far away to the west.

Those families would make of it what they would. She could not control their reaction. She could be honest, she could be complete, she could be truthful and what would happen in Dairapaska would happen.

When she finished her letter, Debbie thought again of what her running away from Shelleen had said to the serfs she left behind. She had some notion of the specifics of what everyone in Shelleen would say, and she likely never would know more. They would talk about it endlessly; she was sure of that.

But Dairapaska, that she would know. Her fleeing her husband and walking onto the trackless steppes with only her three little girls and a little knife and a little dog would be discussed in every cottage for as long as anyone there remembered the story. And they would remember; and they would remember that Debbie had told them what had happened to their own desperately missed daughters.

For the first time, Debbie could understand how a name belonged to one person and one person only. In Kenyatta, she would be Debbie from Dairapaska forever and in Dairapaska? She would be Debbie, the woman traded as a bride who escaped with her life, rescued her children, and lived to tell the tale to everyone who would listen. And in Shelleen, she would be the woman who ran away, stole her children, and died out on the steppes with them. No one else would be Debbie.

Her mother would tell her everything, everything that was discussed and chewed over and passed from serf to serf. All the serfs who resented so much what the daimyo of Dairapaska and the daimyo of Shelleen had done to them and then claimed it was for their benefit would know things they weren't supposed to ever know.

Yannick was wrong, Debbie decided. This *would* make trouble for Dairapaska and eventually Shelleen and then trouble *would* come to Kenyatta when those daimyos got wind of what she had done, and they *would* find out. A story like this would get around like wildfire and like wildfire, it would burn not just the people who had no power. Those daimyos *would* have plenty to say to Remus Kenyatta, and he might be forced to do something other than to tell them to pound sand.

Would he do something to her? Or her daughters? She chewed over this fearful thought and decided most likely not. Like Yannick, he thought she was lucky, both for herself and for the demesne.

Luck mattered. No one ever disparaged a lucky person or tossed aside a lucky object. She had been lucky, Debbie knew that, and now she would use her luck to keep her and her daughters safe. She would continue to help Kenyatta as much as she could, become a valued person in the village, and she would live out her days in Kenyatta, safe, respected, and lucky, and her daughters would too. Her luck would rub off on them.

Remus Kenyatta would have to choose some other way to respond to Dairapaska and Shelleen when they came to complain about her letters and her escape. She had to believe he would not send her or her daughters back and so she chose to do that.

Ghita came to get her for supper and Debbie was amazed at how the time had flown while she wrote and thought.

At supper, she was amazed again. Leon, all smiles, presented her with a kuksa with her name carved into it and a floral garland, along with kuksas for Ghita and Carina and Espe. Each one had their name and flowers carved into the outside of the pale wood.

She was overwhelmed as were her daughters. Despite what Tyr and Harley had said back in the shelter, Debbie had not really believed them.

Leon held up Ghita's birch cup, pale, new and pristine. "See this kuksa? When you grow up, the man you choose to wed will carve you another, just for you. It'll have his name on it and yours, intertwined together."

He held up his own cup, black from decades of use, as did Chika, who was smiling mistily at Leon. Both of their cups, Debbie realized, had their names woven together. She had always thought it was a fancy design but not of any particular significance other than that it was pretty.

That was a change from Shelleen and Dairapaska. You got your one cup and you did not get another unless it was lost or damaged. Debbie decided she liked this custom better. If nothing else, it made sure you had a spare kuksa.

After supper, she walked down to the post office, Spotty prancing by her side, to mail the thick letter to her mother. It would go out in the next day's mail at dawn. Leon had told her that a vaquero rode out every day to Purnell, taking three days for the round trip. They would come back with the mail and anything else important that could be carried in a saddlebag. It was a vital position and one that not every vaquero could be trusted to do; alone, unsupervised, and reliable enough to not get into trouble in the free-city of Purnell or on the road. The chosen vaqueros took their responsibilities seriously. Being selected as a postal vaquero was an honor, one that Yannick had earned and Leon had earned as a young man so long ago.

That night, as she lay waiting for sleep, Debbie wondered again what would happen in Dairapaska when her letter arrived. As she lay in the dark with her daughters asleep beside her, she felt another knot untie itself, thinking of her mother and her family reading her words and knowing how much she loved them and finally knowing, beyond all doubt, how much they loved and missed her.

The days marched forward into early fall, one after another, as Chika and Debbie slowly got everything in the cottage prepared for the long winter. It was so much like Shelleen; you ate what you stored and were glad to have it and by the early spring, you always wished you had stored more.

As they were putting sifted and cleaned grain in crocks and sealing them tightly, Debbie finally asked Chika about something that had been bothering her almost since the day she had met Yannick, something she had not felt safe enough to question before.

"Why does he use the word dirt-eater? And dirt-lords? You farm too; Leon showed me the barley fields he works."

Chika chuckled. "It's the horses, Debbie. Every boy worth his salt in the North becomes a gauchito as soon as he's old enough to try. Not every gauchito becomes a vaquero but most of them attempt it. Being a vaquero is harder, more responsibility and not everyone wants to do the work when they find out how hard it is.

"Far fewer of the men become Hands and the ones who do are all proud of it. They see the world from high on the back of a horse, out on the steppes, moving vast herds of animals around and in all kinds of weather. They're independent, doing what they think needs to be done, and no overseer tells them what to do. A Hand has to manage whatever happens, whatever gets thrown at him and under any kind of circumstances. Hands can't imagine life walking behind a plow, always grubbing in the soil, even if most of them end up doing it as they get older."

Leon had been repairing harnesses next to them, listening to their conversation. "All very true, Chika, my love." He patted her hand.

Debbie asked, very cautiously, "Do you still ride out onto the steppes?"

He grinned at her, the same easy grin that Yannick had. "I do, when it's needful. I'll be working the fall migration. Thing is, Debbie, your bones get old. It gets harder and harder to ride the circuit in all kinds of weather for weeks on end. You get to appreciate a soft, warm bed with your wife next to you."

He sighed nostalgically, his eyes far away, with Chika's hand in his. "The steppes are a young man's game. I loved my time on the steppes and I wouldn't trade it for the world. I help out when I'm needed, I enjoy my grandchildren, all of them, I farm for us now, and I'm respected because I am still a Hand of Kenyatta. That does not change."

Later that evening over the spinning, Chika told her, "girls of the North want vaqueros and Hands as husbands even if they're gone so much of the time. Men who aren't at least a gauchito don't get wives, unless they are very skilled some other way. Vaqueros and Hands are reliable and hard-working and unlike other men, they really appreciate having someone else do the cooking."

Debbie smiled at the wool swiftly becoming yarn in her hands. This wool was fine enough to be worth dying and she carefully twisted it as she spoke, knowing it would be easier for the woman who would knit with it if she took her care with her spinning now. "Tyr did most of the cooking on the journey here. I suppose Harley knows how as well?"

"He does and so does Yannick but only trail food. The youngest of the lads gets to do the cooking and make the tea. No matter what you're doing or where, men have to eat and they like someone else to do the work."

That night, Debbie thought about what Chika had implied. Not every man became a Hand and the ones who did could always marry. So, Yannick could have remarried, if he had wanted to. There would have been some young woman, probably more than one, who wouldn't have listened to gossips like Barb and instead admired the decent, very capable man they saw standing before them.

She was not sure how she felt about that thought and she fell asleep remembering the sound of Yannick breathing, the regular, even rhythm of a man deeply asleep, lying next to her in the shelter.

Every day after mailing her second letter, Debbie stopped at the post office and every day, the Post-Mistress said, "not yet." Over a week after the letter had gone to Purnell, the Post-Mistress said "yes."

As soon as she got back to the cottage and her private alcove, Debbie tore open the letter from her mother. As she had thought, the reaction in Dairapaska had been all mixed up.

All of the families were gladdened by the news that their daughters were still alive and that all had one, two or even three children. These unknown and uncounted grandchildren, the reason for the bride trade, now had names; names that their grandparents and aunties and uncles so far away could add to their own family stories.

The families whose daughters had landed well, to decent husbands and accepting in-laws, were still unhappy about their loss, more unhappy than before, Debbie's mother wrote. Her letter had reminded them of the holes gouged in their hearts. These holes could not be filled with names of absent grandchildren but they were grateful to Debbie for telling them what had happened nonetheless. All agreed it was better to know.

The brides whose husbands had been cruel, whose families were uncaring; those families were angrier than ever. They did not, her mother hastened to add, blame Debbie for being the bearer of bad tidings. Those feelings were reserved for the daimyo of Dairapaska and for the families in Shelleen who had not been able to welcome the girls they had been given. These families too agreed that they would rather know, than not know, what had happened to their daughters.

Interestingly, this had caused some soul-searching, so Debbie's mother wrote, over how the brides from Shelleen had been treated. There had been confrontations and angry words on the parts of the families that had lost their daughters, those that gained brides, and the Shelleen girls themselves. Her mother believed this had cleared the air and, possibly, made things better for the Shelleen girls.

Yes, Debbie's mother admitted, the Shelleen girls knew that Debbie had run away. Too many people knew about Debbie's first two letters for the secret to be kept from them.

She had been approached by most of the Shelleen brides already, tearfully begging her to ask Debbie for news of their own deeply missed families. Could Debbie do this? Debbie's mother provided a list of all of the brides from Shelleen, their names and families, along with who they had been married to and the children they had borne. She added that they understood that Debbie might not know anything about their families, coming from several villages as the Dairapaska brides had, but anything that she did know would be appreciated.

Then came the harder question.

Did Debbie know of any way to write directly to Shelleen and the Dairapaska brides? The daimyo of Dairapaska had his Post-Master checking all the mail for many years now, both incoming and outgoing, to ensure that nothing had been sent to or from Shelleen. Since Shelleen was so far away, no one had any family members who could be written to and who could then write to their own distant relatives and the letters thus pass through multiple hands to eventually reach Shelleen, unknown and concealed from view.

Since Debbie was in Kenyatta, could she solve this problem? Someone in Kenyatta must be related to someone in Shelleen, as the demesnes were part of the same quad. Could she find this person and ask if they would forward the letters?

This question had been asked both by the Dairapaska families and the Shelleen brides. They were united in wanting to send letters to Shelleen and united in their despair and rage at how they had been treated. This is bringing us together in a way that no one had anticipated, wrote Debbie's mother. She did not know what would come of it, other than increasing resentment against the daimyo of Dairapaska, but it was a major change.

The twenty-four families had been united for a long time, despite not necessarily knowing much about each other before the trade. Now, they were uniting with the families that had been given Shelleen brides. As with Debbie herself, there had been overlap between the families that lost daughters and gained brides, but not always and not always directly. Both groups were coming together in ways no one had foreseen at all.

Debbie thought for a long time before beginning her third letter to Dairapaska. She began with saying that she did not yet know of anyone here who had relatives in Shelleen but she would find out.

She plunged into answering what the Shelleen girls wanted to know. The list of names gave her a starting point and as she wrote, Debbie surprised herself with how much she knew of Shelleen. She could not always give information about each specific family, but sometimes she remembered something about their friends or a set of distant cousins.

Debbie wrote and wrote, emptying herself of Shelleen. As with what she had written about the Dairapaska brides, she took care to only write what she knew for sure, of her own personal knowledge.

These letters to Dairapaska were too important to allow any chance of misunderstanding, of passing along false gossip, or of bringing false hope, or worse, more agony to the brides from Shelleen.

When she finished the letter, it was again time for supper and at supper, Debbie asked both Chika and Leon if they knew of anyone who was related to someone living in Shelleen.

"Well," answered Chika after some thought, "I can't think of a single soul. It's because they're agricultural and we're ranching tier. We don't have anything to do with each other. All of our relatives outside Kenyatta are within the North."

Leon agreed. He couldn't think of anybody who had relatives south of the corridor, "unless you go all the way south of the equator to the Southern Ranching Tier. I know for a fact that some doll in Armstrong married a young buck from the Essaretee when he came up North on walkabout and then she rode back across the equator with him to his people."

"I'd forgotten that," Chika mused. "It was quite the romantic story but they'd be even less likely to be related to someone in Shelleen. Let's ask the Post-Mistress after supper, when you mail your letter."

Debbie was astonished at the idea of someone riding thousands of klicks alone to visit the other half of the world, but Chika and Leon assured her that it happened more often than you would think.

"Some young buck drifts all the way north, visits all the demesnes to show off his skills and goes back home south and once in a while, one of our vaqueros does the same. They usually come back and do they have stories to tell!" said Leon.

Debbie caught the important part. "They usually come back?"

"Usually, but not always," Chika said, biting her lip and looking away across the room, as if towards someone who was no longer there and who had not been there for a very long time. "It's a dangerous world, and the Essaretee is a long, long way away. Not all of their young bucks make it back home either."

"But the Sacred Grove? What does the family do?"

"The family waits for ten winters to pass, and if nothing is heard in those winters, not a letter, not a message, then a tree is planted. Every buck who goes on walkabout leaves a lock of hair behind for that reason. It's all you can do," answered Leon. "When our lads go South, they carry messages the same as the Southern lads come North with messages from the families left behind. Sometimes word comes, but not always."

Debbie thought about this; about loss, despair, and the bottomless well of grief, of never knowing and always wondering. She said firmly, "One way or another, I will write to Shelleen and find out what happened both for the Shelleen brides and the families they left behind. Someone has to."

While she was clearing the table for the washing up, Debbie saw Chika and Leon's hands flying and she wished again that she could learn the hand talk. Kerill and Niall had been teaching Ghita and Carina but it took time and practice to learn and she had not yet had the time. She would have to ask Chika for lessons.

At the post office, Debbie dropped her thick letter into the box, the third one to Dairapaska. Afterwards, she asked the Post-Mistress if there was anyone in Kenyatta who could enclose her letter with their own to a relative in Shelleen.

The Post-Mistress was adamant that no one in Kenyatta wrote to anybody in Shelleen, other than official letters on quad business sent by the daimyo and his family. She did not think that Remus Kenyatta would approve of her opening his mail and inserting a letter from Debbie and Debbie agreed. Moreover, the mail from the Kenyatta family went directly to the Shelleen family and they would certainly not pass on mail to their peasants. Debbie shuddered at the thought of a letter of hers being opened by any member of the Shelleen family. That would only stir up trouble.

The Post-Mistress paced in front of the wall of mail cubbies, thinking. She agreed that what the daimyos of Dairapaska and Shelleen were doing was wrong. Mail was supposed to flow unimpeded wherever it came from or where it went.

"Unfortunately," she said, "as you know all too well, daimyos can do whatever they damn well please on their demesne, yeah?"

Debbie sighed and said, "The law is whatever the daimyo says it is."

"You are quite sure that the peasants in Shelleen get mail from outside the demesne?"

"Oh, yes. My mother-in-law had distant relatives in Gish and in Shiraz. Many families got mail from outside the demesne like we did in Dairapaska. It was common. Only Dairapaska mail was refused, incoming and outgoing."

"So people did try?"

"Oh yes, until the old daimyo of Shelleen put a stop to it. He had a man flogged half to death for trying to mail a letter every single day to his daughter in Dairapaska."

Debbie shuddered, remembering his screams from that long ago, dreadful day in the vast, cobblestone square with the manor house looming over it. Attendance had been mandatory, every person in each of the villages of Shelleen, and your age or sickness did not matter. The old daimyo wanted everyone to know his law and the penalty for not obeying.

"After that, people stopped."

"So, they don't check closely, other than to see if the mail came from Dairapaska?" the Post-Mistress asked, her face cocked to one side and her eyes sparkling.

"I believe so," said Debbie thoughtfully. "No one ever said different. In fact, the peasants complained that they could get mail from everywhere on Mars *but* Dairapaska."

"I think I have a solution," said the Post-Mistress looking very pleased with herself for coming up with a way for the mail to go through as it should, knowing as she did a Post-Master's sworn duty and obligation. "Is there a Dairapaska bride who has a good husband and in-laws? Ones you could write to, using Chika's name, who would give the letter to the bride? You could write letters that way, and that person could pass along the information and write back, using Chika's name."

Chika agreed that Debbie could use her name. "Serves those damn dirt lords right, doing this to you girls."

Debbie smiled suddenly, a big, open joyous smile that Chika had not seen before on her face.

"Alice. I'll write to Alice via her mother-in-law. Her husband cares very much for her and she gets along well with her in-laws. They lost a daughter to the trade so they'll have two reasons to do this. It will make Alice happy and it will tell them what happened to Pia."

"My vaquero leaves at first light for Purnell," said the Post-Mistress. Can you be ready by then? The letter will be in Purnell the next morning and in Shelleen soon thereafter."

Debbie was smiling and smiling, unable to stop. "Yes, I know I can, I mean if Chika — you could watch the girls while I write?"

"Of course, my dear. Leon will get the letter to the Post-Mistress as soon as you're finished and it will go out at dawn."

As they walked back to the cottage, Debbie thought about her letter to Alice and her mother-in-law. She would have to be careful in what she said, so she did not stir up trouble or raise false hope.

Tucked back into the alcove, Debbie began her first letter to Shelleen.

She started by asking Alice's mother-in-law, Lupita, to keep the letter and its contents a secret from everyone but the immediate family and Alice. Debbie took care to explain why she had run away, detailing how Aldo had treated their daughters, particularly his refusal of Espe. She did not want to cause more trouble for Aldo's family or for the people who had taken her in and she begged Alice's in-laws to respect her wishes.

Debbie went into some detail as to what she had been writing to Dairapaska and that she would act as an intermediary if Alice and her in-laws agreed. She did not want to get them into trouble with the daimyo of Shelleen. The brides from Shelleen were desperate for news of home but Debbie did not know all of their families. Would the families be interested? Could Alice and her mother-in-law find out, discreetly, so the daimyo did not discover what was being done behind his back?

If they were unable or unwilling to do this, Debbie would understand. She would ask for more information from her mother about the girls sent to Dairapaska and as she received it, she would forward it to Shelleen so at least their families would know what was happening to them, even if they could not answer back.

When she finished, Debbie began her fourth letter to Dairapaska, a very short one. In it, she told her mother what she had done, and she asked for as much information as her mother could provide about the lives of the Shelleen girls. The letters finished and sealed, Debbie brought them to Leon, and he walked out into the cool dark night to the post office to mail them.

That night, as she waited for sleep, Debbie thought about what would happen in Shelleen when Lupita and Alice got her letter. Would it cause the same ruckus as her letters to Dairapaska had? It seemed likely, and perhaps cause even more. She had run away, and taken her children with her, and undoubtedly everyone in Shelleen thought they were a heap of animal-gnawed bones out on the steppes. None of the Shelleen brides had dared such a thing, so her mother had written.

She thought about the risk to herself, and to Kenyatta, when Shelleen eventually discovered her whereabouts and worse, that she had been doing what had been expressly forbidden by both daimyos for the last ten years: passing information to the families of the brides.

The first letter she mailed to her mother in Dairapaska had been like whispering a message to the wind. Debbie had not known if she would get an answer, but she had.

Would she get an answer from Shelleen? As she thought of Pia, whom she had never met, of Fulvia's little sister, Blanca, whom she had never met, of the other twenty-two brides, none of whom she would ever meet, Debbie decided it was most likely she would get an answer begging for information. Those girls' families, she knew from hearing it all the time, missed their daughters just as much as the Dairapaska families had missed her and the other Dairapaska brides.

Her letters to Shelleen were bound to cause trouble, just as her letters to Dairapaska already were. Debbie was fiercely glad, right down to her toes, at that thought. Let her words cause trouble, and eventually, that trouble would reach the daimyos who had brought so much pain, and perhaps, it would trouble them over what they had done.

Time passed and every day she checked the post office and days later, a letter was waiting for her from Shelleen.

Alice's mother-in-law, Lupita, was overjoyed to exchange mail with Debbie. She did not have any trouble at all using Chika's name to fool the Shelleen Post-Master.

She wrote that she was not surprised that Aldo had been such an unpleasant fool. He had always been an unpleasant fool, and only his family's opinion of him had kept his behavior in check. Lupita had already heard the story of him refusing to carve the new baby a cup because she was a girl. Other families in the new village had been writing to their relatives in the old villages; they all knew and they had all disapproved as did all who heard the story.

Yes, Lupita would be discreet and yes, she would do anything to receive news of Pia, and the other families of lost daughters all agreed, even Fulvia's. Lupita promised to be very careful with Fulvia's family, so that Aldo's family would not become more upset than they already were over the loss of their granddaughters. The Acconcios did not, Lupita was sorry to say, seem concerned about Debbie.

Lupita went into great detail about what everyone had to say about Debbie's escape. It had been not a nine-day wonder, or even a ninety-day wonder, but a 900-day wonder. She did not think anyone would ever forget it. People were shocked that it had been Debbie who had run away into the steppes; patient, placid Debbie who never seemed to be bothered by anything. It was widely believed that she and her daughters had died out on the steppes and Lupita promised that she would not tell anyone any different. After all, how could a woman alone with two little girls and a baby survive the endless seas of grass?

Lupita went on to say that she would tell everyone that a

distant relative had figured out a way to pass news from de-mesne to demesne so as to evade the censorship of the mail in both Dairapaska and Shelleen.

As soon as she finished reading Lupita's letter, Debbie wrote her second letter to Shelleen saying that as soon as her mother answered, she would pass along the information. Then she wrote her fifth letter to Dairapaska, telling her mother that, yes, the families in Shelleen were eager to cooperate.

As time passed, Debbie received and sent more letters, passing information between Shelleen and Dairapaska. She had not been that aware of it in Shelleen, sunk as she was in her own misery and mute endurance, but the families of the Shelleen brides felt much the same as the families of Dairapaska and they were reacting much the same. Moreover, to her joy, the Shelleen families were reevaluating their treatment of the brides they had been given.

While Debbie wrote her letters, her daughters made friends and learned Northern ways, and all of them became full, val-ued parts of Chika and Leon's household and the larger village. She got to know Yannick's sister-in-law, Erissa, and Otis's wife, Mandy. They visited the cottage regularly, and Debbie sus-pected they were getting to know her and her daughters for reasons of their own.

As she became more comfortable around Erissa and Mandy, Debbie was able to ask why Chika and Leon were so kind to her and her daughters. It had worried her, this generosity of spirit, and she kept expecting — against all the evidence — that she would be asked to leave. The wounds that Mrs. Acconcio had left, Debbie decided, were still raw and she was borrowing trouble comparing other people to her former mother-in-law. Yannick had asked his mother to take care of Debbie and she had; Chika understood the benefit to Kenyatta as a whole.

When Debbie finally worked up the courage to ask Erissa, she chuckled.

"Maureen is why," Erissa said. "Chika was happy with me marrying Lysander, but we still had our differences. After Maureen showed up, well, Chika stopped getting worked up."

"Oh, yeah," Mandy agreed later with a toss of her head. "Compared to that Maureen, you would have to burn the village to the ground to get Chika mad at you."

Debbie could feel herself relax again and another worry went away. This was a reason she could understand.

The fall migration got closer and closer, the season marched slowly towards the earliest days of winter, and finally, finally, Yannick came home from the poisoned village.

Yannick Returns

O N A COLD, DAMP AFTERNOON, Yannick, Otis, Harley and Tyr, and the three other boys — Josh, Marar, and Azi, who had been a blur at the stone tower — came riding back into the village. They were leading a string of horses laden down with baggage, a pack of wolf-dogs padding alongside them. All of them were dusty, dirty, tired, and very glad to be home.

They scattered when they reached the village, each on his own errand, attracting the attention of everyone they passed. Yannick stopped at the cottage, throwing open the door wide and letting in the chilly, fresh breeze that swept through the air inside the cottage.

"Mom!" he called inside. "We're back. I'm gonna see Kenyatta and I should be back for supper. He may want Debbie to come up to the manor house."

Debbie stared at him as he stepped inside, from where she had been spinning by the masonry stove, Espe playing at her feet.

Spinning was something she took pleasure in; Debbie was proud of her smooth, slub-free yarn though she did not ever say so. Mrs. Acconcio had rarely been able to find fault with Debbie's spinning, although she had not let that stop her from trying. Concentrating on spinning could fill Debbie's mind, blocking thought, feeling, and memory, a gift she had welcomed in the past.

Thoughts came flooding in with Yannick's sudden presence, filling her, overwhelming her, a roil of emotion she could not identify. She almost dropped her spindle from her suddenly nerveless hands. The distaff slipped against her shoulder. She was not sure of how she felt. She had missed him, far more than she thought she would, and here he was, filling the room with his presence, alive, real, here, and no longer just memories of his presence, his warmth, and his concern.

She could not think of anything to say, and she did not want to tell him that she had missed his presence every night beside her, something she had never believed would happen. Yannick had been gone for weeks, far longer than the few days they had spent together riding to Kenyatta and yet she had missed him. He filled her brain with a mad swirl of thoughts and memories, and she could not speak. She could not move.

He saw her frozen by the stove, the baby at her feet knocking over blocks, and walked over with a broad smile for them, for her. "Thought of you every day while we were out there, watching that poisoned village. You knocked over a hornet's nest, Debbie."

She smiled back up at him, her heart filling with joy, pushing out other tumultuous thoughts and then Debbie found words she *could* say aloud. "I never meant to. I'm glad you're back safe, you and everyone."

Yannick crouched down to smile at the baby. "Hey, little one. You've grown." She stared back at him wide-eyed and open mouthed, then decided to smile at this dirty stranger beaming and waving a braid at her.

To Debbie he said, "Did you pick a name for her?"

"Espe. My grandmother said it meant hope."

He smiled again. "A very good choice, and a pretty one. Espe brought you hope and luck, Debbie. I don't mean to run but I got to say hi quick and then go on up to the manor house."

Chika came from down the hallway. She had been quietly watching the two of them with great interest. She ran forward to hug her son, paying no heed to the trail dust or how he smelled.

"I'm so glad you're back safe," she bubbled, full of joy and relief. "Your dad, and all the kids and that Spotty are out in the fields. Do you have time for me to run get them while you tell Debbie how it went?"

"No, I've got to see Remus. I'll be back for supper, Remus

may want both of us back afterwards and the bath house after that." He grinned broadly. "I am filthy from digging in that dirt. Can't sleep in my own bed until I wash it all off."

"You'd best get started then. Debbie and I will put on a feast for you."

"Thanks, mom. Debbie! If Remus wants you right away, I'll send word, yeah?"

"Of course, whatever you need," Debbie replied, not able to take her eyes off of him and unable to say anything else.

Yannick disappeared out the door, closing it against the cold fingers of the wind and the room felt empty to Debbie in a way that it had not been before.

The watery, damp sunshine still seeped in through the windows and spilled on the floor, Espe babbled excitedly as she resumed stacking and knocking over blocks, the fire crackled and spat while the kettle of water on the stovetop steamed, the candle she was sitting by had its flame dance madly when Yannick opened the door and when he left, it recovered, straight and tall again. The yarn she spun felt the same between her fingers, still the same dull cream of undyed wool being transformed from the combed and carded fleece into soft yarn that would be transformed again into something else. Nothing had changed since the moment he had walked in the door.

The room felt empty, but she did not.

"Debbie," said Chika, interrupting her flooding thoughts, "It wouldn't surprise me if they call for you right away. Best you be prepared for that, yeah?"

"Yes, thank you."

Chika was correct. A very short time later, a page came running to the door, panting from his sprint down the hill and through the village. "They want Debbie in the manor house as soon as she can come, Chika."

Debbie was ready, and grateful that Chika had thought ahead. What had Yannick found that he needed her so quickly? There was nothing she could add to what she had already told Remus and his staff.

She headed out the door and up the hill to the manor house, relieved that Chika had sent for Leon and all the kids. That meant she could leave Espe behind and Chika could still make supper without having to keep Espe away from the flames in the hearth, so enticing and colorful.

Espe was learning to crawl and had to be watched every minute to keep her out of danger and mischief.

At the manor house, a page was waiting at the front door for her and she was ushered down the halls and up the stairs to the same room she had been in before. It was the same as she remembered, lined with books and cabinets with the large table in the center of the room.

This time, the room was full of people anxiously studying the samples that Yannick and his crew had brought and talking a mile a minute.

Debbie hesitated at the door, not sure if she should march right in, when Yannick turned and spotted her. "Debbie! You came right away."

He walked over beaming, took her arm and walked with her to the table. "You remember Otis?"

Otis had a speculative expression on his face but he smiled and said, "You probably don't remember me. The lads and I cleaned up your trail back to the way-station, a good thing too."

Debbie smiled her thanks and respectfully made her greetings to Remus Kenyatta and the other members of the family.

"Debbie, we need you to identify people," Remus said. "Yannick thought ahead and had Azi sketch everyone and everything they saw."

Azi waved shyly from the table. Debbie realized that he must have been one of the other lads, the ones that had been left behind with Otis back at the stone tower. He was about the same age as Harley, no longer a boy but still years from becoming a man, with the beginnings of a mustache and a few wisps of hair on his chin. He had long, slim fingers, the hands of an artist.

He brought over a pad of paper, and on every page was a sketch of someone from the new village.

Yannick was looking even prouder of Azi than Azi did himself. "Azi's damn good at drawing and he drew everybody he saw, sometimes a few times. We need you to tell us who they are."

"Of course." Debbie leafed through Azi's drawings. He really was good; she could easily recognize the faces. "This is the village headman." She began working her way through the drawings, putting a name to most of the faces.

Kenyatta found it most interesting that she could not identify everyone. That meant they had not lived in the new village, nor were they the serfs she knew from living in the old village for all those years.

"There were about eighty of us peasants, including the kids, sent out as settlers," Debbie remembered. "The daimyo sent an overseer" — she pointed to his picture — "regularly. He would spend a few days in the village, checking everything we had done, ride back to the manor house and return with some supplies and new instructions. He slept in a tent of his own, well away from the village foundations and the soddys. He had a few servants and they didn't have much to do with us. They did odd things, looking at the rocks mostly."

She pointed to several more pictures. "They were not from any of the villages, I mean they may have been, but they weren't peasant farmers like us. They talked differently and they dressed better."

"Interesting," said Remus. "Hiroshi, recognize any of these guys?"

"I think they may be Shelleen's geologists or assistants. I don't know any of them personally. What did they do, Debbie?"

"They never farmed, but they would go into the fields and scoop up little piles of dirt and take them back to the tent. They collected stones, too, and those would disappear. When the overseer traveled, he always went with a string of packhorses.

"One time — Aldo complained about this endlessly — they had him dig a deep square hole, almost two meters down and two across, and they had him sort the dirt he dug out into layers on tarps they had spread out. Aldo would dig down a layer, about this deep," — Debbie held out her hand, outspread thumb and forefinger making a space — "and put it onto a tarp, and someone else took the tarp back to the tents. How those men complained if the peasants carrying the tarps got the soil jumbled up. They had to carry it as flat as they could. Aldo dug out the layers, layer by layer. It took many days and he got a terrible rash on his hands and arms when he got near the bottom of the hole."

"Hmm," Hiroshi said. "Interesting." He chewed on his lip and ran his hands through his hair.

"How about these men?" Yannick pointed to several more drawings. "They don't look like dirt peasants or the geologists."

He was right, thought Debbie as she studied the drawings. She had never seen these men before, or had she?

"I think these were some of the guards, the ones who made us march to the new village. They were big, scary-looking men and they were always armed. They came from one of the other villages, but they weren't farmers. I'm trying to remember what the midwife told me. They left soon after we arrived and got to work building the soddys and laying out the new village." She tapped two of the faces. "These two stayed to keep an eye on us so we did what the overseer wanted."

"How about this one?" Remus, his face blank, held a drawing of a slim, expressionless man in his late twenties, very well-dressed and groomed for being out in the middle of nowhere.

Debbie studied the drawing. "I'm not sure," she said finally. "I feel like I've seen him before, but not often and from far away. He was not someone from my village, and he's definitely not part of the settlers in the new village and he never came to the new village while I was there."

Remus and Preston's eyes met and their hands flew and Debbie thought again that she had to learn that skill, at least a little.

When they finished sorting through Azi's sketches, Debbie had named all of the settlers he had drawn, including a sullen Aldo, and she had sorted out all of the regular visitors to the village. That left a few, unidentified men, one of whom was the slim, well-dressed man and some others who looked very dangerous indeed.

"The village next," said Yannick. Azi laid out more sketches of foundation walls, paths, soddys, and the village hall, still the only finished building other than the soddys. "I want you to try and place them on Kenyatta's chart, the one you helped make when you first got here."

Debbie looked over the drawings and to her surprise, she remembered who lived in most of them. She placed them on Remus's chart and someone else drew symbols on the chart and then on each drawing so they could be matched up easily. Aldo's pit was placed, as were the tents of the overseer, and the exact distance between the soddys, their well, and the village foundations.

Yannick had kept careful notes on distances and directions and it turned out that Debbie had not been far off on her estimated location of the new village. She did not know where the new fields were, but Yannick did.

When all the pictures had been identified and placed, Remus called a halt.

"That's enough for now. Yannick, I'll want you, Otis, the lads, and Debbie, you too. Be here after breakfast and we'll get started. Excellent work, all of you," Remus said.

Debbie was more than ready to stop. It had already been a long day, she was hungry, she knew Espe would be hungry, and it was getting dark. She walked quietly alongside Yannick back through the manor house, down its long, softly carpeted hallways with the fine pictures lining the walls.

She waited until they were outside before asking him, "Why did you say I stirred up a hornet's nest? I didn't think anybody but Aldo would care that much."

"Don't know about him, but somebody cared," Yannick answered. "Me and Otis and the lads rode out to the way-station first. Otis had messed up your trail but good and the rain finished the job. Even so, he kept watch until he had to meet us at the cairn. Shelleen sent men looking for you, up to the way-station and beyond. They left trails a blind man could follow. It looked to me that they didn't think you'd headed north, that you'd followed the road instead but they couldn't decide which way."

He paused, thinking. "Otis thought that the first search parties were from the village, based on the trails they left. Someone sent word, that overseer probably, that you'd gone missing with your girls and then, he thinks, Shelleen sent the second crew to look for you. Armed men, not peasant farmers, and they had a better idea of what they were doing."

Debbie thought about this. "The only reason he would care is my daughters. And serfs don't run away. That must have been their worry, that other serfs would try and run away after I did."

"I don't think so, Debbie," Yannick replied confidently. "Shelleen cares about that, cause he's got to keep his serfs under his thumb, but I think he's more worried about what you'd tell people about the poisoned village and Remus agrees with me. Serfs can and do run away, but the dirt lords don't usually make such a big deal of it. It's easier to punish the family that's left behind.

Debbie had not considered such a thing before, but she could not find it in her heart to care if Aldo was punished.

"Otis thinks, and I agree, that it took plenty of time for word from the village to reach Shelleen and even more time to get men out there. When they arrived in the poisoned village, this new crew took over. They were a lot more systematic looking for you."

They reached Chika's cottage and Yannick held the door for Debbie. Having been alerted by Spotty's barking, Leon and Kerill and Niall were eagerly waiting for Yannick. The boys rushed for him in their excitement, jumping and squealing. Ghita and Carina were more cautious, time and distance having made them shy with Yannick. Spotty had no such fears and raced around him barking madly.

As they ate a lavish supper, Yannick commenting often how happy he was to eat real food at a real table out of the weather, the questions came thick and fast about his expedition.

Debbie got to ask the questions that had been bothering her.

"How did Azi get all those drawings? How did you see all this and not get caught? And you took all those samples; Alison came over to tell Chika what she saw when the boys rode up to the manor house. Somebody must have seen you with all those horses and the wolf-dogs."

Yannick looked proud of himself. "We're better at it than any of those peasants. Just made sure we saw them first. Azi used the field glasses I brought to do all the sketching. And to get the samples, Otis set up diversions, pulling everyone away from the area we needed to be in."

He laughed uproariously. "That really pissed off those guards. They knew someone was watching them and they had no idea who. That made them even more paranoid and easier to fool."

Leon looked stern. "Don't you think that might cause Remus a bigger problem? Shelleen now knows that someone outside the demesne is paying attention to what they're doing there."

"I thought about that, dad," Yannick answered. "But Remus had to have the samples, and he had to have them quick. It seemed every day we were there, more men rode out from Shelleen and these crews were planned and well-equipped. What I mean is, they started heading out before Otis and I ever got there to stir them up. Shelleen was bringing out a small army and we had to get our samples before they posted a guard every ten meters all around the place."

"So you don't think they knew you were from Kenyatta?"

"Don't believe so. Way-station guys saw us when we watered the horses and they saw us head west down the road as if we were trekking to the pole corridor. They may guess we're from the North, but we didn't identify ourselves and you know how ignorant they are. We all look alike to those corridor types. I made sure we were seen by as few people as we could manage. And yeah, dad, I told Remus all of this. He didn't have a problem."

Leon looked doubtful. "Remus doesn't have a problem now, but he might later on. As his Hand, it's your job to not make his problems bigger, yeah?"

"Too late for that, dad. Shelleen made this problem and thanks to Debbie, Remus knows about it beforehand. There was no way to do this job otherwise and we tried, me and Otis both."

"I suppose it will just have to do," answered Leon with a sigh. "Thinking about it, I don't believe I would have done any different."

"Thanks dad," smiled Yannick. "That means a lot."

When Chika and Debbie began clearing the table for the washing up, Yannick announced, "I got to meet Otis and the lads at the bathhouse. We're all filthy from that poisoned village."

Leon grinned at his son. "I think me and your sons will join you. They need a good scrub anyway and I want to hear more about what happened. Chika, my love, we'll be back later."

Both men and the boys headed for the door and into the cold night, leaving the room suddenly emptier and quieter. When the door closed behind them, Chika said, "and there they go, leaving the washing up for us. Just like men."

Debbie smiled at the flames dancing in the hearth, giving heat, light, movement, life. "Yes, but they're home. And Yannick will smell better after a good scrub."

"True, very true."

Much, much later, after Debbie had settled into her alcove with her daughters and Spotty, who stayed mercifully quiet, and Chika had done the same, she heard Leon, Yannick and the boys come in. She listened to the night sounds of Leon climbing in with Chika and her sleepy acknowledgement, Yannick getting the sleepy boys into their own bed opposite hers and then Yannick padding up to his own alcove to sleep.

It had been vacant since she had arrived at the cottage all those weeks ago. It was odd to think of him lying so close to her, after all those weeks apart and yet he was so much further away than when they had slept side by side in the shelters. Two cupboards and a wall lay between her feet and his head and yet he might as well have been still on the steppes. She could not hear him breathe; she could not feel his long, lean warmth lying next to her.

Debbie did not know what to think and she could not decide why she was feeling the way she was. There was no reason for it. Yannick had been kind, that was true; far kinder to her than he needed to be, even with the chance of getting her daughters for Kenyatta's gene pool. When she thought of the story about Maureen that Chika had told her, what Mandy and Erissa had to say about Maureen, she was even more impressed at how decent he had been.

He still loved Maureen or he could have easily married again. Almost everyone had said so and people like Barb were decidedly in the minority.

Debbie was less sure than ever if she wanted to marry again.

It had been very, very pleasant living in Chika's house, doing what needed to be done without being at the beck and call of some high-handed man. She had the benefits of a man without having to actually manage one. She and her daughters had a home and Chika had told her she could stay as long as she needed to and she and Leon seemed to mean it.

Leon was generally easy to live with and when he was, well, demanding or tetchy, Chika waited on him. Debbie did not have to have anything to do with getting him his tea or making sure his clothes were laid out or doing anything else he wanted done right now. And both of them treated Ghita and Carina and Espe as their own granddaughters.

She had been watching Leon and Chika from the day she had arrived, and gradually, slowly, gently, Debbie had become more comfortable around them. They were openly affectionate with one another, something Debbie had not seen in the Acconcio household. That cottage had always been full of stony silences or cross words. Debbie kept expecting to see that same behavior but she did not. Leon and Chika reminded her, she finally realized, of her own parents. They cared for each other and did not care who knew or saw. It was sad to remember, and she missed her parents even more, but it let her breathe more easily. She had forgotten what it was like to not walk on eggshells.

The kids were slowly becoming a group as they got to know each other. Kerill and Niall seemed to think of Ghita and Carina as their sisters and her daughters were getting more and more comfortable with them. Certainly, they fought like brothers and sisters, which was both heartwarming and annoying. Even Spotty had a place in the household, competing with the cats to catch rodents, beg for attention, sleep where he would be tripped over, and fight over scraps.

Every day, it felt more normal. She was welcomed.

So why did she feel this way now? Uncomfortable and awkward and unsure. Debbie decided it was because she had gotten used to the household being one way and suddenly it was another. That had to be it. That and the fact that, as of yet, no one at Kenyatta knew about her letter-writing other than Chika, Leon, and the Post-Mistress.

She wondered what Yannick would have to say about it, even though he had assured her that it would not matter when they were on the steppes. Would he mention it to Remus Kenyatta? Leon had already decided that it wasn't his place to tell him, Chika agreed, and Debbie certainly wasn't going to march up to the daimyo and tell him that she had been deliberately going against the wishes of two other daimyos.

Neither would the Post-Mistress. She was in the odd position of working for the demesne as a representative of the Martian government. She belonged to Kenyatta just like every other person or animal or building, yet she also worked for the postal service. That changed her views on certain things. She had spent quite a lot of time telling Debbie how spineless she thought the Post-Masters of Dairapaska and Shelleen were, knuckling under to their daimyos and refusing to allow the mails to go through, uncensored and unhindered, as they had sworn to do when they accepted the position.

The Post-Mistress had been taking careful notes of everything Debbie had told her about what both Post-Masters were doing with an eye towards writing it up for the professional journal of postal employees. Debbie's mother and Lupita had been asking discreet questions as to whether or not the ban would ever be lifted and the answer kept being no. They both wrote to Debbie with this information, along with everything they found out about how the mail was examined for potential contraband and forbidden letters.

The Post-Mistress had assured Debbie she would not publish her discussion of the other Post-Masters' lack of professionalism until after Debbie gave her the okay. Neither of them wanted to stop passing the desperately wanted messages between Shelleen and Dairapaska. An essay published in the journal would be read in both Shelleen and Dairapaska (and everywhere else) and wouldn't that start trouble! Not to mention the trouble when the Martian Post Office got wind of what the daimyos had gotten up to.

The Post-Mistress was fairly sure that impeding the mails was one of those things that the charter expressly forbid. There weren't very many barriers as to what the daimyo of a demesne could and could not do, but without a copy of the charter, she could not check. Copies of the demesne charters were not made public for a host of reasons, something else she disapproved of.

Debbie fell asleep thinking about the post office requirements instead of Yannick in his alcove so close by, yet so far away, and she was grateful for the distraction.

In the morning, after a noisy breakfast made more so by Spotty scrapping with the cats, Debbie, carrying Espe in her sling, and Yannick went back to the manor house. As they walked up the hill, she studied his hair surreptitiously.

He no longer tied his hair back in a single long braid but let it hang loose with dozens of tiny braids in it. Each braid was adorned with beads shining against the dark color of his hair. He had said he had as many as Remus and he did. He did not, however, have as many beads as Leon sometimes wore.

Debbie wondered when he had found the time to do this and when he would tell her what all of his beads meant. She had not felt brave enough to ask Leon about something that seemed so intimate. Chika had rolled her eyes and said something about men being such vain roosters, showing off for all the hens and lording it over the other roosters.

She thought of what he had said the night before during their walk back down the hill, about her rearranging her hair from its long braid down her back and flushed again, turning her head so he could not see her cheeks burn. He had noticed. Now she knew what a woman's loose hair implied in Kenyatta but she did not know what *he* meant by his observation and her cheeks burned still more.

When they reached the manor house, the ecologist Avalon was waiting for them in the main hall. She led Debbie to the nursery, a set of brightly painted rooms not too far from the library where the samples and maps were laid out. Avalon introduced Debbie to the nursery maids and her own baby boy, a year old. There were more young children in the room, all playing with an array of toys spread across the brightly patterned carpet.

"Espe will be safe here with the other children," said Avalon. "And when she needs you to nurse, one of the nursery maids will bring her to you just like they bring me Havel."

"He is such a cutie," said Debbie, crouching down to smile at him. "Do you have other children?"

"Two older ones, a boy and a girl," answered Avalon. "Fortunately, they don't need my attention as much anymore as Havel does. We'll probably both spend a lot of time together, nursing our babies." She kissed Havel on his soft dark hair and wiggled her fingers at Espe, making her giggle.

Once they arrived back in the library room, Debbie got to identify stones. Yannick, Otis and the lads had brought back an amazing array of rocks, stones, soil, and sand and, curiously, it was mixed with what Debbie was quite sure were regular stuff that could be picked up anywhere. They had plant samples too, most with the dirt still clinging to their roots.

She was pretty sure of herself, identifying what had come from the poisoned village, and when she wasn't sure, Ghita was sent for.

Harley came back with Ghita and she enjoyed very much being the center of attention as she decided which stones did and did not belong.

Ghita finally asked the question that had been bothering Debbie. "Did you pick these up outside to fool me? This one looks just like the wall outside gramma Chika's garden." She held up a stone that looked like any other stone.

Otis and Yannick smacked palms in triumph. "Told you they'd know." Hiroshi tossed each of them a bead, with a look of chagrin.

"What we did, Ghita," answered Yannick, picking her up and hugging her, "is we collected all kinds of stones, near and far away in the new village. We wanted to see where the boundaries of the poisoned areas are. Every one of those samples has a number and I know where on the map that number belongs. You and your mama are helping us figure out how big the area is and maybe, how big the deposit is."

"Oh. Everybody knew where the edges were," Ghita said confidently.

"No, everybody didn't," answered Debbie. "Nobody knew."

"Mom-mee, the grass was different" Ghita replied, her hands on her hips. "That's why the tents of those men with the overseer were where they were. Their grass was different. Ludo's dad wouldn't let him catch rabbits anywhere the grass was bad so he always went up behind thc tcnts."

"Who is Ludo again?" asked Remus, looking amused.

"The village headman's son. He's a year older than Ghita," said Debbie, finding his portrait in the stack of drawings and holding it up. "I didn't know he caught rabbits."

"Ludo had a *slingshot*. He told me after they got sick eating a rabbit he caught close in, his dad said to go only where the grass was better. He said better grass made better rabbits," Ghita replied pertly.

Debbie said firmly, "you didn't tell me any of this, that you went up behind the tents with Ludo."

"Mom-mee! You said for me and Carina to go play with the other kids so we did. You didn't say where."

Ghita smiled winningly at her mother. "It wasn't far away. We could still hear you when you yelled for us."

"I did not yell."

Avalon thought of her own squabbling children and said, "Ghita, sweetie, why don't you tell us about the grass. This will help us determine the exact boundaries."

After that, for the next two days, Ghita went to the manor house with Debbie and Espe.

By the end of the second day, Debbie and Ghita had been emptied out of information about the poisoned village. Debbie got to know Avalon much better as well, as they sat together with nursing babies at the side of the library, watching the investigation flow around them.

For all of those days, Debbie worked closely with Yannick and the Kenyatta family staff identifying and mapping the area, deciding which plants grew where, which were sown by the peasants and which grew on their own.

Along with the family, she ate breakfast with him every morning and supper with him every evening and then tried to sleep every night, with him so close by and yet so far away.

The close proximity of working with Yannick, walking back and forth with Yannick, living with Yannick in his house and seeing him for hours every evening did not ease her discomfort. Debbie's nights were restless and her thoughts in turmoil.

He always seemed happy to see her, but never anything more. She knew that this was what she wanted. Yannick did not treat her differently from what any of the other unmarried men in the village did. They were all unfailingly politely interested in everything she did. If anything, he seemed less interested than they did; treating her more like a sister than a potential wife.

Debbie knew that they watched her, but she was new, after all. She had not forgotten what Chika had told her, that there would be men who would court her, if she allowed it. She had thought during Yannick's long absence that perhaps she might think about marrying again, but in the end, she had always decided against it. There was no reason to as long as she had a home with Chika and Leon.

She knew that Chika had passed along plenty of information about what her marriage had been like. Debbie understood that everyone would want to know and everyone would then talk about it. That's the way life was in a village so you might as well be honest about what you did. At least then, most people would get their facts straight. The other women in Kenyatta were sympathetic and understanding of her reluctance. No one pushed her to consider a brother or cousin as a possible husband, at least not openly and directly.

Instead, the other village women put their energy into making sure she, and more importantly her daughters, felt accepted and welcomed. They made sure Ghita and Carina met every single child in the villages of Kenyatta anywhere near to their own age. Most of them were boys, Yannick had not been kidding about Northern families running to boys, and all of those boys were paragons of manly virtue and only getting better as they matured. Or so their mothers and aunties and grannies said.

Chika had laughed and laughed when Debbie told her this and said to be grateful that Espe was still too little to be courted as a future wife. Everyone would wait until she was at least two to start pressuring Debbie. This made her roll her eyes but it was something to be grateful for. By the time Espe was two, Debbie decided she might get used to the idea of how all important her daughters were to Kenyatta's future fertility.

Yannick had not been kidding about that either. Everyone she spoke to confirmed it.

And that meant they would not be thrown out when Remus Kenyatta learned about her letter-writing campaign.

Debbie, from reading and rereading the letters that passed through her hands, was more convinced than ever that her actions would cause problems for Dairapaska and Shelleen. Turmoil was bubbling under the surface, where the daimyos would not get wind of it. But they would, it was just a matter of time.

The bigger question was who would say her name first where someone important would hear? All the serfs in Dairapaska knew she was alive and had escaped and, sooner or later, it would slip out in Shelleen that it was Debbie, not some anonymous distant relative, who was forwarding the letters. She knew too many things, current things, things that no distant relative would know and that showed up in the letters. Then word would reach the manor house, via some servant by accident or by someone being questioned about their attitude as they reached for a stone to throw.

That was something else to be uneasy about, when the trouble would come and how many people would be caught up in the resulting investigations. But Debbie knew she would not stop forwarding information. She could not do that to either set of families. She could only be grateful that she had found a safe harbor that allowed her to do this for them.

As she lay there, having woken up from another restless dream, Debbie thought of Yannick again. He had made it possible for her to have this refuge, a home with his family, and acceptance from strangers. She had never believed it possible for a stranger to be so welcomed. Her experience in Shelleen had made her discount even the possibility and yet here in Kenyatta, that thought was proved to be untrue. Moreover, he had made it possible for her to write to her family, to reconnect with them so long lost and desperately missed, and then bring the same joy to all the other unhappy brides.

She lay there in the quiet dark, hearing her daughters breathe and wished there was a way to show her gratitude to him, to thank him for finding her, rescuing her, and bringing her to this safe harbor. Espe stirred and woke up, hungry, and Debbie automatically let her nurse as she thought of what she could do to say thank you to him, more than just words. Espe finished up, burped and fell back asleep, the sleep she would stay in for hours and Debbie let the answer come to her.

There was something she could give him, something he had not asked for, but she could offer it. Debbie wondered if he would refuse her. But if he did, that would be his free choice, she decided, just as it was her free choice to go to him, to lay with him.

She wondered if she would discover what Chika had meant in that conversation weeks ago. Debbie knew that some of the other brides in Shelleen, Alice in particular, had enjoyed what they did with their husbands, even if she, herself did not. Aldo had not seemed to care, but perhaps it was him, and not her who had been at fault. That was a thought she had never entertained before and she examined it with wondering curiosity.

Her decision made, she got up very quietly, as her daughters slept on undisturbed, Spotty lifting his head and then laying it back down, closed the woolen drapes tightly behind her, and slipped down the hallway to Yannick's alcove.

Debbie stood there in the silent, dark hallway, feeling her heart pound in her chest, uncertain again and wondering if she really wanted to do this. She could still turn back, and no one would ever know.

She would do it, she decided, and Debbie climbed into Yannick's alcove, pulling the drapes closed tightly behind her, shutting out the night and shutting herself in with him.

A Growing Intimacy

YANNICK WAS ALREADY AWAKE when she slipped into the alcove and sat down next to him and Debbie suddenly felt very unsure of herself.

He sat up in the bed, barely visible in the velvet darkness and very quietly asked, "Debbie, what's wrong?"

She slid closer to him — she could sense his body heat — and whispered, "Nothing. Nothing is wrong. I wanted to say thank you for everything you've done for me and my daughters."

"You could have done that during the day."

"I wanted to give you something, something more than words. I don't have anything to give you but me."

"You want to lay with me?"

"Yes."

"Debbie," he said patiently, "If you wanted this, you'd be naked and already on top of me. You don't really want to do this."

She swallowed audibly and said, "Yes I do. I want to do this."

He sat up in the bed and turned his back to her. She waited, afraid of what he would say next. She heard the snick of a flint being struck then saw the glow as he lit a small rushlight and set it on the tiny, high shelf overhead. The sudden flare of light was startling. He studied her face, his own revealing nothing of what he thought, what he felt.

"You really want this?"

"Yes."

"Remember that. Lift your arms." And she did, and he very

gently stripped her wool nightgown off over her head. He left his own nightshirt on.

Debbie lay back on the bed and waited for him to climb on top of her like Aldo had, but he did not. Instead, Yannick began to gently kiss her, like no one had since she was sixteen. He stroked her hair, down in its long braid, caressed her body, and she began to relax. He would not just use her and be done with it. It might be more pleasant than that.

He kissed her slowly, gently, like there was nothing more important to do. He ran a hand down across her body, brushing across her nipples. He spent some time caressing her breasts before sliding his hand down until he reached her tummy, and he slid his hand lower, parting her legs and began stroking her there.

Debbie had never felt anything like that before, not in all her experience, and she let her legs fall apart, relaxed, open to his questing hand. And still he kissed her, gently opening her lips with his own, and stroking her with his other hand.

"Why are you doing this?" she whispered.

"You're not ready for me." He blew in her ear and across her neck and she shivered with pleasure.

His hand became more active, more insistent and the pleasure increased as he explored her between her legs and she could feel her hips lifting to his hand of their own accord. Debbie let the pleasure wash over her, rising like the wind before a storm. She would have cried out loud when her climax hit her, but Yannick had his mouth on hers, swallowing the sound.

She lay panting in the dim light, and he smiled down at her. "Like that?" he asked and he kissed her again, more insistently. This time, Debbie returned his kisses, clumsy but willing, and let him explore her mouth as he explored her body with his hands.

Then, to her surprise, he began kissing her down her chin, and began slowly working down her body, kissing and caressing her breasts, then her tummy, and then lower down, at last reaching her most private parts with his mouth.

This was intensely intimate, intensely pleasurable and she wanted more, spreading her legs for his mouth and tongue, wanting more and he gave her more. Debbie emptied her mind, all her thoughts gone, and accepted what she was feeling and enjoying and she moaned as she climaxed again, a wave of intense joy that blotted out everything around her.

She opened her eyes when he got to his knees between her open legs and watched him strip off his nightshirt, showing his lean, muscular body and hard, erect, glistening cock rearing up from its nest of thick curls. He smiled down at her, breathing hard and his eyes dark with lust.

"Now you're ready for me." He bent his head to kiss her again, and she tasted her own sweetness on his lips. His long hair brushed against her face and he thrust his hard cock into her willing, open body. He was big and filled her and it felt good, even better than Debbie would have ever dared hope.

What was left of her rational mind noticed that in this too, Yannick took his time, thrusting into her slowly and as her pleasure increased, he went deeper and faster. Then Debbie stopped thinking and let herself enjoy the rush of pleasure coming over her. Very dimly, she heard Yannick moan and cry out softly as he climaxed inside of her, emptying himself out.

She clung to him in the dim light, tears leaking from her eyes.

"Debbie, what's wrong?" Yannick whispered.

"All those years," she whispered to him. "All those years I laid with that man and never once did he make me feel like you did."

"You should always feel this way," and he kissed her tears away.

Debbie lay with his arms wrapped around her, feeling better than she had in ten years. At last she tried to sit up, to dress and go back to her alcove and sleep.

He held her to him. "Please, don't go, Debbie. Stay with me, please."

"But—"

"I've slept alone too long. Stay with me please." He blew out the rushlight, leaving them in darkness, his strong arms around her, holding her close, but not so tightly she could not pull free if she wanted to.

She thought of Espe, but Espe would not wake until the morning, nor would her older sisters. As long as she got back in time, it would be all right. Debbie relaxed against him, snuggled up closer to his warm, hard body, and let herself sleep with him holding her. Her mind was empty of everything except being next to him, so near, so warm, nothing at all to separate their bodies, nothing to keep them apart anymore.

Morning came abruptly. Debbie struggled out of a deep sleep when the curtain yanked back, light flooding in, and she saw Chika, holding Espe, smiling fondly down at her and Yannick.

"Don't get up, Debbie. This little angel," Chika cooed to Espe "needs her mama."

Yannick sat up, groggy and blinking in the light and the blanket fell away from his nude body down to his waist. "Overslept. I'll get going."

"You will do no such thing," answered his mother tartly. "It's a cold morning and Debbie needs you to keep her and the baby warm, yeah?"

He chuckled. "Yeah, I can do that."

Chika gave Yannick the baby and he in turn passed her to Debbie, then lay back down, his head on the pillow. She automatically took Espe who cooed and burbled at seeing her mother again. She lay back to let Espe latch on and asked, "Where are Ghita and Carina?" She smiled timidly up at Chika, trying hard to pretend that there was nothing embarrassing or uncomfortable about where she had been most of the night.

"Leon's keeping them and the boys busy. And that fool dog, too. I'll call you when breakfast is up." Chika smiled again, looking very pleased, then yanked the curtain closed and disappeared.

"Chika's not mad?" asked Debbie, looking worried.

"No, don't think so. Believe me, we'd know." Yannick chuckled again softly in the dimness. "I feel good. Better than I have in a long time."

He yawned and stretched, then reached over her and Espe to pull back the window drapes letting in the morning light. It fell over Debbie in a wave of soft gold, glinting on her thick braid of hair, all coming undone, and lighting up her olive-green skin. She sighed and enjoyed the rare luxury of lying in bed while other people worked.

Yannick lay beside her, watching her nurse Espe, his hand caressing her hair. "You look so beautiful."

No one had ever said that to her before and that felt good, too. He wedged himself closer, holding her and Espe, and that felt even better.

Later that morning, after everyone had gone to their chores, Debbie and Chika sorted through the heaps of dried, spotted bean pods, shelling them and picking them over for the ones that had to be used right away, the ones to be kept for seed for next year's planting, and the ones that could be safely stored for winter eating.

All four kids were outside stripping the dead vines of the remaining pods, and they kept bringing in more and more basketfuls to add to the quantities already heaped on the floor. Espe was given pots to bang on, in a hopeful attempt to keep her away from the enticing hills of crackly pods. This was a new treat for her and so far, it was working and worth the clamor.

Chika had not said one word to Debbie about discovering her in bed with Yannick. She was not sure what to do, then decided there was no point in pretending it had not happened. Or that she wouldn't like to do it again. Debbie could hardly believe that she had considered such a thought. But she did, remembering his arms around her and his touch and how he felt inside of her. She examined that idea over and over, feeling the pleasurable warmth pooling in her groin as she did so. That was a new sensation, too.

But would what she had done cause a problem?

"Um, Chika? You aren't upset?" she finally asked, after firmly removing a bean pod from Espe's eager clutches and giving her a rattle to shake instead.

"Not at all." Chika looked down at her busy hands shelling a lapful of beans. "Actually, Leon and I had been hoping the two of you would notice each other. We like you more every day, we love the girls like our own and it would be very, very hard to have you leave to some other house. We want you to stay."

Debbie could feel the tears wanting to leak out, and she

forced them back. It would spoil the beans to have salt water spilled on them, and she knew how important they would be, come the thin time.

Aldo's parents had never once said anything to her about how she was welcome in their home. It had not been a surprise when Lupita, in her first letter from Shelleen, had written that they did not seem to care that she was missing. After her first letter, Lupita had not mentioned the Acconcios again, and Debbie had not asked.

"I think you would be good for each other," Chika added. "Both of you can appreciate, more so than most, a decent, caring person."

"What happened this morning?"

Chika chuckled. "Ghita came down to us carrying Espe. 'Mommy's gone. I can't find her and Espe needs her,' she said to me. So I told her I'd take care of the baby, I knew where you were, and I got Leon up and got everybody moving so you two could sleep. Then I brought you Espe."

"You knew?" Debbie was horrified and embarrassed and prayed that she hadn't woken everybody up, and her face showed all of that.

Chika took pity on her and said, "There weren't many places you could go. You would never leave your girls. It was process of elimination so I started with the place I hoped you would be."

"You've all been so kind," Debbie finally said, her nimble fingers never ceasing to sort and shell beans.

"Kind nothing," Chika snorted. "You work hard and Winter knows I can always use another pair of hands around here. And I like your company. You and Yannick enjoy each other, and I hope it comes to more."

Chika looked away over the hills of beans, her expression much colder, then spoke again. "You and that Maureen. It's like night and day. She'd help if she felt like it and then expected a bead from the daimyo to say thank you for just doing what was needful." She looked over at Debbie, meeting her eyes with a much warmer face, her hands never ceasing over her own heap of beans. "Yes, me and Leon both want you to stay."

The door slammed open, bringing with it a cold wind and more baskets of beans, halting the conversation. After the kids scrambled back outside, Debbie looked at the new piles of pods spilling around them and the hours and hours of finicky toil they represented.

"This is so much work, and I know how much it will mean to have them in the spring, but you know? I wish the pile was smaller."

Debbie had never dared to express an opinion like that before. Aldo's mother had not welcomed anyone's opinion but her own. It had been acceptable, barely, to agree with her. Silent acquiescence was considered best of all.

Chika snorted again. "I know what you mean. Tedious, fiddly work. But it'll get smaller and the kids will help shell when the last of the beans are brought in. While we still have some privacy, may I assume you'll keep visiting Yannick? If so, we'll have to ask Ghita to bring Espe to me every morning."

"Oh. I hadn't thought of that. Um." Debbie felt very flustered and took refuge in another basket full of rattling bean pods.

"Better than that worthless dirt-eater, yeah?"

Now Debbie was really flustered and she could feel herself flush to the roots of her hair, remembering Yannick stroking her and his increasingly intimate kisses. "Oh, yes. I can't describe it."

Chika looked amused. "I won't insist. Decide what you're going to do and tell me. And what you're going to tell your girls."

"I'll think on it," Debbie said, her cheeks burning.

"Mommy! We got the last of the beans, and I sent everybody else to finish cleaning up outside," said Ghita, marching in with yet another basketful and slamming the door behind her. She liked being the oldest and being in charge, a change that Kerill — who was used to the same exalted position — was struggling with. He was only a few weeks younger. It made for acrimonious fights, ones that Niall and Carina stayed out of, except when it suited them to encourage the squabbling to distract attention from some bit of naughtiness of their own.

"Oh, good," answered Debbie, grateful for the change of subject. "You're going to help us shell them to get ready for the winter. This is what we look for; the ones we eat right away, the ones we keep for later on, and the very best ones we save for spring planting."

"A different basket for each kind, little dear heart," added Chika, "and be sure to keep the empty pods away from Espe. She'll try to eat them."

"Gram-ma! I know that." Ghita had her hands on her hips, making both women smile. "She puts *everything* in her mouth."

As they worked through the mountains of bean pods, turning them into hills of seeds for using later and much bigger hills of pods destined for compost, Debbie thought about what to say to her daughters. What did she want from Yannick? She wanted to return to him, but what would that lead to?

Debbie automatically answered her daughters' questions, showed them how to efficiently split pods open with a thumbnail and pull out clean beans, and let her mind wander to thoughts of how Yannick had made her feel and how she felt about him.

Chika saw how far away Debbie's mind was and smiled to herself. There was no need to say anything more.

After supper, Yannick found Debbie in a rare moment alone. He stood so close to her, shielding them from the room with his body, and she wondered if he would put his arms around her. They weren't public, not really, as there was no one around at that moment to see them.

She looked up at his face and touched his cheek. He took that as an invitation and bent to kiss her. After a moment of fearful hesitation, Debbie stepped closer to him and wrapped her arms around him, kissed him back, wanting his warmth, his touch, and the feel of his strong arms around her.

He broke away and whispered, "Will you come to me tonight?" His eyes were very dark and intent.

Debbie stared up at him, speechless for a heartbeat and then her body answered on its own accord, as it had responded to his hands and mouth the previous night. She felt that warm wetness pool between her legs, a novel and welcome sensation.

"Yes, as soon as I can leave the girls. Will that be alright?" Her eyes were huge in the soft light.

He kissed her harder, pulling her to his body, and this time he did put his arms around her. Debbie opened her mouth to him, enjoying the intimacy of his kisses. He broke free at last and said, "Yeah, when you can. Let me please you again."

Yannick stiffened and pulled away from her, leaving Debbie startled and hurt at this sudden change. Then she heard the kids milling around, back from outside and she understood. She smiled very shyly up at him. He smiled back and they both let the noise and confusion of daily life wrap around and separate them, knowing it was only temporary.

That evening, as they sat by the fire knitting winter clothing for the girls, Debbie waited until both girls were absorbed in their attempts at knitting. She whispered to Chika that Ghita would bring Espe to her in the morning. Chika looked very pleased and began working a far more elaborate pattern of criss-crossing cables into the winter hat she was knitting for Espe. It had started out, Debbie had noticed earlier, a plainer, simpler pattern.

That night, as she snuggled with her daughters in the cool bed, Debbie told Ghita that if she wasn't in the bed in the morning to bring Espe to gramma Chika. To her great relief, Ghita did not ask questions, nor did Carina. She let them assume she had early morning chores.

Much later, after Espe had finished her last nursing for the night, Debbie slipped down the hallway to Yannick's alcove. This time, she didn't hesitate and eased behind the curtain, stripped off her nightgown and slid into his waiting arms.

He was ready for her, but he did not use her abruptly as Aldo would have. Debbie had wondered if Yannick would give her the same joy he had the night before, and to her great pleasure and gratitude, he did, taking his time to explore her body. She was braver, touching him, stroking him in a way she had never thought she would do to any man. He showed his pleasure in her touch and that made her bolder still.

Yannick had left for the manor house again after breakfast and stolen a kiss on the way out. Debbie did not know how much longer Remus would need him as they studied and discussed what he and Otis had brought back. Every morning, he asked her if she would come to him again that night and so far, she had always said yes. She had never dreamed she could feel the way he made her feel, treasured and pleasured and wanting more.

He would not be here many more nights in the village. The fall migration was gearing up, and he and Otis and the lads would join the men heading onto the steppes to the northern end of the demesne. They would be gone for weeks; long, empty weeks.

Later that morning, Debbie found the feather beds tucked away in one of the deep cupboards and hauled them outside to shake them out and hang them on the clotheslines to air.

She had always had mixed feelings about feather beds. The geese would cry when she plucked their breasts clean of feathers in the spring. She knew it hurt them, however gentle she tried to be.

But in the deep winter, when it was so cold you felt you would never be warm again, the feather beds were so soft, so cozy, and so desperately needed. The geese would grow their breast feathers back over the summer and then in the following spring, Debbie would pluck them again, remembering the biting cold that sank into her bones and wishing there was another way that did not involve suffering.

When a goose or a chicken, any bird at all, was slaughtered, the feathers were kept and sorted for pillows, bedding and fancy work, but there was no denying that goose down was best by far. The down was so valued that only geese got stripped of feathers when they were alive. They were like sheep that way, but it did not hurt the sheep to be shorn. It was just undignified.

It went a long way, Debbie had always thought, to explaining why geese got so mean and edgy, trying to snap at you when you herded them to fresh grass and clean water.

Ghita was now herding geese with the other girls in the village and she had already been bitten. Spotty was turning out to be a big help with herding the geese and when it was Ghita's turn, he always went with her. The geese quickly learned not to snap at Ghita and Spotty did not snap at them in return.

She shook out the feather beds, all six of them, returning

them to warm fluffy fullness. Each one of them would benefit from a few more handfuls of down, but that meant more plucking in the spring. She sighed, remembering how the geese cried and struggled, thought of her daughters already shivering despite their wool nightgowns and wool stockings and wool nightcaps, and shook the feather beds more vigorously.

Thinking of the geese kept her from thinking of Yannick, how warm he was and how warm she felt laying next to him. He was warmer than any feather bed.

It was Yannick's last night at home. Remus and his team had finished with him and Otis and the lads, extracting every last bit of data about the poisoned village for the research into discovering what the daimyo of Shelleen was up to. Come the dawn, he and Otis and the lads would ride to rejoin the rest of the Hands, vaqueros, and gauchitos in the fall migration.

Dinner that night was subdued, even Spotty being quiet. He had picked up the mood in the cottage. Leon had already been gone for many days. Debbie was not surprised at how Chika and Kerill and Niall missed him. The surprise was how Ghita and Carina were pining for grampie Leon as well. It showed her again how they had made themselves at home. They would all have Yannick to miss as well, and for a long time to come.

It would be her last night with him, before he rode out in the morning and Debbie already knew she would go to him, as she had every night before. Her daughters weren't questioning where she went every morning, although she suspected that Ghita and Kerill knew. At any rate, Ghita had not asked and Chika kept all of the kids busy in the mornings with chores.

Debbie knew that Chika had her own reasons for making it possible for her to lay with Yannick. She wanted to see the both of them happy, keep Debbie in the household, and have the possibility of more grandchildren. Every day, Debbie was grateful to Chika for her kindness and this was one more reason.

As soon as she could, Debbie slipped out of her alcove and padded down the now very familiar dark hallway to Yannick's bed. Spotty noticed, as he always did, but he felt that the girls were far more important to watch over than Debbie was. They adored him in a way that Debbie did not and he returned the favor.

Yannick was awake, eager and ready for her. He pulled her into his arms kissing and caressing her, and she kissed and stroked him in return. She was greedy for more of him and he obliged, enjoying her and pleasuring her in a way that Debbie still found hard to believe. It felt so good, laying with him, and each time was better than the last.

"I'm gonna miss you, my Debbie," he whispered "More than I can say."

"You'll be back."

"Yeah, I'll be back." He took a deep breath before continuing. "I need to tell you this, while I still have this time with you."

Debbie felt a rush of fear. He was done with her. She had not been enough. Everything Aldo had ever told her poured over her like icy water. Yannick felt her stiffen, and he pulled her closer to him.

"Nothing to be afraid of, at least I don't think so." He kissed her thoroughly, and she melted against him, all of her stiffness gone.

"I'm falling for you. I didn't think I'd ever trust a woman again after what Maureen did to me."

"Uh, really?" Debbie was astonished and relieved. This was not at all what she had been afraid of. But it was still puzzling. She knew how ordinary she was. Nobody would ever describe her like they did Maureen, a flame in the shape of a woman. "You could have any woman here. Why me?"

He took his time answering her, running his fingers through her loose hair and tracing the lines of her face.

"I remember the first time I saw you, you were so scared. I've never seen anyone so scared as you but you still tried to protect your little girls. You were so brave. You'd have done anything to save them. You'd never walk out on anyone who mattered to you."

He rolled over on top of her, covering her body with his own, a warm, living blanket. She welcomed his weight on her, wrapping her arms around his chest, pulling him closer still.

"The more I got to know you, the more impressed I was.

You are so brave." He kissed her again, slow and gentle.

She could feel her eyes fill with tears, and she fought them back.

"I'm not brave. I put up with what was done to me and I never once fought back."

"Yes, you are. You fought back the only way you could. You did your best, you endured, and when your chance came, you took it."

"I, I, thank you."

"I didn't like it," Yannick paused, remembering, "that you ran away from your man and stole his kids. Bothered me a lot. It didn't make sense to me, a woman like you running across the steppes with little kids you would lay down your life for. I would watch you, as we rode along, and every night out on the steppes. You were as skittish as a wild mare. You didn't trust any of us to do right by you and you still went with us to keep your girls safe. That told me how bad it must have been. You and your girls, barefoot and in rags on the steppes, and all of you jumping at every little noise, afraid to ask a question, shocked by any bit of kindness."

Debbie chose to answer the easy question in his statement. "I didn't dare take anything with us. I didn't want anyone to guess what I'd done. Lupita said in her letter that no one even noticed until the men came back from the far fields in the evening, three days later."

"That was smart of you, to take that head start. But even so, being ignored like that would never happen here." He snorted in disdain, reinforced in his low opinion of Shelleen and its peasants and its customs.

"A woman alone, kids alone, someone would be by to check regularly to see if you were doing okay. Winters are hard in the North and we don't fool around, pretending we can go it alone."

Debbie thought about this. "The villages in Shelleen aren't that much south of here, less than 150 klicks. The winter can't be that much harder here."

"It's probably not. But we're Northerners and we don't pretend we're not. Shelleen and all those dirt demesnes along the divide like to think their winters are easier than they are and so they act as though they were much further south. They're wrong. We hear stories sometimes about what gets found in the spring thaws."

Debbie wiggled under him, trying to wrap herself more tightly around his body. She knew those stories, knew the pain they had caused, and the savage grief that came afterwards and never left.

"I was starting to want you, to care about you as I got to know you. It was hard to ride back out right away, after dumping you and your girls off with my family. Strangers to you. I knew they would do right by you, but you didn't know that."

He sighed, stroking Debbie's hair fanned across the pillow. "But it had to be done, so I did it. And you managed. You made a place for yourself and your girls. And I came back and spent all that time with you and I wanted you more each day."

"You never said anything," Debbie whispered. "I never would have guessed."

He chuckled without any humor. "I learned patience in a very hard school. You were so skittish and I didn't want to scare you. So I waited while you settled in, felt more at ease. I wanted you more every day, hoping you would come to me and you did."

He kissed her again, deeply and she could feel him stirring against her, eager for her again.

"I missed you every night after you left us here," Debbie confessed. "I missed your warmth and nearness, but I didn't, well, I didn't think of this." She moved underneath him, spreading her legs for him and wrapping them around his hips, pulling him closer to her own body.

"I never, ever guessed I would *want* to lay with a man." She returned his kisses with a fervor matching his own. "But you, I wanted to thank you and I'm so glad I did."

"Stay with me."

He began to move slowly inside her, taking his time like he always did, and Debbie responded as she was learning to: with pleasure and enthusiasm and an ardor all of her own.

"Always."

Afterwards, as she drifted off to sleep in Yannick's arms, Debbie felt deeply grateful. He wanted her, and she wanted him back. It was more than enough, for now.

An Interview With Remus

N THE CHILLY, DAMP MORNING, Yannick and Otis and the lads rode out, rejoining the rest of the men of Kenyatta on the steppes for the fall migration.

The village, like the other villages of Kenyatta, became very quiet with most of the men gone. Only the younger boys, the much older men, and the men who could not be spared due to their own jobs were left behind. The Post-Mistress was allowed to keep her four vaqueros and they got much busier on their days in Kenyatta between runs to Purnell, filling in for everyone who had left.

The fall migration took many weeks to get the mixed herds moved down south, plus travel time up to the northernmost borders of Kenyatta. The wild animals moved as they pleased, drifting southwards on their own, and they did not pay attention to the government corridors or other boundaries. Their concerns were more basic.

Once down south, the Kenyatta herds were settled in open pastures, moved regularly as they ate down winter grass, and guarded from predators that also migrated south to avoid the worst of the winter. Only the horses, which were too valuable to leave outside and possibly lose, and the most delicate stock were barned for the long, frigid winter.

Debbie had been told that there was little reason to raise livestock that had to be coddled to keep them alive. The wild herds did not move into barns and most of them managed to survive the freezing snows of winter. It was accepted that not everything would live. The deaths were widely considered to be repayment for the warmth and joy of summer. A sacrifice to the steppes, Leon had said, death to make the soil richer and make the grasses grow tall and lush.

Leon and Yannick would be gone for weeks. Chika missed Leon, which was only to be expected. Kerill and Niall sorely missed their father and grandfather but they had done this before many times and they knew they would be back.

To Debbie's surprise, Ghita and Carina did not stop missing grampie Leon as time passed. More surprisingly, they did not stop missing Yannick either. But that was not surprising, not really, Debbie concluded, despite how much less time Ghita and Carina had spent with him than they had with Leon. He paid far more attention to them than Aldo ever had; he was endlessly patient with them, treating them as valued daughters just like he valued his sons.

Espe knew grampie Leon and Yannick were gone, but unlike the women and the older kids, she did not understand they would come back. Nor did she understand the migration. She remained grumpy and not easily soothed. Teething did not improve her mood or anyone else's.

When Debbie had a spare moment, she desperately missed Yannick. She was grateful that the workload never eased up. It filled the days and made the increasingly chilly nights pass in a blur of exhaustion.

One thing remained unchanged. The mail still arrived as scheduled, as the weather had not yet become severe enough to cause significant delays. Those days would come, the Post-Mistress had said, but not yet.

Debbie read and reread the latest letter from Lupita. The peasants in the new village were frightened and sick.

They knew they had been spied on and no one knew by whom or even if it was still happening. There were widespread rumors of what lived there on the steppes before the settlers arrived and what those unknown residents were doing to drive the unwanted and unwelcomed settlers back to where they came from.

Worse, everyone was coughing and ill, with rashes that refused to heal. All of the crops had failed, even the mint, and everyone knew you could grow mint anywhere. It was a sign, widely believed, that this village was cursed.

The daimyo had been so concerned, wrote Lupita, that he had made a second expedition to the new village in person. He had gone there once before when the spying was at its height, shortly after Debbie's disappearance had been discovered. Lupita believed it was because of the illnesses that he went this time. The daimyo had brought with him wagonloads of mil-rats, blankets, and supplies to get everyone through the winter. The road he had been building did not yet reach the new village but it was getting closer every day, making travel marginally easier.

Lupita reported that the settler's relatives were relieved that their loved ones were getting some help, and angry that they were not being allowed to return home from what was obviously a cursed village.

The problems with the new village were so bad that they had eclipsed the issues brought by the bride trade and Lupita found that amazing. She guessed, and Debbie reading the letter agreed, that it was because so many more families were involved. Even the families of the guards were unhappy, or so the gossip went, because the guards were falling ill, too.

Debbie was deeply grateful that she had run away. If she had stayed, besides all of the other troubles with Aldo, she and her daughters would be ill. She wondered, staring at the letter in her hand, what she should do next. All of her options looked bad.

She had yet to swear fealty to Kenyatta, so technically she had some maneuvering room. Yannick had told her when they were riding to the village from the stone tower so long ago that she would have to do this in order to stay with Kenyatta.

One of the differences between Shelleen, Dairapaska, and the demesnes of the Ennaretee, so Debbie had been told, was that it wasn't automatically assumed you belonged to the daimyo and his demesne.

Instead, you made a public declaration of loyalty and swore fealty to the daimyo and the demesne in front of everybody. The ceremony generally took place four times a year at the equinoxes and the solstices in front of the Sacred Grove and everyone who was eligible pledged during this ritual.

You not only pledged your life and your loyalty in front of the living members of Kenyatta, you swore before your ancestors as well, and you had to speak of your own free will. To go back on your sworn word was a sin and a crime of the first water, a denial of your honor and your family's honor, both before the living vassals of Kenyatta and all the ancestors who still watched over the demesne from the Sacred Grove.

The earliest you were allowed to pledge was when you were sixteen as by that time, it was felt you had some understanding of what you were promising. You had to pledge eventually, usually before you were 25.

People who refused to pledge were forced to leave. You could come back later and swear faithfulness and that was acceptable. You could go to another Northern demesne and swear yourself to that daimyo and that was acceptable as well.

It was not acceptable, anywhere in the Ennaretee, to not belong to some demesne. That was what free-city trash did, and if you refused to pledge your loyalty, a government corridor was where you belonged. The people who did this, while it was not considered a completely respectable choice, did not have their family ties broken. Letters were exchanged, packages were sent, and sometimes, visits were made. Sometimes those people would come back, or their children would return to the demesne and they would swear their loyalty.

There were those who refused to swear fealty, and who refused to move to a free-city and take up a respectable trade. Those men, and they were nearly always men, became bandits, outlaws, wolfs-heads, and every hand was raised against them. A wolfs-head had no legal standing on a demesne anywhere in the Ennaretee and if a wolfs-head caused trouble on a demesne, he would be hunted into the government corridors. A wolfs-head was outside the law and so had no protection from the law, either that of the daimyo or that of the Martian government.

Debbie did not have any idea what a female wolfs-head would do or how one would be treated, and she was quite sure she did not want to find out.

So what should she do?

She reread again Lupita's letter. Lupita was giving so much information about the poisoned village and it was information that Remus Kenyatta could not get for himself. Debbie had already decided that she would swear fealty to him and to the demesne. She could not imagine leaving, not anymore. Her daughters loved it; they had a home with Chika and Leon, and, maybe for all of them, the promise of something more.

She did not think she could return to Dairapaska. Her family and the other brides' families were safe, for now, but if she went back with her daughters, it would be an open insult to the daimyo, one he could not ignore or finesse over. She had been sent away in good faith and then she had run away and stolen children from Shelleen. She had broken the mail blockade. No, Debbie would not be welcomed in Dairapaska and her family could be punished.

Debbie thought of Yannick. She missed him dreadfully, far more than she thought she would. What would he do in such a case as hers? She sighed, making the pages of Lupita's letter flutter as though they wanted to speak with sounds of their own. She knew what he would do and really, it mattered far more what she wanted to do. It was her predicament after all, and one that she had entered into freely, so it was her responsibility to find a solution.

Debbie frowned at Lupita's letter. She would have to begin as she meant to go on. Since the day of the bride trade, so long ago, she tried to do the right thing, the thing that needed to be done, and to endure what happened with a grateful heart and a pleasant face, while her thoughts remained her own. If she meant to swear fealty to Kenyatta, then she needed to behave as a loyal vassal would.

Vassal, that's what they called themselves here in the villages of Kenyatta. Not one person she had met considered themselves to be a peasant, or worse, a serf, and certainly not a dirt-eater. They had all chosen of their own free will to be loyal to Kenyatta and that made them vassals. Very well then, she would behave as a free-willed vassal and not as a bound serf.

Debbie thought of what Leon had said during supper on Yannick's first night back from his expedition to the poisoned village. Did Yannick, via his activities, make things worse for Kenyatta? Was she making things worse for Kenyatta via her clandestine letter writing? This demesne had taken her and her daughters in, no questions asked, and then asked nothing of her that she had not been willing to give. Her actions could be construed as a betrayal and that could mean she and her daughters could be forced from the demesne.

Decision made, Debbie asked Chika that night at supper how she would go about speaking privately with Remus Kenyatta. She could not just march up to the manor house and ask to see the daimyo. He was a busy man, running the demesne, and would not necessarily have time for her. Debbie also knew she did not want to speak to some underling and have her words misunderstood. It had to be Remus Kenyatta and no other.

Chika smiled at her. "Gonna tell Remus about the letters, yeah?"

"Yes, it needs to be done and I'd rather he heard it from me first."

"I'm proud of you, Debbie. I'll send a message tomorrow morning, first thing."

Despite her exhaustion, Debbie passed a restless night, worried if she was doing the right thing and debating what she could possibly say to the daimyo that he would accept. What if Remus became angry and threw her out? She felt her daughters' warmth, snuggled next to her and decided that he would not. She was borrowing trouble by thinking such a thing, comparing him to Aldo's family, when no one she had met so far in Kenyatta had treated her anywhere near as poorly as they had. After that, she was able to sleep.

At midday, a message arrived from the manor house that Debbie had an appointment with the daimyo of Kenyatta within the half-hour. She looked down at her clothes in dismay. She and Chika had been making fermented cabbages again, and she stank of cabbages, brine, and hot peppers. She had on her oldest clothes, the ones she had worn on the trek north from Shelleen, covered with an ancient, stained apron. You never wore good clothes to do as messy a job as this one.

"Chika! I can't go dressed like this. What do I do? I don't have time to change and clean up and still get to the manor house on time."

"Go as you are, Debbie," answered Chika. "Remus knows you got no warning. The kids will be fine here, all of them."

Espe chose that moment to begin to cry for her mother. Debbie sighed right down to the bottom of her toes. There was no help for it.

She bundled up against the cold, put on the sling, tucked in Espe and walked up to the manor house, Espe crying all the way in her own soft wool wrappings. She arrived with a few minutes to spare, enough time to try and sooth Espe. Espe refused to be soothed. She knew what she wanted, and it wasn't a thumb to suck on.

The smartly dressed young page at the door, a new fosterling from Armstrong, curled his lip at her dirty self and her crying baby and led Debbie through a different set of hallways. Espe made sure anyone they passed, despite the closed doors and muffling carpets and insulating tapestries, knew that they had arrived.

To add to her humiliation, Remus was not alone in his office. Preston was there, along with other well-dressed men and women. Debbie assumed they were senior members of the Kenyatta family as they were all older. Other than Preston, there was no one there she recognized from the library of people researching the poisoned village.

Remus stood when she entered, sized up her situation, and said, "Debbie, sit down and take care of Espe. As soon as she's quiet, tell me what you need to say that is so important."

"Yes, sir," Debbie answered. She was grateful that Chika had given her a shawl, and she settled Espe in as quickly as she could. A quietly nursing baby was a relief after the earlier sobbing and wails. It was always a surprise how loud such a little baby could get, although Espe was not so little anymore.

She kept her eyes downcast upon the beautifully patterned carpet of flowers. She hoped she wasn't going to make the nicely upholstered chair, patterned with orange flowers and deep green leaves, dirty with her dirty clothes.

"You know I'm from Dairapaska and I was given to Shelleen as a bride."

"An idiotic way to handle their fertility problems I always thought, yeah?" Remus was relaxed behind his desk. He waved the other people in the office to chairs, where they sat down quietly, watching and assessing Debbie.

This made her even more uncomfortable. She pushed those awkward thoughts from her mind and soldiered on.

"I wrote to my mother in Dairapaska the day after I arrived and I've been writing to her ever since. She writes back and I've told her everything that happened to me including my running away with my children.

"Everyone in Dairapaska knows what I did. And I've been telling all of the peasants there what happened to their girls in Shelleen and I wrote about everything I knew about the Shelleen families for the Shelleen brides."

She stopped and met Remus's eyes briefly, something she still found intensely difficult and deeply disrespectful to do. She did not think it would ever get easier.

"There's trouble in Dairapaska, but it's not out in the open, not yet. The daimyo doesn't know that I went around the mail blockade, telling the families about Shelleen. Or that I ran away, breaking the bargain he made with Shelleen, taking my girls from their father. When he finds out what's going on, and he will, he'll make trouble for you."

"So?" said Remus, unconcerned. "Dairapaska can pound sand. I made no deals with him, I don't care what he does, he is on the other side of Mars, and he has no hold over Kenyatta."

Debbie took a deep breath and focused on the golden heart of a red, red rose by her feet. "There's more."

The room was very quiet and Debbie made herself go on, filling the silence with the carefully chosen words she had fretted over.

"I used Chika's name, she let me, and I wrote to the mother-in-law of one of the brides in Shelleen. I've been exchanging letters with Lupita — that's my friend Alice's mother-in-law — passing her information on the Shelleen brides so she can tell their families what happened to them. She talks to all the Dairapaska brides, too, telling them about their families. Lupita knows who I am, but she thinks no one else in Shelleen knows it's me. Not yet, anyway. They all believe I'm some distant relative who figured out a way around the mail blockade."

Debbie made herself look at Remus again, ignoring everyone else in the room. They were not important.

"Shelleen will cause you trouble. His serfs are in an uproar because I ran away with my girls and because I broke the mail blockade. He doesn't know about me, not yet. It's just a matter of time, and he will make trouble for you. Once he realizes I'm alive and passing letters through Kenyatta, he'll come to you. When he knows I'm in Kenyatta, he'll know it was your vassals who were spying on the new village. I'm the only person who could have told you about it."

She bit her lip and turned her eyes back to the red, red roses woven into the beautiful, disinterested carpet covering the floor. "I want to swear fealty to Kenyatta, but I needed you to know what I've been doing first."

Remus had a blank face that gave away nothing. He waited for her to fill the silence and when she did not, he said, "You do understand that the daimyos will cause more trouble for your own families, both in Dairapaska and Shelleen than they will for me, yeah?" His voice was gentle.

"Yes sir," Debbie answered quietly. "Yes sir, I do. Everyone in both places knows the risk we're taking and everyone wanted to continue to exchange news. It was awful, not knowing what had happened, wondering all the time if you had been forgotten. The girls from Shelleen had just as hard a time as the Dairapaska brides did. It was horrible for all of us, and for all of our families. I'm sorry. I couldn't not do it, and I'd do it again."

Remus smiled at her, his eyes warm. "Such courage you have, and your families, too. I'll accept your fealty at the fall equinox. Debbie, you brought us luck and you will bring us the strength to endure what fortune throws at us."

Debbie sagged in her chair, letting the relief wash over her. Espe had finished nursing and was ready to sit in her lap, quietly Debbie hoped, and watch everyone around her.

"Sir, Lupita tells me many things about the new village and the unhappiness in Shelleen. But overall, I believe things are worse in Dairapaska."

Remus raised an eyebrow. "Why do you say that? Dairapaska has only lost its young women. Shelleen lost its daughters and has to struggle with the poisoned village."

Debbie bit her lip again. "My mother writes that everyone in Dairapaska, not just the families involved in the bride trade, are restless and unhappy, and it has gotten worse over the years. I believe Dairapaska is more poorly managed than

Shelleen. Shelleen should be more unhappy, yet the peasants there managed, there was always enough food and warm clothes for the winter and the obligations to the daimyo were reasonable. I lived there and it does not seem to be as bad, day to day, as Dairapaska sounds in the words of my mother. Even with the bride trade and the cursed village, I believe there will be riots in Dairapaska long before Shelleen."

Remus sat back, unconcerned but not uncaring. "Interesting, but Dairapaska can do nothing to or for Kenyatta. Why do you say cursed village?"

Debbie thought back to what she had read in her letters.

"When I lived there, no one said it was cursed. It was bad, it was out in the middle of nowhere, and everyone thought the new daimyo was insane to do such a thing. Lupita writes that the peasants there believe it has been hexed. They are ill, all of them, with coughs and rashes and stomach troubles. The guards get sick too and have to be sent back to the old villages to get better and they do, within a few weeks of their return.

"And everyone there is afraid of who had spied on them."

Remus smiled complacently, as did Preston.

"The guards are jumpy and the peasants are afraid, always looking over their shoulders. Lupita writes that many of the peasants think witches live there, causing bad luck, and making people sick. The witches are trying to drive the settlers away because it was their home first. She said it got so bad the peasants petitioned the daimyo to let everyone go home for the winter to recover. The daimyo rode to the new village to see for himself and he brought many wagonloads of supplies. But he did not bring new people with him. He has not sent new peasants since his return either, even though the village is laid out for many more families than it has. And he said no to the peasants returning home during the deep winter."

"Now that is interesting," said Remus slowly. "So Airik went back with supplies but no settlers. He's keeping the peasants there alive, but not allowing them to return. What kind of supplies did he bring with him?"

"Lupita said mil-rats, water, medicines, warm clothing and blankets. She said it was very strange that there were no animals, tools or winter seeds."

Preston sat up and said, "Remus, he's keeping them alive,

the minimum he needs to prove he has a going village. I've been researching the charter and if Airik Shelleen can prove he has a settled village, and he can prove he can exploit the lode, he can retain control of his land. The Martian government won't move in and take over."

"That sounds about right, Preston. Debbie, I want you to keep writing to your mother and this Lupita in Shelleen. I want to know anything that Lupita writes about the new village. If you can find out more from her without making her suspicious or putting her in danger, ask for as much information about the new village as she can find out. Come up to the manor house whenever you learn something new, no matter how minor, and ask for Preston."

"Yes sir, I can do that," answered Debbie. "May I ask a question?" She focused on another rose near her feet, as beautiful and as indifferent to her as the other roses woven into the carpet.

Remus gave her an odd look and said, "of course."

"Will this help the peasants in the new village? They didn't ask to do this, any of them. We were forced to go there."

Remus studied the gleaming white ceiling for some moments, then sighed deeply. "They belong to Shelleen. I cannot interfere with how his demesne is being run."

"You interfered when you spied on them!" Debbie shut her mouth in horror. "I'm so sorry. I shouldn't have said that." She cringed back into the upholstered chair, holding Espe tightly enough for the baby to wail.

A ripple of laughter moved through the room and Debbie knew it was aimed at her for being so rude and impertinent to the daimyo and the other members of the ruling family.

Remus winked at her. "So I did, and I did need to be reminded of that. If I can aid them, I will."

"Thank you, sir."

A few minutes later, Debbie was led down the maze of carpeted hallways and outside into the cold, welcome sunshine. As soon as she was safely out of eyeshot of the manor, she sat down on a low stone wall, and shook and shook as she thought of what she had done and said. She wondered if, despite what Remus said, she would be punished for her speech and activities.

At last, she sighed and stood back up. There was nothing she could do about it now, so she and Espe walked back down the hill to Chika's cottage and the waiting mounds of cabbages.

As they tackled the cabbages, Debbie told Chika what happened. Her response was reassuring. "You should be fine. It's good to remind the daimyo what he's been up to, especially if it seems like he's forgetting what he did. We have to be accountable to him and so he has to be accountable to us."

That evening, Debbie studied the waiting blank paper and considered carefully her newest letter to Lupita. Should she ask for news about the new village? She had paid it no attention, other than to pass along the information about the families in it that were related to one of the Shelleen brides. She had carefully ignored Aldo and his very existence, along with the rest of the Acconcio family.

Lupita had not questioned her reticence. She had always had a low opinion of Aldo and the Acconcio family and the events since the forced settlement of the cursed village had not changed it. She had written that she understood why Debbie did not want to be reminded of her unhappiness and all of the reasons she had fled and the subject had been tabled.

Debbie decided to ask Lupita what was happening to Aldo. It would be good if she knew, in case Ghita ever asked about her father. She had not so far, nor did she ask about nonna and nonno back in the old village.

Debbie wondered if she should ask Ghita what she thought about them. Would that stir up trouble? She seemed, her and her sister, to be so much happier now. The forced march across the steppes to the cursed village and the months living there had been dreadful for all of them. Carina had been so little when they had made the march and not much older when they ran away. It seemed to her younger daughter, Debbie thought, that they had always lived with Chika and Leon and Kerill and Niall. Certainly, Espe believed this to be true.

She decided she would do it. It was always better to know. Wasn't that true of all of the families of the brides, both in Dairapaska and Shelleen? They all wanted to know the truth

and damn the consequences when the daimyo of their demesne found out they knew the information he had forbidden
them.

Soon enough, Lupita's letter arrived. Debbie hesitated, fearful
of reopening old memories. She had to make herself slit open
the envelope with her little knife. After all, she told herself, she
would never see any of them again, not Aldo, not his mother,
not his father, not his brother, not his sister. She would never
again have to listen to them telling her all of her faults, despite
what she did to try and please them.

Lupita wrote that she had been waiting for Debbie to ask.
She had not written of these events as she didn't feel it was her
place to cause more pain, reminding Debbie of the people who
had brought her so much unhappiness.

Reports from the villagers to the relatives left behind said
that Aldo was not doing well in the cursed village. He spent
much of his time drinking the raw barley beer when he wasn't
in the fields. He stayed alive but that was all.

Then the daimyo rode out the second time, with many more
wagonloads of supplies. The daimyo had spoken to the gathered peasants, telling them that they would still have to winter
over, but they would have food to eat and would no longer
have to eat what they grew. The road he was building got closer every day, and more supplies would be sent. A new well
would be dug, further away. The water would have to be
hauled to the village, but it would be sweet and pure, unlike
what they were drinking now.

When the daimyo finished speaking, Lupita wrote, Aldo
picked up a fist-sized stone and threw it at him, striking him on
his shoulder. Aldo swore and cursed at the daimyo, screaming
that he would still have a wife and two daughters if only they
had not been sent to the new village to die.

The daimyo had been very angry. His guards beat Aldo and
confined him under guard for the night. The daimyo spoke to
the village headman and the midwife and other people in the
village, so wrote Lupita, and in the morning, he had Aldo
stripped and flogged in front of everyone.

Lupita went on to write that the daimyo told Aldo before he was flogged, while everyone listened, that he had three daughters, as per the midwife and everyone else in the new village. Aldo had caused this problem, so said the daimyo. They were all living under the same circumstances, and no other woman had run away to die out on the steppes with her children. He had no sympathy for Aldo and Aldo would never be allowed to leave the new village.

Back in the old village, Debbie's former in-laws wept and carried on endlessly to anyone who would listen about the loss of their granddaughters. They had only harsh words to say about Debbie running away. Interestingly, they did not mention the baby, only Ghita and Carina. Lupita thought that was very sad and she supposed that it was because if they talked about the nameless baby, it would mean admitting that Aldo's behavior had made Debbie run away and take her daughters with her.

The other villagers did not approve of this refusal to face facts and there were those, Lupita among them, who pointed out to Aldo's parents that there were three granddaughters, not two, and if Aldo had made the baby a kuksa as he should have, named her as he should have, behaved as he should have, then none of this would have happened. These statements were not received gladly by Aldo's family, any member of it, but they were not denied either.

"I think," Lupita went on to write, "that your mother-in-law is starting to realize how much work you did and that makes her angrier than ever. She certainly doesn't feel that *she* did anything wrong. I hope you don't mind my saying what an unpleasant old bitch she is! I pray I'm never that way with Alice and I'm relieved to know that my Pia doesn't have to endure a mother-in-law like yours."

Debbie wrote back to thank Lupita for telling her what had happened. It was unpleasant to know that Aldo had been flogged, but it was not a surprise. He had thrown a stone at the daimyo and struck him. She had heard stories in Dairapaska of a serf doing that and being hung for his offense. It was also not a surprise to hear that Aldo's parents only missed their granddaughters and not their mother. They had never warmed to her, as Lupita did to Alice.

Alice, wrote Debbie, missed her family in Dairapaska deeply, but she had come to love Lupita like another mother. Lupita had not taken out her anger about Pia on Alice. Alice knew this and she appreciated the self-control this took, and the openness and warmth of Lupita's heart. Alice was often congratulated by the other brides on her luckiness in the husband she had been given to; he was as kind as his mother.

Debbie studied the words that she had written to Lupita. She knew they were true. Alice had told her often enough that she was, well, not *happy*. But she was much happier than the other brides from Dairapaska. She had come to care for her husband, she loved her children, and Lupita's family had never once made her feel unwelcome.

Debbie prayed that she had not betrayed a confidence by telling these things to Lupita. The brides, one and all, had struggled with fitting into Shelleen and the families they had been given to. Alice had been the luckiest of them all, and she had never wanted anyone to feel worse next to her own good fortune.

But good things should be acknowledged as well as bad. If you did not celebrate the good things, appreciate them, then they became less important until all you saw in your life were the bad, painful events. This had been one of the ways Debbie had survived. She loved her daughters dearly. She always made a point of enjoying the tiny gifts that life had given her and that was what, Debbie believed, had given her the strength to run away when she had the chance to do so.

After she finished her letter to Lupita and sealed it, Debbie wrote to her mother again, to tell her how much her grandmother's words of wisdom had helped her to cope in Shelleen.

13

The Fall Migration Ends

CHIKA HAD TOLD DEBBIE THAT the return from the fall migration was a big celebration. All of the men and boys who had ridden out to work over the last few weeks would return at about the same time. They would camp on the steppes, waiting until everyone who could, returned, and then they rode back as groups, one group for each of their home villages.

The youngest of the gauchitos in each group would ride ahead to their village and in the center of the square blow his horn, announcing the impending return of the rest of the men and boys. They would ride in with much whooping and hollering and horn-blowing and then the celebration would really begin.

Very little work would be done for several days. Chika rolled her eyes when she said this. "Very little work other than the cooking and washing up, that is. And of course, animal tending, taking care of the kids, and all the other day-to-day chores we have to do. Somehow that gets forgotten in the excitement."

Ghita piped up, "you mean we still have to cut and dry all the apples?"

She was learning to pare apples and trying hard to get a single long strip of apple peeling from an apple rather than many tiny bits. Each apple she peeled would be cored and sliced and then the rings strung on string and hung to dry before the masonry stove. No one would willingly eat dried apples at this time of year when there were fresh ones, but in the dead of winter, they would be a welcome treat.

Carina was stringing the apple rings, separating each ring with spacing knots, as it was felt she was not yet ready to use a little knife to pare an apple. Espe was given mashed apple to smear all over herself, a task she was performing with enthusiasm. Some of the mashed apple even went into her mouth, pleasing her still further.

Chika smiled down at Ghita fondly. "No, dear little heart of mine, we'll take a break for a few days from all that work. I'm worried. Grampie Leon is getting older and he sometimes forgets that. There's always some man or other who doesn't come back, or he comes back injured and I worry it will be him."

Debbie looked up from her coring and said, "It's dangerous? The fall migration?"

"It can be, yeah? A stampede is always bad, and there's the day-to-day risks. The men claim they never get thrown from a horse but sometimes they do. They break bones, get cut up, get bitten by snakes, get sick, attacked by wolves. The list goes on forever."

"Oh." Debbie thought of the shining red snake on the long plod north and was grateful again they had detoured around it, leaving it undisturbed.

"I always get tetchy during the migration. I worry and there's not a damn thing I can do about it except keep getting ready for winter."

Finally, after days more of waiting, the youngest gauchito rode to the center of the village, standing in the stirrups and blowing his horn and waving his hat all the way. At the fountain in the village square, he made his horse rear back and dance, showing off still further and making sure anyone who had not been paying attention knew he had arrived.

Everyone had been waiting for his signal. They poured out of their cottages and lined the square, waving and cheering as the Hands, vaqueros, and gauchitos paraded in on their dancing horses, dirty and dusty from the long weeks away on the steppes.

The parade of riders broke apart as their families saw them, dismounting to greet wives and children.

Chika saw Leon and ran for him. He snatched her up and they spun around in the crowd, hugging and kissing as though they were teenagers again.

Debbie looked around and around for Yannick in the mob of dusty, dirty men and milling horses and barking dogs. She had all of the kids with her, holding Espe in her sling, and Ghita, Carina, Kerill, and Niall hand in hand.

Then she saw him. Yannick at last, smiling through the red and gray dust that coated him from head to toe. Debbie ran up to him, calling his name, ignoring the kids and the stares from the other people and hugged him hard.

He went stiff in his surprise and she recoiled in hurt and confusion.

"I'm so sorry," she said, her eyes downcast to hide her tears as she pulled away. "You want to see your sons."

"No, no, never, you surprised me, that's all." Yannick threw his arms around her and Espe, kissing her hard in front of everyone and not caring who saw them.

The sun came out again, and Debbie kissed him back with equal joy. He had come home and he was in one piece and he had missed her.

He whispered to her as he held her close, "I didn't think you'd want to show everyone. I've missed you so much and you've made me happier than ever."

"Dad! Dad! Yannick! Yannick!" All four kids decided it was their turn and began jumping up and down, demanding his immediate attention.

He sat on the ground and let them overwhelm him with hugs and shouting, all four kids; his own two boys, and Debbie's girls and Spotty leaping around them all, yapping madly.

She made a place for herself in his lap, her arms around his neck and the kids making enough noise to conceal what she whispered into his ear.

"I've missed you terribly, every day, and" – she kissed him again – "at night too."

"Come to me tonight?"

"Always."

"Tomorrow evening. I want to dance for you."

She met his eyes and smiled at him, feeling as though her heart would burst. "Yes, please, dance for me." And she kissed him again, slowly and thoroughly, to show how much she meant it.

Inside the cottage, Chika and Debbie had laid out a lavish feast to celebrate Leon's and Yannick's safe return, delicious things they had been preparing and keeping by, so they would be ready and waiting for the great day. As they ate and drank, Debbie sat next to Yannick holding his hand and feeling as though she had never been happier. He had come home safe, and he wanted her more than she had dreamed he would.

He wanted to dance for her, showing her and everyone how he felt and who he wanted. Debbie knew already some of what that meant and how important a public statement this was.

During her months here, she had learned that there had been plenty of similarities between village life in Kenyatta and Shelleen and Dairapaska. But this was a major difference. There had been dancing and plenty of it in Shelleen and Dairapaska, but not the kind where the men showed themselves off for the women. You danced as couples and groups, although they did that here, too.

Debbie had not danced in Shelleen. She was not asked and she did not volunteer.

Debbie was looking forward to seeing Yannick and the other men dance for her and for the other women. She beamed as she thought of something else she could show him. In Dairapaska, the women sometimes danced for the men and she would dance for him later, and for him alone, because she chose to.

That evening, the men and boys disappeared into the bathhouse to scrub off weeks of dirt, sweat, and grit. Before Yannick and Leon left with Kerill and Niall, he whispered to Debbie, "I want to marry you, my own dearest heart."

The women took their chance to do the same in the women's bathhouse. It was an opportunity to pass along news of who had done what out on the steppes, whose husbands, sons and nephews had excelled and who would be advanced in rank.

Debbie listened to the gossip swirling around her and when she was asked about her kissing Yannick in front of everyone and him kissing her back, she chose to beam but not say any-thing. Mandy and Erissa, in particular, were full of questions as would be expected of the wife of Otis, Yannick's steppes part-ner, and the wife of his brother, Lysander.

Chika was happy too, smiling at the questions and saying how sometimes, things worked themselves out. She showed her open approval of Debbie as they bathed themselves and the girls, acting in every way like a fond grandmother and pleased mother-in-law would. Debbie had not felt so accepted and happy since being forced from Dairapaska.

Not even Barb's pettiness could spoil the moment. Fortu-nately, as Debbie was grateful to notice, Barb turned her atten-tion to talking about how well her own husband had done out on the steppes with his skills and talents and how valued he was by the older Hands.

That night, she and her daughters crawled into their chilly alcove to sleep, all bundled up in wool to ward off the cold and enjoying the warmth of the feather beds.

As they snuggled together in the quiet darkness, Ghita asked, "Mommy, Reay said Yannick might dance for you. What did she mean?"

Debbie had been wondering when Ghita would ask about Yannick. What did she want to say in return? Her daughters had been the most important part of her life for years, the cen-ter of her world, and now they would have to share her affec-tions in a way that they had never had to before.

She debated what to say while Ghita waited impatiently, wiggling and squirming, as she tried to get comfortable and warm.

To their mutual surprise, Carina got there first. "It means that mommy will marry Yannick, dummy! He'll be our dad for real and not just pretend and Kerill and Niall will be our real brothers and gramma Chika and grampie Leon will be our real gramma and grampie and it won't be pretend anymore."

Debbie smiled up at the polished bamboo ceiling, a lighter square in the dark alcove. "Yes, that's what that means, Ghita. Carina is right. Who told you this, dear little heart?"

"Kerill did, mommy. Him and Niall want it too." Carina was immensely pleased with herself for knowing something before her big sister did.

"Yannick and I want to marry. It means we would live here forever, with him and Kerill and Niall and Espe, and gramma Chika and grampie Leon." Debbie studied Ghita's stiff profile in the dim light filtering in around the edges of the wool curtain. "What do *you* want, my angel?"

Debbie did not know how Ghita would answer. She was old enough to remember Aldo and the new village and nonna and nonno and her aunties and uncles back in Shelleen. She never asked about them, never talked about them, and Debbie had avoided bringing them up. She wondered if she should have.

Ghita was silent for a long time before saying anything. Debbie chose to wait for her, rather than try to fill the quiet alcove with words of her own, words that were not Ghita's.

"Stop kicking me, Carina! Let me say my own words. Can Spotty stay with us?"

Spotty was at the foot of the bed, keeping everyone's feet warm and he lifted his head when he heard his name.

"Of course he can, Ghita. He's our dog."

"We're never going back to Shelleen?"

"No, we would live here forever."

"I could be happy here. It's lots better than the awful new village. Mommy? Is it bad that I like Yannick better than father back in Shelleen?"

Debbie hugged Ghita closer, until her stiff little body relaxed against her. "No, dear little heart, it's not. Your father back in Shelleen was, well, not always easy to live with and the new village made things much worse. We won't ever go back there, I promise."

"And we'll never leave gramma Chika and grampie Leon?" Ghita asked plaintively. "I couldn't bear it."

"Never. Gramma Chika already told me that she wants us to stay with them forever."

"Okay, then." Ghita sounded more reassured and she relaxed again, breathing out as if she had been holding her breath from fear.

Debbie smiled and smiled up at the alcove ceiling, enjoying her daughters' warmth and quiet happiness next to her.

Ghita broke the silence, as they were just drifting off. "Yannick doesn't make you cry, mommy. Not like father did."

Debbie blinked. She had thought she had done a better job

of hiding her feelings in front of her daughters. "No, he doesn't," she answered slowly. "Not ever, and I don't believe he ever will."

"Good." Ghita wiggled around some more and then fell asleep.

Debbie lay awake a long time after that, listening to her daughters breathe, with Espe nuzzled close to her. She fretted over what else Ghita remembered from Shelleen about how her mother had been treated and if that was why she never talked about her old home.

Much later, she woke again when Espe wanted her, and when Espe was finished nursing and fell asleep, Debbie slipped out of the alcove and padded down the dark hallway to Yannick's alcove.

He woke as soon as she entered and pulled her to him, kissing her fiercely.

"I've missed you, more than I thought possible."

He was ready and eager for her, on top of her and inside of her within minutes and Debbie to her joy discovered that she was just as eager for him.

In the morning, after an exceptionally noisy breakfast, made more so by the cats teasing Spotty, Chika found a quiet moment to explain to Debbie what would happen that evening. "I don't want you to be unprepared. It's quite a show the men put on for us, and peacocks that they are, they want to be appreciated when they show off."

Debbie smiled down at the thick, heavy parsnips she was scrubbing, thinking of Yannick and how he would look dancing for her. "I don't think that will be difficult."

Chika sighed. "I'm borrowing trouble, I know. It's that bitch Maureen. She would make him wait, make him think she would reject him and in front of everyone too! Don't wait too long, but you do want to wait long enough to make him want you more."

"How will I know?"

Chika grinned at the roots she was scrubbing. "It's pretty obvious." Debbie could feel the heat rise in her cheeks and she flushed at Chika's implications.

"Will Leon dance?"

Chika looked pleased and contented, a faraway look in her eyes. "Not tonight, but he will tomorrow night. I still remember the first time he danced for me. He was so handsome and he looked so delicious. What a good time we had afterwards."

"Why not tonight? Oh. Oh!"

"Yes, oh. All of us grandparents drew straws to see who would get to chaperone all of the little ones in the biggest barn. All the kids who aren't old enough to participate will be having a party of their own, well away from the adults. Leon and I got short straws so we'll be supervising along with the other shortstraw couples. All of us old folks will trade off nights for the week while you younger people have a very good time indeed."

Chika grinned wickedly at Debbie. "You can be as noisy as you want to be and you don't have to stay in the alcove."

This made Debbie even more flustered, and she focused all her attention on making dumplings to top the stew bubbling on the hearth and left the parsnips for Chika to scrub.

That afternoon, Yannick and Leon took up their chairs by the fire, their long, long hair clean and loose. They each had a bowl full of colored beads in front of them on the table, Leon having quite a few more than Yannick did.

Chika showed Debbie how to comb out Yannick's hair, make the tiny braids and plait in the beads. It was astonishingly intimate, combing and braiding, with so many opportunities to stroke his head and neck. As they worked, Yannick told Debbie what each bead was for, who gave it to him, and when.

"Our beads are our record of what we do in this life," he said, holding up a deep blue one. "We wear them so everyone can see our deeds. When I go to the Grove at the end of my days, they'll go with me in my hair, every last one." He caught Debbie's hand and pulled her into his lap.

He held out a narrow braid before her, the one that hung at his left temple. It had three beads on it and was the one she had plaited second. "This is where your bead will go, along with ones for Ghita and Carina and Espe. My wife, my daughters and my sons, in my hair forever more."

Debbie had seen those beads in his hair since the day she had met him, but this time the top bead was different. It had been scratched up, its previous glossy lime green now dull and drab. She touched it. "This one is damaged."

"It's Maureen's bead, the one her father gave me. I'm not married to her anymore, I haven't been for years, and it's time I showed it." Yannick frowned at the remaining beads in the bowl on the table, running his fingers through them and letting them spill back into the bowl.

"She was part of my life, she bore my sons and I won't pretend that she didn't exist. So I wear the bead but now it shows what she did."

Debbie looked dismayed. "My father can't give you a bead for me."

Leon reached over to pat her hand. "I've already taken care of that, my dear. Welcome to the family."

He held out a gleaming bead of polished bone, creamy orange tinged with red and purple. "I thought this would do. It reminded me of the sunset and since Dairapaska is to the west, it seemed appropriate."

"Nice, dad. Very nice." Yannick took the bead and held it up to the light, turning it between his fingers and admiring the way the splotches of color looked like early twilight clouds on the horizon. "But I'll carve my daughters' beads myself, yeah?"

"Of course, my boy. Wouldn't dream of it."

Chika rolled her eyes at Debbie in amusement. "And from now on, when you do up Yannick's braids, you'll get to hear the story behind each and every bead until you know their history better than he does."

Leon grinned up at her. "Because I'd forget! I need you to remember for me."

"It's traditional, mom! It's how we pass down our stories," Yannick added with a grin.

"You love it, my dearest heart, and you'd miss running your fingers through my hair, if I quit wearing my beads." Leon blew kisses up to his wife and leaned back into her bosom.

Chika laughed. "Well that's true, my dearest heart. I missed you every day you were on the steppes and I'll do your beads every day to keep you home."

It was almost time when Harley stopped by the cottage. He had more beads in his hair than Debbie would have guessed for his age. He came charging in, looking for Yannick alone and finding everyone on their way out instead.

"I, uh, wanted you to know that I'm gonna dance for my girl," Harley said.

Yannick and Leon both studied him with concern and disapproval, making Harley lose some of his sureness in his course of action.

"You are, huh," said Yannick. "Does she know this?"

"She put my beads in!"

"Her daddy know about this?"

Harley looked annoyed. "I can't tell him, he'll have a fit."

Yannick sighed with great patience. He put his hands on Harley's shoulders, keeping him from turning away.

"Harley, think. What kind of fit do you think her daddy will have if you surprise him like this? Dancing for his little girl? If you don't have the stones to tell her parents what you're gonna do, you shouldn't be doing it."

Harley looked thoughtful but said, "You sound like my dad."

"I should hope so."

Chika leaned in and added, "Does her mama know? If your girl can't tell her mama, she's not old enough for you to dance for her."

Cornered, Harley looked around for support but did not find it in any of the adults in the room.

"Harley, lad, get your girl and go find her parents. Don't surprise them," said Yannick. "Tell them and take the consequences."

Harley sighed, an exaggerated, exasperated, weary sigh indicting everyone else in the room as being too old and set in their ways to understand.

"I'll think about it," he finally answered.

"You do that."

After Harley left, not having gotten the answer he was hoping for, Leon said, "good work, boy. It's nice to know you listened to me."

Yannick grinned. "I listened. I may not have done what you wanted, but I always listened."

"A fine young cockerel, desperate to strut for the hens," Chika whispered to Debbie and they both smiled.

The last task to perform was to take the kids to the largest barn in the village. There were piles of hay to sleep on along with plenty of blankets, tables of goodies, and games of all kinds. Debbie could see that much work and planning had gone into keeping the kids occupied and then, eventually, exhausted so they would sleep deeply.

Every child in the village was there, and she was grateful to see that Ghita and Carina fit right in, racing to see their friends, matching Kerill and Niall with their joyful shouting. There were plenty of teens in there as well, helping to supervise. Many of them seemed ambivalent about the evening ahead. Were they still little enough to stay in the barn or were they more like adults?

She caught a glimpse of Harley and his girl smooching in a corner. So, they had not chosen to be adults yet. One of the older women approached them, disapproval oozing off of her in waves, and they hastily separated, looking guilty.

Chika took Espe, her tummy full, and carried her over to where the other babies were corralled and she joined in the noisy group, trying her best to stand up and crawling when she couldn't.

"Debbie, I'll keep Espe all night and bring her to you in the morning," Chika said. Espe was eating well-mashed and stewed grains so she knew that she would not go hungry.

Debbie made her goodbyes and with the other women and walked away from her children, looking forward to the exciting night ahead.

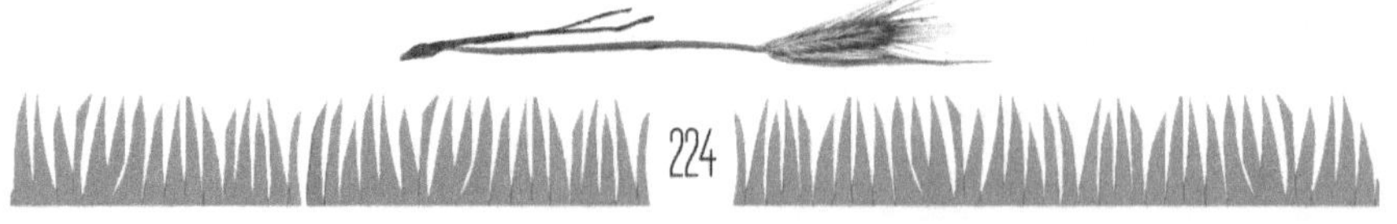

The dancing would take place in the village's center square, well lit with lanterns overhead and a bonfire in the middle. Tables had been set out, with treats and savories to eat, and plenty of apple-cider to wash them down with. Debbie had a sip, blinked, and knew at once why the kids in the barn had been given something different to drink.

The men and older teenage boys were off somewhere else, getting peacocked out, every single bead in place, and dressed in their finest. Debbie was told that for a few of the young men, this would be their first time dancing and for their girls, their first time watching. It was reassuring for Debbie, knowing that she would not be the only woman in the group who had never been there before, even if she was oldest member of that select group.

She was thrilling with anticipation as she joined with the other women, some of whom, like Erissa and Mandy, were becoming friends. Debbie knew she was looking her best in her embroidered kirtle with the low-cut neck and the full sleeves, with wide bands of more embroidery at the hems and an edging of feathers. All the women were in their festival best, old and young, and they all had ribbons and more feathers in their elaborately plaited hair.

Someone began the drumbeat, the horns sounded and the night began.

The women gathered in a wide circle and watched the men parade in to the sound of drums and clapping. Debbie had never seen anything quite like it. The men danced in, athletic and graceful, swinging their long hair and the beads swished and clattered.

They didn't wait to heat up from dancing. Despite the cool air, tunics were being stripped off fast, showing off muscular, bare chests and rippling biceps coated with a sheen of sweat to catch the eye still more. There was a murmur of approval when Yannick came in last.

She couldn't tear her eyes away from Yannick. As he spun and leaped into the air, his eyes always found her own. He danced for her, showing off his body, his strength, his virility, his need and desire for her. It was a celebration of masculine beauty and joyful, earthy lust. It was sensuous, fluid, and lewd, all at the same time. It was exciting to watch, in more ways than one.

And yes, Chika had been right. You could tell how much a man was enjoying himself, dancing for you, and what he was thinking of doing with you.

Debbie found herself clapping along with the women, laughing and shouting, and when Yannick singled her out, dancing for her and her alone, she surprised herself and him, and everyone. She stepped away from the women and began dancing with him, mirroring his movements, and never taking her eyes off of his face.

She danced like she had not danced since she left Dairapaska so long ago. She danced the way the women did in Dairapaska, showing their joy and love and public commitment to a man.

They spun around and around each other, never quite touching. That would come later; for now, they danced for each other and for the night to come.

Eventually, Debbie and Yannick made their way back to the empty cottage. They staggered and sang as they walked, like everyone else in the village. The apple-cider that had been passed around had added to the mood. Debbie spared a thought towards the wisdom of getting all of the little kids out of the way. They did not need to see this.

She stumbled, and Yannick helped her to her feet, then pressed her hard and suddenly against the wall of someone's cottage. He was still stripped and damp with sweat, despite the rising chill.

He kissed her hard, greedy for her and she let him have her, all of her, exploring his mouth with her own, rubbing her body against his. Someone shouted nearby, a shout of triumph and joy, women laughed, and then another hoarse cry from someone else, and Yannick pulled back enough to shake his head to clear it, the beads swinging and clattering, his long hair draped across his shoulders and hers.

"I gotta get us home, or I'll do you right here."

Debbie did not spare a thought as to what he meant and pulled his mouth back to hers. He kissed her again, and then picked her up and carried her back to the empty, waiting cottage. She floated in his arms and looked up at the ribbon of stars that seemed to cover her like a blanket.

He spared a moment to bump the door closed behind them, then carried her to his alcove, jerked the curtain all of the way open, and threw her onto the bed. He stripped off his pants and he was achingly ready. She had torn off her blouse and skirt and she spread her legs wide, ran her hands across the mounds of her breasts, and lifted her hips to him.

Debbie had never felt so wanton before and she reveled in the freedom. Yannick plunged himself into her and rode her hard, until she screamed in pleasure not caring who would hear, her cries of ecstasy joining the other sounds outside the cottage.

It was a night to remember, and there would be six more to come.

Debbie woke up in the morning, her breasts full and aching for Espe. As she stretched and stirred, enjoying the feel of her body against Yannick, he woke up ready and eager for her again.

"The baby," she gasped. "Chika will be bringing her."

"She'll be fine. Let me love you again and then we'll get the kids."

Debbie looked up at Yannick bending over her, his hair loose and brushing against her body, enjoying the sensation of the beads against her skin. His eyes were full of lust and yearning need. Espe could wait a little longer.

Six more days of dancing and celebration and eating and drinking followed. Yannick danced every night for Debbie, thrilling her with his maleness, his virility, his sheer physical beauty and strength. Unlike the first night, she did not join him in his dance. Chika had not been the only woman to tell her the morning after that this was not acceptable behavior as the turn of the season dancing was only for the men.

As with other Kenyatta customs, Debbie chose to comply and

instead she danced for Yannick privately in the cottage where no one could see. Her only regret was that she did not have the finger chimes and ankle bells she would have worn in Dairapaska. She would have to ask her mother to mail her the set she had left behind when she had been chosen for the bride trade.

The second night, they were joined by Chika and Leon in the dancing. Leon was older and grayer, but he danced with the same joyous abandon that Yannick did. As with most of the older men, he could not leap as high. Nor could the older men bend over backwards quite as far as the younger men could, letting their long hair sweep the dance floor, but they did not let that stop them from trying.

They separated afterwards and Chika and Leon did not join them in the cottage. That was theirs alone. Debbie did not ask where Chika and Leon went, but she assumed that they managed to find something to do in the privacy they found.

Not everyone was so private and Debbie saw again the forethought in exhausting all of the kids in the village during the day, and then sequestering them in the biggest barn for a party of their own, all night long. As eager as she was about coupling with Yannick, she did not believe she would like to be as public about it as some of the other villagers were.

On the last day of the equinox, the inhabitants of all four villages in Kenyatta gathered in the clearing before the Sacred Grove. A bamboo dais had been set up, with tables loaded with food along one side of the clearing. Pennants and flags snapped in the breeze and garlands of barley straw intertwined with leaves had been draped from pole to pole. There were several hundred people in all, men, women, children, and barking dogs to add to the noise and merriment.

Yannick had told Debbie what would happen. First, the people ready to swear fealty would do so. That would be followed by declarations of marriage. Everyone in Kenyatta, the living and the dead, would stand witness to what was sworn before them: the declaration of loyalty and allegiance to Kenyatta and the declaration of love and commitment to a marriage partner.

It was customary to use your own words, so Yannick had said. That way you said what you meant, and you meant what you said. Pre-set words, words that were written by someone else, did not mean much. What was valued was the sincerity of words that came from your own heart and soul.

Debbie had thought long and hard on what she was going to say, practicing when she had a moment and there was no one around to hear her stumble over what she wanted to express. She hoped she was ready.

She thought again of how she and Yannick, with Leon and Chika, had gone out the day before and walked to the Sacred Grove. With the Grove-Master and the Grove-Mistress accompanying them, they had walked around to all the trees that held the lives of Yannick's family who had passed on to the next stage of existence. Before each tree, she and Yannick declared that they would marry on the last day of the fall equinox ceremony. With the Grove-Master and the Grove-Mistress, they discussed what a marriage would entail and stories were told of the lives of the family members who had come before them and watched over them from within the quiet trees. Debbie thought it strange but also oddly calming. The trees were serene and detached from the tumultuous emotions of the living. They encouraged a longer view, of thinking towards a future far away.

They dressed in their finest garments for the parade down to the grove. The men and older boys were wearing every bead they owned and Debbie marveled anew at how proudly they lifted their heads while carrying that added weight. It still amazed her that they could dance, with hair so loaded with beads. The thought raced past of Yannick, sweaty and half-naked, dancing for her in public, and then later in private.

Espe in particular looked adorable in her kirtle embroidered with flowers and her knitted hat with the pair of pompoms looking like big fluffy ears. Debbie's mother had mailed her the bright pink yarn for the pompoms, a color that no one in Kenyatta was able to dye. Espe's pompoms caught every eye as her grandmother so far away in Dairapaska meant for them to do.

Even Spotty had a ribbon around his neck.

Leon and Chika, Yannick and Debbie, with Debbie carrying Espe, were followed by Kerill and Ghita, Niall and Carina. They were joined by Yannick's older brother Lysander, his wife Erissa, and their children and all of the family cousins from the villages of Kenyatta. Debbie and her girls had met all of them, at one time or another, but this was the first time they were together. Erissa told Debbie again how pleased she was that she had come to Kenyatta and how happy she and Lysander were that she and Yannick were marrying.

Remus Kenyatta and the senior members of the Kenyatta clan were waiting by the dais, along with the Grove-Master and the Grove-Mistress, in their long robes of undyed wool, trimmed — as was customary — with wide forest-green bands at neckline, cuffs, down the front, and at the hems. Debbie had been told that no one else in the Ennaretee wore that color.

Remus was resplendent in a full-length cloak of feathers in every shade of blue and flame orange. He raised his hands for silence and the crowd settled enough for him to be heard.

"Another successful fall migration, thanks to all of your hard work. And this year, Debbie of Dairapaska has brought us luck! There were no serious injuries or deaths this year."

He waved to Debbie, standing near the front of the crowd with Yannick. The mob of vassals turned as one to look at her and cheer, embarrassing her deeply. She had not known that Kenyatta would single her out like this.

To her surprise, Yannick swept her high into the air and sat her up on his shoulder, supporting her easily and making sure everyone in the crowd could see her. Debbie did her best to smile and wave and not fall down as the people around her cheered lustily.

When the noise subsided, Yannick let her slip down beside him, back on her own two feet. She hissed at him, "Don't you ever do that again!"

He grinned at her, unrepentant. "Everybody wants to see you, Debbie. You brought us luck. This was the easiest fall migration in years." He kissed her soundly, bringing more cheers and shouts.

It seemed to Debbie that it was extremely unlikely that her presence had made one particle of difference to the fall migration as she had not participated in any way. But good luck was good luck and it should never be taken for granted or it would disappear, and so she chose to be grateful that the migration had gone so well.

She had decided long ago that she would never tell anyone that she brought luck to Kenyatta, but she would not stop anyone from believing it either. It made her and her daughters' positions more secure with the daimyo if he believed, like everyone else, that she was lucky.

A letter from Lupita had arrived that morning, reminding her again of what the daimyo of Shelleen might do or say to Remus Kenyatta. So far, the knowledge had not slipped out that Debbie and her daughters were still alive and not piles of dry bones on the steppes, that Debbie had broken the mail blockade, and that Debbie had told Kenyatta about the poisoned village. It was a worry, never far from her mind, and she hoped it would remain just a fretful concern.

Yannick suddenly scooped her up again, startling her and breaking her train of thoughts. "We've got to go up next, Debbie. You and me are first."

She stared at him, open-mouthed. She had known that she would swear fealty to Kenyatta in front of everyone and that she and Yannick would vow their love and their life to each other in front of everyone, but the impact of doing it in front of a large, noisy crowd of well-wishers had never occurred to her.

He carried her to the dais, mounted the steps, walked across the platform and didn't set her down on her own feet until they were in front of a smiling Remus and every single other person in Kenyatta judging by the noise of the crowd when they saw her on the dais.

"Ready, Debbie?" asked Remus. He turned to face the crowd, waved his hands for silence and when he got something approximating that state, proclaimed in a voice trained to carry over a crowd.

"Debbie from Dairapaska, you will belong to Kenyatta now and forever. You will owe Kenyatta your life and your loyalty, and in return, Kenyatta will owe you your support and your care for all time. I will have as many obligations to you as you will to me. If I fail in my obligations to you, to all of my people to guide them, to guard them, to lead them to a better, brighter future, then I fail myself, I fail my family, and I fail Kenyatta, now and forever. Will you swear, Debbie of Dairapaska, your faith, loyalty, and trust to Kenyatta?"

She nodded, unable to speak.

He smiled and tossed his head, making his beads clatter in his snowy hair. He did not have as many beads as Yannick, and not nearly as many as most of the older Hands in the crowd around them.

"Then kneel before all of Kenyatta and swear your oath."

Debbie knelt down before him, with Yannick standing proudly behind her. It was a surreal experience to state in words what was assumed but never spoken in Dairapaska and Shelleen of what peasants owed to the daimyo and the demesne.

Of far more importance in both Dairapaska and Shelleen was that there was never an open statement of the duties and obligations of the daimyo to his family, to his people, and to his demesne. The duties and obligations always seemed to flow in only one direction and it was never down, only up. This way was far better.

All those thoughts ran through her mind. The crowd quieted down and as soon as she thought everyone close by could hear her, Debbie said, as loudly as she could,

"Yes, I will swear my life and my loyalty to you, Remus Kenyatta representing the demesne of Kenyatta, now and forever. I am obligated to you as you are obligated to me. I will do my best to fulfill my duties and to honor the trust and faith you have placed in me. I swear this, Debbie from Dairapaska and Shelleen, in front of everyone in Kenyatta, the living and the dead, now and forever."

"Well done, Debbie," Remus cried, and he lifted her to her feet. To the crowd he cried out, "Debbie is one of us! A free woman choosing to swear her loyalty to Kenyatta, now and forever! Make her one of your own, all of you."

The crowd roared its approval. Remus let them cheer, then raised his hands for quiet.

"Debbie has something more to do, yeah?" he asked the crowd.

"Sure does," answered Yannick, loud and clear and jubilant.

He waved up his parents, all of the kids, and all of his close family and they gathered around him and Debbie. Chika was carrying Espe, and all of the women in the family from her on down to Espe were crowned with the last flowers of autumn.

Yannick kneeled in front of Debbie, holding out a garland of flowers that Leon gave him. "I love you, my Debbie, now and forever. Will you do me the honor of joining my family and being my wife?"

She smiled and smiled and cried "Yes! I will. I love you, my Yannick, now and forever. I am honored to join you and your family to my own."

He stood up and swept her into a deep kiss before everyone and then carried her down from the dais, their family following them. They were enveloped by the crowd, all offering congratulations to both of them, on their marriage, and on Debbie swearing her loyalty to Kenyatta. She was one of them now and could not be turned out unless she betrayed the demesne.

There were a few other young men and women who were ready to swear fealty to Kenyatta. Debbie cheered for them all, and she especially cheered and applauded when Harley stepped forward.

He swore his loyalty to Kenyatta with words of his own and then was recognized as a vaquero with all of the rights and duties of the position. The pretty young lady he had been kissing in the barn several days earlier ran up onto the dais as soon as Remus finished with Harley, and she hugged and kissed him in front of the approving crowd.

Yannick grinned at them and said to Debbie, "Harley must have finally talked to her dad. We'll see him tonight, dancing for her."

Then it was their turn to go up on the dais again. After everyone had sworn their fealty, after the other marriage declarations were made, it was time to show to everyone in Kenyatta, the living and the dead, the babies who had been born since the summer solstice celebration. Their proud parents and grandparents showed off their infants, all of whom were overwhelmed into terrified wailing by the noise and commotion.

Although they were not babies, Ghita, Carina, and Espe were also presented to Kenyatta. They were new members of the demesne and so had to be recognized by everyone as belonging, now and forever. Debbie had to wonder if anyone was left in Kenyatta, including the dead in the Sacred Grove, who had not known who her daughters were before this ceremony, considering how every woman with young sons, nephews, and grandsons had made a point of seeking her out and having those boys meet her daughters. Ghita enjoyed the enthusiastic cheers, waving at everybody joyfully, Carina shrank back against Yannick and did her best to smile at the mob, and Espe burst into noisy wailing, as loud as any of the babies who had gone before her.

The rest of the day passed in a happy blur for Debbie of dancing and singing and eating and drinking and that night, as Yannick predicted, Harley danced exuberantly for his girl.

The weather turned colder, and it became more and more imperative for Debbie and Chika to prepare for winter as life settled back into its routine. The difference was that they were a family now, all of them. Ghita and Carina had shyly asked Yannick if they could call him dad like Kerill and Niall. He had joyfully accepted, as did Debbie when Kerill and Niall asked her if she could be mom.

The days passed on, one after another and with every day, the night came on sooner and lasted longer and got colder. It would snow sometimes, on and off, teasingly light, like the finest white sugar being sprinkled across the steppes. Eventually, the snow would not stop coming and with it would come the deep, bitter cold that sank into the bones of the living and the dead and never left until spring.

The household had closed up for the night, everyone tucked up in their beds. Chika had begun heating flannel wrapped bricks by the stove and they were a welcome source of warmth at night, keeping feet warmer while the beds slowly warmed up.

Now Debbie knew why every window had floor to ceiling wool drapes. They kept out the cold, as did the alcove curtains, making the winter easier to bear.

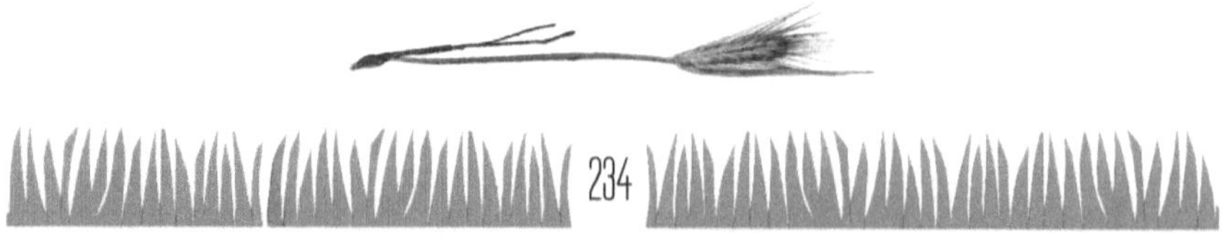

Debbie bolted awake from a sound sleep to the sound of someone pounding on the front door and Spotty barking hysterically.

Yannick was on his feet, scrambling out of the alcove and running for the door. "Stay in the hallway Debbie! Keep all the kids back."

He stopped long enough to pick up a heavy staff as he made his way through the dark room to the door. The last light from the banked fire did little to light the space. Leon was close behind him, carrying a lantern that spread a welcoming glow to help identify who was who. He also picked up a heavy staff. From the way they carried them, Debbie could see they knew how to use them.

In the dim light, she could see Spotty barking ferociously at the front door. Debbie spared a moment to be grateful to Spotty who had warned them and did not let a threat approach them unawares. She watched from the hallway with Chika, the kids clustered behind them. Everyone was awake, and she could only be grateful that Espe wasn't crying. Carina wanted to, but Ghita was holding her, trying to calm her while Debbie tried to keep Espe quiet.

Spotty had not barked like this in months and that meant a stranger, someone who might be a danger to them all.

14

A Late-Night Visitor

T HE POUNDING ON THE DOOR rose in volume. Yannick took a moment to light a second lantern to pierce the darkness. He pulled the bar from the door and swung it open to the cold, black night and whoever waited on the other side.

He stood in front of the open door, raising his staff high. Spotty raced besides him and outside, barking ferociously and tried to bite the strangers who stood there.

"What do you want!"

"You Yannick? I got someone to see you. And call off your damn dog!" came the answer.

Spotty was stymied in his search for biteable flesh by high leather boots, leather leggings, and long leather coats but he was not allowing that to stop him.

Debbie heard the stranger and cringed; desperately afraid it was someone from Shelleen, someone who had discovered somehow that Yannick had been the one who spied on the poisoned village. Instead, she heard something quite different.

"Hello, Yannick. Been a long time." It was a woman's voice, sultry and low, with a purring quality that made Debbie think of tabby cats playing with mice and enjoying every moment of the terror they caused in their unwilling toys.

Even in the poor light, Yannick looked stunned, as did Leon but neither of them lowered their staffs. If anything, they raised them higher.

Chika whispered to Debbie "All my ancestors, it's that damn bitch, Winter save us all. Keep *all* of the kids well away from her."

Debbie hustled her daughters and Niall back down the dark hallway to their alcove. She looked around for Kerill but did not see him.

"Where's Kerill?" she hissed at Chika.

"Gone for Otis," Chika whispered back. "Through the root cellar."

Debbie whispered to Ghita, "Do not let Carina, Espe, or Niall come down the hallway! Stay there in the alcove, quiet as mice. No sound."

Ghita's eyes were huge and frightened in the dim hallway, but she nodded and shoved her sisters and brother back and into the alcove, yanking the curtain shut, concealing them behind the layer of cream wool.

Debbie and Chika edged down the hallway to see what was happening. Debbie was deeply grateful that Espe wasn't crying. She could hear Ghita softly playing peek-a-boo with Espe and Carina to distract them and prayed she would continue. The sounds of peek-a-boo were not nearly as loud as crying children would have been and it would have been heard over Spotty's yapping outside.

"What the hell are you doing here, Maureen?" asked Yannick, his voice shocked and hostile.

"I brought you your son," she replied silkily. "I knew you would want him, and I have no desire for any child of *yours*. You know that after what you did."

"My son?!"

"May I come inside? It's so cold and you wouldn't want *your* son to suffer, no matter how you treated *me*."

On cue, a baby, a very young one by the sound, began to wail. It was a thin, weak sound, and it did not last.

"Who is that with you, Maureen? Tell me now."

"My escorts and bodyguards. You can't be too safe these days. They can wait outside."

"You never did think of anybody but yourself, Maureen," said Chika in a strained voice. "They're not Northern. It's freezing cold and getting colder."

"Oh Chika, how I missed your wise counsel."

"She's right and you know it," Yannick growled. "Leon, take Maureen's escorts down to the pub and get them something to eat and a round or two to keep out the cold." Yannick added hand gestures, turning his body slightly so the strangers wouldn't see.

"We don't drink on duty," answered the leather-clad stranger over Spotty's yapping. Spotty was keeping him and his partner busy, as they fended him off while trying not to break his legs with their staffs.

So they weren't here to harm them, thought Debbie, at least not right away. They were not going to cause trouble if they could avoid it.

Leon answered dryly, "Not to worry. It's just apple-cider."

"Uh-huh. And is this apple-cider made of apples?" The stranger at the door sounded politely disbelieving about what northern peasants drank in the winter to keep out the cold.

"Mostly apples. Might be some pears in there."

Leon grabbed his heavy sheepskin coat off its hook, pulled it on over his nightshirt, and yanked on a pair of boots over his night stockings and headed out the door, still carrying his staff.

He turned around in the lane, silhouetted by the light spilling from lanterns being lit in the cottages around them as their doors opened. Spotty's barking had attracted the hostile attention of the other villagers and the bodyguards, not being fools, realized that armed men were watching and gathering to see what they did.

"Are you laddies coming with me or you gonna freeze out here?" Leon called out, making sure everyone, seen and unseen, could hear him. "And it'll get you away from the dog. Bring the horses. We'll tie them up in the shelter at the pub. Get them out of the cold."

Both bodyguards looked at Spotty, leaping almost chest-high in his fervent desire to sink his fangs into soft flesh, and yapping to deafen the living and awaken the dead. They batted him away, kicking at him and missing, and he responded with renewed vigor. There was sound of barking in the distance.

"Kennel-Master will be letting out the pack very soon," Leon added.

"That okay with you, miss?" called the first escort over Spotty's barking.

"Yes, yes, yes, just get on with it and give me and my child's father some privacy. When I'm finished here, I'll come get you and we'll leave this little slice of frozen hell." The sensuality in Maureen's voice did not quite conceal her contempt for everyone around her.

Her bodyguards looked at her, then at each other, shrugged, and followed Leon down to the pub, along with a more than a few armed villagers who were not looking as hostile as they had before.

Spotty was split between following or staying. After racing back and forth yapping, he chose to bolt down the hallway to Ghita and the other kids, snarling and snapping at Maureen when he passed her. They had become his first priority, now that the major threat had left. He remained in the mouth of the hallway, growling and alert, and never took his eyes off the stranger.

Maureen strutted into the room, dropping her heavy coat onto the floor for someone else to pick up. Yannick closed the door behind her, keeping out the cold, and ignored her coat.

Debbie saw her clearly for the first time, the lantern light illuminating her face and form. As Chika had said, she was stunningly beautiful, with vivid green eyes and — extremely unusual for a Martian — gorgeous apple-red hair that set off her emerald complexion to perfection. Her hair made a fluffy cloud of curls around her face, past her shoulders, loose and flowing and unrestrained by any braid or ribbon. It was shocking to see, in more ways than one.

Not many Martians had red hair and most of those who did looked dreadful. No matter what their complexion, ranging from yellowy-green to the upper-class emerald to almost blue, red hair nearly always clashed. Nearly every woman dyed it to a more harmonious color. Only men who could not be bothered left their hair red and there weren't many of them.

No wonder Chika had said Maureen looked like a flame in the shape of a woman. Her unbound hair set the stage, her voice insinuated itself into your ears, and you could not tear your eyes away.

She was so distracting that Debbie started when Yannick spoke. His voice was very cold.

"It's been years, Maureen. That is not my son, you liar."

"Still stating the obvious, Yannick? Of course it's not."

The tiny baby she was carrying wailed again, the lost, sobbing sound of an infant who had already learned he was going to be ignored. Debbie flinched and she could feel her milk swell in her breasts. Espe had cried like this whenever Aldo was around and would not allow her to rush to her side. Whoever this baby was, Maureen did not care much for him.

Maureen sauntered to the best chair and sat as if she owned the cottage, her back ramrod straight and tossed her head, making her hair swing freely. She held the whimpering baby carelessly in her lap, paying it no attention. "Do put down that staff. I won't hurt you."

Yannick turned slightly away from Maureen's view and his hands flew. Chika answered the same way, then pushed Debbie back deeper into the shadows of the hallway.

"Still doing that silly handtalk, Yannick? It hasn't been *that* long so I haven't forgotten how to speak it. I know you remarried and that must be your blushing bride cringing in the hallway. Do sit down and stop looming over me."

Yannick did not sit down.

"Explain this baby."

Maureen curled her lip up at him. "You know that I've been traveling Mars, going wherever I felt. I took up with this man, very wealthy; you know how much I enjoy the good life. *He* was fun, my gods was he fun, until he wasn't. So I left and now here I am." She smiled up at him, fluttering her lashes seductively and running her right hand flirtatiously through her unbound hair, ignoring the baby in her lap.

Yannick looked unimpressed. "I am not this baby's father. Maureen, there is a book full of information you aren't telling. Why aren't you giving this baby to his father?"

For the first time, Maureen looked uncomfortable and she turned her face away from Yannick and studied the lantern's flame.

"Because *that man* was and is a monster. I knew it at the time, but I knew I could handle him. And I did, until I couldn't anymore and then I left. *He* is not suited to raise a child. *He* is not suited to be responsible for anything alive."

"Why me? Explain."

"I want the baby to grow up to be a Steppes Rider, like his brothers." She smiled complacently up at him, back in control, but Yannick did not smile back.

"Every last relative of yours in Lynch would be thrilled to take this baby in and make him a Steppes Rider, no questions asked. You know that. *Why me*?"

Maureen looked more than uncomfortable. She looked

afraid, hunching over, no longer the queen on her throne.

"It's *him*. The baby's father. *He's* an equator lord in his forties and he has never, ever fathered a child successfully. Not one of his partners, and there were plenty, got past a miscarriage. Most didn't even make it to late flowers. *He's* looking for me now, for the jewelry and cash I took with me, but he'd get over that, eventually.

"I did not know I was pregnant when I left, and when I discovered I was, I expected late flowers. Then I expected a miscarriage but that didn't happen either. I had to hide while pregnant, waiting for the baby to be born.

"If *that man* knew he had fathered a son, he would move the planets to get him back. If *he* ever discovers I carried *his* child to term, he'll go looking for my mother first. *He* knows about her. I can't take the baby to Lynch or to anywhere in the North except here."

Maureen looked up at Yannick. "Everybody in the North knows how I feel about you." She curled her lip up again in contempt, once more a queen contemplating a filthy serf.

"Even if it were to get out that I was pregnant, no one would ever believe that I would come to *you*. If *he* finds out, he'll race to my mother and there will be no baby, no rumor of a baby for him to trace, and my mother will be safe."

Yannick said patiently, "You never did think things through, Maureen. Lynch wouldn't let someone like that on his demesne. Your mother, your relatives and this child would be safe enough."

Maureen snarled, her face a mask of rage and she clenched her fists. Debbie watched her become a queen at bay, facing her enemies.

"The current daimyo of Lynch is a spineless bastard and he won't be up to the fight when *that man* comes calling. He's that powerful. The daimyo would lose the proxy fight over what happened next, but my mother would be the one to suffer. I won't take that risk."

Chika spoke up, her voice still oddly strained. "Much as it pains me to say this, Maureen is right. The current daimyo of Lynch is a stopgap while the branches of the Lynch family fight it out. He knows it too."

Maureen smiled coolly over at Chika. "My mother keeps me

up to date on what happens here just like she keeps you up to date. Thanks ever so for your detailed letters. They've been most entertaining, reminding me of all the reasons I left this wasteland."

She turned her attention back to Yannick, dismissing the very existence of her former mother-in-law. "Congratulations on taking up with some dirt serf. That works out very well for me. You have a temporary bed partner and a baby wouldn't be a huge surprise."

Yannick looked as angry as Debbie had ever seen. "Maureen, if you're gonna spit poison at my Debbie, you can leave now. Put the baby in the baby wheel in Purnell and be done with it. He'll disappear and some family will be forever grateful for this gift."

Maureen sat back in open surprise. Debbie, watching quietly from the hallway out of sight, could see that she had not been expecting this response from Yannick. She wondered if Maureen really had expected him to agree to whatever she wanted, especially since a child was concerned.

The baby began to wail again, and Maureen jiggled it roughly, making it cry louder, a despairing sob that died down quickly. Her face became a snarling mask of distaste.

Debbie flinched, memories cascading over her of all the times she had desperately wanted to take care of Espe and being forced to ignore her because of Aldo. She had had to listen to Espe's wails of despair, feel the pain in her engorged breasts and in her aching heart and know that it was wrong what he was making her do. She could not listen to another unwanted baby whimper in distress.

She pushed past Chika and strode into the room. She stood in front of Maureen, feeling like a peasant clod compared to the beautiful woman glaring up at her and said, "Give me the baby, he's hungry and dirty and needs to be cared for."

Maureen smirked up at her. "You must be the dirt wife. Saint Debbie, doing good for all. Take him."

Maureen lifted the baby to Debbie and she took the wailing infant and sat down with him by the masonry stove seat where it was warmer, ignoring Maureen, Chika, and most of all, Yannick.

She could not do it. She could not ignore another hungry,

neglected baby. Debbie hugged the baby, cooing to him, cuddling him, and when he seemed to calm a little, she opened her nightgown and let him suckle at her breast. He lunged for her, despite her being a stranger and not his mother, and Debbie realized how desperate and hungry he was. She glared up at Yannick, daring him to stop her.

"So you're not such a doormat after all," said Maureen. "I'm amazed. That man beat me once and I left as soon as I could yet you put up with years of abuse. Congratulations on finally growing a spine."

"Shut up, Maureen. Debbie is more of a woman than you will ever be," said Yannick. "Debbie? Do you want to keep this little one and raise him as our own? Espe's still nursing and it'll be a lot more work, most of it on you."

Debbie looked down at the baby nursing with the vigor of the starving. The baby was oblivious to everything other than filling his tummy while he had the chance. He could not have been more than eight days old. He still had that raw, unformed look and was much skinnier than he should have been. She looked back up at Yannick.

"Yes, he'll die with her and she won't care."

He pulled over a stool and sat next to her, studying another child being thrown away by Maureen. He turned back to his former wife, every line of his face and body showing his distaste for her.

"I don't know that anything you've said is true."

Maureen scowled and on her, it looked beautiful. "I wouldn't be in Kenyatta otherwise. I don't want him and I will not let *that man* have him. He's half Steppes Rider. Make him all Steppes Rider and keep my mother safe."

Debbie asked, "What is his name?"

"Vengeance," answered Maureen harshly.

They gaped at her. Debbie found her voice first. "No, absolutely not. We can name him Geance, if it's not on the lists."

"I see you got sucked into that stupid-ass superstition," said Maureen. "Well, I don't really care so do what you please."

She stood up gracefully and sauntered to the door, picking up her coat on the way when Yannick made no move to get it for her. "Time for me to go. I remember where the pub is, so you don't need to go with me. Did you know, Yannick? I stayed with you longer than any other man."

Maureen smiled winningly up at him while he watched her warily, standing between her and Debbie and the baby she had abandoned without a quiver. "I cannot believe the time I wasted on you, time I will never get back."

She opened the door and stepped out, slamming it behind her with unnecessary force, leaving the sound of the baby nursing greedily.

Debbie looked up from the baby to see Chika and Yannick watching her closely.

"I'm sorry," she apologized. "I had to. Aldo made me make Espe wait whenever he was around, and it tore me apart listening to her cry."

Yannick leaned over to kiss her gently. "I will always love you, my Debbie, now and forever. We have another son, yeah?"

Chika leaned in for a closer look at the baby. "He'll be a little darling, won't you, Geance. Debbie, that is a much better name than Vengeance. I will never understand how that woman thinks."

"Mom, write to India, let her know what happened, that Maureen came by, but don't tell her about Geance. See what she says about Maureen having an affair with some equator lord, if it's true or not."

"Do you think she lied?" asked Debbie.

"I don't know," answered Yannick heavily. "I just don't know. Maureen lies whenever it suits her but she doesn't put herself out for anyone, ever. She rode out here with a newborn and hired guards in late fall, they must have come from Purnell, and she wouldn't have inconvenienced herself like that without a damn good reason. Not her."

Chika pursed her lips, looking very unhappy. "She may not have been lying. India wrote that Maureen had a short affair that ended badly some time ago. She didn't know much about it, as Maureen wouldn't tell her the details or where she was. And you will notice that Maureen was very careful to imply to those escorts of hers that this baby was yours, not some other man's."

"Terrific." Yannick sighed deeply. "We'll have to pray that she did a good job of covering her tracks. It would be just like her to give us Geance and then let slip to the equator lord where he is."

He stopped, and then started to laugh. Debbie and Chika both looked puzzled.

"Damn, I'll owe Otis a round at the pub. He said this would happen when I met him back at the cairn after dropping Debbie and the girls off here. He'd asked me what I was going to do with you" – Yannick put an arm around her and kissed her on her forehead – "and I said I'd do nothing because Maureen would come home to me. You should have seen his face. Did not believe me about her at all, he never did. Then he got this look and told me that as sure as the sun rises in the east, if Maureen ever got wind of me moving another woman and her kids into my home, she would be back to make trouble."

He laughed some more, low and rueful.

There was a double knock at the door and Yannick was on his feet at once, staff back in his hand, and he opened it carefully. Spotty raced across the room to see Kerill had returned with Otis and he returned to his guard post at the hallway.

"I saw *her*," said Otis. "So *she* came back." He mouthed the word 'bitch' to Yannick but did not say it aloud in front of Kerill.

"Dad, are you and everybody okay?" asked Kerill. "I got Otis as quick as I could."

"We're fine, Kerill. Come meet your new baby brother. His name is Geance."

Otis and Kerill both started. It was hard to say who looked more surprised.

"So that was what that was about, then?" asked Otis, his eyebrows up into his hairline. "I saw the two bodyguards leave with Leon, and I waited with Kerill until *she* left. *She* went prancing down to the pub, flinging her hair and swishing her hips like nobody's business. Yannick, every single person in Kenyatta, dead or alive, will be talking about this by the end of the week and everyone in the nine-square will know by Winter Solstice. Bring me up to date."

"Daddy?" Ghita peeked out of the hallway. "Can we come out now?"

"Ghita, my dear little heart, get your sisters and your brother. You got a new baby brother to meet."

While the kids gathered around Debbie, along with an avidly sniffing Spotty, Yannick quickly brought Otis up to date.

He finished with "We'll tell everybody what Maureen said. This is our son. He is now anyways, mine and Debbie's. I'll give the truth to Remus. He'll have to know, in case some equator lord comes calling."

Otis looked over at Debbie, marveling. She had Geance on her other side, and Espe was demanding her share as well. The four older kids were clustered around, talking a mile a minute about what they had done while the strangers were there and how brave Spotty had been. Chika had made tea and was refereeing; making sure nobody spilled their cup onto either baby.

"You couldn't have found a better wife than her. Debbie brought you luck too."

Yannick looked deeply content, and went back to sit next to Debbie, one arm around her, all the kids making room for him. "Yes, she did."

Otis grinned suddenly. "You owe me a round."

"Sure do."

"You went from two kids and no wife to six kids and a wife in half a year's time. Amazing, yeah?"

"Yeah, sure is. Gets noisy, though. Real noisy. My dad should be back soon to tell us what he got out of the bodyguards at the pub."

"Filling them up with apple-cider, yeah?"

"Oh, yeah. They won't know what hit them." Both men grinned at each other. Chika snickered. Debbie smiled too, thinking of how deceptively good the apple-cider was. Children were never allowed to drink this kind of cider and adults had to be careful.

"I'm gonna go down to the pub," said Otis. "See how your dad's getting on, yeah?"

"Mandy gonna be okay with that?" asked Yannick.

"She sure will, cause she'll be the first to know everything that happened. I'll talk to you in the morning; compare notes with what Leon heard."

"So I get the gouge second?" asked Yannick with an upraised eyebrow.

"'fraid so since Mandy comes first. Debbie, you made the right choice. This little one should be a Steppes Rider, like his brothers will be." Otis tousled both boys' hair and headed out into the cold and the dark.

Carina yawned suddenly, followed by Espe.

"Time to get you kids back to bed," said Chika. "Your mama's gonna have her hands full with Geance tonight." She took a sleepy Espe from Debbie and led them all down the hallway, followed by Spotty, leaving the room suddenly empty and quiet.

Debbie had already discovered that Geance wanted to cling to her. It was not a surprise, she thought. Maureen had done nothing for him other than the minimum needed to keep him alive. She wondered, taking a sniff, when was the last time he had been cleaned or bathed.

Yannick was wrinkling his nose too. "I think this little one needs a quick scrub and he'll be sleeping with us. Think he'll let go and come to me?"

Geance whimpered, unhappy to let go of Debbie, but he allowed himself to be cradled in Yannick's arms, giving her a chance to stretch and look for a change of clothes in one of the cupboards.

Finally, they were tucked back into the alcove, Geance clean, dressed, fed, and showing signs of sleepiness. Yannick had lit the rushlight and they lay quietly in the dim light, letting the infant relax between them, feeling safe and cared about for the first time in his short life.

They heard the door open again and Leon stagger in, sounding somewhat worse for wear. The night sounds of Spotty racing to investigate were followed by Chika tsking and getting the cottage closed up, and her getting Leon back into their alcove and tucked in for the night.

"We'll have to see Remus tomorrow," said Yannick.

Debbie laughed softly. "I would have never guessed that I would talk to any lord so often, let alone the daimyo. He must be getting tired of us."

"It's what he signed on for, my own dear heart." He stroked her face gently, and even more gently, ran his hand over Geance's head. The baby was wearing a knitted hat that Kerill and Niall had both worn long ago, along with a soft, well-worn bunting, leaving his legs free to kick.

Yannick took a deep breath and blew it out softly. "I need

you to understand that I would never cheat on you and if I was crazy enough to do something like that, it sure wouldn't be with Maureen."

"She's so beautiful," said Debbie softly. "I've never seen anyone so beautiful." There was no comparison between Maureen's looks and Debbie's and she knew it.

Yannick snorted. "Beautiful on the outside and ugly as sin on the inside. But you don't see the inside, not at first. I knew she was trouble when I saw her the first time, sashaying around the village square like she owned the place, and I was fool enough to say so in front of her. Like waving a flag in front of a bull.

"I don't know what happened, Debbie. I wanted nothing to do with her, I had Tamar, and it's like she cast a spell on me. I couldn't do enough for that woman; I would have done anything for that woman. I was getting ready to build that woman a house of her own, something that would have put my family in debt to the daimyo for two generations, and still whatever I did, it wasn't enough. It was almost a relief when Maureen left me, except she stole my boys. I felt like I could think again."

He sank back into the bed, his eyes closed, his face full of the pain of remembering.

"I thought I would die when she stole my boys from me. When she gave them back, I was so grateful. And then she left, and I was even more grateful. I was afraid I'd have to take *her* back, to get my sons back."

"Chika said you'd always tell people Maureen would come home," said Debbie, not sure if that was the right thing to say, but she needed to know why he had said it.

Yannick chuckled without any humor. "I did that for two reasons. It kept people away, I didn't think I could ever trust a woman again after what Maureen did to me and, well—" he looked away, shamefaced.

"I was using it like a spell. Maureen never would do what you wanted her to and if I said she'd come home to me, she wouldn't. Foolish, I know. Magic's not real." He sighed deeply.

"There's some who think Maureen is a witch and I don't know that I could disagree. I look back at my life with her and I can't understand what happened and why I did what I did. I wasn't sane."

He kissed Debbie on her forehead, her cheeks, and then her soft mouth, aching with tenderness, then reached up to snuff out the rushlight, leaving them in the velvety darkness.

"I know it will be hard, having another little one so close in age to Espe. But I'm glad," he kissed Debbie gently again, "you chose to help him. You are beautiful, my Debbie, on the out-side and the inside. Geance's our son now and he always will be, now and forever."

Breakfast was very late. As soon as there was some quiet, Leon told the other adults what had happened at the pub.

"Those bodyguards were from Purnell and they did *not* want to be here, doing this job. Andrew and Dave were their names. The owner of the firm they work for fell under Maureen's spell. Andrew — that's the heavy-set one with the scarred face — said he kept expecting the owner to change his mind over coming uninvited onto a demesne. Apparently, that Maureen gave the owner a pile of cash and jewelry, plus a sworn promise that they'd not be bothered or enslaved by Kenyatta if they were in and out quick."

Chika rolled her eyes. "The lies they tell in free-cities."

"The real reason the owner took the job was the baby. Maureen gave him this story about Yannick taking a mistress."

Yannick scoffed and Chika laughed. Debbie was shocked at the very idea.

"And he expected Maureen to take second place to the new woman, share the same cottage and everything. So she up and left, but she didn't know she was pregnant. When the baby was born, she took one look at him and swore she'd never raise any child looking like his damned father. She wanted the baby to go to his father and the slutty mistress."

Debbie sat there open-mouthed, while Chika laughed again.

"So the owner took the job. Andrew said the owner did check with the hospital and the midwife and the Purnell police and they all agreed that Maureen had had the baby, not stolen it from some other poor woman. She gave him more money, so's he didn't make arrangements in advance with Kenyatta, to be met at the border. Said she didn't want the slutty mistress

...," Leon winked at Debbie.

Debbie was laughing by this time. She would have never in her life dreamed that she would be someone's idea of a slutty mistress.

"... to have a chance of saying no to the baby. Andrew and Dave both thought getting a child returned to his father was the reason the owner finally took the job, but the money sure didn't hurt. They rode out for Kenyatta and Maureen was, in Andrew's words, 'a terrible mother, a royal pain in the ass, and he could understand why Yannick took a mistress cause he would have too if it meant getting rid of Maureen.'"

Everybody laughed.

"They enjoyed the cider."

Yannick laughed.

"And they were happy to talk and eat away from the cold. The more cider they drank, the more they talked. Maureen showed up, and she was fit to be tied, seeing them in the pub, eating and drinking with the rest of us. Got half the village in there, I'd guess, listening to them talk. She would have ridden out right then and there."

"It's pitch dark and freezing and they didn't know the road," said Yannick, shaking his head. "She just doesn't think."

"Andrew knew that and he put his foot down. Said they'd been given assurances they could stay the night, no trouble from Kenyatta if they did so, and they'd leave first thing in the morning. Maureen looked around the pub and everyone there knew who she was and she wasn't getting any support from anyone."

"Not a surprise," said Chika. "There aren't many in the village who think kindly of her. Not after what she's done."

"Otis came in and introduced himself and did they give him an earful about how Maureen had treated that baby and them! Andrew and Dave agreed that if you'd refused the baby, they'd have taken him to the baby wheel in Purnell or home to their own wives rather than let Maureen keep him one *minute* longer than necessary. Andrew was ready to beg Kenyatta for a wet nurse, he's got kids of his own and he could not stand seeing Maureen do the minimum needed to keep Geance alive. Keep in mind that the both of them knew they were trespassing and could be legally taken and held by Kenyatta and they would still have asked for help."

"My goodness," said Chika. "Maureen must have been awful if two free-city men would have gone to the daimyo without permission. All those free-city folks are convinced that they'll be hung for trespassing if they put so much as a toe outside a government corridor."

"Like I said, my own dearest heart," Leon held onto Chika's hand, "Andrew and Dave were ready to speak to Remus if it meant keeping the baby from Maureen. They should have left at dawn."

Yannick snorted. "With all that cider in them?"

Leon grinned. "Maureen was gonna motivate them, I'm sure. When I left, she was asking Sal for buckets of water so's she could wake them up at dawn. She doesn't want to stay in Kenyatta one minute longer than she has too. She's foresworn and she knows it."

Chika sniffed with disdain. "Like that ever bothered her. She swishes around a demesne and expects every man to fall under her spell."

Leon smirked. "It's not working so good anymore. She's not as young as she used to be, and word has gotten around. I don't believe Maureen could go anywhere in the North now, other than back to Lynch. She'd be turned away and she knows it, yeah?"

"Is she a wolf's-head?" Debbie asked.

"She should be," answered Yannick, looking offended. Leon had the same expression on his face. "If any man had done what she'd done, he'd have been hunted down everywhere in the North. She lies, she stole my kids, she steals, and she swears allegiance and never means it. She swore allegiance to Kenyatta and then walked off without a backward glance."

"I still don't know," added Chika, looking equally disapproving, "why Satran let her stay so long. I suppose she charmed him like a snake and he believed her lies. Winter knows that vaquero did."

"Met him a while back," said Yannick leaning back in his chair. He looked amused at the surprise on Chika's and Leon's faces. "He had nothing good to say about Maureen and apologized handsomely for believing her. He said Satran knew she was fertile and they hoped she would stay and have more kids for the demesne."

"Like me," said Debbie softly. It was what Yannick had told her when he had met her, all those months ago near the stone tower.

"You brought us luck, my own dear heart, my Debbie, and don't forget that. And you have never once lied to anyone. Don't forget that either." Yannick's voice was gentle and he leaned over to brush his lips on her hair.

"I'm sure you've noticed," said Leon, "that we don't have enough women to go around. Not every man can marry. That means we tend to cut someone like Maureen more slack than we should. She's a Northern woman, she knows how it stands with us, and she, well, she takes every advantage she can."

Chika sighed gustily. "I have to give the devil her due. She could have left little Geance in the baby wheel in Purnell and no one would have ever known. She's Northern enough to want him to be a Steppes Rider."

"And ornery enough to choose me and Kenyatta, instead of any of the other Northern demesnes. She could have still done that and walked away," said Yannick. "I will never understand why that woman thinks the way she does."

Another Interview With Remus

ATER THAT DAY, YANNICK went along with Debbie, Chika, Espe and Geance to the Names-Mistress. Moswen was waiting for them in her snug cottage and she had already heard much of the gossip.

"I insist you tell me everything," said Moswen as her granddaughter poured the tea and her daughter brought forth the rolls of names, laying them carefully out on the table dedicated for their use.

"I had an affair with Maureen and this is our baby," answered Yannick without a flicker of emotion on his face or in his voice.

Moswen set down her kuksa, stained black from decades of use, and laughed until the tears came. Her daughter and granddaughter laughed, too.

Yannick sat stone-faced with Espe in his lap as his wife and mother joined in.

When she had recovered, Moswen said, "Try again. The truth this time. I'm very discreet so you need not fear that I will ever tell."

Chika was looking very pleased. "I told you she wouldn't believe Maureen's lies for one minute."

"We'll have to be honest with a few people, but we do not want this story to spread," said Yannick and Debbie nodded vigorously. "We need to keep this little one safe."

"I see. Maureen angered the wrong person?"

"Something like that," replied Yannick, and he plunged into the story.

When he was finished, Moswen said, "Oh, my. I think you

can be sure that Maureen won't let slip she had a baby to this equator lord, whoever he is."

"Why is that?" asked Debbie. She had become very curious about Maureen. She was so unlike anybody Debbie had known, and she could not figure out how or why Maureen thought and acted as she did. No one's opinion mattered to *her*. She acted as though other people's needs did not exist. It was very strange.

"Maureen may not care what happens to other people but she cares what happens to her," answered Moswen. "She'll realize that if this man discovers she had a child by him, not only will he want the baby back, he'll want her back."

"He'd be crazy to do that," said Yannick flatly.

"No, he wouldn't. He'd have a woman who was fertile with him," Moswen said.

"If she could have one baby by him, she could bear more. He would not have to be nice about it either. Maureen is still relatively young. As long as she couldn't escape, he'd have the promise of more children and for years to come. A lord of the equator expects to get his own way, always. This one will not be different."

Debbie felt ill. That would be on par with the bride trade she and the other young women of Dairapaska and Shelleen had endured, perhaps worse. They had been wives, even if not by choice, and they had the freedom of the village they lived in. If he found her, this man would never allow Maureen even to leave his house. For the first time, she felt a twitch of sympathy for Maureen.

"I hadn't thought of that and I should have," said Chika slowly, catching the flash of pain on Debbie's face. She patted Debbie's hand reassuringly. "I'll write India and tell her to tell Maureen this. That will guarantee that Maureen won't ever tell anyone about the baby."

"A good idea," said Yannick. "Do it right away."

"Now then, let us move on to more pleasant matters," said Moswen. "Did Maureen give this little one a name? He looks like he will have lovely eyes." She chucked the baby under his chin and he stared at her with wonder, cuddled safe in Debbie's arms.

Debbie grimaced. "She did. Vengeance."

Moswen sat back appalled, as did her daughter and granddaughter. "Moons and stars in the Winter. She was furiously angry at that man. I could understand naming a boy Courage or a girl Truth, but Vengeance?"

Yannick grinned. "Debbie already settled on Geance and we like that fine."

Moswen closed her eyes and drummed her fingers on the table while everyone around her sat quietly, sipping on their tea. Yannick let Espe sip tea from his kuksa, blowing it cool and holding the cup for her, and Debbie was deeply grateful for how fortunate she had been. Aldo had never shared his cup like that with Ghita or Carina when they were little, although other family members regularly had.

Moswen came out of her trance. "I think Geance has never been used, not here in Kenyatta and possibly not in the nine-square. It has a new sound, one I am not familiar with. My daughter and I will confirm this when we go through the name rolls. When I know for sure, I will tell you."

"Thank you, Moswen," said Debbie. She had chosen a name for a second child and it had been accepted. A warm glow of contentment spread through her and not just from the hot mint tea.

On the way back to the cottage, Otis spotted them and came running up the lane.

"They're gone, a few hours back."

"When did they leave?" asked Yannick, lifting Espe up so she could see all around her. She made a grab for Otis's beard and he stepped safely out of range, and then waved his braid at her, making her giggle.

Otis laughed roughly. "Not at dawn, that's for sure. Sal at the pub told me Maureen was tearing mad. She was ready to pour buckets of icy water on Andrew and Dave to get them going and Sal wouldn't let her. Said they'd have more trouble moving, if they were frozen to start with."

Yannick shook his head. "Maureen never did think."

Otis went on, "Sal got them up, fed them a hot breakfast and plenty of willow bark tea to wash it down with for the headaches, and made sure their horses were ready to go."

"Very nice of her."

"Sal wasn't about to accommodate that Maureen, and it paid off handsomely for her. Andrew asked for receipts for everything, including all the cider they drank last night and then he paid the tab in hard coin."

Yannick, Chika, and Debbie stopped short at that.

"My dad said he paid," said Yannick.

"True," said Chika. "And we'd be owing Sal for quite a while, paying it back. What happened?"

Otis beamed. "Apparently, professional escorts and body-guards like these two get reimbursed for what they spend. That's what they told Sal. They'd have taken up Leon on his offer and not charged their company, except they were both so mad at Maureen and their boss. Everybody here treated them decent, made sure they didn't have trouble with Kenyatta, and they appreciated it. So Sal got hard coin and she is very happy."

"And we don't owe Sal?" asked Chika suspiciously.

"No, not a penny," answered Otis. "Well, except Leon's tab, that you still owe. She made Maureen pay her own way too and in advance."

"I can live with that," said Yannick, smiling broadly. "We all can."

Once home, a steady stream of visitors came by to the cottage, all eager to see the new baby. Debbie showed off Geance and to everyone she said, "He's our baby, mine and Yannick's."

She understood perfectly well that everybody knew the baby had arrived under unusual circumstances but she and Yannick presented a united front and that was what mattered.

As Moswen had said earlier that morning, "a baby's parents are the people who raise him."

Everyone who came by agreed with that sentiment. There would be gossip and plenty of it, but in the end, Geance was their son, now and forever.

Everyone was told that the baby needed to be kept safe from Maureen, but the reason was not spelled out.

Chika quietly told Debbie "the neighbors think the worst of Maureen as it is, and we'll take advantage of that fact. No need to bring in some equator lord and confuse the issue. People will understand that Maureen wants the baby to be a Steppes Rider like his brothers. Why would you want a boy to be anything else?"

Debbie thought of what the farmers of Dairapaska and Shelleen would have to say to that, smiled, and agreed with Chika. She was a Northerner now, sworn to Kenyatta, and so her sons would be Steppes Riders, all of them.

Debbie silently worried over when the summons would arrive from the manor house, although the rest of the family seemed unconcerned. Surely by now the daimyo would have heard something and as it turned out, indeed he had.

Spotty sprang into action when a page banged at the door, interrupting them at dinner.

Leon dragged a yapping Spotty away from the page, another new fosterling from Satran, to the lad's open relief. The page must have heard that part of the story and expected Spotty to savage him, tearing out his throat.

"Kenyatta wants Yannick and Debbie up to the manor house and he wants them quick. He is tearing mad," sputtered the page, still out of breath from the run down the hill and dodging Spotty at the door.

Yannick sighed. "I was wondering when the gossip would reach the manor house."

"Shouldn't we have said something right away?" asked Debbie.

"I would have, if there'd been a problem," he answered. "Those bodyguards of Maureen didn't cause harm to us, they didn't want to be here in the first place, and they left as soon as they could. Telling Remus last night would have brought harm to them, most likely."

He kissed Debbie, then Geance. "I'd rather apologize later than ask permission to do what I know is right. It works out better."

Yannick looked over at Leon and their hands flew for a moment and Debbie watched, trying to follow what they said. She only caught a few signs, not enough to understand what they had said. Brother. Cousin. Uncle. Or so she thought.

"We're gonna bring everybody," announced Yannick. To the page he said, "Run on back to Remus and tell him we're on the way."

"Everybody?" Debbie squeaked.

"Yup. Show of force, yeah?" he answered. Leon had already pulled on his sheepskin coat and run out the door, as did Kerill in the other direction.

It took some time to round everybody else up, get dressed for the weather, leave Spotty shut up in the cottage to his and the tabby cats intense, vocal disapproval, and walk up the hill to the waiting manor house.

They were met in the courtyard by Leon, Kerill, and Yannick's brother Lysander, sister-in-law Erissa, and their kids as well, plus quite a few of the cousins and other relatives.

"As many as we could round up on short notice, yeah?" said Leon with a wink.

It took more time to show off Geance again to all of his new relatives from the safety of Debbie's arms. She had already discovered he fussed less if he was carried, by her, continuously. Debbie took a moment to be grateful that Chika was carrying Espe. It would have been much harder to carry both babies, especially as Espe was getting to be a wiggly toddler.

Yannick led the way to the front door, and down the now-familiar hallway to Remus' office.

He knocked for admittance and led the way again, and the group filled the room in behind him.

Remus sat scowling behind his desk and watched a small army of his vassals come in, of every age, and said testily, "Did you have to bring everybody you are related to?"

"No sir, I did not," replied Yannick. "Didn't have enough time to do that."

"And why was I not told, at once, that free-city trash had come onto my land last night?"

"Well, sir, I did not believe they were a danger to the demesne. They brought us our new son as was right and fitting, and they left the next morning, without causing anyone trouble."

"Your new son. I was told that Maureen of Lynch set foot on my demesne, that forsworn wolf's-head, and you let this happen?"

"I did not know it was going to happen until it happened and then I dealt with her. She gave us our son, she spent the night in the pub with her escorts and they left first thing in the morning. Those two bodyguards from Purnell paid Sal in hard coin for their tab, too."

"I heard about the coin. I did not hear they left at first light. I was told that it took some time to get those two moving and off of my land with that woman."

"Well sir," Yannick conceded, "they didn't leave as early as they should have, I'll grant you that, but they had drunk plenty of cider the night before so I believe they should be forgiven."

Remus turned to Leon. "You, one of my oldest and most reliable Hands, took those two Purnell men to the pub and got them drunk?"

"Just cider, sir, you know that. It's made of apples! That makes it good for you," Leon said, mustering all of his considerable charm. "I do not feel that I should be held accountable for the weak constitutions of free-city men who are unable to hold their cider as a man should."

"I see. Furthermore, I was told they were given assurances that Kenyatta would allow them to leave, without complaint, cost, or discipline and by one of my own Hands! *You*, in point of fact."

"I did indeed do that, sir," answered Leon easily. "They brought me my newest grandson and I felt that I owed them a debt. Why, they could have dropped little Geance off in the baby wheel in Purnell and we would have lost a future Steppes Rider, a lad who will be a loyal Hand of Kenyatta just like his brothers, his daddy, his uncles, his cousins, and his grandfathers going back to the founding of Kenyatta."

Debbie could feel bubbles of hysterical giggles wanting to push their way to the surface and she urgently tamped them back down. She wondered how the other adults were keeping such calm, easy-going expressions as they faced down the daimyo of Kenyatta. She also wondered how long it would be before the first baby started to cry or one of the intently listening kids made some noise.

"Did Maureen steal this child to cause trouble?"

"No sir, she did not," answered Yannick. "The Purnell men brought her here only because she had the baby in Purnell as attested to by the midwife, the hospital, and the police, and she wanted to return him to his father as is right and fitting."

"*You* are this child's father?" Debbie had never seen anyone with eyebrows raised as high as Remus' were.

"I am now sir. A child belongs to those who raise him and I intend to raise little Geance to be a Steppes Rider and a Hand of Kenyatta, like his brothers, his cousins, his daddy, his uncles, and his grandfathers going back to the founding of Kenyatta."

"And you, Debbie. You are this child's mother now? You are accepting this child from *that woman*?"

Debbie felt pinned to the carpet by his glare, but she said, "Yes sir, I am. Geance needs me. He was hungry, dirty, skinny, and was developing a rash. That woman barely kept him alive, and she would have let him die. I couldn't let that happen."

"Who is the father of this child?"

"I am, sir."

Remus tapped his fingers impatiently on the desk as he glared at Yannick. "You have been nowhere near *that woman* for years. Everyone in the nine-square knows this. Who is this child's father if it is so right and fitting that he be given to his father to raise?"

"Well, sir, that's quite a story," Yannick said.

"I'm sure it is. Get started on the telling of it."

Yannick looked around the room confidently, meeting the eyes of the Kenyatta family members in attendance. "It would be best, sir, if I did the telling of this story with the understanding that it does not leave this room."

"It seems to me," said Remus, "that you have far more gossiping family members in this room to worry about than I do."

His second, Preston, and two other senior family members had been quietly sitting at the side of the room, witnessing the meeting. There was a much younger man as well. Debbie thought she recognized them from when she had come to confess about her letter writing, but she could not be sure.

"That is true sir."

"Then get on with it."

Yannick plunged into the story and when he got to the part about the equator lord, Remus sat back, suddenly intent. The other Kenyatta lords also sat up, listening closely.

When he finished, Remus asked, "Chika, you witnessed everything Maureen said. Was she truthful?"

"Yes, sir, I believe she was. India of Lynch writes to me regularly of what Maureen does and she said Maureen had an affair that she would not discuss and that it took place near to the equator. Maureen was very careful in what she said in front of the Purnell men and she would not have put herself to any trouble if she didn't think she had to, for her own safety."

"Why Yannick? Why Kenyatta? Maureen made her feelings very clear on *that* subject." Remus's face was twisted with distaste.

Chika frowned at the roses in the carpet before answering. "I believe it was to cause as much trouble as she could, for people she could trouble. Whatever Yannick chose would bring problems to him and to the family and at the same time she would deny the equator lord his son. She could have given the baby away anywhere, no questions would have been asked and we would have known nothing, the equator lord would have known nothing, and little Geance would have been safely anonymous. She didn't do that."

Yannick added, "She wanted to name him Vengeance."

Remus looked appalled, as did the other Kenyatta family members.

"That could have been aimed at me, as well as at the equator lord," Yannick said. "If I didn't take the child, I would forever know what I did was wrong, wondering what happened to little Geance and if I did take the child, it could have caused problems for me and Debbie, now and down the road."

He tightened his arm around Debbie and said, "But Maureen doesn't know my Debbie. She has a big heart and she knew that Maureen lied."

Remus considered this. "And down the road? If this equator lord were to discover that Maureen bore his son and threw him away?"

"We will ford that stream when we come to it, sir. My family will never say anything as to where Geance came from. He was a gift given to us by Winter and our ancestors and no one needs to know otherwise."

"Debbie, let me see this baby," Remus commanded.

Debbie slowly walked to the desk, carrying Geance. He was awake and looking around and she knew that as long as she held him, he would probably not fuss too much.

Remus and the other Kenyatta lords looked him over closely, especially his deep-green eyes, rimmed in a lighter green, and when they were finished, he dismissed Debbie and she went to stand next to Yannick, pushing up against him for comfort. He put an arm around her and Geance and steadily watched Remus. He and the other Kenyatta lords were speaking together, in tones low enough so that Debbie could not hear what they said.

"I don't know," said Remus finally. "I'm not sure who this equator lord could be as we rarely have doings with any of them. Geance's eyes are unusual, but that means nothing. Many people have unusual eyes."

He tilted back his head to study the ceiling. "Maureen and her escorts are long gone, yeah?"

"Yes sir, they are," answered Yannick. "They'll most likely arrive in Purnell tomorrow at mid-afternoon."

"Leon, you swore to them that Kenyatta would cause them no harm?"

"Yes, sir, I did."

"Did you say anything about the firm that employed them?"

Leon looked startled, but answered, "No sir, I did not."

Remus said, "I cannot allow any security firm in Purnell to think they can ride onto my demesne as they please. I will not say anything about those two men, Andrew and Dave. They did as they were ordered to, as loyal employees, and they spent as little time as they could on my land and caused no harm to anyone.

"The company's owner, however, needs to know that I will take action against him. Moreover, the Purnell mayor and the free-city council need to understand that this is unacceptable behavior on the part of any company in Purnell."

Debbie stiffened against Yannick. She bit her lip and made herself say, "Sir, may I ask that you please not do this?"

Remus gave her a searching look and said, "And why is that?"

"That Maureen may not have done a good job of hiding what she did," Debbie answered, keeping her eyes firmly on the roses in the carpet and avoiding Remus's sharp eyes.

"If that lord finds out, he will cause trouble for you, more trouble than a security firm in Purnell would, more trouble than Dairapaska could or maybe even Shelleen. If you complain to the firm, they may investigate Maureen and discover why you were angry about a baby being returned to Kenyatta. And if that Maureen's story is true, then little Geance isn't closely related to anyone in Kenyatta other than Kerill and Niall. He'll be fertile, whoever he chooses to marry."

Preston leaned over and whispered something to Remus. Remus said, "That may be true or it may not. We won't know for decades. And yes, an equator lord could cause more trouble by far for us than Dairapaska ever could, or Shelleen. This matter is finished, for now. You may go, all of you."

"Thank you, sir, for hearing us out," said Yannick and he bowed his head to Remus, as did all of the members of the family except for the babies. He led them out of the office, down the thickly carpeted hallways, past the colorful paintings and tapestries, and outside the manor house. No one said anything until they were well away from the building and could not be overheard.

Leon broke the silence first: "I think that went well."

"As well as you could have hoped for," agreed Yannick with a smile.

"But, but, but," sputtered Debbie, "he didn't agree to anything! Remus could still ask us to leave, he could have us beaten or doubled our obligations."

Yannick put his arms around Debbie and Geance. "My own dearest heart, Kenyatta isn't one of those dirt demesnes. Remus expects us to be honest and straightforward in all our dealings with him and we were. Remus expects us to look out for the best interests of the demesne and we did. We did not lie, we explained ourselves, and we showed, all of us, what was in the best interests of the demesne."

"Yannick's correct, Debbie," added Chika. "And you did well, too. You reminded Remus that he has trouble ahead of him with Dairapaska and Shelleen and the last thing he needs is another demesne adding to his troubles."

"Remus may be spitting mad, but he's boxed in," said Yannick. "If Maureen showed up tomorrow, that would be a problem, *for her*. Not us."

"I believe Remus will let this slide," added Leon. "Those two from Purnell caused us no harm, they paid their bills, and they are now obligated to Kenyatta. They know they were treated fairly and they will tell people that in Purnell, which benefits us, and Remus knows that, too."

"Remus was as angry as I have ever seen him," said Yannick.

"But we did not lie to him, ever. He already knew what had happened, I figured he would, he just didn't have all the particulars. Now he does. He's one of the better daimyos in the North and I am not saying that because I'm sworn to Kenyatta. Remus has always kept his word to us and I cannot say that about some of the others."

"Don't you be worrying about this, Debbie," said Leon. "Remus has a very good idea of how valuable you are to the demesne. You've brought us luck and fertility and information, all very valuable things, and Remus knows it."

"But you said he's so angry! What will he do?"

Leon, Yannick, and the other relatives considered this, their hands flying. Debbie thought again how annoying it was to be left out of a conversation. She had been taking lessons from Chika but she couldn't follow this conversation at all.

"I believe," Yannick said finally, "that Remus will work out that anger by doing some thorough inspections over the next few weeks. We'll pass the word, make sure everything is right and tight before he gets there to check."

Leon said, "I know Remus wasn't jumping up and down, screaming and throwing things, but successful daimyos don't get to be daimyos by showing off. They use their anger as a tool to get things done. We'll just help him along."

Debbie had to be content with that, but it was so different from what she had grown up with. Everyone was so casual about it.

She spoke about it again later with Chika.

"I just can't believe how relaxed everyone is about speaking to the family! To the daimyo! No one in Shelleen or Dairapaska would ever dare speak to the daimyo or to the family other than to say 'yes, sir'."

"Debbie," Chika replied, "I think this difference is because Remus and the rest of the Kenyatta family spend their time out on the steppes like the vassals do. All Northern lords spend plenty of time in the saddle, and they see how competent the Hands are. The Hands are expected to do what's right, to think on their own and, well, that bleeds over into everyday life."

Debbie thought about Chika's statement for the rest of the day as she moved through the endless work, made more difficult since she could never put Geance down, which made Espe, in turn, more demanding. Shelleen and Dairapaska before that were primarily farming demesnes. Every day was much like the one before it, changing slowly and gradually with the seasons. The daimyo and his family did not trouble themselves with the peasants and certainly did not work in the fields with them, shear the sheep, butcher the pigs, or bring in the hay.

She had not known that the younger men in the Kenyatta family had ridden out for the fall migration until Chika told her. They slept on the ground and herded the livestock along with everyone else. In fact, Chika had said, they had less status out on the steppes as they weren't as skilled and everyone knew it. They did what they were told, so as to not endanger the people around them.

And when the family members rode out, they saw, first-hand, how skilled and resourceful their vassals were. That changed their thinking, in a manner that the farming lords did not have available to them.

Debbie let herself be content with this explanation, but it was still very different and very strange.

16

Troubles In Dairapaska and Shelleen

G EANCE BEGAN TO CAUTIOUSLY, warily, settle in, but he did not ever want to be out of her arms. Debbie was not surprised, as Espe had not wanted to be set aside when she had her mother's attention either.

Debbie was deeply grateful that she had been able to rescue Geance, giving her a son without the bother of a pregnancy and, she could hardly believe she had the thought, grateful that she understood why he behaved as he did. He had been neglected and abandoned, and it reminded her of the early days with Espe back in the poisoned village. Aldo had made her abandon Espe, leaving her baby to sob in despair as she waited for her turn for attention, attention that was often a long time in coming.

Geance slowly began to recover, and she never left him alone. He was always being cuddled by someone, and he grew and thrived. Debbie was even more grateful that Yannick did not expect her to put Geance in a corner to sob, unattended and ignored. He tolerated Geance needing her with good humor, saying that babies grew up fast, and they should enjoy this precious time.

She was also deeply grateful to Chika. Chika made it possible to care for two nursing babies, plus the other kids and she was equally good-humored most of the time. And when Geance and Espe were napping at the same time, a rare occurrence, Chika made it possible for Debbie to have private time with Yannick. They were both intensely grateful for that thoughtfulness.

The weather turned colder and colder and the days grew

shorter and shorter, as the year ground its slow way toward the Winter Solstice. This would be another big festival as it was in Dairapaska and Shelleen. Winter Solstice marked the beginning of winter and the promise of spring, so very far away. The days would gradually begin to get longer, the nights shorter, a minute here and there, even though the weather would get much, much worse.

Despite being not that much further north than Shelleen, it was much colder and Debbie enjoyed Yannick's warmth every night, keeping her and Geance cozy. When she took the feather beds outside to shake back into fluffiness and then laid them back on the beds, she thought of the geese crying in the spring, made her apologies to them, and planned which ones she would pluck first for their down.

Despite the wool stockings and nightcaps, the heated bricks, the wool curtains, and no one sleeping alone in one of the snug alcoves, the nights were freezing and every night they got colder. It was cold enough that, to her amusement, she caught Spotty sleeping in a heap with the tabby cats in front of the fire, something that none of them had been seen to do before. The cold brought them together, forcing a truce that might last until spring.

Letters continued to arrive from Dairapaska and Shelleen on an almost daily basis and she continued to pass along stories of what the families were doing to their lost relatives so far away.

Her mother and Lupita both pointed out how much the residents of Shelleen and Dairapaska were getting to know about each other's demesnes. This would have never happened without Debbie breaking the mail blockade. It gave her pleasure to know that, in her own small way, she was helping the two groups understand each other better.

Both sets of brides and their families, the new and the old, were getting along better. They still could not write to each other directly, but there was hope now that if one thing had changed, other things could change as well.

Debbie read each letter with pleasure and passed along the contents. She kept each letter carefully stored in a high cabinet to keep them safe, and she would refer to them when a question came as sometimes she already had the answer and did not have to wait for a response. With each letter, she also learned so much more about all of the families, information about their lives that she would have never known.

Debbie felt that she, too, was growing closer to all of the brides and their families despite being so far away, even the ones from Shelleen. In her misery, she had had little to do with anyone outside the Acconcio family and the other Dairapaska brides. Despite living for ten years there, she had still been a stranger in Shelleen. That was no longer true.

Then the letters from Dairapaska stopped.

Debbie wrote several more times to her mother, begging to know what had happened, but no answer came. She asked the Post-Mistress if she knew of any news from Dairapaska but Dairapaska was so far away. It was a minor agricultural demesne far off in the west and the wider world did not trouble itself with its affairs. The Post-Mistress had heard nothing.

She wrote to Lupita, asking if she had heard anything at all but Lupita had not.

At last, Debbie steeled herself and walked to the side door of the manor house, following the path that she knew very well now. She asked for Preston, as she had so many other times and he expected that she had some information about the poisoned village as she only spoke to him when she did. But this time, she did not.

Debbie asked Preston if he had heard anything of Dairapaska but he did not know either. No word had come to Kenyatta from the daimyo of Dairapaska nor had the doings and affairs of Dairapaska been nosed out into the wider world.

Preston said, "A demesne can be a private as it wants to be. No demesne is required by the charter to spread its private business to the newspapers and magazines of the free-cities. Nor do they have to stay connected to the Sky-net terminals. If I hear something, I will tell you."

Debbie spoke to Yannick and he, at least, was able to give her practical advice.

"Stop writing, Debbie," he said. "There's problems going on or your mother would have written to you and if not her, then some other relative would have stepped into her place. That tells me they can't send a letter to you. Don't send another letter to Dairapaska because it may be some harm may come to your mother if you do."

That was cold comfort indeed, but Debbie could see the wisdom in Yannick's advice. She did not want to draw unwanted attention to her mother. Instead, Debbie waited to see if word would come from Dairapaska.

She wrote to Lupita of her decision and her regrets that she could not help the families any more with news of Dairapaska, as no news was forthcoming. Lupita, to her surprise, agreed with Yannick.

Lupita wrote that the Shelleen Post-Master had noticed that she had an active correspondence with Kenyatta, a ranching demesne and not an agricultural one as would be normally expected. She had not told Debbie of this before, as she had not wanted to worry her.

The Post-Master thought her correspondence very odd, since he knew that she had never done this in the past and indeed, no one in Shelleen had relatives in Kenyatta despite it being just across the government corridor. She had told him that she had struck up the acquaintance via an advertisement for a pen-pal and that her pen-pal in Kenyatta liked writing letters as much as she did and what business was it of his anyways?

Lupita bluntly told him he was not supposed to get in the way of the mail, even though he was doing just that, keeping her from writing to her daughter Pia in Dairapaska. How could he consider himself a Post-Master when he censored the mail? The Post-Master, to her intense relief, looked ashamed of himself and backed down.

Lupita wrote she would explain to the families that something was wrong in Dairapaska and if news came, she would share it. They would have to be content with this sop, as what choice did they have?

Perhaps, wrote Lupita, someone noticed that your mother was busy sending and receiving many letters from Kenyatta and stopped her. It was wrong and everyone knew it, but that was the way it was. Facts had to be faced, head on. Pretending differently did not make them go away.

Debbie read Lupita's letter and was forced to agree. They were both right, Yannick and Lupita, and she would have to wait and see what happened in Dairapaska.

Nonetheless, every day she walked up the hill and checked

with the Post-Mistress, carrying Geance bundled up against the increasing cold in soft wool and softer sheepskin, and every day, the answer was the same. She walked back down the hill, empty-handed and disheartened.

And then the answer changed. A letter arrived at last from her mother in Dairapaska.

Debbie took the letter with shaking hands and carried it back down the hill to the cottage. She shut herself up in the alcove, as she had so many months ago, the first time she had received a letter from her mother.

She had two differences from that first letter. She had Geance instead of Espe in her lap, and she now shared Yannick's alcove. She could look out the window to the west, as she had before, and watch the same sun set over the horizon that would, many hours later, set over Dairapaska.

She slit open the letter with her little knife and began to read. When she had finished, Debbie read it again, with tears running down her face.

Terrible things had happened in Dairapaska. The peasants had been unhappy for a long time. The bride trade had ripped open wounds that had never closed. Debbie's letters had helped the bride trade families but overall, the peasants of the demesne were deeply suspicious of the daimyo and what he wanted from them.

The demesne had been poorly managed for many years, and the obligations and duties demanded of the serfs were getting harder to meet. They were being raised and raised again for no reason that anyone could see. Moreover, no benefits came back down to the people who did the work and grew the crops.

But even so, people had managed.

Then the daimyo announced to all the villages that since the bride trade with Shelleen had gone so well, with so many children being born, that he was arranging another one and this one was with an agricultural demesne even further away, both well to the east *and* south of the equator. As before, the girls would be chosen as the overseers saw fit, and no contact with the other demesne would be allowed. And he would not take 24 girls. He would take 48.

The overseers reading the announcements were stoned. The peasants rioted and the overseers and other representatives of the Dairapaska family were beaten. The manor house was set on fire, along with many other buildings, but only the ones that belonged to the daimyo and his family. There had been looting.

Several people were killed, and many more injured.

Fighting had raged for weeks, before being put down by hired troops from the free-city of Renolds, which took more weeks. The Dairapaska guards and security men were from the villages and this time they were going to lose daughters and sisters to the bride trade and they did not like it any better than the farmers did. Most of these men fought alongside the peasants and not against them, causing further turmoil.

The hired troops had no such concerns and they were ruthless, with more injuries, deaths and rapes spreading in their wake.

When the fighting stopped, the investigation by the Dairapaska family began. The daimyo was forced out. It seemed, wrote Debbie's mother, that the family had realized that things weren't being run as they should have been. It had certainly taken them long enough to notice what anyone with eyes would have seen: the demesne was poorly managed, the peasants poorly housed and fed, and resentment ran deep and strong.

The mismanagement was understood better by the peasants than they would have under normal circumstances. The letters Debbie sent had said many things about how Shelleen was managed and the brides from Shelleen had confirmed how things had been done back home. This caused more resentment against the ruling family. The serfs had long suspected that things could be different, and now they knew that they *were* different in other demesnes. The Dairapaska way was not the only way, despite what they had been told.

When Debbie read this, she saw the wisdom of how Remus ran Kenyatta. He was regularly out and about, and he knew all of his vassals. She saw Kenyatta family members on a routine basis in the villages and, as with Remus, they knew who they were speaking to and they knew something about their lives. It was sensible that the male family members went out onto the steppes to assist with the migrations as well as all the other work. They knew and spoke to their vassals and valued them for their hard work and skills.

The vassals of Kenyatta were real people to their daimyos,

unlike the serfs of Dairapaska and Shelleen. Debbie had never seen, other than at a distance, any member of the Dairapaska family and the same was true in Shelleen. She certainly had never spoken to them. She did not exist as a person to any of the aristocrats. None of the serfs did. They were interchangeable and did not matter as individuals. They were sheep, waiting to be sheared. They were geese, waiting to be plucked. You did not ask sheep what they wanted. You did not consider the feelings of geese.

Debbie's mother wrote that the daimyo had been found guilty, by the family, of financial malfeasance. She carefully printed the strange words so there would be no confusion. The gossip in Dairapaska said this meant the daimyo had stolen much of the demesne's money. Debbie's mother wrote that the peasants believed this was part of the reason the daimyo was forced out, but only part.

The real reason was the bride trade and the raw anger it generated in the serfs. Never before had all of the villages of Dairapaska united as one and fought the family, burning the manor house and its buildings and killing some of the family. Peasants had been slaughtered too, by the hired forces from the free-city of Renolds, so there was plenty of death to go around.

The Dairapaska family had to give an acceptable reason for the forced exit of the daimyo and they had to cool the furious rage of the peasants.

Someone had finally noticed, so wrote Debbie's mother, that there were far more peasants than ruling family. The Dairapaska family was hugely outnumbered by a furiously angry mob, a mob that did all of the work, a mob that was strong and armed with axes, scythes, sickles, flails, and pitchforks, a mob that was rapidly coming to the conclusion they had nothing left to lose.

So there was a new daimyo installed in Dairapaska. He cancelled the planned bride trade. He began an investigation of what had been done by his predecessor, looking at things that should have been noticed before. Many of the more onerous obligations had been rescinded, but not all of them.

This investigation had also led to the realization that the families of the brides, both sent and received, were far closer than they would have been expected to be, scattered as they were among the villages of Dairapaska.

The new daimyo had discovered the mail blockade had been broken and that it had been Debbie and her mother who had done it. Debbie's mother did not know who had told him. Many, many people had known, so it could have been anyone. She guessed it was probably someone trying to protect a family member, and she did not blame them for doing so.

The replacement daimyo now knew mail had been passed back and forth, in direct conflict with the ruling passed by his predecessor. He knew that Debbie, a traded bride, had stolen her children from Shelleen and run away. He knew that she had not died out on the steppes as would be expected. He knew that she and her stolen children were alive and living in Kenyatta. It was believed that if he had not yet done so, he would be speaking very soon with the daimyo of Shelleen about Debbie and what she had done.

Previously, the daimyos of Dairapaska and Shelleen had had little contact with each other after the bride trade was concluded. It had not been felt necessary. Peasants were interchangeable and it was like breeding livestock. You did not ask the ewes which ram they preferred. The results had been good; more babies being born and the promise of more to come down through the generations. That was why the previous daimyo had wanted the second bride trade, with far more young women involved, and devastating far more families.

No one knew where he was and the family was saying only that he had retired. It was widely speculated in Dairapaska, since he had not been seen, that he had been retired to a grave. Debbie's mother wrote this was, at any rate, the hope among the peasants.

This hope was possibly true, since many of the low servants in the manor house were village girls and they would tell their families what they had seen and heard in the manor house when they went home for a visit. The previous daimyo was nowhere to be seen and, in the past, he had always been seen, quite a bit more in fact than the girls liked. Every female servant in the manor house quickly learned to be wary of him.

Much of the information that Debbie's mother was passing along came from one of the parlor maids, invisible to the ruling family, yet seeing everything they did as she cleaned up behind them.

The new daimyo was cleaning up the mess his predecessor had made of things. He had not yet, to Debbie's mother's knowledge, contacted either Kenyatta or Shelleen with his complaints about Debbie but she believed that he would.

He had decreed that Debbie's mother could continue to write to Debbie and pass information, but, and Debbie's mother underlined that word several times, no one was allowed to write to Shelleen directly. The other daimyo had to give his permission first and as everyone knew, the law was what the daimyo said it was.

It was possible, even likely, wrote Debbie's mother, that other families in Dairapaska would write directly to Debbie. These families had not written to Debbie before since no one wanted to draw attention to Kenyatta by sending it a flood of mail. An avalanche of letters to a demesne halfway around Mars, one located next door to Shelleen, would have been thought suspicious and so Debbie's mother had discouraged those people who had wanted to write directly to Debbie.

Debbie's mother believed she was being allowed to write to Debbie because the cat was already out of the bag and, she underlined these words several times as well, it had been brought to the daimyo's attention by someone -- but no one knew who -- that the mail blockade was illegal as per the charter.

Debbie's mother had regularly pointed out this fact to the Post-Master, as had all of the other bride trade families and it seemed he had taken it to heart and had passed along the information. The new daimyo did not need the additional problem of someone telling the Martian government that Dairapaska had been doing something that could allow their charter to be revoked. So he threw a sop to Debbie's mother, that she would be allowed to write to her daughter and keep the bride trade families connected; hoping, so Debbie's mother wrote, that no one would tell Barsoom.

Debbie took a moment to be grateful to the Post-Mistress for telling her this theory so long ago. She would have to let the Post-Mistress know her guess about the charter must be true or why would the daimyo of Dairapaska still allow Debbie's mother to write to her? If it was false, he would not care if he blocked the letters and someone told the Martian government that he was doing such a thing.

The new daimyo had to punish some of the peasants for the rioting and so, even though he had rescinded many of the more onerous duties and obligations, he did not relax those requirements on Debbie's family or on any of the other bride trade families.

This was an acceptable compromise to the ruling family apparently, and it was acceptable to the bride trade families. They had all been afraid members of their families would be sent off the demesne to the Dirac mines or be hung. The obligations and duties, despite the burden they caused, were preferable to death.

An uneasy peace lay across Dairapaska. Everything was out in the open, no longer hidden or denied. It was hoped that this daimyo would be a better manager than the last one. Certainly, so went the gossip, the family had been put on notice they needed their serfs to be, well not happy, but at least reasonably content with their lot in life.

Debbie's mother finished her letter begging Debbie to be careful and to write Lupita in Shelleen what had happened so she, too, could ready herself for the troubles ahead.

Debbie sat for a long time after she had read the letter a second time, thinking of what this would mean. She was roused for supper and she ate silently, a fact that was noticed by the family.

The kids were sent off to play and the adults, with Espe and Geance who could not be sent off to visit their cousins, discussed the contents of Debbie's letter from Dairapaska.

Debbie, after much tea and sympathy, decided she would go back up the hill in the morning to tell Remus what had happened in Dairapaska. It was her duty as a loyal vassal to let him know if trouble was coming. Yannick insisted on going with her, even though she had made the trip many times by herself.

"This trip is different, Debbie," he said. "It's not gossip about the poisoned village. You'll be reminding him of the wider world and what it can do to Kenyatta. He needs to know, but Remus is like everybody else. Needing to know doesn't mean he wants to know."

In the morning, they walked back up the hill, following the lane winding between the cottages. Yannick carried Espe, snugly wrapped in wool and sheepskin and Debbie carried Geance, equally snug in his own layers. Geance could not be left behind; Espe had fussed enough that they decided to bring her, reminding Remus of the luck and fertility Debbie had brought to Kenyatta.

It had snowed again and the village boys were shoveling the paths clear, loading the snow into carts and hauling it away to the fields and out of the village, making room for the snow still to come. Ropes were already being strung up between cottages and gates and barns and outbuildings, along every path in the village.

"Why are they doing that?" asked Debbie, glad of a distraction. She had not seen this before. Her breath made clouds in the air and the cold bit into her face. They were passing behind a cottage that blocked the icy fingers of the wind, making it easier to speak.

"We don't pretend Winter's not hard," answered Yannick. "Still got to do everything, especially with the animals, and a blizzard does not change that fact. The ropes mean you have something to hold onto when the wind screams, trying to knock you down, and you can't see your hand in front of your face for the snow. No ropes mean someone can get lost and freeze to death in their own kitchen garden."

Debbie ran her mittened hand along the rope, heavy and thick, that ran alongside the path to the manor house. "They should do this in Shelleen," she said. "I know two years ago that happened to an old woman in the next village. They found her body buried and frozen under the snow."

They continued on up the hill to the manor house side door, and this time Debbie asked for Remus as well as Preston.

Once settled into the office, Debbie gave her mother's letter to Remus to read and when he had finished, he silently passed it to Preston. When they had both finished, Remus gave the letter back to Debbie.

"I should pass this around to some of the other daimyos at the conclave," he said with a grimace. "Not all of them can understand that peasants are not just sheep to be sheared. Cut too close and you draw blood."

Debbie had a sudden flash of plucking the geese and the blood droplets welling up on their bare, ruddy breasts, but she chose not to say anything. It had to be done, but it was best to do it gently, and give the geese plenty of time to recover, with fresh grass and clean water. Geese could be plucked for many years without injury if you were careful and gentle. They never got to like it, but they managed, laying eggs, raising more geese, and living out their lives. Then they got old and you slaughtered them and ate them and took *all* their feathers. It was what geese were for.

Remus sighed and shook his head, making his beads clatter. "I appreciate the warning. At the same time, Dairapaska can't do anything to me or to the demesne. They're on the other side of the pole corridor, too far away to matter. Politically, they're farmers, not Ennaretee ranchers, so we don't work together in the conclave. They can pound sand for all I care. Don't worry about them, Debbie."

"Well, that's all fine and dandy, Remus," said Yannick. "But what about Airik Shelleen? If Dairapaska gets Shelleen stirred up, well, you got to work with them. They're part of our quad, part of our nine-square. You cannot ignore them."

Remus grinned at his Hand's impudence while Debbie cringed inwardly. She could not get used to the casual way the Hands interacted with the Kenyatta family, and what might be acceptable in the village square seemed much less so inside a fancy chamber inside the grand manor house.

"This is true, but Shelleen has to work with me as well. He's got big problems coming up with the Martian government and he needs Kenyatta on his side, along with Satran and Armstrong. He can't pretend, like those dirt-eaters usually do, that we don't exist. Ozigbow to the west and Gish to the east will support him, as they always do. But we control the north side of the corridor."

"You figured it out then? What the poisoned village was about?" Yannick asked.

Remus sat back in his big chair, looking very pleased. "We did and we could not have done it without Debbie telling us it existed in the first place and you getting us all those samples. You brought us luck, Debbie, and saved me a major headache. I'd have had to support Shelleen, as would Satran and Armstrong in this matter, but I know why I'm doing it, I've been able to prepare for it, and there won't be any surprises."

"May I ask what it was, sir?" said Debbie hesitantly.

She was grateful for the change of subject, more since it reminded Remus he thought she was lucky, and she was very curious as to why the poisoned village had been established. There had to be a reason for such a dreadful, wasteful thing to happen.

"Of course, my dear. Airik trained as a geologist, Shelleen has a few of them on staff as it has long been known that there are valuable ores on the demesne. As they find them, Shelleen has exploited them."

Debbie had known about the tin mine, since one of the Dairapaska girls had been married off to a miner. During the letter writing, she had learned of other small mining operations on Shelleen, digging out a variety of minerals from deep under the soil, thus enriching the demesne.

"This lode, however, and Airik recognized what it was, is of critical importance to the terraforming. The poisoned village lies atop a deposit of Red Mercury."

Debbie had never heard of such a mineral. Yannick shrugged and said, "So?"

"So, Red Mercury is so valuable that the charter allows the Martian Government to take over that portion of a demesne that has a deposit," replied Remus. "They can keep the land until every last drop is extracted. Then and only then, the ruined land is returned to the demesne. The family gets nothing in return and they have to bear all the costs of restoring the land, a process that can take a century."

Debbie opened her mouth, then closed it again.

Yannick, equally shocked, said, "I thought the Four Hundred owned their demesnes, lock, stock, and barrel, and nothing could ever be done to take them away. That was the deal, yeah?"

"Yeah, that was the deal," said Preston, answering for Remus. "But the devil is always in the details. The charter our ancestors signed ran to dozens of pages of very fine print. There's some bizarre stuff in there. The part that matters to Shelleen, and to us, is the clause about supporting the terraforming.

"The terraforming keeps us all alive, and we have to keep it going, no matter what. We still have centuries ahead of us before the process becomes self-sustaining."

Remus sniffed. "More like millennia, I'd say."

"I'm going with a best-case scenario, Remus, and you know that," answered Preston, glaring at him.

"Best case or not," said Yannick, interrupting what looked like to him an ongoing argument of long standing, "we'll all be long dead so it don't matter to us. What matters is what's Shelleen gonna do now?"

Remus and Preston shelved the argument, to the relief of everyone around them.

"If Airik can prove he is already using that land, if he can prove he knows the scope of the deposit, and he can prove he knows how to extract the Red Mercury, he can keep control of his land and he will be paid for the Red Mercury he mines by the Martian government. He can also claim environmental costs to restore the land after all the Red Mercury is pulled out," said Remus.

"I intend that Kenyatta come down on his side, along with the rest of the nine-square and Purnell. I don't want to set a precedent that the government can come and take over, I know the other daimyos will agree, and I really don't want to start a mining rush."

Remus let them think over what he had said, watching them closely as they took it in, as did Preston.

Debbie puzzled over the last part. A mining rush?

Yannick stood up suddenly, startling Espe. He let her chew on a braid to sooth and distract her, as he began pacing back and forth, trampling the roses.

"Damn. I did not think of that. The lode is close to the corridor, an easy ride or a day's walk into Shelleen. It's 150 klicks or more from Shelleen's power base. They won't be able to control access and every wanna-be-rich miner will head out and move in. Shelleen can't control the steppes, the incoming hordes won't know where the lode is and the land will be stripped down to bedrock."

Remus looked even more pleased, knowing that his Hand had understood the underlying issue.

"That's what I'm afraid of," he replied. "The Martian government would be bad enough, but amateurs swarming in would be far worse. They'd flood the corridor, flood Purnell, and spill over onto *my* land. I know Airik doesn't want that, no one would. He'd lose control of massive amounts of his land, end up with squatter camps everywhere, and since it's all on his land, he'd have to pay for every last penny of the damages, maybe even in the government corridor, too."

"What about the people in the village?" asked Debbie. It seemed to her that was what mattered. "They're suffering now, and they'll suffer more."

"They will indeed," answered Remus. "Another reason for Airik to retain control. Red Mercury is extremely toxic. It's why even the terraforming fungi were struggling. Amateurs will spread that poison everywhere, killing themselves and killing the land around them. Right now, it's in only a small area."

Preston added, "A handful of Red Mercury can contaminate a hectare of land."

Debbie gasped. "They'll poison all of the land, not just where the village is."

"Amateur miners will," said Preston. "Professionals will do a better job of containing the Red Mercury. They don't want to spill a single drop because every drop is needed for the Magnetrons. Amateurs just want to make a pile of money and walk away from the mess they leave."

"I think, Debbie," said Remus, "you do not need to worry about what Airik Shelleen has to say to me about you running away, you stealing your former husband's children, or your breaking the mail blockade with Dairapaska. He has much bigger problems."

"No," she answered slowly, "I suppose I shouldn't. But the villagers, what about them?"

"That I don't know; what I do know is I will not bring you up to him," Remus said, and she had to be content with that.

Then he added something that added even more to her concerns.

"I do not want you to tell Lupita, or your mother for that matter, about the Red Mercury. This is confidential information. I believe it will cause far more problems for Airik if there is a panic."

Debbie stared at him for a moment, then said, "The peasants in the poisoned village need to know what is happening to them, sir."

"And they will," said Remus patiently. "Give Airik Shelleen the maneuvering room he needs."

"This is wrong," said Debbie, her jaw trembling, "and you know it, but I will do as you ask."

She did not say anything of consequence to Remus after that, refusing to look at him or anyone else in the room, answering yes or no as needed. She focused her attention on Geance who, to her gratitude, decided he needed her attention. As she had hoped, no one disagreed that what a baby needed took priority over anything else.

On the walk back down the hill, away from Remus, she could not stop herself from talking about how dreadful it was that the villagers, people she knew and lived with, were being used to further Airik Shelleen's ends. The presence of Espe and Geance, warm and safe in their arms, made her think of the babies there, and how they were suffering.

Yannick listened patiently and waited until she had run down. Then he said, "I know all that, my Debbie. It's wrong. But a panic would be worse and if word gets out, and it will, Shelleen will get an influx of fortune hunters as well as an internal revolt. Why don't you write and ask Lupita if the milrats and the new well are helping? Suggest to her that the villagers eat nothing that isn't shipped in, only drink from the far wells, and sweep and wash every day to keep the dust out."

Debbie thought about it. "I suppose that will help."

"It will help, my Debbie. Does everyone wear gloves when they work the fields? They should and those gloves should be used only when they work. Similarly, all those villagers should wear water-soaked bandanas over their faces when they're out and about. It can't hurt and it may help. It being winter will help too. They're probably not outside grubbing in the dirt."

"I suppose."

"People need to believe they can help themselves. If the villagers don't feel so helpless, they'll cope better. You know that, yeah? Write to Lupita soon as we get back and tell her so."

That evening, Debbie shut herself up in the alcove and wrote to Lupita.

She wrote down everything that had happened in Dairapaska, not just what had happened to families involved in the bride trade. She related about her mother being allowed to continue writing because what the Kenyatta Post-Mistress believed seemed to be true. She begged Lupita to be careful and to warn the other bride trade families to be careful.

Then she wrote about the poisoned village, telling Lupita she believed that the less physical contact the peasants had with the air, the soil, the water, and the plants that were there, the healthier they would be. Debbie wrote that, although the village was probably not cursed and that there were probably no witches, it would do no harm to have as little to do with the place as possible and it could help.

She reread her letter, studying the black ink markings on the dull white paper, and prayed that her concern and care would shine through the matter-of-fact words. There did not seem to be anything else she could do.

This time, Yannick took her letter to the Post-Mistress, out in the cold dark night so it could go out into the world as the sun rose, rather than wait another day.

17
Word Slips Out

D EBBIE WAITED ANXIOUSLY for a letter from Lupita and more anxiously over what she feared Lupita would have to say.

The response came quickly, obviously written and mailed the day Debbie's letter had arrived.

Lupita wrote that she was not surprised at the riots in Dairapaska. She found the idea of doing another bride trade — and with 48 young women! — to be horrible. She wrote that she would not be surprised by riots in Shelleen if such a thing were to be done to the peasants.

She thanked Debbie for her advice about keeping safe in the poisoned village. The villagers were eating only mil-rats, and it was helping, as was the winter. Nothing had changed there. No new people were being sent, but no one was being allowed to leave, either. New soddys had been built further away, and that helped too, along with the new wells.

Then Lupita got to her real concern. She had heard nothing about the mail blockade being lifted but, as with Dairapaska and Kenyatta, many of the young women of Shelleen worked in the manor house as lower servants and so the peasants had a fairly good idea of what their betters were getting up to. She would hear and quickly, if Dairapaska contacted Shelleen even if the official announcement took longer.

Her fear was that the daimyo of Shelleen would not wait on complaints from Dairapaska to speak to Kenyatta. Word had slipped out that Debbie was alive, her daughters were alive, they were living in Kenyatta and that it was Debbie who had broken the mail blockade. So far, only the peasants knew, not the Shelleen family, but that was just a matter of time.

Gossip ran both ways and there was always someone looking to curry favor with the ruling family.

What happened was that Lupita's daughter-in-law, Alice, had been confronted by Fulvia Acconcio.

Debbie grimaced at the memory of her sister-in-law. Fulvia had never gotten over her resentment of Debbie. Seeing her every day reminded Fulvia, every day, that her little sister, Blanca, had been chosen for the bride trade. Fulvia had cared deeply for Ghita and Carina — she had no children of her own and her bitter envy did not help the situation — but she would have been just as happy if their mother fell over dead in the streets and often said so, if it meant that Blanca could return to Shelleen.

It seemed that Fulvia's mother was very ill and was likely to die. Fulvia went to Alice and begged her to tell how she could write directly to Blanca.

Did Alice know? She was a bride from Dairapaska and Lupita's daughter-in-law so she *should* know, and she *should* tell what she knew.

The family did not want to go through Lupita and the distant relatives who were forwarding the mail to Dairapaska. They had to write directly to Blanca, as the things they had to say had to be kept private. They would not allow even a single sealed sheet of paper to be sent via Lupita as they did not want her or the forwarding relative to steam it open and read the contents.

Lupita wrote that she found this to be extremely offensive as she had been discreet over everything she had passed along. The stories she knew about the things that people got up to in their spare time! She never gossiped about what she learned, despite often being asked.

Alice did not like Fulvia and she did not like how Fulvia had treated Debbie, but that was not the problem. The problem arose when Fulvia told Alice that she did not want to do to her mother what that bitch Debbie had done to Mrs. Acconcio, abandoning her in her hour of need and stealing and murdering her grandchildren.

Lupita wrote that Alice and Fulvia had gotten into a shouting match with Alice telling Fulvia that Debbie had been a saint, putting up with that vicious old bat and that Fulvia should have been nicer to the person who took some of the pressure off of her and who had given the family their only grandchildren. Debbie had never wanted to come to Shelleen but she, like Alice, had made the best of it anyway. Did Fulvia want her little sister to be treated like Debbie had been? Was Fulvia too stupid to see that Debbie being gone put most of the burden of dealing with Mrs. Acconcio on her?

Fulvia had screamed back that the only sad thing about Debbie being torn apart by wild beasts on the steppes was that her adored little nieces had been devoured too. Fulvia had only named Ghita and Carina, ignoring the baby, and that had enraged Alice still further.

Alice had screamed that this was why Debbie had left! The precious proud Acconcio family would not, could not accept the third daughter, little Espe. And Debbie leaving was why Fulvia's family had been able to exchange news with Shelleen about Blanca along with the other bride trade families! Debbie had broken the mail blockade and if Fulvia had a lick of sense, she'd be grateful to her as should everyone else in Shelleen.

Fulvia, so wrote Lupita, had not taken this well, attacking Alice while yelling that she was a liar, and then it all came out: that Debbie and her three daughters were alive, that Espe was the name of the third girl (not a name that the Acconico family would have ever chosen), that they had found refuge in Kenyatta, that Debbie had broken the mail blockade and not some mysterious distant relative of Lupita's, and that Debbie had married again, to a much better man than Aldo Acconcio would ever be.

By this time, sadly too late, Lupita had been summoned and she forcibly dragged the two enraged women apart. Lupita was upset with Alice and furious with Fulvia. She sent Alice home and hustled Fulvia over to her mother's cottage. There, Lupita wrote, she confronted Fulvia and her family and told them that they were putting at risk the messages being sent back and forth between Dairapaska and Shelleen.

Did they want that? Did they? To not only never have contact again with Blanca but to also deny this small comfort to the other families caught in the bride trade? What would the other families say to them if and when they discovered that Fulvia and her family had made sure they could never communicate with their own lost daughters again? Had they thought of this?

If word got out, it would reach the daimyo and he was sure to crack down on the letter-writing as breaking the blockade had been against his rules and everyone knew it. He was equally likely to punish the families involved too! Did they want that?

It was only because of Debbie's bravery that they had any contact at all! Lupita told Fulvia and her family that she missed Pia every day, and every day she said prayers that Debbie continue to pass along letters. She, Lupita, understood as well as anyone what it meant to lose a loved daughter and be handed an unhappy stranger in return. She had made a place in her heart for Alice who had not asked for anything that was done to her, as Debbie had not, as Blanca had not, as Pia had not, as all of the other girls had not.

Lupita told Fulvia and her family that they had not done one thing to make Debbie's life easier and that they should be ashamed of themselves. Would they want their Blanca to be treated the same way they had treated Debbie? Would they?

Lupita wrote that, to her amazement, the family seemed to take her words to heart. At any rate they promised, all of them, to not say anything more to anyone. She did not know how long the situation would last as the cat was out of the bag. Fortunately, Fulvia's husband Enzo had been working in the fields so if Fulvia could keep her fool mouth shut, the Acconcios would not find out instantly from their oldest son.

Unfortunately, Fulvia and her mother both had mouths as big as the great outdoors!

Despite her dismay, Debbie had to laugh when she read that part. Fulvia had never been able to keep quiet unless Mrs. Acconcio was around. She had to say whatever was on her mind, no matter how trivial or unkind it was, and she always had something to say. Debbie had not missed Fulvia one bit.

It was possible that Fulvia would keep quiet as the one thing that did matter to her was her little sister Blanca. Lupita thought this might do the trick and Debbie had to agree. But Lupita hastened to add that Debbie needed to know this could change, and she needed to be ready.

Debbie wrote back, thanking Lupita for her warning, and repeated what her mother had written about the riots and what her mother had said about maybe, perhaps, the chance that the mail blockade would be lifted. If everyone could keep quiet, the Shelleen family might never discover mail had been exchanged in direct opposition to their dictates and so no one would be punished.

After she mailed her letter to Lupita, Debbie wondered if she should continue on up the hill the rest of the way to tell Remus that Shelleen might complain. After some minutes of going back and forth in the tiny post office, she decided to say nothing. Remus already knew the possibility existed, so there was no point in reminding him again.

Several days later, another letter from Lupita arrived. Fulvia had not been able to keep her fool mouth shut, and she had blabbed out the story in the most public way possible. Every peasant in every village in Shelleen heard the story, it was far too juicy not to pass along at once so it leapt from cottage to cottage like thatch set ablaze, and it was just a matter of time before word made it up the hill to their betters.

Lupita wrote that she almost couldn't blame Fulvia. Almost.

Mrs. Acconcio had been getting nastier than usual with the Winter Solstice approaching, carrying on endlessly about her lost granddaughters and how deeply she would miss them during the celebrations. As always, she refused to admit that there were three little girls and not two. She had then lit into Fulvia about her being barren and why didn't she bear grandchildren? What was wrong with her? She should have borne a son for the family! She was no better than that heartless bitch Debbie! Debbie had produced only the two girls and then she had murdered them on the steppes and Fulvia, useless daughter-in-law that she was, had borne no grandchildren at all. Fulvia was just as bad as that worthless Dairapaska slattern.

This had not gone over well, so wrote Lupita.

Debbie knew this gossip well. Her mother-in-law had never been very nice to Fulvia, everyone knew it, and when Debbie had arrived, it had taken much of the pressure off of Fulvia. Mrs. Acconcio had always told everyone that Fulvia was a sterile disappointment; the fault could not have been Aldo's brother Enzo of course, despite the fact that everybody knew none of the Acconcio children had produced grandchildren until Debbie came along.

Fulvia had finally had enough verbal abuse from Mrs. Acconcio.

Fulvia screamed back that if the precious Acconcios had been nicer people none of this would have happened and Debbie ran away because of how nasty that precious Aldo was to her and she was still alive with all *three* granddaughters and Mrs. Acconcio could live with that fact forever. She'd made everyone around her desperately unhappy, and if Fulvia could have run away across the steppes to escape her, she would have!

Fulvia then went on to tell Mrs. Acconcio, at the top of her lungs, that Debbie had been the one who had been writing letters to tell everyone what had happened to their daughters and sisters, Debbie had been the heroine, Debbie who had been despised for her very existence was a better woman than Mrs. Acconcio would ever be.

Lupita deeply regretted that this had happened, forcing her to tell Debbie this story, but for Fulvia, it was like lancing a boil. All the poison spewed out, years and years of a slow accumulation of hate, resentment, and bile.

Even more regrettable was that Fulvia and Mrs. Acconcio had not had the decency to have their argument behind closed doors as Fulvia and Alice had done. They had their screaming match in the center of the village at the fountain, with a good portion of the resident peasants as a fascinated audience.

Lupita had begged everyone not to say anything more, as did the other families involved in the bride trade. But the cat was out of the bag for good and racing for the barn, never to be captured again, and it was just a matter of time before the daimyo was told.

In fact, Lupita wrote, she wouldn't put it past that stupid Mrs. Acconcio to march up to the manor house and demand an audience to get her granddaughters back. She was so selfish that she would not think about the bride-trade families and what would happen to them.

Lupita did not know what to do, other than to warn Debbie trouble was coming and to beg, again, for calmness and peace in the villages and for all the damn fool villagers to keep their mouths shut and wait a while longer. If Dairapaska let the blockade drop, then it was a surety that Shelleen would do so as well.

Debbie wanted to faint when she read Lupita's letter.

She took the letter to Yannick and told him what Lupita had written. It was time to bother Remus again, to let him know that Shelleen would come calling this time for sure.

Yannick was exasperated, but not at Debbie. "Some people do not know when to keep their damn fool mouths shut."

Chika was more disparaging and pointed out how much better off Debbie was in Kenyatta, out of that roiling snake pit of gossip, and didn't those people have anything better to do with their time?

Debbie chose to not say anything to that, as she had quickly learned how much gossip swirled around in Kenyatta, particularly about their family. The arrival of Geance had made sure that everyone who hadn't already been talking about her and Yannick was doing it now. He shrugged the gossip off, saying only that he'd been talked about worse. Debbie found it annoying, but there was nothing she could do about it other than to smile and politely correct errors of fact.

And no, people did not have anything better to do with their time.

Debbie no longer believed that people were different from demesne to demesne and now she thought they were much the same in the free-cities as well. They talked continuously about each other as what could be more fascinating than what other people got up to in their spare time? It certainly wasn't the work always needing to be done.

She did agree that she was far better off in Kenyatta in every way. She had only to look around her to know that. Yannick's loving, Chika's caring, Leon being amusing, and all of the kids, starting with Kerill and ending with Geance bounding about reminded her every day.

In the end, Debbie decided it was better to get it over with and warn Remus. Espe was old enough to stay behind with her gramma Chika and so only Debbie, Yannick and Geance made the chilly trek back up the hill, over the shoveled paths lined with knee-high walls of snow and up to the manor's side door.

Debbie still found it awkward to speak to any member of the Kenyatta family, especially when she came bearing bad tidings. It was different when she had news about the poisoned village. She spoke to Preston at the door and then disappeared back to the village below and her own business, leaving behind the concerns of the ruling family.

She did not like being one of the ruling family's concerns.

They were admitted, and Yannick led the way down the familiar carpeted hallway to Remus's office. Considering the situation, it was surprisingly pleasant to be in the manor house as it was quiet, without the sounds of squabbling children, a yapping dog, and hissing cats.

It was not any warmer than the cottage was, which Debbie did not think was a surprise. The building was huge, and she had often wondered how they kept it warm in the winter. The masonry stove kept the cottage at a quite-acceptable temperature, particularly after the day's baking. She and Chika rarely had to break the ice on the buckets of water in the morning unless the night had been colder than usual.

Chika had told her that would change as they headed into the deep winter. Then, no matter how much you baked during the day, the cottage slowly got cold later on. You could not afford to burn precious charcoal all night long to heat the whole, empty cottage when everyone was tucked up into a sleeping alcove and so the fire was banked for the night and the cottage slowly got colder as the heat faded away. It made for chilly mornings that encouraged you to get the fire started and the tea on faster.

Remus did not look happy to see Debbie yet again. He had several other family members with him, some she recognized and some she did not. Preston and Hiroshi were both there, making her feel marginally more comfortable. They were grouped around the large table, studying more charts and other documents.

"What is it this time?" Remus asked, his voice testy. "I do not have time for this shit. I would have never guessed that one woman and three little girls would take up so much of my life."

Yannick frowned at him and said, "My Debbie swore fealty to you and she's keeping her faith. You wanna know what's coming charging at you or not? I should think you would be happy to not be surprised."

Debbie cringed against him. She could not believe Remus would allow Yannick to speak to him like that.

Remus looked more tired and unhappy than ever, against a backdrop of carefully blank faces, but he said, "You are correct. I don't need any more surprises. Tell me what happened."

Debbie made herself tell him about Lupita's latest letter.

Remus rolled his eyes. "Do none of these peasants have anything else to do? Are they incapable of keeping their damn fool mouths shut?"

Debbie was unsure of how to answer those questions. The peasants of Shelleen and Dairapaska as well as the vassals of Kenyatta always had plenty to do but that did not stop them from talking. Talking made the work go faster and passed the time. She chose to say nothing other than to nod her head, a gesture Remus could interpret as he chose.

Yannick did answer. He said, "People love to talk, they live to talk, and there's some who wouldn't be able to stop talking if they were at death's door. It won't be long before Airik Shelleen hears that his missing serf and her stolen kids are alive and well and living in Kenyatta."

Remus said, "I appreciate being told, but I won't worry about it. Airik's got bigger problems. It seems that he has to keep the village going during the mining operation, start to finish, to hold onto the land."

That made Debbie look up and speak. "But that will make life worse for the villagers."

"Probably," replied Remus. "But if Airik wants to keep control of his land for his family, he'll sacrifice the lives of a few peasants." He sat back down in his chair and watched Debbie stonily.

"I would too, if it meant keeping out the Martian government and keeping out squatters." The Kenyatta family arrayed around the room nodded in agreement, equally stone-faced and implacable.

Debbie did not know what to say, as she stood there rooted to the floor and struggling to breathe. She knew those people in the poisoned village, some of them fairly well, and none of them deserved what was happening to them.

"I know you got to make hard choices, Remus," said Yannick, his voice cold. "But these are people, living and breathing, and I don't believe that should be forgotten. We aren't Olde Earthe, to use and use and use until a man or woman is used up and dead and use what's left for making soap."

He dipped his head and added, "By your leave, Debbie and I will head out and let you attend to business."

Remus dismissed them and they walked out through the silent corridors, silent themselves.

When they were well away from the manor house and could not be overheard, Debbie said, "That is awful. Not one of those villagers asked to be moved there, anymore than any of us asked to be traded as brides."

"I know. But I also know that the Shelleen family, if they have half a brain between the whole pack of them, have got to keep hold of the demesne. If Airik won't do it, someone else will. Someone not so nice."

"I don't see how it could be worse," fumed Debbie, thinking of the dreadful soddys and how miserably gloomy, cold, and damp they would be in the winter.

Yannick sighed. "Airik's trying to keep them alive, sending the mil-rats and keeping them from working the fields. Do you think there's others in Shelleen who wouldn't care, who'd just send fresh peasants to replace the ones who die?"

Despite the cold, Debbie stopped walking and sat down on a low wall. She thought about the gossip she knew about the Shelleen family and what she knew of the Dairapaska family. "Yes," she answered at last, "there are some. They wouldn't bother keeping anyone alive, even though that would lead to bigger problems down the road."

"Try and remember that and remind Lupita to tell the villagers to keep clean and well away from the bad area. There's not much else we can do right now."

"It's all so wrong. How can we say we're better than Olde Earthe when we do this?"

"I don't know, my Debbie." He lifted her to her feet and wrapped his arms around her and Geance, and they stood there in the pale winter sun for a long time.

18

New Pressures

A FEW DAYS LATER, DEBBIE was summoned to the manor house. The page delivering the message refused, as always, to tell her why, but she could guess. The daimyo of Shelleen must have finally said something to Kenyatta. She bundled up Geance and pulled on the heavy sheepskin coat and heavy boots to trudge back up the hill. The day was grayer than usual and snow was threatening again. The wind tore down from the north, whistling around the cottages, and it cut her to the bone. It brought with it the smell of ice and a promise of a deeper cold to come.

She missed Yannick desperately but he had been out working, and she could not take the time to fetch him. Chika sent Ghita to look for him, so she could only hope that he got the message in time to meet her before she went inside the manor house. Despite the biting cold, she did not hurry on the long walk up the path to the top of the hill.

Debbie reached the courtyard of the manor house, shoveled clear of snow and soaking up the warmth of the sun. She paused to admire the work that had gone into moving the previous day's snowfall so quickly, with strong arms and backs, and then carting it away to the fields. The stones heated quickly in the sun and would radiate heat all night long, warming the courtyard and the manor house wings wrapped around it.

She was raising her hand to knock at the side door when she heard Yannick call out to her. Debbie turned and saw him running towards her. He was catching his breath when he got to her and she knew he must have run the whole way from wherever Ghita had found him.

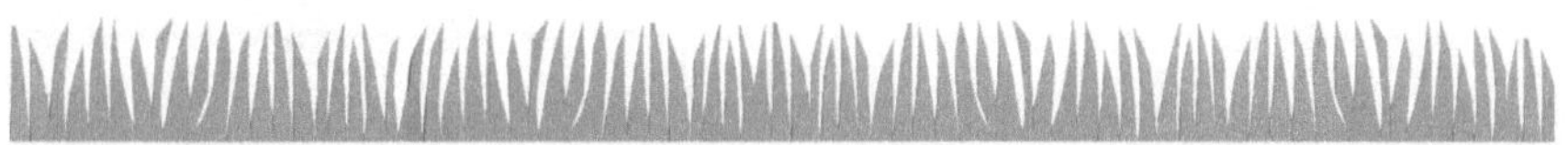

He caught her up in his arms and kissed her soundly and she fell into him, feeling safe and loved and much better able to face Remus Kenyatta and whatever he had to say.

Yannick took Geance from her, saying, "My turn, I think." Just as he had always done with Espe, he waved his heavy braid at Geance, letting the wide-eyed baby try to clutch it tightly in a mittened fist.

"Hey, buddy. It's daddy. How's my boy?" Geance was learning to smile and burble and his joy at seeing Yannick gave them a moment's respite from fears about the upcoming interview.

As they walked in, Yannick asked her if she had any idea of why Remus had summoned her.

"No, nothing," answered Debbie. "Lupita hasn't written anything new, nor has my mother."

They were admitted into Remus's office and once again, there were several family members in attendance. Debbie was getting to recognize more of them, but she still did not know their names. She would have to ask Yannick. He knew all of the family and what they did on behalf of the demense.

One person in particular stood out among the older family members. Yannick had told her he was a Kenyatta cousin who was being groomed for bigger things. He had always been present, other than during the fall migration, listening intently but not speaking. Well, Debbie could understand that. Listening in the background and keeping your own counsel was a good way to find out what was going on. She had relied on this method for years to survive in Shelleen.

"Ah, there you are, Debbie, prompt as always," said Remus, looking jovial. "And I see you managed to find and bring my Hand, as well."

"Couldn't let my Debbie enter the wolf's den on her own, Remus, you know that, yeah?" answered Yannick with an easy smile.

She pushed herself a little closer against him, feeling more uncomfortable than usual while carefully keeping her eyes on the patterned carpet. By now, Debbie knew the pattern of flowers entwined with leaves far better than she would have liked. It was a very pretty carpet with its deep green leaves, crimson and scarlet roses, and thorny vines sprawled against a paler green background. There were even tiny yellow flowers scattered in the background, like daisies in grass. She saw the flowers sometimes in her dreams; the roses would move, dropping their petals like blood spattered on grass, but they refused to speak clear words about the future.

"Word has finally gotten around," said Remus. "Dairapaska called me to bitch about Debbie breaking the mail blockade against the express wishes of both the daimyo of Dairapaska and the daimyo of Shelleen. I told that fool, newly minted I understand?"

He looked over questioningly at Debbie, and she nodded vigorously.

"I told that fool that Dairapaska had nothing to do with Kenyatta and reminded him to read his charter regarding mail service. I reminded him that if, somehow, that little fact of him denying mail service to his peasants were to get out, he'd have far more problems than he has now. I told him that there should be no repercussions regarding Debbie or her relatives coming from the Dairapaska family."

Debbie looked up and said, "thank you, sir. My family appreciates it as do I." She dropped her eyes back to the roses at her feet.

Remus said, "That was the easy one. Airik Shelleen also contacted me this morning. He is not happy. It seems that one of his longtime peasant families, been there since the founding of Shelleen, lost its grandchildren and wants him to get them back. Both of them, which I found interesting, as I knew there were three and said so. He thought that was interesting as well, especially as he already knew there were three, despite what he was being told."

Debbie firmed her jaw, looked up from the carpet to meet his eyes and said, "I won't go back and I won't let my daughters, any of them, be taken from me." Yannick tightened his arm around her. Even through his thick clothes, she could feel the tenseness in his muscles

"I told Airik you had sworn fealty to me, something you did not do to Shelleen at any time," Remus said. "This matters. I refused Airik and he made the counteroffer that you could take your girls to Purnell and meet the Acconcios there."

"Absolutely not!" Yannick answered harshly. "They'll steal my Debbie and my girls, you know that! You got no control over Purnell, it's a free-city, and there's nothing you could do if they dragged her back to Shelleen to be beaten or worse."

Debbie was horrified at his outburst, despite the joy that surged through her on knowing he would defend her to the daimyo of Kenyatta.

Remus looked pained. "Give me some credit, Yannick. Debbie has been good luck for Kenyatta, and I won't give her up and Shelleen cannot make me."

He smiled then, baring all of his teeth, and Debbie was reminded of how the wolf-dogs had looked out on the steppes, the sunlight glinting on their fangs.

"I told him I knew about his Red Mercury mine. And I told him he needs me on his side, along with Armstrong and Satran when he negotiates with the Martian government."

Debbie could feel Yannick relax against her slightly. "Thank you, sir," she said. She shifted Geance to a more comfortable position and wondered what else she should say. A few words of gratitude seemed so inadequate in exchange for her safety and that of her daughters. But there *was* something she needed to know and she wanted to it know badly enough to ask the daimyo.

"May I ask what happens to the peasants in the poisoned village?"

"They're being taken care of. Besides being interested in the fact that you have three daughters, not two, Airik was also interested in how I knew about the lode."

Debbie steeled herself again. "How are they being taken care of, sir?" She kept her eyes respectfully on the too-familiar carpet, focusing on a bloody rose near her feet, its petals spread to reveal a hint of its delicate, golden heart.

"Just won't let that go, will you," Remus answered, letting his irritation show. "The serfs have to stay there, close enough to meet the requirements in the charter. As the mine expands, the village will be moved so as to be as far away as is legal and no closer. Airik will keep them fed so they won't have to eat anything grown in the poisoned soil."

Yannick shifted his weight against Debbie and she chose to say, "thank you, sir." She felt him relax again and knew she had said the right thing.

"Tell me, sir," asked Yannick, "Shelleen figure out Debbie

told you about the village?"

"He supposed she told me something along the lines of witches hexing the village. Now, I know and he knows that this is not possible so I explained I had other ways to find out what was happening."

"He knows we spied on him, doesn't he," Yannick said. He did not comment on the possible existence of witches.

"Yes, he figured that one out. He can't do anything about it as he needs me too much. We could keep out squatters, us, Satran, and Armstrong, and he can't. Airik needs us enough to swallow his pride for the good of the demesne."

"So my Debbie and my daughters are safe and sound and home-free?"

Remus sat back in his chair, his face blank again. "Well now, I will have to give Airik Shelleen something in exchange for Debbie and the girls but I have not yet decided what that thing will be. I do have to work with him, both now and for years to come. He's smart enough to know I'd support him in his negotiations with the Martian Government as would Armstrong and Satran. Debbie is a minor issue and I want to keep it that way."

Debbie did not think of herself as a minor issue and the safety and happiness of her daughters was certainly not minor to her, nor she knew, was it minor to Yannick and the rest of the family.

She wondered if there was a solution, something that Kenyatta could give that Shelleen would accept, something that would benefit them both. The letter-writing had brought the demesnes of Dairapaska and Shelleen closer in unexpected ways. Perhaps there was something here in Kenyatta that would do the same, bringing it closer to Shelleen.

If she could think of something, it would make her more valuable and thus less likely to be discarded as a sacrifice needed for the health and safety of the demesne. Remus had made it very clear that what mattered to him was the whole of Kenyatta and if sacrifices had to be made, they would be. You do not ask the sheep how they want to be shorn. You do not ask the pigs if they want to be butchered.

Debbie shelved those uncomfortable thoughts. She would have time to consider what would be helpful for her situation and maybe, would be helpful to the unhappy residents of the poisoned village. Was there a possible solution that would do all of those things?

"Debbie," said Remus, startling her from her musing.

"Yes, sir?"

"Do you want to know what is happening with your former in-laws?"

Debbie set her jaw, thinking of Aldo's mother, her voice sweet as the scent of a rose and every word barbed with thorns. This was an easy question to answer.

"No, sir. I do not. I am part of Kenyatta and my in-laws are here."

Remus looked pleased, as did Preston and the other senior family members. Against her back, she could feel Yannick shift his weight, hugging her a little tighter, and he was pleased as well.

After they were dismissed, they walked back down the hill to the snug cottage in the village below. Once safe inside, Debbie ran to Chika to hug her and tell her how much she meant to her, that this was home and always would be, now and forever.

That night, cuddled up in the alcove, their breath visible in the cold air, Debbie asked Yannick, "What will Remus do?"

"I don't know. He's not happy; we've been causing him problems."

She started to say something and he kissed her then said, "I know, it's not something you or me meant to do. Remus is glad to have you and the girls, but it's still something he has to manage, along with every other part of running Kenyatta. Having to do something doesn't mean you always want to do it, yeah?"

Debbie thought of plucking the geese in the spring and hearing them cry and how bright the blood droplets shone against the soft white down and their now-naked skin. She wiggled closer to him and Geance, under the delicious, life-giving warmth of the feather bed their suffering made possible.

"Yes, you're right."

Winter Solstice arrived at last. Like in Shelleen and Dairapaska before that, it was a week of worship, singing, celebration, games and feasting, marking the beginning of winter and the promise of spring returning again, despite it being so many months away. Every day grew longer by a few precious seconds and every night grew shorter by a few seconds more. Debbie knew that as the days crept forward, the seconds would add up to minutes, enough to truly see that the morning came earlier and the deep night would fall over the village later, lit by the glitter of the icy stars and the frozen moons racing past each other as fast as they could forever.

Much about this time of year was similar to Shelleen and Dairapaska. They exchanged simple gifts. Debbie knitted sweaters using the patterns she knitted in Dairapaska. They looked very different from the knitting done in Shelleen and Kenyatta, which used elaborate cables and twists in a single color to make a complex design. In Dairapaska, and she had to have her mother mail her the patterns, colored yarns were knit into a tapestry of animals and flowers and geometric designs, with the yarn floating free and hidden inside the sweater until that color reappeared again in the design.

For months, Debbie had collected, traded, saved and sorted the undyed yarns into their different shades of cream and tan and beige and gray, until she had enough to knit her sweaters. Kenyatta, like Shelleen, did not dye most of the wools and linen, only what was used for embroidery. Finely dyed wools and linen were reserved for the ruling family as it was more costly and did not wear as well in daily use. As she knitted, she resolved to get the seeds from the dye plants of Dairapaska to give to Chika and the women of Kenyatta. The patterned sweaters she knitted did not look like the brightly colored sweaters she remembered from Dairapaska but they looked nothing like the sweaters of Shelleen and Kenyatta. She knew that everyone who saw them would know she had done the work and no one else.

Other things were different. The men danced for the women again, this time inside one of the barns as it was far too cold outside, no matter how vigorously they danced, to strip down and show off for their admiring audience. Debbie, like other mothers of young babies, made arrangements and trades so they all could enjoy the dancing and what came afterwards. As before, this was an event very strictly segregated by age just as the Fall Migration celebration had been.

Later on, in private, Debbie danced for Yannick, wearing the ankle bells and finger chimes her mother had mailed her and his response was everything she could have hoped for.

As with the Fall Equinox, oaths of fealty were sworn, marriages publicly declared, and babies born since the Fall Equinox presented. Debbie and Yannick got to show off Geance to the crowd, ensuring everyone in Kenyatta, both the living and the dead, knew he was one of them. Debbie chose not to point out that she did not think it likely *anyone* in Kenyatta didn't already know about Geance. It seemed to her everyone in each of the villages had stopped by at least once to see this remarkable baby who had arrived in the middle of the night, dumped off by the notorious Maureen of Lynch. Instead, she smiled and told everyone how happy she was that she and Yannick had little Geance as their son, destined to become a loyal Hand of Kenyatta like his brothers, his father, his uncles, and his grandfathers on back to the founding of Kenyatta. Since this was quite true, it was a very easy thing for her to say.

Another high point during the week was letters bearing welcome news from Dairapaska and from Shelleen. The mail blockade had been lifted for the families.

Debbie's mother and Lupita both sent letters that arrived the same day and both said the same thing. Their respective daimyos had decreed that their Winter Solstice gift to their peasants was to allow them to write letters, as they should have been allowed to do all along. There were more traditional gifts as well, but to the bride-trade families, this was what mattered the most.

Debbie's mother and Lupita also wrote that their next letter, the one they were writing after this one to Debbie, would be to their counterpart so far away. Debbie smiled as she read this, knowing the two women would enjoy writing to each other. They both knew so much already about each other's lives and now they would be able to communicate directly. Lupita added in her letter that she had already written to her daughter Pia, a letter she started as soon as the families in Shelleen had been given the glad news.

Debbie wondered if anyone would write to her from Dairapaska and Shelleen and sure enough, letters began arriving from the bride-trade families, from multiple members within each family, thanking her for her efforts. Each of the other forty-seven brides wrote as well, as grateful as their families, both new and old, for this chance to reconnect directly with those who had been lost to them so long ago. Every day brought more mail and the Post-Mistress commented that she would have to assign Debbie a bigger mail cubby if this flood kept up.

Even Fulvia Acconcio sent a short, grudging note.

Debbie answered every letter she received, including Fulvia's. As she wrote her responses to the families in Shelleen, she was surprised at the savage joy that filled her with every word she laid on the paper, the ink shining black against the dull cream. No one in Shelleen would ever again think of her as silent Debbie, dull Debbie, drab Debbie, patient Debbie who did not seem to care what was said to her, Debbie who had no spine, Debbie the ox.

No one else in the Acconcio family wrote to Debbie, and she did not write to them. That part of her life was over and she saw no need to revisit it. She had rarely spoken when she was living in their household and now, Debbie thought, her silence could continue to speak for her.

The end of Solstice was marked in another way, one that made it more important to enjoy every day, every hour, every minute and every touch. It was Yannick's turn to go back out onto the steppes to the winter pastures. He and Otis and their crews would be gone for many weeks. It would be bitter work in bitter weather, repeatedly testing their toughness and endurance. Chika told her that some men and boys did not return whole from the winter pastures and some men never returned at all. Prayers would be said daily for their safe return, as they were said for every man and boy who rode out into the winter storms for the good of the demesne.

With Yannick gone, each night brought with it a deeper cold than she had ever known and Debbie was grateful again to the geese and the sheep who sacrificed their down and wool so her children could stay warmer.

With the Winter Solstice over and Yannick gone, life returned to its normal routine, all the things that had to be done to keep body and soul together, while trying hard to keep out the cold. Every day, the stored food in the root cellar, the larder, and the dry stores grew imperceptibly lower until suddenly in mid-winter, it was apparent that spring could not come fast enough.

Every meal was enjoyed, there was nothing wasted and nothing was ever left over. Pangs of hunger did not make the cold easier to bear.

The cold grew crueler still over the weeks, the deep winter arrived and with it came the thin time, the hungry time, the starving time. Every day, Debbie and Chika debated what to prepare, as they sorted through potatoes, turnips, swedes, and other roots that needed to be eaten before they spoiled, checked stored grain for insects, hoping to not find too many, picked over beans, checked cheeses for mold, inspected the fermented vegetables and salted and dried meat, and prayed for an egg from the chickens.

Spotty earned his keep in the root cellar, catching and eating the rats that the cats missed. He was hungry, and they were delicious. When he caught a rat, he would tear it to bits and swallow every bloody scrap, right down to the tail and eagerly go hunting for more. Debbie did not envy him his rats as she had in the poisoned village so long ago, and she prayed daily that she would not be in that position again as the winter deepened and grew colder still.

They were hopeful they had stored enough food for the worst of winter, enough to last until the earliest days of spring when planting could begin again and when the chickens would give a few eggs. Then, no matter how economical they were, the food would finally run out. As it was, it would be a near thing and they would have to borrow from family and neighbors to eat while waiting for the early harvests.

Chika reassured Debbie they could borrow from relatives and neighbors, who would be repaid in other ways. Even, she said, as early as the following winter if they had an insect infestation or sickness in their own cottages. It was routine to help the neighbors and relatives as they would help in their turn when it was needful.

The rapidly lowering food stocks made another decision easy. Debbie and Chika agreed they would double the size of the kitchen garden in the spring despite the additional work that would require at every stage, from planting to harvesting to preserving. They needed more of everything, particularly as six kids grew up fast and ate more and more every day. Much time was spent deciding what to grow, where, and how to make room for it in the storage spaces. Debbie resolved to ask her mother to send her seeds from plants she remembered from Dairapaska, despite their not, perhaps, being winter hardy in Kenyatta. Chika had warmer parts of her garden, areas that might allow them to grow these new foods and herbs that could be preserved to add more flavor and color in the long, cold winters ahead.

More weeks passed and it became apparent that Winter was beginning to loosen her icy grip. Every day, Chika and Debbie contemplated the stores in the root cellar and the attics and the larder, checking and rechecking every corner, every crock, every flask, every sack, to be sure nothing had been missed. The season had moved deep into the thin time and the stores in the root cellar were very low, they would not last until spring, and it would soon be necessary to borrow.

At last Yannick, Otis, and their crews returned from the winter pastures, their places being taken by other Hands and their crews. It was a great joy for Debbie to welcome Yannick home, to see him again, talk with him, and snuggle up in the alcove bed with him.

He had been home for a week. The family had sat down to supper, hungry as always at this time of year. They were enjoying very much how the last of the sharp, spicy cabbage went with the dried beans and salted meat, when the knock came at the cottage door.

Spotty sprang into hysterical action, and he did not calm

down so Debbie knew, even before Yannick got to the door, that it was not a relative or friend. It was someone else, someone they did not know.

Someone else turned out to be a page from the manor house, one of the new fosterlings, this time a lad from Aguillero. Some of the Kenyatta lads had been likewise fostered out, Avalon's son among them, ensuring that the lords of the demesnes of the North all got to know each other as they grew up. The page refused to come into the cottage and escape the cold until Spotty had been dragged off protesting vigorously, leaving Debbie to wonder what silly story he had been told by the older boys up at the manor house.

"Yannick? Remus wants to see you in the morning, first thing. He's got a big project for you," said the page. He looked young and nervous, not much older than Kerill.

"A project? The snowdrifts are still man-high on the steppes. What does he want?"

The page gave him a hunted look and said, "Sorry, sir, I just deliver messages. He didn't say."

Yannick and Leon exchanged worried glances. The page eyed Spotty, being firmly held down by Kerill although that did not stop him from growling, and refused tea or supper, saying he had to get back up the hill right away.

As soon as he left, Yannick said, "I got to talk to Otis, right after supper. If Remus wants me, he'll probably want the both of us."

"Do you know what it could be?" asked Debbie.

Yannick sighed, looking unhappy. "No idea. I'll find out tomorrow." He refused to speculate, but Debbie noticed that he and Leon did talk, their hands flying too fast for her to follow despite the lessons she had been getting from Chika. Chika did not look happy either.

That evening as they sat spinning, while Ghita and Carina carded the creamy wool, Debbie asked Chika, but she refused to speculate. "No use borrowing trouble," was all she would say and then changed the conversation to how did Debbie manage to knit colored patterns like flowers and snowflakes? This was a conversation they had had before and it showed Debbie how uneasy Chika was.

The next morning Yannick set off for the manor house,

wearing the patterned sweater she had knitted him for Winter Solstice, the white snowflakes standing out against the gray wool.

"Got to show it off, yeah?" He kissed her soundly and said goodbye to everyone as though he did not expect to be back for some time.

Hours later, he came back spitting mad.

"That *bastard*! And I can't refuse without betraying my oath. He just *had* to remind me who's the boss. An honor, he says. No one else can do as good a job. I'll be representing Kenyatta, he says. Putting Shelleen permanently in our debt, he says. All true, every last word of it and I do not want to do this."

Yannick swore and stomped and carried on and eventually, over supper, calmed down enough to explain the honor he had been assigned.

"You all know that very early spring's the thin time. Hardest time of the year to get by, all the food stocks are low and getting lower and not much besides greens will grow this soon." Yannick was not saying anything that they did not already know and Debbie wondered why he was saying it at all.

"To make it through, you got to spend all year planning and preparing." Yannick held up a spoonful of beans and barley, mixed with salted meat. "You two worked as hard as any man out on the steppes to keep us fed."

"Quite true," replied Chika. "It's always nice to know what we do is noticed." Debbie nodded in agreement.

"Get to the point, boy," said Leon.

Yannick scowled at his beans. "That poisoned village, they didn't prepare for the winter. They couldn't because anything they managed to grow was ruined, not fit to eat. Airik Shelleen sent mil-rats and plenty of them to keep the villagers alive. He can't anymore, not now."

Debbie sat back, startling Geance in her lap, making him whimper. "They'll starve. What happened?"

She noticed how closely Ghita and Kerill were listening. Both of them were now old enough to notice how the family food stocks were getting lower. Ghita in particular was old enough to learn how to manage a household and she was intimately involved, every day, with what Chika and Debbie did.

"Shelleen had a road built from the villages out the 150-plus klicks to the poisoned village. Those winter storms we had tore it all up to hell and back. It'll be weeks rebuilding it and they have to wait until the weather gets better to start. Meantime, it's damn hard to run wagons out. They have to use pack horses and you can't move as many goods, not enough to keep everyone fed."

"They're trapped," said Debbie. "It would be closer to walk to the way-stations in the corridor."

"These people can't do that," Yannick answered. "Shelleen won't let them off the demesne, on account of that says to the government he can't make a go of the village if they go taking handouts from the government. If he can't make a go, then he cedes control of the lode and he won't do that, ever."

"What's this got to do with you?" asked Leon. "As if I couldn't guess." He looked away across the room, rapping his hands on the table in agitation.

Yannick smiled sourly. "I'm one of his best Hands, which is true. I've been to the poisoned village, spent a few weeks there. I got me and my crew in, we spent weeks there watching and living off the land and we were fine, and I got my crew out, with not a hair on our heads mussed. Remus wants me and Otis to go back."

"Go back! And do what?" asked Leon. "You can't move in pack horses loaded with mil-rats any faster than Shelleen can."

Yannick glared at the table, fixing his ire where he could since he could not fix it on the person who had earned it. "I am gonna collect that mixed herd that was going to Purnell in the spring to be slaughtered. I am going to move that herd, all those mixed critters, and get them from the farthest winter pasture down to the corridor, across the government road, and into Shelleen to the poisoned village. Those villagers will be eating that herd, until Shelleen can get through with building the road. Oh, and I'm gonna bring in everything else I can, out on pack horses. Probably dig wells too, to water the stock and dig dew ponds as well."

Leon blew out his breath very slowly. "Madre Winter. You'll be gone for weeks, the railroad won't like you crossing the tracks with the herds, they always get pissy when you block the trains, and the road people will hate you.”

“Yup. Oh, and I got to work around them all, so as to not let people wonder what I’m up to.” Yannick glared again, this time at nothing in particular, and Debbie guessed he was envisioning how difficult it would be to achieve this special honor.

“Who is paying for this?” asked Chika.

“Shelleen will be, with the proceeds from his Red Mercury lode.”

Yannick and Debbie had told Leon and Chika what was happening in the poisoned village and why, but outside of the Kenyatta family, no one else other than Otis and the lads knew.

Yannick speared the kids with his eyes, each in turn, and said, “You will not mention this outside this house,” and waited for and got their nods of acknowledgement.

Leon rolled his eyes. “IOU’s you mean. Remus is betting the Martian government will pay Shelleen and Shelleen will pay him, yeah?”

“Yeah. But what he’s really doing is making sure Shelleen is beholden to Kenyatta for the next hundred years.”

“Maybe, if they remember. A new daimyo can change everything,” Leon said sourly.

“But why you?” asked Debbie. “You just got back and you weren’t supposed to go back out on the steppes so soon.”

Yannick looked even more sour. “It should be someone else, but it’s true that I have been there, that I know what to avoid, without him having to tell even more people what’s going on. And, I will see and know what Shelleen’s been doing with the poisoned village since I last was there. Me and Otis were there for weeks, we know everything about it. We’ll see, better than anyone else could, what has changed.”

Leon drained his tea and set his kuksa down with a thud. “Let me guess. The real reason is Remus is the boss and he wants you and Debbie to know it.”

“Yup, and everyone else too. He’s cut us slack, and now he’s reining us in, and making it look like an honor and a privilege!”

Chika snickered without any humor. “Which is why he’s still the daimyo, even though he’s been getting on in years.”

“Remus went over all kinds of things, everything he thought I’d need to know and everything he wants me to look for. It’ll be a big job and it won't end until Shelleen gets that damn road repaired and a few wagon trains of supplies moved along it. It's likely to lead to bigger and better things too, another reason I should be *honored* to do this." Yannick began moodily stirring his beans as though hoping to divine a future more to his liking in them.

"What bigger things could there be?" asked Debbie.

"Working with Shelleen to keep out squatters, patrolling the corridor from Armstrong to Satran, spending time in Purnell and working with the government there, all on Remus's behalf. I'd be his eyes and ears on the ground. The list must be as long as your arm." Yannick did not sound enthusiastic.

"You can't say no to this," said Leon with a sigh. "You'd be making Kenyatta better for everyone, making it an important part of the quad in a way it's never been before, and keeping the overflow from the mine out of our land. Government control or not, there'll still be squatters and claim jumpers and Shelleen is made of dirt farmers. They cannot patrol their own land the way we can."

Yannick drained his cup of tea and Debbie poured him another, watching the mint leaves unfurl in the boiling water and wishing she knew how to read them. They told her nothing, other than it would be a messy, complicated job.

"This is what the oath of fealty really means, doesn't it," said Debbie. "You do what has to be done and you don't count the cost."

Yannick smiled at her, the first time he had smiled since getting back from the manor house. "My own dearest Debbie. I wouldn't be doing this job if I hadn't met you, it would have gone to someone else, Pello most likely. Meeting you made us know, before it happened, what the future would bring to Kenyatta. And I will do this job for you, because you are worth everything to me."

She snuggled up next to him. "I'll miss you every day and every night. When will you have to leave?"

"It'll be a few days. Otis and I have to make arrangements for crews to go with us. We'll need more than just our own. I've got a long list already. I should be back by mid-spring."

He took Geance and Espe both into his lap, hugging them to him. "Espe's already walking and by the time I get back,

Geance'll be crawling. I'll miss it. I'll miss all my kids growing up."

Kerill said, "we'll tell you everything, dad. And when it warms up, maybe we can ride with grampie to meet you for a few days."

"That's true, it'd be a good experience for when you go out as a gauchito. Ghita? You want to ride out with your brothers?"

"Of course I do! I can ride as good as Kerill now," she answered stoutly. Leon smiled in amusement but did not say anything. Kerill glared at Ghita and mumbled under his breath, making her stick her tongue out at him, leading to louder words and then a kick. The next few minutes were spent restoring order at the table.

With the return of calm, Chika sighed down to her toes. "Well, it's an ill wind that blows no good. The food will last a bit longer with you gone."

Debbie eyed her over the table and said, "I'd still rather Yannick stayed home."

"I know. As would I."

After supper, the kids were sent off to do the chores, allowing Debbie to say something that she had not felt like bringing up earlier. Now seemed the time, as the adults settled into the evening's work.

She looked shyly down at her spinning, her hands never stopping. "There will be other opportunities to see little ones learn to walk."

The other adults turned to stare at her.

"Are you?" asked Yannick, looking astonished and gratified. He set down the spoon he was carving for Espe, his hands stilled by his surprise.

"Not yet, but Geance is starting to eat some real food. My cycle will start again."

Chika started humming to herself over her own knitting, a sign that Debbie had learned meant she was happy and thinking of the future.

Leon said, "More grandchildren! Why I'll soon have more grandkids than anybody else in Kenyatta. With Lysander and Erissa's, I'm already at eight and counting!" He leaned over to kiss Debbie's cheek. "And don't you fret if the baby is a boy or a girl. Either one would be a blessing beyond measure."

"Let's get there first, dad," said Yannick with a laugh. "I'll be up to the manor house or out and around every day until I leave. Plenty of time ahead of us, yeah?" He winked at Debbie, making her flush with pleasure.

The next few days flew by, filled with preparations, and then Yannick, Otis, the lads and a few other crews rode westward to the far winter pastures, not to return for many weeks.

The cottage was much emptier with Yannick gone, and the nights for Debbie grew colder still, despite the weather ever so slowly shifting back to the spring.

Debbie's Dilemma

AS ALWAYS, SPRING DANCED in on her own terms, not attending to anyone's desires nor arriving a moment earlier to better suit anyone's needs. Winter shifted away slowly, grudgingly upon her teasing approach and the days grew marginally longer as the nights grew infinitesimally shorter. The weather changed imperceptibly, randomly, dramatically; whimsical as ever, and as the season progressed, no word came from Yannick or Otis as to what was happening so far away in Shelleen at the poisoned village.

Word finally did come, but indirectly.

Debbie received a letter from Lupita that Yannick and his crews had arrived in the poisoned village, news that Lupita had been told by one of the family members who had gotten their own letter from a trapped relative, starving and isolated on the frigid steppes. The overseer had finally been able to reach the poisoned village and had been able to return afterwards to the manor house and the villages of Shelleen, bearing news of what had happened to their far-away kin.

Starvation had been terrible. A few of the peasants had died; the youngest and the sickest and the oldest, as would be expected, and those people, sadly, might have died anyway. Even under the best of circumstances, not everyone survived the winter. Nevertheless, it looked like everyone else would live, now that Yannick of Kenyatta had arrived and the herds he brought with him were slowly being slaughtered and eaten down to their boiled bones, the bones cracked and sucked emptied of their rich, fatty marrow.

In her letter, Lupita asked Debbie if this was her Yannick?

He had not, according to the letter that had been passed around the villages of Shelleen, admitted to anything other than knowing who Debbie was and that she and her daughters had indeed found refuge in Kenyatta. Lupita thought this very sensible as his presence was less likely to cause trouble with Aldo Acconcio, who, by all accounts, was not doing well.

Moreover, Lupita wrote, this also kept Yannick and his crews from being pestered constantly by villagers wanting to know every last detail of Debbie's new life and, more importantly, how she had been able to walk away into the endless seas of grass with two little girls, a baby, a little dog, a little knife, no man to help her and yet live to tell the tale. Lupita believed that life in the poisoned village was so miserable that there were others there who would have taken the chance and run away to a new life in one of the free-cities, if only they knew how Debbie had managed such a feat.

Lupita wrote that it was most unlikely the daimyo would want to encourage this information to spread around and that Yannick, no matter what he might have thought of Shelleen personally, did not want to go chasing after runaway serfs out on the steppes. He had more than enough work to do already, by all the accounts *she* was being given.

Debbie wrote back to Lupita that yes, he was her Yannick and yes, he did not wish to cloud the issue with the peasants in the poisoned village. He already had too much to do keeping them alive in a very difficult situation while they all waited for Shelleen to rebuild the road. She knew he did not need the interference of idle speculation and, even more, did not want the gossip.

Then Debbie asked the question that had her most concerned. Had the daimyo of Shelleen yet addressed publicly why he was so insistent on keeping the village alive? If the trapped villagers knew there was a reason, despite being forced to live in a cursed area, it might make it easier for them to manage. It grated on Debbie that she could not write to inform Lupita what was happening. She could only ask carefully worded questions and hope that Lupita would be guided by Debbie's questions into asking the correct questions on her own.

She waited impatiently for an answer from Lupita and one

came several days later.

No, the daimyo had not said anything official, but there were rumors flying everywhere in Shelleen. Something had been discovered at the site of the poisoned village and it was of critical importance to the health and well-being of every single resident in Shelleen, from the highest to the lowest. The Shelleen family was in turmoil over what was happening; the poisoned village overshadowed most of the family's business and discussions.

Lupita wrote that the ruling family didn't quite grasp how much of their business their peasants knew. They seemed to believe that since *they* paid no attention to the housemaids cleaning up after them that the housemaids paid no attention to them. This was not true, of course, but the housemaids, their families, and, in fact, all the serfs of Shelleen felt no need to enlighten the ruling family. Doing so would cut off what little information they had; information that sometimes, as in this case, had taken far too long in coming.

The ruling family had been unusually careful in their discussions for months, even to the point of cleaning up after themselves. This was an important fact, Lupita wrote. It demonstrated how serious the issue was. But at long last, bits of information the family did not want made public had slipped free.

Knowing there *was* a reason, even if the serfs did not yet know the details, made things easier to bear. It meant the daimyo was not being heartlessly cruel, criminally stupid, and wasting resources that could be much better spent elsewhere. It seemed the ruling family had been *forced* to establish the poisoned village, something they were openly unhappy about, and this made the peasants of Shelleen somewhat less resentful than they had been.

Lupita also wrote she would not tell anyone Yannick was married to Debbie. That information could wait until the current crisis was dealt with. She would wait until Debbie gave her permission and, in the meantime, quash those rumors as best she could.

There was other news from Shelleen as well, something that concerned Debbie very much, making her fears rise up again. With Aldo lost to the poisoned village and never to return, the

Acconcios were more desperate than ever to get their grand-daughters back. They were pushing, as much as serfs could push, for some punishment or other to be visited on Debbie for running away and on Kenyatta for taking her in.

Lupita wrote that this was remarkably stupid on the Acconcios' part as Kenyatta's men were even now keeping the unfortunate residents of the poisoned village alive. The relatives of those unhappy residents also felt this way and they were refusing to aid the Acconcio family in any manner. The bride-trade families were in full agreement. They did not see the need to punish Debbie for running away with her daughters; why, Debbie running away meant they had gotten news of their own daughters lost so long ago and still so far away. The Dairapaska brides and the families they had been married into agreed wholeheartedly and for the same reasons.

This meant the Acconcios — formerly a proud, respected and long-established family — were being avoided, even shunned. Lupita found it difficult, she wrote, to feel much sympathy for them. They had brought it upon themselves. What else did they expect? And yet they expected the daimyo of Shelleen, a man who listened only to his own counsel, to listen to *their* demands just as they expected the families involved in the bride trade and the families with relatives hanging on by their fingernails in the cursed village to accede to *their* demands and ignore the needs of their own kin.

This showed, Lupita wrote, a serious misunderstanding of reality. Their pride got in the way of facing facts.

Debbie had to agree, but her agreement did not change reality for her either. She had to face facts, too. The Acconcios *did* have a point; several points in fact, each one large enough that the daimyo of Shelleen could not avoid noticing them, despite their source.

She had stolen their granddaughters, the only children left to the Acconcio family. With no possible heirs, their name would be lost and their land reclaimed by the Shelleen family to be redistributed as they saw fit. This was always a serious matter among peasant families. Who would get that land? How would it be parceled out? What trouble would this cause when some were enriched and others were not? Would a third son be elevated, allowing him to found a new line? Would multiple families each receive a small piece or would one large family group receive it all? The ramifications of divvying up the Acconcio holdings would be felt and discussed for generations.

Moreover, by taking their granddaughters, Debbie had also stolen long-term fertility from Shelleen, the planned-for result of the bride trade. Debbie's daughters, whomever they would have married in Shelleen, would have borne many children, followed by many more grandchildren. Now her daughters would give their hoped-for fertility to Kenyatta. That they would do this of their own free will, choosing whom they married, did not change the fact Kenyatta benefited and Shelleen did not.

And finally, there was the other point, one the *Acconcios* might not be making, but it was clearly seen by everyone else, as evidenced by Lupita's letter about Yannick arriving in the cursed, poisoned village and what those trapped villagers wanted to ask him the most. If Debbie could run away across the trackless steppes, with her three little girls, her little dog, her little knife, and live to tell about it, then anybody could.

That meant for Shelleen, for Dairapaska, and anyone else who heard the story — and Debbie was certain that every person in Shelleen, Dairapaska, and, yes, Kenyatta too, who had kin outside their home demesnes had written about this story to those far-away relatives — knowing it could be done revealed a door that didn't exist before. You could escape. You could choose to stay of your own free will or you could take your chances and choose to leave, knowing that if Debbie could survive, alone but for her little children and without any aid from any man, then you might be able to as well.

This was not, perhaps, a problem for Kenyatta and the other Northern Ranching Tier demesnes. Their Hands, their vaqueros, even their gauchitos knew very well how to live on the steppes, how to find food, water, and to navigate across the unending oceans of grass, vast and mysterious beyond knowing. Yet they did not run away; not to the free-cities in the government corridors nor to other demesnes. Debbie had asked and the answer, from everyone she had asked, was the same. "We like it here in Kenyatta and have no reason to leave."

This was — she was sure from her months of daily living

and daily observing — because Kenyatta gave his vassals no reason to leave. He could not compel them to stay, but he could make their lives acceptable enough that they wanted to remain. This was a very different thing altogether from what Debbie was familiar with. Having twice watched Remus Kenyatta swear fealty to his vassals, something that everyone here considered normal, right, and fitting, Debbie saw what she had not seen in Dairapaska nor in Shelleen. The daimyo, along with every member of the ruling family, considered *all* of Kenyatta to be part of his clan and therefore worthy of care.

Kenyatta had vassals and not serfs. This was not true of Shelleen, and it was even less true of Dairapaska.

Shelleen was, at least, well managed. The daimyos of Shelleen thought of the people living there as peasants and serfs, lesser than themselves, but they also considered them to be of value. Sheep had to be cared for to extract the most wealth. Uncared-for sheep died of disease, gave poor wool and scanty milk, and delivered stillborn lambs, leaving the owner with nothing at all. People were livestock, and like any resource had to be husbanded carefully, to encourage growth and good results and wealth.

Dairapaska was not well managed. Debbie had not realized how ground down the serfs there were until after her escape to Kenyatta. The resented, daily burdens imposed by the ruling family had been normal, what everyone expected; and in Shelleen she had been so miserable that she could not see the differences between what she was used to and what was expected of a serf there. Once in Kenyatta and recovering from her misery, she could examine what she had seen and heard and remembered and the differences became clear.

The flow of questions and answers from the letters she shepherded brought the rulers' differences into even sharper focus. There had been no riots in Shelleen over the forced settlement of the poisoned village, no open revolt from peasants who had decided they had nothing left to lose. Lupita had commented in her letter that she was surprised at how there had been no riots in Shelleen over the poisoned village. Until she had been told of the riots in Dairapaska, she had not considered doing such a thing. No one had.

The peasants of Shelleen had enough residual trust to believe that the actions of the daimyo were of benefit to the demesne as a whole. The new rumors flying about said the demesne had been forced to settle the cursed village; their faith was justified.

The daimyo of Shelleen had been told about the riots in Dairapaska. All the daimyos on Mars must have heard about them by now. Did this make Airik Shelleen lay uneasy in his bed at night? Perhaps he did not worry because he knew he cared enough for his serfs that they had *not* rioted, despite the provocation of the poisoned village. This would not be true of other daimyos, who might be very uneasy, indeed, as the story raced around the planet via conversations and letters.

Did the daimyo of Shelleen wonder how many of his serfs would slip away at night, through the seas of grass, and disappear into the government corridors? Did any of the other daimyos wonder and fret?

Once a serf was in the corridor, the property of the Martian government and not under the control of any demesne, he was, in theory, a free man. Thinking this over, Debbie supposed that daimyos could and did send their own men onto the steppes to retrieve runaways as who would ever know they had trespassed? The steppes were vast and only the grass witnessed what you did on them. Runaway serfs could vanish forever. Some would make it to the government road and some measure of safety; other serfs would die on the steppes but they would die free.

Yannick believed the dirt lords relied on a potential runaway's concern about the family left behind. But if Debbie could run away with little children, then a serf did not need to leave his family behind. He could take his wife and children with him. Other family members left behind might be prosecuted, but not the way an abandoned wife or children would be.

Debbie's escape was serious, more serious than Yannick believed and more serious, she thought, than Remus could understand. He did not worry over his vassals vanishing into the steppes because they would not do such a thing. Nor did he fret about what Dairapaska would say or do; that demesne was too far away to matter.

But Shelleen was different. Shelleen and Kenyatta had to work together because of the Red Mercury lode. What would the daimyo of Shelleen have to say to Remus Kenyatta if his serfs ran away and worse, if they decided to escape to Kenyatta? The problem of one serf and her stolen daughters might be swept under the rug. Many serfs lost forever would not be acceptable and thus could not be ignored.

As Debbie fretted over this dilemma, she realized her first fears upon being discovered by Yannick were well founded. Her escape would matter. News would spread far and wide and eventually many other daimyos might put pressure upon Kenyatta to make an example of her so they could demonstrate to their own restive peasants that they could not flee without unpleasant consequences.

Debbie thought and thought as she labored through each passing day, doing everything that was needful, while she waited for Yannick to return from the poisoned village. There had to be a solution, something she could offer to Kenyatta to give to Shelleen, a solution of enough value that both daimyos would not care what was said to them about her. She had stolen fertility from Shelleen and she had proved to the world escape was possible. What could be of enough value to pay for those things? What could she provide that would prove to Remus Kenyatta *and* whomever replaced him as daimyo that she and her daughters were lucky for the demesne? What could she give to Shelleen so the daimyo would not care about her and would not care about what other daimyos had to say to him?

Chika and Leon both noticed Debbie's worried introspection. But when she spoke of her concerns, they dismissed them.

"Remus will tell them dirt lords to pound sand," Leon said with a laugh and a hug. "They don't matter one bit, not to him and not to anybody in the North."

"No use borrowing trouble, Debbie," Chika said soothingly, patting her hand. "I know it's a worry but I don't see what you can do that would repay Shelleen short of going back and we, all of us, don't want you to ever do such a dreadful thing."

But it felt to Debbie that Remus could not just tell the other daimyos to pound sand; he had to work with them on occasion and telling other people to pound sand did not make them want to be cooperative. Debbie also did not feel as though she was borrowing trouble. It was coming all on its own, she could feel it, as she lay awake at night fretting and missing Yannick. She was grateful every night that Geance was with her as his own needs distracted her from her concerns, sometimes enough that she could let go and sleep and dream of Yannick's touch.

The worry ate at her, distracting her from the ongoing work of enduring through the last, hardest weeks of the thin time. Spring, that capricious, heartless jade, teased and cajoled and disappointed as she always did and then, just as suddenly, she was all smiles and joy with soft breezes and gentle rain. But warmer days did not make the food stocks grow any higher nor did increasing sunshine make it less needful for Debbie and Chika to ask for scare roots and barley from the neighbors who did not have much to spare. Nor did the shorter nights make the new greens in the earliest beds in the warmest corner of the kitchen garden grow any faster. They, like Spring, took their time and did as they pleased.

That morning, Debbie and Chika had asked for and received a crock of oats, suitable for porridge. Alison, well known for her fastidious housekeeping, had tightly sealed the crock and stored it away carefully the previous fall. Nonetheless, when Debbie and Chika opened it, the surface was crawling with repellent life, alive with little worms and weevils.

Debbie grimaced at the sight of the groats moving and shifting, the little worms wiggling up to be seen and then disappearing again downward under the trembling surface. She had never been able to sift weevils from flour without her stomach objecting; she would swallow the bile and do the job, however distasteful, as it had to be done. Nobody could afford to throw away flour. Sifting through these oats bid to be a worse job.

Chika swore under her breath at the heaving crock of oats. "I'll have to tell Alison right away. She won't be happy. Some of her other stored grain may be contaminated too."

"Let me find the coarse sieve," Debbie said, wanting to postpone for a moment or two the task waiting before her. She turned away from the crock, not wanting to study it further. She would see it up close soon enough. "I'll get started and clean the groats as best I can."

Chika sighed gustily. "Don't bother, Debbie. It's chicken feed now. They'll love it and might even give us some eggs in exchange. I'll trade those for another crock of grain."

Debbie said wonderingly, "you don't want me to sift out the crock? The chickens can eat the bugs and we'll still have the groats." She would miss some of the bugs, no matter how careful she was. It was a disgusting thought, but there you were. You did what you had to do to keep food in your belly.

"We're not *that* desperate," Chika said dryly. "Not this year. The harvest wasn't as good as it could have been, about average truthfully, but that means there's enough to go around so we don't have to eat grain better suited for poultry."

Debbie sat back on her stool, her mind awash with astonishment. This set her thinking again, and slowly, she started putting together the pieces that might answer her dilemma.

She had helped Chika prepare for winter almost from the day she had arrived. She knew very well what to do; she had been taught from her earliest years by her mother in Dairapaska and then had done much the same in Shelleen under Mrs. Acconcio's exacting and meticulous tutelage. Kenyatta was further north than Shelleen, and it had a harsher, longer winter. Like in Shelleen and Dairapaska before that, you had to work hard all spring, summer, and fall to ensure you had enough to eat over the winter when nothing would grow.

Chika had an extensive kitchen garden, as did every woman in Kenyatta. It was comfortingly similar to Shelleen and to Dairapaska, although not all the plants Chika grew were the same as Debbie remembered. She tended her garden, harvesting and cooking from it, and preserving the extra beans, tubers, cabbages and the like for the winter. Chika had not panicked when Debbie had arrived with her daughters; bringing extra mouths that had to be fed. She had fed them every day and still stored as much as she could harvest.

At no time had Chika worried the family would starve during the endless winter. She knew, as she often told Debbie, there would be shortages and they would run out and they would have to borrow food from the neighbors. But she never once worried there would be *no* food available. Enough was grown, every year, for the vassals to make it through the winter with a comfortable margin. That margin would let Chika borrow for the family and they would, in turn, repay those whom they borrowed from as was needful later on.

Debbie had seen the barley Leon had grown, harvested, and stored for the winter, the oats that Alison's husband had grown, the rye that Lysander's in-laws grew, the buckwheat that Otis' father grew. The men of Kenyatta, retired from the steppes, grew a wide variety of grain and pulses and roots, since you never knew in advance which ones would thrive and which ones would yield poor harvests. The weather could not be controlled, insects would come, disease would come, birds would come, and you would not know until the harvest which crop had been the best to grow for that particular year.

The farmers of Kenyatta, like the farmers of Shelleen and the farmers of Dairapaska, hedged their bets by growing many grains and trading among themselves. They did not rely on just their vast herds of animals, all mixed up together. In fact, as Debbie considered this strange line of thought, they grew as many crops as the farmers of Shelleen and Dairapaska did, and as varied a selection. And as in Shelleen and Dairapaska, their animals were used for their milk, their wool, their meat, their hides, horns, feathers, bones. Nothing got wasted, ever.

The herds of Kenyatta were huge and varied, far more so than what Shelleen or Dairapaska had. But the men of Kenyatta did not slaughter their bounty of animals wantonly. They did not use them in place of plants. They used them in addition to what they grew, either in the fields of roots and grains and pulses, or in the kitchen gardens their mothers, wives and daughters ruled, the hedgerows of berries, the orchards of fruits and nuts.

In the months she had been living in Kenyatta, Debbie had eaten and enjoyed more meat than she had eaten during her entire previous life. From the first bite of hare, roasted on the steppes, she had reveled in the taste and satisfaction. It had become normal.

Kenyatta had vast herds of all kinds: cattle, sheep, goats, llamas, horses, kazzowarys, pigs and many other kinds that Debbie had never heard of before. That did not include the wild herds of antelopes and gazelles that roamed free. That did not count the poultry in the villages of Kenyatta; chickens, geese, ducks, and pigeons. It did not count the rabbits, nutria, and guinea pigs in the kitchen gardens. There were many more wild flocks of birds beyond count on the steppes and sometimes those were eaten, too.

Yet despite this bounty of animals, most of them lived out their lives and were not raised specifically to be slaughtered for food. The ones that gave wool and milk were shorn and milked to provide for the villages, yet they did not necessarily end up on the supper table, at least not until they could no longer offer wool and milk in abundance.

Why did Kenyatta have so many, many animals? They had far more than Shelleen or Dairapaska did, despite not having more people to feed. In Shelleen and Dairapaska, there were plenty of animals, yet only the herdsmen spent most of their time with them. A village family would have rights to a set amount of milk from the village goats, they might raise a pig or three for the fall slaughter, they would have a hutch of rabbits, a coop of chickens, they would have rights to so much wool. In some ways, it was the same in Kenyatta.

Yet there were so many, many, *many* animals. And Yannick had told her that Kenyatta paid attention to the wild ones as well, directing them as best they could to where they wanted them to go.

Did this tie in with what Yannick had told her so long ago, out on the steppes? They kept the animals to feed the soil so the soil might feed them. In Shelleen and in Dairapaska, too, the farmers rotated their crops; one year a grain, the next pulses, then a root of some kind and they did that here too. But in Kenyatta, those rotations were alternated every single year with the land lying fallow and then used for pasture.

The farmers of Shelleen did not. They did not have enough animals to do that. Fields would lay fallow, then get used for pasture only as they became worn out. They were then fed with compost and manure, but never as much as the fields of Kenyatta received; there weren't enough animals to generate that much manure. Debbie had been told that the great barns alone, when scraped clean of rotted dung in the spring, would cover every kitchen garden in every village with a thick layer. And there would be manure left over, to be used wherever it seemed most needful.

The fields of Kenyatta, Debbie realized, neither the grain fields or the kitchen gardens, were never allowed to wear out. As she pondered over this marvel, her hands never stopping at whatever task she did, the worry lines on her face smoothed out. Debbie did not notice this, but Chika did.

Debbie began to notice other differences and she began to ask careful questions as she went about her days. The men of Kenyatta, in their fields, were not as careful in their farming practices as the serfs of Shelleen. The women of Kenyatta in their kitchen gardens, despite their careful attention, were not as tense as the farm wives of Shelleen. Why was this? They both farmed. They were all equally dependent on the vagaries of the weather. Insects preyed on their crops as did flocks of birds. They were careful, the farmers of Kenyatta, yet they did not obsess as did the farmers of Shelleen.

Part of it, Debbie supposed, was they knew they would never starve. As with the mixed herds that Yannick had moved from the farthest winter pastures across the government corridor to feed the starving serfs in the poisoned village, the vassals of Kenyatta knew they could eat the animals they so carefully raised if it was needful.

But even so, why did Kenyatta and the other northern demesnes have so many, many huge herds of mixed livestock? They could never eat them all. They did not even eat most of them. They did not raise them all to be sold to far-away markets for other people to eat them, although that could have been done. They had to have another reason.

And a few mornings later, as Debbie crouched in the soil in the kitchen garden, thinning the very earliest sharp greens to be eaten and giving what she left behind more room in which to grow larger, she saw the reason.

She turned over the soil in her hands, over and over, studying it and breathing in its scent. It was alive. It was full of life, rich and fecund and smelling of earth and fertility and more life to come. The more she looked, the more she saw; large creatures like the worms and many much smaller bugs, wrapped around the thick network of roots and humus, threaded throughout with the filaments of the terraformers. The soil itself was alive.

Debbie sat back on her heels in the warming sunshine. The

low stone walls soaked up the morning sun and they blocked the winds, making the corner she was in warmer than it should have been. The earliest spring greens flourished here, growing thickly and tall, sprouting from seeds that Chika had sown in the fall and then overwintered. The rest of the kitchen garden was still sleeping under layers of rotting leaves. The fields that Leon planned to till for barley, weeks from now, were still sleeping under their dense layer of winter-killed grass, the result of several years of pasturage.

This soil though, like many such warm patches in the kitchen gardens of Kenyatta, had already come back to life. It was not waiting any longer. It felt Spring reaching to it with her sunny warm hands, enough so that the earliest greens were willing to risk a hard frost. Even that, Debbie knew, might not be enough to kill these hardy greens with their roots reaching deep into the slowly warming soil.

This was what Yannick meant; that Kenyatta used their animals to feed the soil so the soil could feed them. So he had said and Leon had said, Kenyatta and all the Northern demesnes husbanded their soil as carefully as they did any other resource. They were as careful in handling their soil as they were with their water.

Debbie thought back to Aldo, trying to see him with new eyes. She could say many things about him, although she never did, but he was well regarded as a careful, competent, and skilled farmer, as were his brother and his father. They were, in fact, far more fastidious in their practices than Leon was. Yet Leon's yield of barley was as great, for the land he worked, as what Aldo would have expected from his own efforts.

Mrs. Acconcio, and Debbie could say many things about *her*, was as fastidious as anyone Debbie had ever seen about managing her kitchen garden. Yet Chika, who was far more easy-going on the subject, had harvested as much for the winter as Mrs. Acconcio would have done.

Debbie studied the soil in her hands, squeezing it between her fingers and breaking apart the clumps. She remembered vividly the dead, greasy sand in the poisoned village. Everywhere they dug, the soil was thin, scanty, and unpleasant to the touch. It smelled off, sour, not like the rich earthiness of Chika's kitchen garden. There were few worms or other bugs and they somehow never looked healthy, if a worm could look healthy. The roots of the few poverty grasses had been straggly and discolored, with lesions marring the larger ones.

She thought of the changes in the land as she and her daughters and Spotty had plodded north all those months ago. The grasses had changed, growing thicker, taller, and far more varied with every klick they had walked. At first, the changes were not so great from the rest of Shelleen, once she had left behind the poisoned village and the dead soil surrounding it. But they had crossed the road in the government corridor and there, Debbie had seen more dramatic changes. She had not stopped to dig in the soil as why would she? At the time, she had other things on her mind.

But thinking back she saw that the plants told their own story, as did the insects, the birds, the little rodents that Spotty caught more and more often. That soil was better and so was everything else that lived in and on it. Yannick said this was soil Kenyatta used for its own herds as no one else was using it and the result of their usage showed.

She also remembered the soil from her old village in Shelleen. Mrs. Acconcio's soil had not been this dark nor had it smelled quite so sweet. Debbie thought back to the fields that Aldo had worked. She had gone out many times to hoe and weed, and she did not think it looked the same as Leon's barley fields, thick with worms and full of rich, dark crumbles.

Debbie considered the peasant farmers who had been chosen to settle the poisoned village. They, all of them, had known what decent soil was. They had complained endlessly about the soil. She knew Aldo was well regarded for his skills in growing a wide variety of grains from uncooperative land while managing the vagaries of the weather. For the first time, Debbie began to seriously consider why he and the other men had been specially chosen by the daimyo from among all the peasants of Shelleen.

The midwife's husband was easy. He was a carpenter, the only non-farmer in the group. His wife had to go, for the health of the other women in the group, so he was chosen, too. As a midwife, she had also taken care of everyone's basic health needs.

Of the other men selected, the ones from Debbie's home village were like Aldo: well regarded for their farming skills and their ability to coax a better return from the land than the other men. Were the men from the other villages the same? She would have to write to Lupita and ask, but Debbie thought she already knew the answer.

The daimyo of Shelleen had known what the soil was like and he had tried to give the peasants he sent a fighting chance. She thought back to what Preston and Hiroshi had said when she had first gone to the manor house. Airik Shelleen had been trained as a geologist, not as a farmer. He would know soil, but not as a farmer would. He had misjudged the soil in the poisoned village. It had defeated his plan of the villagers being able to support themselves by their own efforts. But when he realized this, he sent mil-rats to feed them, and when he could no longer do that, he asked Remus Kenyatta for help to keep the peasants of the cursed village alive.

This recognition shocked Debbie. Airik *wanted* to keep them alive; he wanted to husband his resources and not waste them. The serfs of Shelleen mattered to him. Perhaps not as family members, but they had value and he did not want to discard them out of hand. Yannick was correct. There were daimyos who would not have cared. They would have sacrificed the lives of their serfs if it meant retaining control over their land. Remus himself had said as much.

The daimyo of Shelleen thought ahead, thinking of what he had to do to keep control of his land. The daimyo of Shelleen valued his resources; enough so he did not want to unnecessarily sacrifice the lives of his serfs. The daimyo of Shelleen was willing to bend his pride enough to ask the daimyo of another demesne for assistance to keep serfs alive; something that Debbie knew, from countless stories, was highly unusual.

Did this mean that, possibly, the daimyo of Shelleen would listen to her? A runaway serf who stole fertility from him and said to the wider world that escape was a real possibility and not a hopeless dream?

Debbie studied the soil spilling from her hands, the soil she was kneeling on. This was why the Northern demesnes had those vast herds of animals. Those animals were used to build up the soil so it would feed them all. They were as much a part of the terraforming as the lichens and algae and funguses that

Olde Earthe had seeded on Mars centuries before. She had watched the few goats and chickens in the poisoned village as they struggled to survive. Had similar animals struggled the same way during the earliest days on Mars so long ago, when Olde Earthe had begun the vast, millennia-long project of transforming a world of airless, arid red sand into a world that would support life in the open air?

She did not know *why* the Northern demesnes took such care with their animals when the agricultural demesnes did not, even though both regions were equally dependent upon the soil under their feet. But Debbie could see the results. Life in Kenyatta should have been harder than life in Shelleen. It was farther north with a longer, harsher winter just as Shelleen was farther north than Dairapaska, with a longer, harsher winter. Yet Kenyatta, with its more challenging climate, did not do just as well in keeping everybody fed. It did a little better.

Debbie realized what she could offer to the daimyo of Shelleen in exchange for her life and the lives of her daughters.

If he accepted her idea, the idea of a serf, he would enrich himself and Shelleen for generations to come. If he accepted her idea, he would be more beholden to Remus Kenyatta than ever, proving her value and luckiness to Kenyatta. If Shelleen demonstrated that he could improve his land, enriching himself and his peasants, then the other agricultural demesnes in his own nine-square might follow suit and honor him for it. That, too, would make them beholden to Remus Kenyatta, further enriching him.

Debbie could give fertility to the daimyo of Shelleen.

Improving the fertility of the lands of Shelleen for all time would more than repay him for the loss of her own fertility and that of her daughters. This would be a gift of such bounty that it would repay him for the knowledge that escape was possible for the serfs in Shelleen. If the land was improved, so that no one would go hungry, then they, like the vassals of Kenyatta, would have less reason to leave. Their lives would be improved.

She thought back to the grain maidens that the peasants of Dairapaska and Shelleen made at every harvest; something that, to her astonishment, the vassals of Kenyatta did not do. The grain maidens were brides of the land, symbolizing the hope of future harvests. Her idea, if accepted, would make her the bride of all of Shelleen; every person, every animal, and every hectare of soil would be wedded to her.

It would take time; years, Debbie thought, if not decades. But time would pass whether she did anything or not. She would go in the morning, after she had finished thinking about how and what she wanted to say. She would ask for an audience with Remus Kenyatta and tell him what she wanted said to the daimyo of Shelleen.

Debbie's Decision

EBBIE THOUGHT OVER HER plan carefully for the rest of the day and throughout the evening. She could find no flaw in what she had to say. She did not see why Remus would refuse to see her as he never had before. She could not ferret out a reason why he would refuse to pass on her idea to the daimyo of Shelleen. It benefited him and all of Kenyatta. Her coming to him, as a loyal vassal of Kenyatta with a way of enriching Kenyatta, would prove her value and her luckiness to the demesne. He would never send her or her daughters away. And yes, if the nine-square was enriched and working together better than it ever had in the past, he would tell other daimyos, from outside the nine-square, to pound sand and he would be backed up by the daimyos of Halverson, Winzlow, Aguillero, Armstrong, Satran, Ozigbow, Gish, and Shelleen. They would all benefit in so many ways.

The ultimate acceptance of her plan would depend on what she had deduced about the daimyo of Shelleen, a man she had never met, had never seen other than the picture Azi had drawn when Yannick had spied on the poisoned village; a man as far above her in the hierarchy of Shelleen as she was ranked above the rabbits in the hutch and the sheep in the meadow. His actions spoke for him, and Debbie could only pray that she had judged his character accurately. Was she right? Was she lucky? His response, an answer she would not receive directly as such a man would never speak to her, would tell her.

Debbie chose not to discuss what she wanted from Remus as she did not want to involve Chika or Leon. She did not want to hear what they had to say. This was her plan, her idea, and hers alone, and she did not want to muddy it nor become fearful over what she wanted to do: request the daimyos of two demesnes to do as she asked. Chika and Leon would be supportive, she was sure of that. The daimyos were quite capable of feeling differently about the words of a serf, however clever those words might be.

She thought suddenly of the Acconcios, her former in-laws. If her idea was accepted by the daimyo of Shelleen, he would tell them to pound sand over their stolen granddaughters. The thought filled her with savage, angry joy. Not once in all those years had anything Debbie said or done been valued by them. Even the grandchildren she bore them might have been delivered by a ewe in the meadow for the gratitude *she* had received. Her silence had spoken for her during the Winter Solstice, when she had written to so many other people in the villages of Shelleen but not to them. If the daimyo of Shelleen accepted her idea, it would speak great volumes to them about her worth, a worth they could no longer ignore or belittle.

What would Yannick say? She could not ask him. He was still toiling out at the poisoned village and would not return until Shelleen rebuilt the road between the poisoned village and the manor house villages and began moving wagons of provisions to the isolated, trapped serfs. But Debbie thought she knew what he would say. Yannick would approve and tell her to try.

That night, as she lay waiting for sleep, Debbie thought over her idea again, turning it back and forth and examining it for flaws. She was grateful that it filled her mind and kept her from missing Yannick so much. Spring was slowly, slowly warming the steppes, dancing her complex back-and-forth dance with Winter. The Spring Solstice was approaching, and she prayed that Yannick would be back in time to dance for her.

In the morning, she bundled up Geance, clean and fed and amused into sleepiness, and walked up the hill in the chilly sunshine to the manor house as she had done so often before. Debbie had chosen not ask for an audience in advance, feeling if she did, it would give Remus time to wonder what she wanted. She had seen him many times now, studying the rich carpet she stood on in his office until she knew every petal of the blood-red roses, the curve of every thorn, how the deep green leaves concealed and revealed the roses with their delicate, golden hearts, the tiny yellow flowers scattered around them like stars in the sky, but almost always, Remus had sent for her.

At the side door of the manor house, she knocked as she had so often before, but this time, to the surprise of the servant who answered, she asked to see Remus and not Preston.

While Debbie waited with Geance, now asleep, the servant summoned a page to lead her through the hallways to Remus. The boy turned out to be the young lad from Aguillero who had brought the request months before, that Yannick was to attend Remus in the morning. That meeting had led to Yannick's endless absence, as he rescued the starving inhabitants in the cursed village. Debbie hoped that the lad's presence was not a bad omen and then chose to regard it as a good one. Yannick was saving lives at the behest of the daimyo and indebting Shelleen to Kenyatta.

The page stared at her, trying to place her and then remembered.

"Oh. You have that dog. Is he with you?" the lad asked, his face worried.

Debbie smiled reassuringly. "No, Spotty would be barking his fool head off and you would have heard him long before I ever got here. He's with Kerill and Ghita, hopefully not getting into mischief. I need to speak with Remus."

The lad took a moment to peer around her, checking the truth of her words, and Debbie had to wonder again what silly stories the older boys had been telling him. He was very young and might believe them. She added, "Spotty likes to bark but he isn't dangerous to anyone who isn't a danger to us."

The boy looked openly doubtful. "I saw those teeth, begging your pardon, miss."

"You know," Debbie said thoughtfully, "you should come down to our cottage and have Kerill introduce you to Spotty. Then the other fosterlings will see how brave you are."

She watched his emotions fly across his face as he stood, hand on the wall. It was so hard going to a strange place, where you knew no one and he was not much older than Ghita or Kerill. She knew he was doing what was expected of boys of ruling families and was well treated, but he had to miss his own family desperately. He would not see them again for a year or more.

"I promise Spotty will behave," Debbie added warmly. "You can come by any time you're free from duties and play with Kerill and Niall, Ghita and Carina. Did you know that Ghita and Carina aren't from here? We're from Shelleen and everything is so different from what we were used to. I know my girls would like to meet you."

The page smiled at her suddenly, his face lighting up. "Thank you, miss. I'd like that. I'll take you to Remus now. I think he's not busy."

Debbie followed the page down the familiar hallways, marveling as she always did at the intricate tapestries and vivid paintings that adorned the walls. It was a pleasure to see them again and enjoy their beauty. Like the glittering stars at night, the fluffy clouds by day, the tapestries and paintings were beautiful for their own sake and their beauty did not diminish if they were ignored. They did not have to be admired to remain beautiful. They simply were. The art reminded her of herself; the endless years of existing in Shelleen. She had worked hard and endured to the best of her ability. Her efforts went unnoticed or were dismissed, but that did not change the fact she had made those efforts, every day. That mattered and therefore so did she, and she tried to draw some strength from this thought. She would need it to face Remus.

The page stopped at the now-familiar door and knocked for admittance. A secretary called for him to enter and so the page opened the door for Debbie.

She steeled herself and walked in, trying for Yannick's easy, confident stride and failing. She could not walk that way, she was not him. She was only Debbie. She thought of her daughters, of all her children now, Kerill and Niall and Geance, as well as Ghita and Carina and Espe, and then she was able to walk more confidently. Preston was there, as always, and surprisingly, Avalon, and, as always, there were others she recognized but did not know. She ignored them as they did not matter, other than as witnesses to what she had to say. Only the daimyo of Kenyatta mattered.

Remus sat back, surprised and irritated at her unexpected appearance, and said, "What is it now that you can't speak to Preston? I've no word from Yannick and I don't expect any."

Debbie bowed her head respectfully and answered, "Yes, sir, I know that. I need to speak with you and I need you to speak afterwards to the daimyo of Shelleen."

"Oh, you do."

"Yes sir, I do. I have thought of a way to repay him for the fertility I stole from him, to repay him for my escape, and it is a way that will benefit Kenyatta." Debbie did not dare meet his eyes but she was able to speak clearly and carefully, not shouting but not whispering either.

Remus watched her for an endless time, time drawn out like the string of a bow, tighter and tighter, until it felt to Debbie as though the room would snap. But she stood there, rooted to the carpet like a tree in the Sacred Grove, and she did not fall back or move. She endured like the woman she was, a peasant, a serf, someone who was bred to endure, continue, live. She had the mute patience of an ox, inured to disparagement and stony silences. She had more patience than he did.

"Get on with it then," Remus said, irritated and, although he would never say so, the tiniest bit impressed by Debbie's stoicism.

"Thank you, sir," Debbie replied. She launched into what she had seen and observed: the soil of Shelleen and the soil of Kenyatta and the soil she did not observe directly but deduced via the changed grasses growing upon it in the government corridor that separated and connected the two demesnes. She had worked in the fields, walked through them, and she was intimately familiar with the land that surrounded her. Debbie did not ride upon a horse or sit at her ease in a carriage, so she saw, close-up, what others did not see from their loftier, faster vantage point.

She spoke of what Yannick had told her of the vast herds of Kenyatta being used to build soil and how Shelleen and Dairapaska, despite being agricultural lands, did not follow those practices.

Then she spoke of how Kenyatta could offer the services of his herds to enrich the soil of Shelleen, feeding his own animals, overwintering them in gentler climes, while returning life-giving fertility to Shelleen's lands. Doing so would put Shelleen into his debt, while benefiting them both.

As Debbie spoke, carefully and slowly as she had planned out, Remus grew thoughtful and paid attention, setting aside the yellow glass paperweight he had been toying with. So did other members of the Kenyatta family in the room, the ones who had paid little attention to Debbie at first although they would not have ignored the same words if they had come from Yannick, a Hand of Kenyatta.

When she finished laying out her idea, Debbie said, "thank you for hearing me out."

Remus considered her for a long, long moment and as before, Debbie stood silent and still, other than cuddling Geance. He was awake again, gazing around him, wide-eyed but quiet, something that made Debbie intensely grateful and she wondered how much longer that blessed state would last.

She waited for Remus to speak, confident in her own patience and was rewarded when *he* spoke, breaking the silence.

"Why do you believe Airik Shelleen will accept my offer?"

Debbie felt a surge of triumph at his response, and more joy that she had spent so much time considering this question and thus had an answer ready for him.

"Because he is a geologist. Because he knows something about soil but not as much as a farmer would. Because he sent skilled farmers to the cursed village, so they had a chance of succeeding. Because he cared enough about the peasants in the cursed village, even though they failed, to keep them alive. If the daimyo of Shelleen cares enough to ask your aid to keep them alive, then he cares for all of Shelleen and would welcome making his own land better, benefiting both his family for the future and their serfs."

There was another long, long silence as Remus considered her response and Debbie, as before, stood quietly, waiting, her eyes fixed on the heart of a rose. Geance did not want to be quietly held anymore and began to fuss. Debbie tried to sooth him, but like Espe before him under similar circumstances, he knew what he wanted, and he wanted it now.

To her infinite relief, Avalon broke the silence of the adults and said, "I'll take Debbie to the nursery. By your leave, Remus?"

He nodded his approval at her, Avalon rose from her own seat, and smiling at Debbie and Geance, she led them from Remus's quiet office, down the quiet hallways and into the noisy, cheerful, brightly painted nursery. Debbie did not speak to Avalon as they walked down the hallways but concentrated her attention on keeping Geance soothed until she could give him what he wanted; her milk along with her full attention. She was well aware that of the various Kenyatta family members who had been present, only Avalon could be counted upon to understand, in her bones, what a baby needed.

Once the two women were seated comfortably in the nursery, Geance happily suckling away, Debbie said, "Thank you Avalon. He had a full tummy and wanted to sleep when I arrived, but, well." She smiled ruefully and Avalon returned the same smile.

"Babies do as they please," Avalon said. She smiled lovingly at her own little son, Havel, who was trying to climb into her lap and ignoring the nursery maid hovering behind him. "Geance is growing so fast. Such lovely eyes he has."

"Yes, he does."

"You spoke very well, Debbie. When Geance is finished, do you want to return to Remus's office?"

Debbie thought about this and decided she did not need to. "I've said everything that was needful. I'm sure Remus has many things to do."

"He does," Avalon replied. "I think you may have given him more of a gift than you know."

"What do you mean?"

"Remus is getting up in years," Avalon replied. "I won't speak of our family's business more than that. If you are correct about the daimyo of Shelleen, then Remus may also benefit personally."

Debbie considered this and chose to say, "I am grateful. Remus has been very kind to me and my daughters, welcoming us to Kenyatta."

She did not ask further questions and instead asked about Avalon's Havel, who had decided that he was hungry too. This led to a long discussion about what Havel was learning compared to what Espe, a little younger, was learning to do. They compared notes on keeping toddlers out of mischief, although

Avalon, being a member of the ruling family, had far more assistance in this matter than Debbie did.

Debbie tabled the matter of Remus but she would revisit it when she got back home to the cottage; it was not her place to do so in the manor house, and she felt she had already overstepped many boundaries. Besides, Chika and Leon were far more attuned to the gossip about the Kenyatta family than she was, knowing who and what to ask. It would be better to ask *them* later on, as it was always better to not let the ruling family know either your ignorance or your knowledge of their personal doings.

Safely back in the cottage, Debbie finally allowed herself to shake, tremble, shudder, and then unburden herself to Chika about where she had been. She had done it. She had faced Remus, explained herself, and it was in his hands. Would he speak to the daimyo of Shelleen? It was his choice, not hers.

Chika was astonished and pleased by Debbie's plan and her boldness in presenting it to Remus.

"You may have done him a good turn, Debbie," Chika said thoughtfully over soothing cups of mint tea. "Remus is getting on up in years. I know he won't want to leave the demesne a mess to clean up after he moves on. Whoever succeeds him as daimyo will have to work with Airik Shelleen and the easier *he* is to work with, the better it will be for all of Kenyatta, yeah?"

Debbie stared into the dancing flames in the hearth as she breathed in the reassuring scent of mint. "The law is what the daimyo says it is and a new daimyo means new laws."

"True, but a smart daimyo won't go changing things that work well and benefit the demesne. We'll see what happens."

Debbie did not hear back from the manor house, either for good or for ill. She decided this meant Remus was considering her idea; if he had been angry, he would have said or done something by now. Every day passed like the day before; full of work and hope that Spring would come again and this time decide to stay.

Then a letter arrived from Lupita.

This was no longer a common occurrence. Since the mail blockade had been lifted, Lupita no longer needed to ferry information on a regular basis as the families could correspond between the demesnes as they pleased. She only wrote directly to Debbie if there was something important between the two of them and their families.

Debbie settled herself comfortably into the alcove she shared with Yannick with Geance cuddled up against her to nurse and looked into the setting sun as she had so often done before. She slit open the letter from Lupita with her little knife and expected to read family news, something about Alice perhaps and her new baby son.

But this letter was not about that at all. As she read, Debbie's eyebrows rose higher and higher in astonishment. She read the letter again slowly, to be sure she had understood what Lupita had written. After the third rereading, Debbie sat back and stared out of the window at the sun hiding below the horizon, its last rays painting the sky with bloody crimson smears and angry purple bruises.

She felt a smile of triumph blaze across her face. She had been correct. She had judged the character of the daimyo of Shelleen as best she could on limited information and her judgment had not been found wanting. There was every chance that he would act on Remus's suggestion about cooperation between the demesnes. The well-being of Shelleen did matter to him, more than she would have ever believed.

Lupita had carefully organized what had happened, as it took place over many months; bits of information seeping out gradually and then everything revealed at once. Since Debbie's disappearance, the daimyo had asked many questions about her and, as it turned out, that led to questions about the new village and how it had been set up, provisioned, and managed. Over time, he asked the right questions of the right persons and those persons, over time, had become eager to talk to someone who would listen. Anger, despair, and resentment had fueled those conversations. There had been little left to lose and so certain truths had come out of hiding at last.

Airik Shelleen had not been happy with his discoveries.

He had been so unhappy that the entire Shelleen family had

been put on notice, a notice that did not escape the observations of the housemaids, dusting the rooms and emptying the chamber pots and serving the meals. They could not help overhearing what the Shelleen family had to say to each other, often shouting loudly enough to be overheard without any effort at all on the part of the maids.

Only the daimyo did not raise his voice, but then, he never did. His fury showed as ice, rather than as fire.

Apparently, the pressure to set up the new village out on the steppes was even greater than had been previously understood by the peasants, wrote Lupita. The Shelleen family had narrowly averted losing control of their land to the Martian government by its hasty, forced settlement. Yet, despite knowing how desperate the situation was, an uncle in the family had chosen to shortchange the wagonloads of supplies the villagers needed for the first long trek outwards and feathered his own personal bank account instead. He had been a leader in the Shelleen family's financial affairs department, delegated to act on the daimyo's behalf in this matter, and his position allowed him to hide his thievery.

At every point since then, he had skimmed off money needed to pay for supplies and, since he was a valued member of the family, senior in the hierarchy and important within family politics, his doings had not been questioned. No one could believe that any member of the Shelleen family would deliberately put everyone else and the demesne at risk. Yet he had.

As the family learned the details, so did the peasants of Shelleen, via their daughters who served as maids. But, as Lupita wrote, the peasants did not expect anything to come of it. Howard Shelleen was a member of the ruling family and nothing would be said or done to *him*, other than behind closed doors, and possibly not even then. His position kept him safe from any repercussions.

Then, so Lupita wrote, an announcement was read in all the villages. Everyone, with exception only for severe illness or childbirth, was told to assemble in the morning on the stone plaza facing the manor house. The reason was not given but everyone knew that the stone plaza was only used for important, demesne-wide news.

This was the same plaza on which Debbie had been assigned

to Aldo all those years ago. She still remembered the look and feel of the stone cobbles, hard and cold beneath her feet.

Rumors flew and virtually every peasant in Shelleen made the trek to the plaza to see what their masters had in store for them. Very little good had ever come out of announcements at the plaza and there was no thought, Lupita wrote, that this would be any different.

Lupita and her family got up before dawn to walk to the plaza from their village, along with everyone else who could attend. At the appointed time, the vast majority of the peasants from all the villages of Shelleen – other than from the poisoned village so far away out on the steppes – filed in, to wait and quietly socialize while ignoring as best they could what might happen next.

Then Lupita recognized, to her immense surprise, the headman of the far steppes village, with his wife and two other men and their wives from that village. She had not known they had traveled all the way back, she who now knew every piece of news in Shelleen as soon as it happened. Nor, it seemed, did any of their families left behind who rushed to where they stood on the plaza when they saw their sorely missed relatives. There were cries of joy at the reunion; tears, hugs, and every other form of long-pent emotion allowed free rein during this unexpected and most-welcome reunion.

As Lupita watched, amazed, she finally noticed something else erected on the plaza, something that was normally only erected when required and thankfully, it rarely was. A wooden dais had been assembled overnight and the thick, black whipping post reared up from it. As the excitement of seeing the representatives from the far steppes village settled and the dread of why everyone had been called forth spread, more and more of the peasants saw the same thing that she did. Silence thickened as fear spread and the crowd became sullen and downcast. Someone would be punished, that was certain.

The Shelleen clan filed out to their own upholstered chairs under an awning to shade them from the sun. Their seats faced the wooden dais so they could not miss what would happen next. Surprisingly, every seat was filled. Then, the daimyo of Shelleen strode to the carved wooden podium, well-dressed but not showy as other members of the family were. The crowd of peasants grew quieter, children were shushed, babies given nipples or fingers to suck, and through it all, the ruling family of Shelleen sat as still and silent as their peasants stood, as fearful and apprehensive from the looks on their faces.

The daimyo spoke, his voice low, clear, carrying, and cold as ice. He told the waiting crowd of peasants and aristocrats of his deep shame over one of his own family putting the entire demesne of Shelleen at risk because of greed.

This was something, so wrote Lupita, that she would have never expected to hear from any member of the Shelleen family. What came next was even more unexpected. The daimyo told the waiting crowd that it was Howard Shelleen who had done this, naming his name so that everyone present would remember his sin and tell the tale for generations to come. Members of the family, Lupita wrote, cringed in their seats as the daimyo spoke, their own shame and humiliation etched upon their faces.

She did not think Howard was present, looking for him among the ruling clan under the awning and not seeing him, this fact confirmed by whispers from peasants in the crowd who knew him on sight. Lupita wrote she thought he had been spared that humiliation in front of the entire demesne and been sent into exile.

Instead, Howard was led into the plaza, his wrists chained behind him. He was a white-haired, older member of the family, someone who would normally be cloaked in dignity and fine garments. Today, he wore a simple white shirt over dark pants no better than any village man, and he stumbled as he walked. A pair of impassive guards forced him up onto the dais and to the stunned amazement of the crowd, tied him to the whipping post, his arms outspread and his face against the post. He shook and trembled and did not fight them, tears leaking from his eyes and catching the sunlight.

Lupita expected, so she wrote in a shaking hand, that Howard Shelleen would be visibly and verbally shamed before the peasants he had wronged, the family he had endangered, the demesne he had put at risk, and that would be the end of it. He would be released and walk away into exile into whatever place would accept him.

Instead, the daimyo waved a hand and the Whip-Master

came out, his black hood concealing who had been chosen for this duty. Even then, Lupita wrote, she expected that Howard would be released after being given a fright, seeing how he whimpered at the sight of what approached him.

But instead of freeing him, the Whip-Master cut Howard's shirt from his cringing body, stepped back, and raised his thick arm and struck Howard across his back with the upraised leather whip, leaving the first bloody welt, scarlet across his emerald skin.

Howard screamed and a woman among the Shelleen family screamed as well and fainted in her seat. The Whip-Master paused and turned to the daimyo whose face remained cold and stony. The daimyo looked over his assembled, horror-struck relatives, then waved the Whip-Master to continue. Howard Shelleen received nine more strokes, screaming continuously, until with the tenth stroke, he collapsed into a faint.

At that point, the daimyo waived his hand again, and the Whip-Master cut Howard Shelleen free from the post and he crumpled onto the bloody, wooden platform. He was loaded, not gently, into a waiting litter, and carried off into the manor house.

The daimyo of Shelleen, the youngest daimyo Shelleen had ever had, went back to the podium to address the crowd of open-mouthed, gaping peasants and his waiting, appalled family.

"I will not," he said facing the seats of his shocked and gasping relatives, his ringing voice filling the silent, waiting plaza so all the astonished peasants could hear him as well, "tolerate treason or betrayal of the demesne of Shelleen from anyone. *We* are supposed to set the example. *We* have the duty to protect and guide the demesne for generations to come. *We* rule Shelleen, *our* family, yet Howard betrayed us all with his greed. *We* have everything we need. *We* want for nothing. The Martian government cares nothing for us, our history, our land, our people. *We* do that. Let me remind all of you that they are waiting for our mistakes so they can rob us, take control of our land, and poison it for all time. Howard would have let that happen. *I* will not."

He turned back towards the peasants, his back to his own family. His face was carved from green ice, Lupita wrote. "*I* will not betray Shelleen. *I* will do what I must to keep all of us safe and secure. *I*, Airik, daimyo of Shelleen, pledge this to you, my people."

He walked from the stone podium and the assembly was over. The family left their seats, some visibly struggling to contain their horror, tears, and grief. The woman who had fainted was carried back inside the manor house. She was Howard's wife, so Lupita wrote, tarred by his actions despite no fault of her own.

The peasants took some time to disperse back to their own homes and villages as they thought about what they had seen and heard. It was many hours walk for some of them and there would be much to discuss on the journey homewards. The peasants, Lupita wrote, were uniformly shocked at seeing a member of the ruling family whipped like any serf. More than a few of the men present pointed out, unkindly, how poorly Howard Shelleen had borne up under the whip. He had no spine, no strength of character, and those men who had felt the kiss of the whip were gratified at their own tough endurance compared to his. It was proof, as if anyone needed it, that the Shelleen family was not a superior form of humanity as some of them liked to claim.

Lupita finished her letter with the family news Debbie had expected, its importance washed away by the larger story of Howard Shelleen's betrayal of the demesne and his punishment. Word of what the daimyo of Shelleen had done would, Debbie knew, spread like wildfire. Lupita wrote to tell her what had happened, and it was a sure bet every single other peasant in Shelleen had also sent a letter off at once to every relative they had outside the demesne to ensure this story was told and retold.

Debbie's smile blazed again, thinking of those letters reaching Dairapaska where, eventually, the ruling family would hear of what had been done to Howard Shelleen.

Debbie pulled a sleepy Geance closer to her and considered what would happen next. Should she speak to Remus again about Lupita's letter? Should she, she wondered, prod Remus to speak to the daimyo of Shelleen about her own idea? No, Debbie decided. Remus had already heard her so there was no need to push him further. And now, she was sure of it, the daimyo of Shelleen would accept her plan. It would benefit both demesnes, Shelleen would be strengthened, and she and her daughters would have paid their debt in full. They would be free.

She left the alcove to her own, deeply loved family waiting for her at supper and could not stop smiling. She and her daughters were freed from any obligations to Shelleen. What a story to tell them over supper! How stunned Chika and Leon would be. Debbie smiled again, harder. Soon, tomorrow even, letters would race from Kenyatta across the Ennaretee and then further out. Leon at the pub and Chika at the bathhouse would ensure the story's rapid spread. It wouldn't take long before all the peasants on Mars knew what Howard Shelleen had done and soon thereafter, their ruling nobles would know how his family had not swept his theft and betrayal under the rug.

Even Yannick, so far away from everyone in the poisoned village, would be told as soon as the village headman and the others returned. Those peasants, who had suffered even more than they should have, would soon know and curse the name of the man who had made their lives worse.

More days passed and then, in the late afternoon, Yannick, Otis, and their crews, tired and dirty, came riding back into the village. The daimyo of Shelleen had rebuilt the road to the poisoned village and the wagons of provisions were on the move at last, resupplying the serfs, trapped and isolated no longer. His job there was done.

At the cottage, Yannick was greeted with joy and relief. He was alive, he was unhurt, and he had taken no damage from the poisoned village that he knew of. When the flurry of greetings and welcomes was done, Yannick asked for quiet.

"I got to talk to Debbie. Mom? Can you take the kids, all but Geance, over to Lysander and Erissa? It's important."

Chika's eyebrows raised and her hands flew and Debbie was again struck by how annoying it was to have the conversation flow around her and not be a part of it. She did not catch many words. Ghita was concentrating hard but Yannick had taken care to turn his body so neither she nor Kerill and Niall could see his flying hands clearly. They were openly puzzled but still trying hard to understand what their father was saying that he did not want them to know.

Finally, Chika said, "Fine. Supper'll be late though."

Yannick smiled a bit and said, "Not a problem."

Debbie felt fear flood over her again. What had gone wrong that he had to speak to her right away, in private? What could not wait for the night and the privacy of their alcove?

She motioned for him to sit next to her, Geance in her lap, by the hearth, but he did not. Instead, Yannick paced as Chika rounded up the restive, disappointed children, bundled them into coats and finally got them and Spotty out the door to visit their uncle and auntie and their cousins instead of seeing their father as they wanted to. Chika's own silence spoke of her own emotions, but as to what they were, Debbie was unsure. Chika knew something of what Yannick had to say, something that Debbie had to wait for.

When the cottage was quiet and empty, Yannick said, "I got things to say, my Debbie. I don't want to say them. I don't want to burden you but I am a Hand of Kenyatta and I swore an oath to represent the demesne in everything I say and do."

He paused and began to pace again, back and forth. She watched him in apprehensive silence.

"I met Aldo. He made a point of seeking me out, let me be clear." Yannick stopped again and this time he sat down next to Debbie and hugged her to him, despite the filth that coated him from the days of journeying from the poisoned village to come back home.

She hugged him back tightly, not caring about the dirt, overjoyed to be with him, knowing that whatever it was, his own affections had not changed during his absence. She was amazed at his anger on her behalf.

Yannick pulled away and stood back up, his face set and his shoulders tense.

"I will not repeat what that man said to me about you. If I had not been there as a Hand of Kenyatta and representing Remus in everything I said and did, I would have killed him for what he said about you." Yannick glared fiercely at the flames dancing in the hearth, staring into them as if seeing something else other than what was in the room.

He sighed and sat down again, searching for words he did not want to say, and Debbie reached for him, reassuring him with her own quiet presence and gentle touch.

"That man wanted me to give you something. He asked me to swear on my name, on my honor that I would do so and so I am doing that."

Yannick stood up again and walked over to the bag he had brought with him and took out a kuksa, the wood bright and pale in its raw newness. He stared at it, his face twisted with distaste.

"He wanted the baby girl he had rejected to have this kuksa. He chose a name and carved the kuksa. Debbie. What do you want to do with this?"

Yannick handed her the kuksa and Debbie took it with a trembling hand. Aldo had refused Espe, had wanted her to die and now, after all that had happened, he wanted to name her and claim her. She took the kuksa and read the name Aldo had carved into the wood, paler still against the paleness of the cup.

She stared at it for a long, long silence and Yannick let her. He did not speak, he did not put words into her mouth, he let her have the space to think and speak of her own free will. He sat down beside her again, calmer now, and put one arm around her and in the other, he took Geance, cuddling his youngest son.

"Angela," Debbie said at last, reading the name that Aldo had finally chosen for the daughter he had initially refused. "He wants to name Espe Angela." She could not stop her voice from shaking with fury and rage and hurt. She wanted to vomit up everything she had eaten for the day and from the day before and the day before that.

"It's a pretty enough name, but Espe has a name of her own," Yannick said.

"It is an awful name," Debbie forced out, past the sharp-edged stone blocking her throat. "Angela is the name of his mother, and there was never a woman less like an angel than Mrs. Acconcio."

Yannick smiled crookedly at her. "I swore to that man I would give you the kuksa. I did not say to him what you would do with it. What do you want to do with the kuksa, my own dearest heart?"

Debbie turned the cup over and over in her hands, watching the pale, raw wood catch the light from the dancing flames, but not their life and warmth. If Aldo had behaved as he should have, all those months ago, she would still be struggling in the poisoned village. The hardships might have killed one of her daughters. She would have met Yannick as a rescuer and he would have been nothing more to her than that, nothing like the man he was to her now. She would not have stolen her daughters and run away, taking her chances on the steppes. She would not have the family she had gained, Chika and Leon, Kerill, Niall, Geance, and the larger circle of kin who had welcomed her with open arms. She would never have written her first letter to Dairapaska and discovered that her mother was still alive and how much her family there missed her. She would not have broken the mail blockade and reunited, via paper, the brides of Dairapaska and the brides of Shelleen with their families, lost and far away. She would not have come up with a plan to bring Kenyatta and Shelleen closer, for the benefit of both demesnes, although she did not yet know what would come of that plan.

Everything, everything about her life now would be different if Aldo had behaved as he should have when his youngest daughter was born.

She stood abruptly, walked the few steps to the hearth, and stood for a moment, seeing a different life in the flames and then Debbie tossed the kuksa into the fire, sending up a spray of sparks. She watched it sink into the hot, red embers, the flames gently teasing the wooden cup, wrapping themselves around it and the cup caught and began to burn.

Yannick stood and came up behind her and put an arm around her as together they watched the kuksa burn.

"They say that fire destroys and it does, but it can bring life too," he said.

Debbie leaned into him, letting him support her weight. She could not speak, only watch a different life turn to ash.

Yannick chose again to fill the quiet. "I carved a bunch of kuksas for Maureen. She'd get tired of the one she was using and want another, something new. When she walked out, I burned them all, one by one. Each one that I burned, burned my soul a little cleaner. I spread the ash in the garden and pissed it into the ground. I kept Kerill and Niall's cups as a talisman, hoping and praying that they would come home to me and they did. You did the right thing, my Debbie."

"I should hate him and I do," Debbie said softly. "But I will be grateful to Aldo. Because of who and what he is, I am here now." She waited a heartbeat. "If and when we have another daughter, I will not let her be named Angela."

Yannick laughed then. "Not a problem. We'll let someone else choose that name and cleanse it." He kissed her soundly, leaving smudges of trail dust on her face and Debbie did not care. When he broke away at last, Debbie said, "We should fetch the kids back. They'll be desperate to see you."

My own Debbie," Yannick said. "My own dearest heart. Now and forever."

On the walk down the winding path through the village over to Lysander and Erissa's cottage, Debbie told Yannick what she had said to Remus and that Remus had yet to tell her what he would do.

Yannick thought it over. "A good plan, I think. I saw that land of Shelleen's. Their daimyo would be a fool to not take up Remus's offer. Lot of work for us, but a reward at the end." He stopped short and added, "you are well shook of that place. Terrible, just terrible. I'll tell you all about it tonight at supper. And then the bathhouse afterwards to get cleaned up."

He smiled at her, lingeringly. "I missed you more than words can say. I thought about you every night and every morning and exactly how I wanted to say hello again."

Debbie flushed and said, "I missed you, too. Don't take too long to get washed up." She stood up on tiptoe to whisper something in his ear that made him laugh and say, "I like the sound of that!"

Yannick spent the entire next day with Remus and the Kenyatta family, going over everything he did and saw in the poisoned village. When he returned, he had news for Debbie. Remus had discussed the ramifications of her idea with the family, they had agreed to it and he had presented the idea to the daimyo of Shelleen.

Airik Shelleen had responded, and his answer was yes.

21

The Daimyo of Shelleen

WITH YANNICK HOME AGAIN, things settled back into their routine, other than the added work of expanding the kitchen gardens and Leon's fields for the upcoming winter. The Spring Solstice arrived, with all of its celebration and joy over the return of light and warmth to the world. Debbie was grateful, during every minute of the weeklong celebration, that she did not have to stand on the dais again in front of everyone in Kenyatta, the living and the dead, for either herself or her children.

Remus made the announcement that the upcoming fall migration, still half the year away, would continue across the corridor and into the northernmost lands of Shelleen. The slightly easier climate would ensure that more of the herds would survive the winter. He also said that, although no formal announcement had yet been made, Shelleen and Kenyatta would be working far more closely than ever before, to the mutual benefit and need of both demesnes. This was not a surprise to anyone. Everyone in Kenyatta knew what Yannick and Otis and their crews had accomplished in the poisoned village. The vassals of Kenyatta speculated that something else was going on to drive this unusual detente, the poisoned village being the first open symptom, and this something would be revealed in due course to the wider world. In the meantime, they talked about it endlessly, chewing over every scrap of information until the last bit of juice had been extracted.

Debbie had asked Remus to keep her name out of his speeches and he had graciously agreed. He did remind the crowd that she had been lucky for the demesne and this was another aspect of that luckiness.

She had to wonder if everyone in Kenyatta would agree with his assessment when Shelleen made the announcement to the wider world of the Red Mercury lode. Debbie decided that they would, if only because it would allow the Hands and their crews to control the potential flood of get-rich-quick squatters from despoiling Kenyatta's own lands.

Soon after, the spring migration began and Yannick, along with Leon and most of the other men, left to begin the long process of moving the flocks and herds to their northern pastures.

The spring migration had ended at last, with its usual pleasures for young and old. Yannick and Leon had been home a few days, settling back into their usual routines, when rumors began to race through the villages of Kenyatta. Big things were happening: fancy supplies were being ordered in and the manor house was being scrubbed from top to bottom, its grounds and gardens brought back into the best, most showy order. Important people were coming to call on the ruling family. It became known that Satran and Armstrong were sending large delegations, both families *and* their senior Hands *and* their crews. Then *the* message came down to the household from the manor house, brought by a panting, excited page.

The daimyo of Shelleen, along with his staff, was leaving Shelleen and coming to Kenyatta for meetings with Remus, apparently participating along with Satran and Armstrong. As part of his visit, he insisted on meeting Debbie. The meeting would take place the day he arrived. He did not reveal his reasons to Remus, or so the page claimed upon being questioned by Yannick.

Debbie was not looking forward to meeting Airik Shelleen.

She fretted and worried as she could not understand why he wanted to meet her. As the daimyo, Remus Kenyatta was the person who mattered. The Kenyatta family would be making the arrangements for enacting her plan and working closely with the Shelleen family. The Hands of Kenyatta, with their crews, would be the people who did the work, along with the Hands of Armstrong and Satran. The animals herded across the government corridor would donate their fertility. *She* had no part in any of those actions. Why would the daimyo of Shelleen care about meeting her?

She could only be grateful that Yannick would be by her side. He had insisted on being included, getting into, well, not quite a shouting match with Remus, but it certainly seemed one to Debbie. The daimyo finally backed down agreeing it was right and fitting for a woman to be accompanied by her husband when meeting potentially dangerous strangers.

Yannick's presence almost made up for the even more distressing news that the daimyo of Shelleen had insisted she bring her children with her to the meeting.

Yannick was not happy about that part of the message either and told Remus so in no uncertain terms. He decided, and Debbie did not argue, that their children included everybody so that meant Kerill, Niall and Geance as well, and to make it easier on Debbie, having to wrangle six kids in the manor house in front of their betters, he insisted that Chika and Leon be brought along to assist. He would have brought every other relative they had, packing the manor house out to six degrees of consanguinity if he could have gotten away with it. As it was, these relatives, along with Otis, their crew, and much of *their* kin, ended up loitering on the grounds of the manor house on the great day and gossiping with the Hands of Satran and Armstrong and their crews.

Chika and Leon were equally unhappy; about both the daimyo of Shelleen's visit and what that might mean for their family and his urgent desire to meet Debbie and their grandchildren.

The great day arrived at last. The entire family were dressed in their festival best, waiting in the vast main hall of the manor house. Yannick and Leon had every bead they owned woven into their hair, and Kerill was wearing his first beads, the ones that said who his father and grandfathers were. They were dead quiet, sitting on the bench outside the door, waiting for

Remus to finish conducting his initial business with the daimyo of Shelleen, Ghita and Carina, Kerill and Niall had all been carefully instructed on how to behave so as to not shame the family.

Espe was asleep in Debbie's lap and Debbie hoped she would nap the afternoon away. She had made sure that the other kids had played and played plenty with Espe to ensure her having a good, long, deep sleep.

Geance was good and tired as well, and asleep in Chika's arms.

Chika put her foot down so Spotty, to his intense, vocal disapproval, was handed over to the Kennel-Master, ensuring that the meeting between the vassals of Kenyatta and the daimyo of Shelleen would be quiet along with the cottage remaining undamaged and the neighbors left in peace. He did, however, make the most of his imprisonment, which the Kennel-Master discovered weeks later when his prize bitch delivered her much-anticipated litter of prize puppies, and they were not the ones he had planned for.

At last, the family were admitted to Kenyatta's private office where the daimyo of Shelleen was waiting, along with Kenyatta at his desk.

At first sight, he did not look like much. Airik Shelleen was surprisingly young for a daimyo, slim to the point of thinness, almost weedy if you were unkindly comparing him to the size of the bodyguard standing patiently in the back of Remus's office. He wasn't particularly tall, either. Azi had drawn his features accurately all those months ago, yet his sketches did not capture how Airik Shelleen stood apart, remote and sufficient unto himself. Debbie noticed his eyes, cooler than any she had ever seen. His eyes, she thought, observed everything and then judged what he observed by some standard not her own.

She felt a sudden shock of recognition, something she had barely thought of since she had run away from the poisoned village the previous summer. Spotty had seen a snake on their journey, slim and red, its scales shining in the sun, and he had barked to warn her of the creature. Airik Shelleen reminded her of that snake, dangerous but only when disturbed and only when he chose to be.

To her further shock, she recognized the people behind

him, sitting stiffly on the padded bench at the side of the office. They were her in-laws from Shelleen, Aldo's mother and father. The Acconcios looked miserable and out of place. They had become withered, old and gray, decades older in the year that had passed.

"I am Airik Shelleen," said the daimyo, waiting until after Leon and Chika got the kids settled on a bench as far away from the Acconcios as they could manage, while still remaining inside the office. The daimyo of Shelleen's voice was a pleasant tenor, with the unemotional edge of a knife in it, that useful tool that does not care what it cuts.

He stepped forward to meet them and to Debbie's astonishment, he addressed Espe, sleeping in her arms.

"So, you are the little one who caused such a crisis for Shelleen, for Kenyatta, and for Dairapaska so far away. So small to cause such great troubles."

Yannick, standing behind her, tightened his arms around Debbie and she could feel his fury at being forced to expose her and their children to this man.

"You are Debbie, of course. You have become a great heroine to many people."

The daimyo of Shelleen inclined his head to her, surprising her again. She did not know what to say so she said nothing, keeping her eyes respectfully down. She focused on the blood red roses in the carpet; it had been freshly beaten clean and their delicate, golden hearts were laid bare before her as they never had been before.

"And this must be Yannick. How full of rage you look. You would slash me open from gullet to groin to defend your family and never once count your own cost, would you not?"

"I would and it would be worth it," answered Yannick, looking him dead in the eyes. Remus Kenyatta didn't look overly happy with what his Hand had to say, but he said nothing himself.

Shelleen turned back to Debbie's former in-laws, his expression much less warm, and it had not been warm to begin with.

"Do you see this? This man has known Debbie and her daughters for barely a year and yet he stands ready to lay down his life for them. This woman carried your grandchildren and yet you, in all those years could not make her welcome, could not accept her into your family."

Debbie's mother-in-law opened her mouth, and Shelleen held up a slim, surprisingly calloused hand.

"Do not speak," he said.

"If you could have found it within yourselves to throw her a few crumbs of affection over the years, I would not now be standing here. If your son had been kind to the woman who bore him his children, she would still be with him, along with your granddaughters, and with the promise of more children to come. If your son had been able to accept this little baby girl, there would not have been death and riots in Dairapaska."

This time, Debbie's father-in-law opened his mouth and Shelleen again held up his hand.

"Interrupt me and I will have you flogged as I did your son. I interviewed many, many of your peers and all agreed. You and your wife could not accept Debbie into your family; you tolerated her only because of the children she bore. She did not cause trouble, she listened respectfully to you, she did what was needful, as she was asked and as she was told, never shirking her duty. Yet you and your family could not find it in your hearts to admit her into the precious, proud Acconcio family."

His voice took on a colder tone. "There are no grandsons in the Acconcio line. Your older son is barren, as is your daughter and if your daughter had borne sons, they would be claimed by her husband's family. Because of how you could not accept the gift that was given to you by my predecessor, when your sons die the land held in trust by Acconcio since the founding of Shelleen will revert back to me, to dispose of as I see fit. The name of Acconcio will be lost from the cadastre, but it will not be forgotten. It will become a byword in Shelleen for ungratefulness."

He turned back to Debbie. She had to forcibly keep her mouth closed at his words, words that warmed her as few words had. While he had been speaking, Espe had woken up and she was staring all around her at the rich colors in Kenyatta's office and the people she had never seen before, especially the stranger approaching her.

"Little one, I have a gift for you." He held up a fine gold chain, with a blood-red drop of light hanging from it. The daimyo of Shelleen waved the chain in front of the toddler, making the gem catch the light in the room and flashing like fire. Entranced, Espe grabbed at it, burbling and giggling with glee.

Debbie gasped and recoiled, and Yannick pulled them both further back and away from the daimyo of Shelleen.

"She doesn't need your poison," he said.

Shelleen smiled a small smile, and a hint of warmth reached his eyes. "It is a ruby, and not what you think. I swear this, I, Airik, daimyo of Shelleen. If you like, you may have this confirmed by Kenyatta's geologists. It is for Espe for her dowry, to use as she deems needful in years to come."

Debbie looked up at Yannick, and he bent down to hear her whisper. She stepped forward, carrying Espe, and he let her go.

"Thank you, Lord Shelleen. Espe will treasure your gift."

Espe grabbed for the bright stone and Debbie let her clutch the chain for a few minutes, waving it around and making the stone flash. She gently pried it from Espe's chubby hand and waved the ruby drop before the mesmerized, reaching toddler.

"I can't let her hold something like this for very long, sir. She'll try to put it in her mouth," said Debbie, and she dared to meet Shelleen's cool hazel eyes and smile at him.

He unbent enough to smile at her and at Espe. "You have a grateful heart, Debbie. It will always serve you well."

"I'm gonna have this checked, see if you're lying about this not being harmful to my daughter," said Yannick.

Kenyatta, who had been watching from behind his desk, winced.

Shelleen however looked approvingly at Yannick. "I would expect nothing less from a Hand of Kenyatta, a man of courage whose first concern is the well-being of his family."

He stepped back to the desk and said, "Remus? I have no further need of Debbie or her children or her man."

Debbie bit her lip, thinking of what to do. She had been watching her former in-laws and their silent agony. They stared at Ghita and Carina, seated across the office, with hungry, needy eyes. Despite how they had treated her, they had adored Ghita and Carina and they would have loved Espe, she was sure of it.

As she had hoped, the daimyo of Shelleen had indeed told the Acconcios to pound sand over their stolen grandchildren and, astonishingly, he had gone to the trouble of doing it in front of her. She thought of how angry he must have been to drag them here to Kenyatta, punishing them still further, as it was a sure bet he had already spoken to them in Shelleen. Debbie also thought of how desperate, despite the circumstances, her former in-laws must have been to see their granddaughters, as lost to them as if they had been sent away to Dairapaska. They would not have had any choice over the journey as the daimyo got what the daimyo wanted, but still, they saw their deeply missed granddaughters again. The daimyo of Shelleen had managed to punish and reward at the same time. She thought of her own parents so far away in Dairapaska, grandparents too, and ones who would never see their grandchildren other than through the drawings Azi had sketched and the words Debbie had written.

"Sir? My lord Shelleen? May I ask a favor of you?" Debbie asked diffidently.

Shelleen turned back to her, remote and expressionless again. "You may."

She kept her eyes focused on a golden-hearted rose in the carpet, its petals spread to reveal nearly all of its innermost self. "Would it be acceptable for my daughters to write to their nonna and nonno in Shelleen? And for them to write back? They always loved their granddaughters and wanted the best for them."

Debbie's former mother-in-law began to sob quietly into a handkerchief, while her husband sat stiffly beside her, his face turned away from the people in the room. They had never been an affectionate couple and Debbie was astonished to see him reach for his wife's free hand and she let him take it.

"You have a generous spirit as well as a grateful heart, Debbie," Airik Shelleen replied. "You and your daughters may write letters as you see fit. You are, after all, a famous letter writer."

He gazed coolly at her former in-laws, huddled and distraught on the padded bench. "Perhaps the Acconcios will even write to you in return, if they are able to unbend their pride."

He paused and everyone in the room paused with him, waiting for what he had to say. "If you like, Debbie, I will allow you some time with the Acconcios. I will be in Kenyatta for many days, conducting my business with Remus and the other daimyos. The Acconcios will not be leaving Shelleen again so this will be the last time they ever see their granddaughters."

Debbie glanced over at Ghita and Carina. They had been sitting with Kerill and Niall, bookended by Chika and Leon to ensure they all behaved. All four children had behaved very well, sitting quietly with a minimum of wiggling and whispering and leg swinging, and it left her almost lightheaded with gratitude and relief. Geance was still asleep. She wondered how much longer their perfect behavior would last.

She raised her eyebrows questioningly at Ghita. Did she want to do this? Carina, Debbie knew, barely remembered nonna and nonno and now she had gramma Chika and grampie Leon to dote on her, along with a host of other adoring relatives.

But Ghita, Ghita's situation was different. Debbie did not know her daughter's mind at all as she stubbornly refused to speak of the past.

Ghita looked over at her nonna and nonno, who stared back at her with red-rimmed, hungry eyes, their faces desperately pleading. She had been the adored and cosseted apple of their eye since the day she had been born, and she did remember and miss them. She also well remembered how often they, her father, uncle Enzo and auntie Fulvia, and auntie Camille (but never uncle Steig) had been dismissive and belittling towards her mother.

She stared at them for a long, long moment, the center of attention and then decided to follow the example her mother set.

"I would like to, mommy. And I'll write letters too. But I want all my brothers to come with me and Carina and Espe. All of us. If they won't take all of us, they get none of us," Ghita said firmly and clearly, pinning her nonna to the wall with her eyes.

Watching her daughter's single-minded determination, Debbie was struck by a memory she had always pushed away, of a story she had never liked to hear but had often been told. Almost from Ghita's birth, everyone had said how much Ghita looked like her nonna as a baby and as Ghita grew, everyone had told Debbie how much Ghita resembled her nonna as a young girl, in both looks and actions. No one ever told Mrs. Acconcio what to do, starting with her own husband, and Debbie could now admit that perhaps Ghita did, in some small way, take after her nonna.

Mrs. Acconcio stared at Ghita longingly, then at Carina, then up at Debbie. The world waited around them, the room struck still, the people statues where they stood. Ghita stood rigidly in front of her brothers and sisters, her arms akimbo, staring at her nonna, her normally mobile face carved stone and her eyes bright with tears.

Then Mrs. Acconcio spoke, her voice as sweet as ever, a melodic voice whose tone that in Debbie's experience never matched its words, and the room breathed out.

"Of course we will. What a lovely idea, my precious Ghita. You and your sisters are a credit to your mother."

Acknowledgments

I want to thank everyone who helped make 'The Bride From Dairapaska' possible. My beta readers Anne Simmons, Angel Raser, and Eileen Wilson all pointed out flaws, holes, and inconsistencies in the story leading to the book you hold in your hand. Their careful, thoughtful reading and extensive notes made this a much better book than it would have been otherwise.

My cover artist, Jake Caleb (jcalebdesign.com), gave me wonderful art showing Debbie and her daughters lost in the steppes.

Denise, the interlibrary loan librarian at our local library, got me all the books I could ever need on esoteric subjects such as terraforming.

All the dogs I have known and loved, but particularly Fido who I still miss, Muffy who slaughters groundhogs while ignoring rabbits as beneath her skillset, Mariah who really can leap waist-high, and Maxie, who would never allow anyone to set foot on her territory without alerting everyone for a quarter-mile around.

And of course, my dear husband Bill. He believed in me when I didn't.

About the Author

Odessa Moon has at various times painted, sewed, served in the Navy, worked as a sales clerk and cashier, taken care of her family, and gardened with enthusiasm. She reads extensively, especially on subjects like medieval history, the class struggle, colonization, and resource depletion. While growing up, she read piles of science-fiction and fantasy and often wondered what the authors hand-waved away about how difficult it really would be to terraform another planet. The series, "The Steppes of Mars" is her attempt to combine all those interests.

When Ms. Moon is not writing, she is working on improving the soil in her own garden and planting trees in her municipality.

Visit Odessa at Peschel Press (www.peschelpress.com) or her website at OdessaMoon.com. She can be reached at odessa@peschelpress.com or written to at Peschel Press, P.O. Box 132, Hershey, PA 17033.

If you want to learn more about her books, sign up for the Peschel Press newsletter. Visit peschelpress.com or odessamoon.com and look for the sign-up box.

And if you like this book — or even if you don't — could you leave a word or two at the online book retailer of your choice? Reviews sell books, and she would appreciate it.

The Complete, Annotated Series

<u>Available in Trade Paperback and Ebook editions</u>

Return to your favorite novels by Agatha Christie & Dorothy L. Sayers with added material exclusive to these editions!

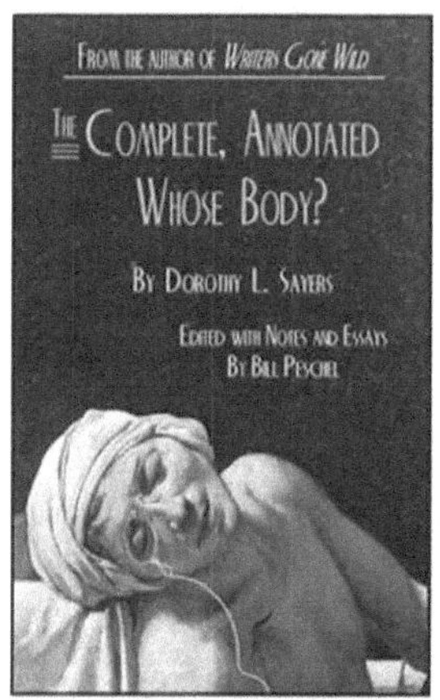
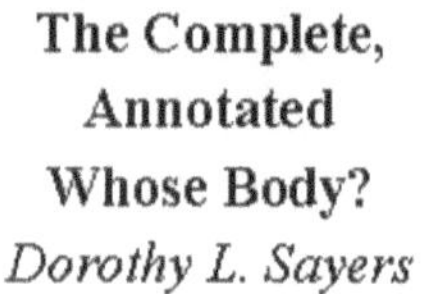

The Complete, Annotated Whose Body?
Dorothy L. Sayers

Sayers' first novel introduces the witty Lord Peter Wimsey investigating the mystery of the body in the bath. Three maps and essays on notorious crimes, anti-Semitism, Sayers and Wimsey, plus two timelines. *282 pages.*

The Complete, Annotated Mysterious Affair at Styles
Agatha Christie

Mystery's most auspicious debut, Christie was only 25 when she introduced Hercule Poirot! With essays on Poirot, Christie, strychnine, women during the war, plus chronology and book lists. *352 pages.*

The Complete, Annotated Deluxe Secret Adversary
Agatha Christie

Christie's conspiracy thriller in which Tommy and Tuppence —based on herself and her husband?—fight socialists plotting to ruin England! With art from the newspaper edition and essays on thrillers and her 11-day disappearance and more! *478 pages.*

The 223B Casebook Series

<u>Available in Trade Paperback and Ebook editions</u>

Reprints of classic and newly discovered fanfiction written during Arthur Conan Doyle's lifetime, with original art plus extensive historical notes.

The Early Punch Parodies of Sherlock Holmes

● Parodies, pastiches, book reviews, cartoons, and jokes from 1890 to 1928.
● Includes 17-story cycle by R.C. Lehmann.
● Two parodies by P.G. Wodehouse, and a story by Arthur Conan Doyle.
● Essays on Punch, Lehmann, Wodehouse, and an interview with Conan Doyle. *281 pages.*

Victorian Parodies & Pastiches: 1888-1899

With stories by Conan Doyle, Robert Barr, Jack Butler Yeats, and J.M. Barrie. *279 pages.*

Great War Parodies and Pastiches I: 1910-1914

With stories by O. Henry, Maurice Baring, and Stephen Leacock. *362 pages.*

Edwardian Parodies & Pastiches I: 1900-1904

With stories by Mark Twain, Finley Peter Dunn, John Kendrick Bangs, and P.G. Wodehouse. *390 pages.*

Great War Parodies and Pastiches II: 1915-1919

With stories by Ring Lardner, Carolyn Wells, and a young George Orwell. *390 pages.*

Edwardian Parodies & Pastiches II: 1905-1909

With stories by 'Banjo' Paterson, Max Beerbohm, Carolyn Wells, and Lincoln Steffens. *401 pages.*

Jazz Age Parodies and Pastiches I: 1920-1924

With stories by Dashiell Hammett, James Thurber, and Arthur Conan Doyle. *353 pages.*

The Rugeley Poisoner Series

A 3-book series from Peschel Press reprinting seminal works
about Victorian poisoner Dr. William Palmer

The Illustrated Life and Career of William Palmer 1856	The Times Report of the Trial of William Palmer 1856	The Life and Career of William Palmer of Rugeley 1925
• A "quickie biography" written to cash in on the trial.	• A trial transcript created by the Times newspaper, edited, corrected, and annotated.	• Written by a doctor who interviewed witnesses and jurors.
• Gossip about Palmer's family, betting scams, and the stews of London.	• More than 50 original woodcuts restored to better-than-new condition.	• Rare photos and art not seen since 1925.
• More than 50 restored woodcuts.	• Essays on the trial judges and barristers, glossary of medical terms, and index to witnesses. *426 pages*	• Annotations define medical and legal terms and clarify obscure points.
• Essays on medical training and racing.		• Essays on Palmer's impact on modern culture, strychnine, and Rugeley today. *227 pages*
• Excerpts from Palmer's love letters. *225 pages*		